The odex was a thin grey disk; Togura could just have spanned its diameter with his outstretched arms. Seen side-on, it appeared to disappear entirely. Seen from an angle, it acted as a mirror, reflecting the surroundings.

'Stand in front of it,' said Brother Troop.

Togura moved round in front of the odex, which hung in the air, standing knee-high off the ground without any apparent means of support. As he came directly in front of it, the mirror surface broke up into discordant cascades of colour and light. These shimmered, swirled, stretched, contracted and pulsed.

'Is it angry?' said Togura, warily.

At his words, a puff of red mist broke loose from the surface of the odex. It twirled lazily in the air.

'Who knows?' said Brother Troop.

Also by Hugh Cook

THE WIZARDS AND THE WARRIORS

and published by Corgi Books

THE WORDSMITHS
AND THE WARGUILD

or
The Questing Hero

Hugh Cook

CORGI BOOKS

THE WORDSMITHS AND THE WARGUILD
A CORGI BOOK   0 552 13130 X

Originally published in Great Britain by Colin Smythe Limited

PRINTING HISTORY
Colin Smythe edition published 1987
Corgi edition published 1987

This book is set in Plantin

Corgi Books are published by Transworld Publishers Ltd.,
61-63 Uxbridge Road, Ealing, London W5 5SA, in Australia by
Transworld Publishers (Australia) Pty. Ltd., 15-23 Helles
Avenue, Moorebank, NSW 2170, and in New Zealand by
Transworld Publishers (N.Z.) Ltd., Cnr. Moselle and Waipareira
Avenues, Henderson, Auckland.

Reproduced, printed and bound in Great Britain by
Hazell Watson & Viney Limited,
Member of the BPCC Group,
Aylesbury, Bucks

THE WORDSMITHS
AND THE WARGUILD

CHAPTER ONE

Sung was a land which was famous far and wide, simply because it was so often and so richly insulted. However, there was one visitor, more excitable than most, who developed a positive passion for criticising the place. Unfortunately, the pursuit of this hobby soon led him to take leave of the truth.

This unkind traveller once claimed that the king of Sung, the notable Skan Askander, was a derelict glutton with a monster for a son and a slug for a daughter. This was unkind to the daughter. While she was no great beauty, she was definitely not a slug. After all, slugs do not have arms and legs – and, besides, slugs do not grow to that size.

There was a grain of truth in the traveller's statement, in as much as the son was a regrettable young man. However, soon afterwards, the son was accidentally drowned when he made the mistake of falling into a swamp with his hands and feet tied together and a knife sticking out of his back.

This tragedy did not encourage the traveller to extend his sympathies to the family. Instead, he invented fresh accusations. This wayfarer, an ignorant tourist if ever there was one, claimed that the king had leprosy. This was false. The king merely had a well-developed case of boils.

The man with the evil mouth was guilty of a further malignant slander when he stated that King Skan Askander was a cannibal. This was untrue. While it must be admitted that the king once ate one of his wives, he did not do so intentionally; the whole disgraceful episode was the fault of the chef, who was a drunkard, and who was subsequently severely reprimanded.

Again, the traveller was in error when he claimed that the kingdom of Sung was badly governed. In fact, the kingdom was not governed at all. Indeed, even to imply that there was such a thing as the 'kingdom of Sung' was, to say the least, misleading.

The question of the governance, and, indeed, the very existence of the 'kingdon of Sung' is one that is worth pursuing in detail, before dealing with the traveller's other allegations.

It is true that there was a king, his name being Skan Askander, and that some of his ancestors had been absolute rulers of considerable power. It is also true that the king's chief swineherd, who doubled as royal cartographer, drew bold, confident maps proclaiming the borders of the realm. Furthermore, the king could pass laws, sign death warrants, issue currency, declare war or amuse himself by inventing new taxes. And what he could do, he did.

'We are a king who knows how to be king,' said the king.

And, certainly, anyone wishing to dispute his right to use the imperial 'we' would have had to contend with the fact that there was enough of him, in girth, bulk and substance, to provide the makings of four or five ordinary people, flesh, bones and all. He was an imposing figure; 'very imposing', one of his brides is alleged to have said, shortly before the accident in which she suffocated.

'We live in a palace,' said the king. 'Not in a tent like Khmar, the chief milkmaid of Tameran, or in a draughty pile of stones like Comedo of Estar.'

His remarks were, in due course, widely reported.

From Prince Comedo came the following tart rejoinder:

'Unlike yours, my floors are not made of milk-white marble. However, unlike yours, my floors are not knee-deep in pigshit.'

The Note from Comedo came promptly, for, pirates and sea monsters permitting, a few days by sea could take one from

Estar to Sung. Receiving that Note, Skan Askander placed it by his commode, where it would be handy for future royal use.

Much later, and to his great surprise, he received a communication from the Lord Emperor Khmar, the undisputed master of most of the continent of Tameran. The fact that Sung had come to the attention of Khmar was, to say the least, ominous. Khmar had this to say:

'Your words have been reported. In due course, they will be remembered against you.'

The king of Sung, terrified, endured the sudden onset of an attack of diarrhoea which had nothing to do with the figs he had been eating. His latest bride, seeing his acute distress, made the most of her opportunity, and vigorously counselled him to commit suicide. Knowing Khmar's reputation, he was tempted – but finally, to her great disappointment, declined. Nevertheless, he lived in fear; he had no way of knowing that he was simply the victim of one of Khmar's little jokes.

In an effort to avert disaster, the king of Sung made the following law:

'Skan Askander, king of Sung, ruler of Ravlish East, emperor of the Lesser Teeth and of the Greater, rightful heir of Penvash and of Trest and of Estar, scourge of the Hauma Sea and lord of the Central Ocean, will and must and does with respect and piety thrice daily honour an image of the Lord Emperor Khmar, most noble and esteemed Overlord of All Lands and All Peoples for All Eternity.'

This law was obeyed, one of Khmar's far-flung coins serving as an image until a statue could be made.

Thus, thrice daily, Skan Askander bowed down to his idol, the graven image of the distant emperor of Tameran. Khmar, hearing this, sent him a present – a wine skin containing the death-blood of a traitor. The skin was many days in transit; the condition of the contents on arrival are better imagined than described. However, the king thanked Khmar for his gift, and sent him a side of bacon in return.

Skan Askander ordered the wine skin, bereft of contents, to be paraded in front of his household once a year, at a solemn ceremony at which all present were to take or affirm an oath of fealty to the distant emperor.

This was done.

So it is clear that at least two of the king's laws were effective. Furthermore, obedient to his written commands, the sun rose in the east and set in the west; the moon waxed and waned; the tides rose and fell; the winds swept in from the open oceans and brought generous helpings of rain to his scrabble-rock kingdom.

Nevertheless, most of the laws passed by the king were widely flouted, or obeyed only by accident. He decreed that everyone should wash their clothes and their bodies at least once in every lunar month; scarcely one person in a thousand obeyed. He had more success with a law forbidding people to sleep by daylight, but no joy whatsoever with a ludicrous statute — he was drunk at the time he signed it into law — which endeavoured to compel people to obtain written permits from the state to authorise their births, deaths and marriages.

As for the king's wars, death warrants and taxes, these were never fought, executed or raised; indeed, most of the king's putative subjects never heard of those wars, death warrants and taxes. In fact, many of them lived out their lives without hearing of the king.

For, if the unvarnished truth be told, the borders established with such exactitude by Skan Askander's part-time cartographer were, not to put too fine a point upon it, fatuous. In the continent of Argan, many leagues to the east of the king's palace and piggery, the lands of Trest and Estar had their own rulers, while Penvash was commanded by the Melski, green-skinned monsters who had defeated the king's ancestors in a disastrous war which had permanently undermined the credibility of the monarchy.

To the south, the islands of the Greater Teeth were under the sway of the Orfus pirates, those gentlemen occasionally known — but only to themselves — as the Honourable Associates of the Free Federation of High Sea Sailors. Skan Askander's claim to rule the Greater Teeth was spurious; even the fishermen and fisherwomen who inhabited the low-slung sandy islands of the Lesser Teeth defied him, for they lived independently, acknowledging no rulers whatsoever.

As for the eastern end of the Ravlish Lands, where the king had his home, most of it was effectively under the control of the barons who lorded it over huge country estates, or was supervised by self-governing towns which had persuaded the world to describe them as 'city states', though few had a population of more than two thousand talking heads.

To return to our unkind traveller, who so maligned the unfortunate land of Sung, it has now been demonstrated that there was no truth to his claim that the kingdom of Sung was badly governed. His statement was not just untrue but impossible, for, as there was in practice no such thing as 'the kingdom of Sung', the question of its governance did not arise.

The traveller, out of ignorance or malice, made another mistake when he claimed that the main amusements in the kingdom of Sung were scavenging gorse, drowning in peat bogs and playing at fumble in the smothering fog.

The non-existence of the kingdom in question has already been amply demonstrated, which in itself serves to prove the allegation false. Assuming that the traveller was speaking of that eastern part of the Ravlish Lands commonly known as 'Sung' scarcely improves matters, for the statement would still be false both in its substance and its implications.

The traveller's accusation implies that Sung was a dull, foggy area dominated by gorse and peat bogs and inhabited by dull, provincial people at a loss for any reasonable form of entertainment.

Nothing could be further from the truth.

As a matter of fact, less than 7 per cent of the arable land was covered in gorse; in contrast, horse thistle, gripe and barbarian thorn accounted for 22 per cent between them, with another 12 per cent being dominated by snare, clox and blackberry. Overall, only 3 per cent of Sung was peat bog, a full 50 per cent being bleak-rock uplands, or trackless forests where ravening wolves would ravage the unwary, leaving the stripped skeletons to become bones of contention between bad-tempered porcupines and rabid foxes.

And to say that Sung was foggy! That was ridiculous. Foggy days were few and far between, there being only 10 days of fog a year, compared to 275 days of rain. Water is essential to life, so the inhabitants of Sung were particularly favoured and fortunate, for they were copiously supplied with this commodity, which was delivered free of charge or taxes.

Let it also be known that, contrary to the traveller's declaration, the amusements of the people were many. The principal pastimes were hunting, feuding, fighting and fornication. Drinking and gambling were also very popular. Certain hobbies, including fishing and rat-fighting, also had large followings, and, on occasion, the people found time for dancing, music and banqueting.

The inhabitants of Sung also had their own unique cultural heritage, the intricacies of which were seldom appreciated by outsiders; it included lively games such as 'Stone the Leper', and detailed religious rituals such as those laid down for strangling unwanted children and disposing of aged relatives.

Clearly, the unkind traveller whose comments have been the subject of this analysis did Sung a great wrong when he slandered it so unforgivably.

So who was he, and what were his motives?

The disgruntled tourist was none other than the renegade wizard of Drum, who lived on a high and barren island in the dangerous strait separating the continent of Argan from the Ravlish Lands. The wizard of Drum had passed through Sung frequently on his various peregrinations, and, for one reason or another, had never been very pleased with his reception.

Once, indeed, he almost became the victim of a game of 'Stone the Leper', which was unfortunate, as his incontinent reaction left fifty people dead and an entire village in smouldering ruins. It must be admitted, also, that the wizard of Drum was one of the victims of the Devaluation, which occurred shortly after he had been paid 5,268 punts for work he had done for the Wordsmiths and the Warguild. After that incident, he swore never again to have anything to do with Sung, or even to set foot in the place.

The Devaluation, which ruined many people, was the direct result of swine fever.

While the kingdom of Sung was at best a legal fiction, and the king of Sung little more than a handy butt for the jokes of most of his people, the currency issued by the king had for many years enjoyed great respect and stability.

King Skan Askander was passionately interested in pigs, which he bred on a large scale. The currency he issued was backed by pork, and consisted of elegant ceramic dials marked 'one rasher', 'five rashers' or 'fifty rashers', and of thin bronze disks which each declared that 'This Punt Will Be Redeemed By The Royal Exchequer For One Side Of Bacon'.

Then came the great swine fever epidemic of the year Askander 32. In the consequent and inevitable Devaluation, a punt became worth a single rasher of bacon, and the minor ceramic coins became worthless. Hence the wrath of the wizard of Drum, who, besides being rather partial to pork, had seven hungry dragons to feed.

While the wizard of Drum had nothing good to say of Sung, there was some good that could be said of it. There were no droughts and no deserts; the land was free from scorpions and crocodiles; nobody died of thirst and nobody of heatstroke; there were no forest fires, and there was virtually unlimited stone for building with.

Furthermore, despite the weakness of the king, the ferocity of the barons, the strictly parochial interest of the city states and the local penchant for feuding and fighting, the land was protected by a rough and ready form of law and order administered by the Warguild. The wizard of Drum once described the Warguild as a club for the promotion of amateur archery; while it is true that the Warguild held archery contests, with wine and women as the prizes, there was much more to it than that.

The Warguild was a league of the more aggressive barons who had made a mutual defence treaty to protect the realm. It had been formed thirty years previously, when the land had

13

been plagued by bandits and warlords; having routed out those nuisances, the Warguild now occasionally exercised itself by undertaking mercenary forays, or by serving as guards with Galish convoys.

Many Galish convoys passed through Sung, as the main long-distance trading route, the Salt Road, ran through the land. Furthermore, convoys often wintered in Sung. The Galish found it attractive first and most importantly because the king was too weak to levy any residency taxes, and, second, because the local patois was a form of Galish, albeit much modified. Indeed, some generations previously, this land had been colonised by a number of Galish convoys at a time when war, plague and famine had made trading particularly difficult. The lifestyle of the inhabitants of Sung was now wildly different from that of the Galish traders, to put it mildly, but, when they spoke, they still found each other mutually intelligible.

If there had been any problems in mutual understanding then the Wordsmiths, now busy perfecting their command of all known languages, could surely have translated. The Wordsmiths, an organisation slightly older than the Warguild, had formed their alliance shortly after the discovery of the odex, which, in the year Askander 35 — three years after the Devaluation — was held in the Wordsmiths' stronghold in a city state in the mountains, a town known as Keep, which boasted a population of a full 5,000 souls.

Not far from Keep was the estate of Baron Chan Poulaan, who, on a certain night in the season of autumn, was keeping a close eye on his son Togura, who was dancing with the girl Day Suet. Now the Suets were a family from Keep, a powerful banking and trading family which actively supported the Wordsmiths. Baron Chan Poulaan, head of the Warguild, considered himself to be, in some respects, de facto ruler of Sung; he was suspicious of traders, bankers and of the Wordsmiths, and saw the family Suet in particular as a potential rival for influence and power.

At this stage, it is worth noting that the palace of King Skan Askander lay close to the city state of Keep. The Suets were, therefore, in a good position to make a grab for any residual powers commanded by the royal family. It was said that one of the boys of the Suet family was bravely romancing the king's daughter, Slerma, who, at sweet sixteen, was alleged to weigh in at sixty bushels.

Baron Chan Poulaan had already determined that his son Togura would marry the king's daughter. He had come to a private agreement with Skan Askander, and had already informed Togura that he would soon be betrothed to Slerma.

Watching Togura and Day, Baron Poulaan noted how closely they held each other when the dance came to a clinch, and frowned.

CHAPTER TWO

The banquet was in full swing. Buoyant with drink and excitement, Day and Togura danced to the skirl of the skavamareen. In the clinch, he brushed against her soft breasts, which flushed out against her light woollen chemise. Her sly little fingers dared his hard-fleshed buttocks, then stopped because:

'Your father's watching us.'

'I love you,' said Togura.

'No, really, he's watching us,' said Day. 'He doesn't look happy.'

'Kiss me. Kiss me quick!'

'Not here!'

As the music ended, she pulled away from him. He pursued her through the crowded hall. He chased her out through the main doors, and then, giggling, she allowed him to catch her.

They kissed.

Her mouth was warm and yielding. His embrace savoured the curves of her back and her buttocks. Moths danced around the doorway lanterns. The night was cool but he was hot, his lust shafting hard within his trews. He smelt her hair, her skin, her perfume.

He burped.

'Really!' said Day, breaking away.

She poked him in the belly, provoking another burp. She

poked him again, teasing him with cunning jabs which he was helpless to resist. As he flinched, she giggled.

Then kissed him.

Seriously.

'Your father was watching us,' said Day, breaking the kiss. 'He wasn't happy at all.'

'He can shunk his cho and scavenge it,' said Togura, using the local gutter argot.

'Togura Poulaan!' said Day severely.

From inside the banqueting hall came a rowdy burst of laughter which rose above the general hubbub. What had so amused the banquet guests? Togura, knowing his people well, guessed that probably someone had been debagged, or that a helpless drunk had vomited over someone of high importance.

The laughter died down and the music started up again. A drone joined the wail of the skavamareen while a sklunk back-thumped and a chanter whined.

'My lady,' said Togura, with a formal bow. 'Shall we dance?'

'Talatashee,' she said, assenting.

They danced the vigorous kola-ka-skee, kicking their heels and whirling on the changes, inventing partners for the passages known as romance and the flora — for the kola-ka-skee, of course, is for a foursome.

While they were dancing, an old man tottered into the lamplight. They danced on, until, disturbed by his silent scrutiny, they broke apart and turned to face him. He was a tattered vagrant with a ravaged face and a dirty grey beard.

'It is night,' said the old man in a thin, querulous voice.

'No,' said Day smartly. 'It's day.'

'Do you mean to make fun of me, little smut?' said the old man.

'Talatashee' said Day.

'Tala-shee? Now what's that, young lady? Yes or no?'

He was clearly a foreigner.

'Who are you, old man?' said Togura.

The old man leaning on his shepherd's crook, was about to answer when the music escalated to a stormburst crescendo. A

17

thrum began to gallop, a kloo honked harshly, a krymbol crashed and scattered, a skittling nook began to campaign against the skavamareen and a plea whistle hooted.

'What,' said the old man, 'is that appalling noise?'

'Music,' said Day. 'Don't you like it?'

The old man sniffed.

'The miscreants perpetrating that dismal cacophony should be fed to the dragon pits,' he said.

Togura could not figure him out. His manner was bold, and had, indeed, a hint of lordliness about it. Yet he was clearly a tramp of one kind or another. He was wearing a roughwork patchwork skirt, which finished above his knees, and a battered short-cut weather cloak of the type favoured by fishermen. His boots were coming apart at the toes, exposing his feet.

'What are you doing on my father's estate, old man?' said Togura.

'Child, I had the misfortune to be shipwrecked here,' replied the ancient.

'Shipwrecked!' said Togura.

Day giggled.

'Don't laugh, gamos,' said the old man, naming Day with the Galish word for a female horse, which was upardonably vulgar.

'Why you—'

'No, Tog,' said Day, holding him back.

'Did you hear what he called you?' said Togura, burning with anger.

'She heard me, boy,' said the old man, in his stilted, strangely accented Galish, so unlike the smooth-flowing local patios. 'How about some hospitality for a shipwrecked mariner now?'

'If you find yourself afloat, then hard liquor's to answer, not the sea,' said Togura. 'In case you didn't notice before you started drinking yourself silly, you're up in the mountains, not down by the coast.'

'I know that,' said the old man steadily. 'Now have a little pity on poor old Pitilkin and show him a bed for the night. I've

18

sailed from Chi' ash-lan, and that's a hearty journey my boy. Chi' ash-lan to Quartermain, that's a fair old step.'

'You're not in Quartermain,' said Togura. 'You're in Sung.'

'Ah!' said the old man, eyes bright with revelation. 'That explains everything. The barbarities inflicted on the human ear in the name of music. The provinical manners of the local peasants. The—'

'Are you calling me—'

'Tog,' said Day. 'Don't argue, you're only encouraging him. He's a poor harmless old man. Why not have the servants show him to a garrow for the night? Alternatively—'

At that moment a rowdy party came barrelling out of the banquet hall — seven or eight reeling drunks laughing and jostling as they staggered out into the fresh night air. Amongst them was Cromarty, Togura's hefty half-brother, who was three years his senior.

'Why, hey!' said Cromarty. 'It's Spunk Togura and little girl Day. Hitting the eiderdown tonight, chids? Getting in some of the old kerna tamerna?' His cronies guffawed and ribbed each other. Then Cromarty saw the stranger. 'This is new, boys, hey hey? What ho! I say, grandad, past your bedtime, isn't it? Shall we put him to bed, boys? Hey what?'

'You can help me fix my ship if you would,' said the ancient mariner. 'If not, I'll do it by daylight once I've slept.'

'A ship, hey. A ship? Boys, this we have to see. Snaffle the lantern, Lanks. Nids, you salvage the other.' On Cromarty's orders, the two lanterns guarding the banqueting hall's entrance were snaffled and salvaged. 'Come along, grandad,' said Cromarty. 'Show us your ship. Coming for a sail, Day? Come along now!'

Cromarty's bounders seized her.

'Let her go!' said Togura.

He waded into them, flailing wildly, but he was grossly outnumbered. The scungers grabbed him, and he was frog-marched into the night. As they swaggered along with lanterns swinging wildly, the drunks roared out the Kanover drinking song.

'Where now, grandad?' said Cromarty.

'This way,' said the ancient mariner. 'This way!'

Gaining a small knoll, the drunks dropped Togura face-first into the long rough grass. This, of course, was dew-damp, and appeared to contain more than the usual quota of gorse.

'What ho!' said Cromarty. 'The ship, hey?'

Getting to his feet, Togura saw, by lantern-light, a clutter of sticks which looked like a gargantuan parody of a crow's nest. Cromarty hefted one of the heavier sticks.

'Careful with that, boy,' said the old man sharply. 'That's the rudder.'

'Rudder, hey? Then this is the jakes, suppose, suppose.'

And Cromarty hauling out his penis, began to piss on the sticks. The old man swiped at his buttocks with his shepherd's crook. Cromarty, startled, lost control of his shlong, and pissed all over his pants.

'You klech!' shouted Cromarty, tucking away his shmuck. 'You ornskwun vig of a hellock!'

And he gave the old man a push, sending him reeling back into one of the drunks, who dropped the lantern he was holding. It smashed, leaving them with a single light.

'That's enough, Cromarty!' said Togura. 'You're disgracing the estate!'

'Why so,' said Cromarty softly. 'Our little Spunk Togura is riding the angers, hey? All up and on about the precious estate. It's my estate, little boy! I'm the one who inherits.'

'Then behave yourself until you do,' said Togura manfully. 'Now pack your rabble out of here. Go!'

'Not so swell, my hearty,' said Cromarty, unshipping a knife. 'Not so swell.'

Togura was unarmed. He grabbed for a stick, but one of Cromarty's scungers stepped on it.

'Cut him good, Crom!' said one.

'I will,' said Cromarty, his face turning ugly. 'Oh, certain, certain. It's ribbons for little Togura!'

'No fighting, children,' said the old man, trying to inervene. 'Pitilkin doesn't like fighting.'

'Stand aside, grandad,' said Cromarty, giving him a hearty push.

'Kill him, Crom!' yelled an eager admirer.

'I will,' said Cromarty. 'For sure.'

And he moved in on the attack. He slashed at Togura, who leapt backwards. Cromarty advanced. He was good with a blade. Even when drunk, he was good.

'Stop this!' screamed Day.

She tried to intervene, but was restrained. Cromarty's mobsters had their blood up. They were shouting:

'Into him, Crom!'

'Scallop him!'

'Finish him!'

Suddenly the old man swung his shepherd's crook. The stout wooden shaft smashed Cromarty's wrist. Quick as a flash, the old man demolished the surviving lantern. There were shouts, roars and cries of pain in the darkness. Togura hit the dirt and stayed down. Someone trampled over him, fleeing for shelter. He heard the vicious whistle of the old man's stick slicing through the air.

Then it was all over. Cromarty and his friends had fled. They could be heard swearing in the darkness; then, as their cries diminished in the distance, Togura became aware that music was still playing in the banquet hall. While he was in danger of getting sliced and diced, his father's guests had been amusing themselves all unawares of the drama taking place out in the night.

'Tog!' called Day, loudly, almost directly overhead.

'Here,' said Togura, feeling for her in the darkness as he tried to get to his feet.

His blundering hand slid straight up her dress to the warmest part of her flesh. She screamed. He jerked his hand away as if it had been burnt.

'Tog,' said Day uncertainly. 'Was that you?'

'Me,' admitted Togura, blushing in the darkness.

'What the feck and fuckle did you think it was, girl?' said the ancient mariner. 'An octopus? Come on, children, pull yourselves together.'

They did not answer, for they were now embracing.

'Tog, oh Tog,' said Day, holding him close and tight. 'I was so worried. Are you all right?'

'Fine,' said Togura. 'If only I had a blade! I would've cut him from spleen to kidney. I would've—'.

'Leave your heroics till later,' said the old man sharply. 'If we can't work on the boat tonight, I want to get to sleep. Where's my bed for the night?'

'You've got a nerve!' said Togura, who bitterly resented the fact that it was this querulous old madman who had just saved his life or his beauty, or maybe both.

'Come on,' said Day. 'Don't be nasty. I'm sure we can find him a place to stay for the night.'

'Oh, all right then,' said Togura. 'Let's go.'

They went back to the banquet hall, where they met Quail the rouster. He was bearing a lighted candle, which he was trying to shield with his hand. As they drew near, he recognised them.

'Master Togura!' said Quail. 'Have you seen the doorway lanterns by any chance?'

'Why, has someone lifted them?' said Togura.

'Yes. Some of your young friends, perhaps? That little sod Cromarty was on the muck tonight.'

'Is that so?' said Togura. 'Well, a couple of lanterns isn't the end of the world. Tell me, man Quail, can you bed down this gentleman for the night?'

Quail peered at their ancient mariner.

'Are you sure we want to house this individual, Master Togura?'

'Pitilkin sleeps quietly,' said the old man, his voice quavering. 'No trouble, no trouble.'

'Just for the night,' said Togura.

'It won't do any harm,' said Day.

'Well . . . just for the night then,' said Quail, doubtfully. 'There's probably a spare garrow at the backstop, if the incest twins haven't bedded themselves down for the night. Otherwise, I'm afraid, it'll be the stable.'

'Thanks,' said Togura, turning to go.

'Oh, and Master Togura — if you see Cromarty and his spry young brags, ask them about the lanterns, will you?'

'We will,' said Day. 'Thanks for everything.'

Togura took her hand, and they walked off into the night together. His hopes were high, but they were soon to be disappointed: he did not lose his virginity that night.

CHAPTER THREE

'I don't suppose you know how your brother damaged his wrist,' said Baron Chan Poulaan.

'I don't keep track of his business,' said his son Togura.

The baron harrumphed, but did not press the point.

The two were riding side by side. They were on a road, or what passed for a road in those parts, which led to the city state of Keep. The baron was riding a brindled mare and his son was riding a donkey. Following on behind, riding Kloggles the Mule – and it took a brave man or a foolish man to venture that – was Prick, the baron's venerable secretary.

'The fog seems to be closing in,' said Togura, looking around.

'I'd noticed that,' said his father.

'Perhaps we should stop till it clears.'

'We might be here all day,' said his father. 'We'll go on.'

And they did.

Visibility swiftly became zero. The road abruptly became peat bog. After floundering around in the mist for a while, they staggered out of the bog, hauling their animals along with them, only to find themselves waist-deep in flourishing gorse. The baron cursed and struck out with his sword, accidently clouting Prick with the flat of the blade.

Fortunately, it then began to rain, causing the fog to dissipate swiftly. Unfortunately, they found themselves on a small gorse-covered island surrounded by peat bog.

24

'There's the road!' said Togura, pointing to an indeterminate ribbon of mud and stones lying some distance from the island.

'Your powers of observation astound me,' said the baron grimly, leading the way back into the bog.

Kloggles the Mule was most reluctant to leave their little island, but, after a savage battle with no holds barred, they forced him back through the bog to the road. By this time, they were mud from ankle to shoulder. Fortunately, the rain was rapidly becoming a solid downpour, suggesting that they might be able to strip off their dirty clothes, take a shower in the rain then change into clean clothes. Unfortunately, they had no clean clothes to change into.

'I think,' said Togura, 'That perhaps this is not the best of days on which to go and visit the king.'

'You are young, my son,' said his father, 'But not entirely devoid of wisdom. Come, let us make for home.'

And they retreated back down the road, which was rapidly becoming a quagmire.

The next day, in fine clear weather, they set out again. The road was muddy, but they reached the outskirts of Keep in good order. It was then that they encountered what appeared to be a free-floating monster.

In some places, this apparition might have been taken for a ghost, a hallucination or a trick of the light, but this was Sung, and they knew the intruder for what it was — an ilps.

The ilps was very large.

It had seventy-nine teeth, shared between two mouths of generous dimensions.

Five of the teeth were poisoned.

It stank of rotten oranges.

Its fingertips smoked with blue light.

'Who are you?' said Baron Chan Poulaan, speaking roughly.

'Ska,' said the ilps.

'Where do you come from?'

'Ska. Nanesh stel.'

It was fading rapidly.

'Where were you born?'

25

One of its mouths collapsed.

The baron assaulted the ilps with harsh, insistent questions. Disintegrating under the attack, it started to retreat. But he followed, urging his horse forward, asking one question after another. Finally, battered to death by his verbal assault, it broke apart into a dozen rainbows, which scattered into discordant chords of music.

Nothing remained but the smell of rotten oranges.

'That was a large one,' said Prick.

'They get larger all the time,' said the baron. 'And more numerous. Unless someone brings the Wordsmiths to heel, we'll have a regular disaster on our hands.'

The Wordsmiths claimed that their precious odex held all the knowledge of all the ancient long-lost civilisations which had existed before the Days of Wrath. They claimed to be learning how to control and manipulate the odex, but all they had produced so far was a string of distorted monsters.

Baron Poulaan could reasonably claim to be the most powerful man in Sung, but that meant little; as yet, he lacked the power to challenge the Wordsmiths, for his fellow barons were not yet convinced that the odex was a bad thing.

Brooding about the ilps, the odex and the Wordsmiths, the baron led the way into Keep, passing between mountainous slag heaps. They passed a few houses then a mine shaft. A fire was burning by the shaft, helping to draw stale air up from the depths and keep the miners alive. A creaking bucket lift was bringing up gemstock ore from the veins which ran far underground.

'Dismount,' said Baron Poulaan.

They went by foot thereafter, leading their mounts through the tilted, canting streets. After five generations of mining, which had hollowed out a considerable portion of the rock beneath the town, the whole urban area was very slowly subsiding. Hence the odd angles of the streets, which were buckling and twisting, and the nightmarish angles of the shops and houses.

After a slow and dangerous journey, they reached the far side of Keep and set off for the palace of King Skan Askander, scourge of the Hauma Sea and lord of the Central Ocean. They had gone through the town rather than around it because Baldskull Mountain lay on one side and Dead Man's Drop on the other.

Once out of town, they mounted up again, but soon had to climb down to lead their animals past a massive subsidence in the road, which was only slowly being filled in with slag.

'That's new since I was here last,' said Baron Poulaan. 'And that was scarcely a month ago.'

One day, he expected to come this way and find that the entire town of Keep had fallen into a hole. He would not be unhappy when it did. After all, his estate never saw a single flog or splorin's worth of the town's mining profits. He had no love for the earthgrubbing miners, or for the merchants who fattened on the profits of the trade in opal, topaz, jade, japonica, russellite, kolzaw, fuze, buff, celestine and carnelian which the miners recovered from the gemstock.

'My lord!' said Prick, pointing. 'Ahead! The palace!'

'I saw it some time ago,' said the baron.

Togura, who had never been this way before, looked for the building of white marble which so many people had spoken of, but could not see it for the fences, sheds, huts and granubles of the surrounding piggeries.

Shortly afterwards, they were shown into the presence of the king, who invited them to dine with him.

'We will be having swedes, rutabaga and the kidneys of several pigs,' he said.

'We will be honoured,' said Baron Poulaan.

'And, dear baron,' said King Skan Askander, 'my darling daughter will be dining with us, so your son will have a chance to meet his future bride.'

Togura nerved himself for this ordeal. But he was confident that it could not be as bad as people had led him to believe. After all, Slerma was only sixteen years old; there was scarcely time for her to have grown to the monstrous size which she was alleged to have attained. She was probably just a little fat and sludgy. Well, he could endure that – he thought. It would mean that he would one day inherit the palace and the piggery,

27

which would be a valuable asset once it had fully recovered from the effects of the swine fever which had caused the Devaluation.

If Slerma was no great beauty, she would doubtless welcome the attentions of a real man like himself. She would at least be a real woman, hot and wet in the right places. She would complete his sentimental education and initiate him into manhood.

They were shown into the dining room. The king seated himself on a couch, which creaked ominously beneath his weight. Then he snapped his fingers, and a young woman entered. Togura's face fell. This was Slerma? She was worse than he had expected. She was more than plump: she was positively bloated.

'My wife,' said the king.

And the young woman bowed to them.

Togura was relieved.

'Where is Slerma, dear?' said the king.

'She's just coming now, my lord,' said his wife.

'Ah, there you are!' said the king. 'Hello, Slerma. Meet our new guests.'

As he was speaking, a vast and slovenly giantess was in the process of forcing her way into the room. She was huge. She was gross. She was impossible. Togura wanted to scream and run, but found himself paralysed by fear.

'Is this it?' she said in a thick, slurred voice, eyeing him with disapproval.

'Yes, my dear,' said the king happily.

'There's not much to it,' said Slerma, laying one prodigious paw on Togura's shoulder.

She squeezed. He felt as if he was being crunched by a vast nut cracker. Then, just before she did permanent damage to flesh and bone, she released the pressure.

'There's no meat on it,' she complained. 'I want Guta.'

'No!' said her father sharply. 'You cannot marry the baker's boy. I forbid it.'

'He's a real man,' said Slerma. 'Not like this – this thing. Do you speak, thing?'

28

'I am articulate, intelligent and proud of it,' said Togura, finding his voice at last.

'What does articulate mean?' said Slerma.

'It means,' said the king, 'that all his working parts are in good order.'

'They'd better be in good order, thing,' said Slerma, addressing Togura. 'I'm a girl with big appetites. Remember that! Once we're married, you'd better be faithful, too. Or I'll kill you.'

'Now dear,' said her father mildly. 'Don't frighten him. He's a good little boy. I'm sure he'll behave himself.'

'Far too little!' said Slerma. 'Not like Guta.'

'I'm sure you can fatten him up,' said the king. 'In fact, now is as good a time as any to start.'

He clapped his hands, and their meal was brought in. There were two or three plates apiece for Togura, the baron and Prick, a number of heavily platters for the king and his wife, and a large trough for Slerma.

Togura found his appetite had failed him.

'Eat!' ordered Slerma, filling the room with the ominous rumble of her thick, slurred voice. 'Eat! Food is good for you!'

Ad she set an example, gouging out huge handfuls of swede, rutabaga and kidney, slapping them into her mouth then swallowing, apparently without chewing. Togura tried to see if her teeth were missing, but failed. It was impossible even to tell whether her vast, wallowing face had a jawbone. Seasick folds of flesh swayed, buckled and lurched as she ate. Technically, some of that flesh must have belonged to her cheeks and some to her chin, but such distinctions vanished in the awesome slurry of fat which constituted her face.

'You're not eating!' she bellowed.

She seized Togura and plastered his face with kidney. Some went up his nose, some squeezed its way into his mouth and some fell into his lap.

'Eat!' she yelled, hurting his ears.

She gave him a shake. If she used any more force, she was going to dislocate bones. Togura tried to wriggle free, but it was impossible.

'Eat, thing!' hissed Slerma, spraying him with spittle.

To his dismay, he began to weep, crying with hot tears of agony and shame. Slerma gave him another shake then tossed him to one side.

'Your son insults us,' said King Skan Askander, his voice going very cold.

'Togura!' shouted Baron Poulaan. 'Pull yourself together!' His son got to his knees.

'I hate you!' he said, clenching his fists. He sniffed.

Then he took another look at Slerma, and suddenly vomited. Then he fled.

CHAPTER FOUR

Towards the end of day, Baron Chan Poulaan finally managed to locate his son Togura, who had taken refuge in the Murken Hotel. This building, the victim of a subsidence, looked just about ready to fall over. Outside, huge timbers shored up the walls. Inside, the place was a maze of props and cross-struts. As the baron entered, the building was alive with hammering; it had taken an alarming lurch sideways that afternoon, and emergency reinforcements were now being put into place.

The proprietor, a foul-smelling hunchbacked dwarf with a huge goitre, directed the baron to Togura's room.

'Take me there,' said the baron.

The dwarf flattened his nose against the back of his hand, which, in those parts, was an emphatic gesture of refusal.

'I don't venture upstairs,' said the dwarf.

The baron saw the wisdom of that as soon as he started up the rickety stairs, which creaked and groaned beneath his feet, imploring him for mercy. Reaching Togura's door, he hammered against it with both fists. A slow dust of powdered dry rot began to sift down from the beams above; alarmed, the baron stopped hammering.

'Togura!' he yelled. 'I know you're in there.'

Silence from within.

The baron threw his shoulder against the door. The floor shook, the stairs creaked alarmingly, but the door held.

31

'Come out, boy,' shouted the baron.

From within, a muffled voice responded:

'Go away!'

'Open the door, so we can talk.'

Silence replied.

'Come on, open the door!'

There was a pause, then confused sounds from within. Then the door was opened a crack. The baron, with a roar, threw his weight against it. A crossbeam overhead ruptured, showering him with sawdust. But the door still refused to admit him.

'What have you done to the door?' demanded the baron,

Togura replied, but the baron, sneezing vigorously because of the sawdust in his nose, failed to hear.

'What was that?' he said.

'You heard me,' said Togura.

'I suppose you've wedged the door with a baulk of timber.'

'That's what I said.'

'You're not going to cry again, are you?' sneered the baron, hearing the distress in his son's voice.

'Go away,' said Togura.

'I will not go away,' said his father. 'You will open the door, quit this place and come home with me. Then, once we've had a little talk together, we'll go back to the palace. To see Slerma.'

'No!' howled Togura. 'No, no, not that. I'd rather die.'

'Stop being melodramatic,' said the baron impatiently. 'I can't see what you're making all this fuss about. When all's said and done, she's a healthy young girl with a moderately wealthy father.'

'She's obscene.'

'Many men like their women a little plump. After all, you've got to have something to hold onto once you get in the saddle.'

'A little plump! Paps, that woman's a horse, a cow and a whale all rolled into one. She's—'.

'Don't call me paps,' snapped the baron, who hated hearing that kind of tiny-tot talk from his son. 'It's time to grow up,

Togura. Be a man. You're not going to kill yourself, so you'll just have to live with the life you've got.'

'Yes, I want to live. That man-eater would kill me. I—'

'Stop that! Togura, face facts. You're not going to inherit. Cromarty gets the estate. If you marry, you get the king's title and his property once he dies. He's an old man, he can't last much longer.'

'Neither will I if I—'

'Enough! Listen! Soon, Togura, this wretched town of Keep is going to fall into the ground or slide into Dead Man's Drop. The king's property will be more valuable than ever then. Anyone wanting to mine the gemstock will have to—'.

'I won't sell myself for money,' shouted Togura. 'I want to marry a woman, not a walking slime pit.'

'You don't have much option,' said the baron.

'If I have to, I'll go down to the coast and sell myself to the first slaver passing through. I'd rather—'

'This nonsense has gone far enough,' said the baron, cutting him off. 'Open this door properly and come out. We're going home. Now!'

'No.'

'No?'

'No!'

'No!!??'

'No!!!!'

'By the sperm of my ancestors,' raged the baron, using the most fearsome oath he knew. 'You'll come out of there right now or suffer the immediate and unlimited consequences. No son of mine is going to defy his father like that.'

'Push off, paps,' said Togura, all defiance.

The baron then assaulted the door vigorously. A chunk of rotten wood fell from the ceiling, and one of the risers of the stairway split open, but the door itself was solid, and held. Finally, cursing and muttering, spitting sawdust and swearing ferociously, the baron retreated downstairs. He took rooms for himself and for Prick, paying the ground floor premium; they would spend the night there, and deal with Togura in the morning.

Togura, alone and lonely in his room, barred the door then cried himself to sleep. The bed on which he slept was a huge, solid and incredibly ancient affair made of stout timbers standing waist-high off the floor; as he slept, he was a small crumpled island of misery in an ocean of dirty linen. Bed bugs, oblivious of his emotional agony, feasted merrily on his helpless flesh.

Sleeping, Togura dreamt that he was in a castle which was under siege. Invaders were attacking the main gate with a battering ram. The sullen thud and thump of the assault began to undermine his composure. The ram charged again, hitting the door with a crash so loud that it woke him up.

Togura, starting from sleep and blinking at darkness, stared in the direction of the door. Someone was demolishing it. With a final crash, the door splintered and gave way. A faintly aromatic smell of ancient timbers percolated through the room. Outside, on the stairway, some large animal was breathing heavily with a kind of wet, guttural wheezing.

'Paps?' said Togura uncertainly.

'Prepare yourself, little man,' said the animal, in a thick slurred voice.

'Slerma!' screamed Togura.

The animal outside made strenuous efforts to enter, but failed. The doorway was too small.

'Slerma,' said Togura, in a shaky voice. 'I'll do anything you say. Just don't hurt me, that's all. I love you.'

He was answered by a scream of rage.

'Love? Love! Little man, I'll kill you! Guta will kill you. How dare you make love to his Slerma?'

Too late, Togura realised his fatal mistake.

'No, Guta!' cried Togura. 'I didn't mean it. I don't want Slerma. I don't want anything to do with her.'

'Liar! You were seen. Their serving girl told me. You were seen. Embracing! Deep in her charms, her arms enfolding you. She fed you with her own magnificent hand.'

'Guta, I really don't want her. She's appalling. She's hideous. She's a mass of flab and sausage meat. She makes me sick, she—'

34

'You insult my darling. My true love. My fondest dream. The one and only real woman in the world. Animal! I'm going to kill you!'

The building shook, timbers groaned, the roof strained, and Guta forced himself into Togura's room. As darkness crashed toward him, roaring, Togura rolled out of bed and took cover underneath the bed. Guta, finding the bed in the night, hoisted himself aboard and began to trample it with his knees. He roared out incomprehensible obscenities as he sought for his victim.

Frustrated at finding nothing, Guta tore the sheets apart. Then he grabbed hold of the mattress and ripped it open, spilling mouldy old straw and bracken into the night, together with bedbugs, lice, dead spiders and a virile colony of the kind of red ants that bite. Then he began to jump on the bed.

Just before the bed splintered and gave way, Togura rolled out from underneath and sprinted for the doorway. He tripped, fell, recovered himself, barked his shins against something, cracked his head against a low-lying beam, then gained safety. At least for the moment. Where now? Up, down? Togura ascended, pounding up the stairs, thinking the fearsome young troll behind him would not dare to attempt the increasingly fragile heights of the Murken Hotel.

He was wrong.

Hauling himself back out through the doorway, Guta started up the stairs after Togura. He began to gain on him. Togura strove for extra speed. But Guta was fast and ferocious. He grabbed hold of Togura's foot. Togura screamed. The stairs collapsed. Guta roared. Screaming and roaring, the two plunged downward to their doom. Guta landed first, smashing his head open and breaking his back, which killed him. Togura landed on top of the corpse of his recently deceased rival. A shower of rotten wood rained down on the two of them.

Togura became aware of doors opening. There was a muttering of voices in the darkness. Then the proprietor came on the scene. The hunchbacked dwarf was bearing a candle, an evil-smelling stump of black wax which burnt with a greenish-blue light, filling the air with smoke and shadows. The dwarf was doing his best to restrain a huge rat which he had on a short leash. It was the size of a mastiff, had blood-red eyes and razor-sharp teeth, and was slavering as it strained against the leash, which was attached to a collar ringed with spikes of sharpened metal.

The dwarf surveyed the damage.

Then he kicked Guta in the head.

'Leave,' said the dwarf.

The dwarf knew that Guta was a valuable catch. The city state of Pera Pesh, a fishing town of some one thousand people down by the coast, had put a price on his head. He was wanted, dead or alive, for a variety of crimes including grave robbing, necrophilia, the theft of a small whale and the destruction of a small stone bridge which he had incautiously walked across. The reward would more than compensate for the cost of repairs.

'I'm going right now,' said Togura, with what fraction of his voice he had so far been able to recover.

'Togura,' said a loud voice from one of the darkened doorways. 'You come here this instant.'

It was his father, the formidable baron.

Togura got to his feet, and fled.

CHAPTER FIVE

Togura found refuge in a fire watcher's hut by a mine shaft. It gave him at least a modicum of shelter against the cold autumn weather. Exhausted, he slept. He woke, once, to find something gnawing at his boots. He kicked it away. Hissing and spluttering it retreated; after that, he found it hard to get back to sleep again.

At dawn, a fire watcher arrived, a big, gruff man with a red beard and bloodshot eyes, and big dirty boots, one of which had marked Togura's backside by the time he made his escape. Outside, a light drizzle was falling. Miners, with pick axes and shovels slung over their shoulders, were trooping to the climbing shafts.

Shivering, Togura wandered off, wondering what to do now. He had already considered turning to Day Suet for help, and had rejected the notion; he was too proud to beg, and, in any case, doubted that her family would welcome him if he came as a beggar.

The streets of Keep were dangerous, as always, for housewives were going through the morning routine of emptying chamber pots out of the window. Ducking and dodging, Togura escaped with no more than a few stray licks of splatter. His zigzag course through the drunken streets brought him to the very brink of Dead Man's Drop.

Togura stood on the Edge, looking out at the dim grey horizon now soured by stormclouds. The ground dropped away sheer to the pinnacles of the Claws which would receive his body if he jumped, fell or was pushed. Between the Claws and the enclosing horizon lay the leagues of the Famines, a regular wasteland of scoured rock and eroding hillsides speckled with colonies of gorse, clox, snare and barbarian thorn. Down in the hollows there was the occasional glint of lake or slough.

Far below Togura's feet, some nimble birds darted through the dull-weather sky. They, at least, had homes to go to, and regular occupations to follow.

Overcome by a sudden access of self-pity, Togura considered throwing himself over, but decided against it. The pleasures of self-pity were, for the moment, far too sweet. Besides, he still had some money left. It would be foolish to suicide before spending all his cash.

Turning away from Dead Man's Drop, Togura walked down the street. He had only just departed when the piece of stone he had been standing on fell away, almost soundlessly, and toppled into the gulf. Hearing the faint sound the stone made when it slipped away, Togura turned. But, seeing nothing, shrugged, and went on his way.

Two streets from Dead Man's Drop, Togura bought some roasted chestnuts from a street vendor, a crippled hag with a festering rupia despoiling the skin beneath her left eye. She tried to cheat him. They argued. He swore. She cursed him. They parted on bad terms, he with her chestnuts and she with his money, both convinced that they had got the worst of the bargain; rounding a corner, he kicked at a cat with ringworm, swore again, then stopped to eat.

As he ate, he began to feel better.

As Togura savoured his chestnuts, he watched two raff-taff street dogs fighting. Then a man came hurrying down the road; after him came a hunting harridan dressed in harn, who screamed abuse at him.

Togura thought to himself:

– Now what was all that about?

He was accosted by a rough, burly swordsman of middle years, who spoke to him in a strangely accented Galish:

38

'Which way to the king's palace, boy?'

'Who is it who wants to know?' said Togura.

'Barak the Battleman, hired killer and trained assassin,' said the swordsman.

That was a lie. The stranger was, in fact, Guest Gulkan, sometimes known as the Emperor In Exile. He was the son of Onosh Gulkan, the Witchlord; he had been wandering the world for years now, travelling to places as far distant as Dalar ken Halvar and Chi' ash-lan. He lied about his name because there was a price on his head in many parts and places.

'The palace lies that way,' said Togura, pointing firmly, and hoping that he was right; at the moment, he was more than a little disorientated.

'Thank you, lad,' said the stranger, and strode away with an easy, rolling gait.

Togura watched him go, struck, momentarily, with horror. The king was angry with him! The king had hired an assassin! He was going to be hunted and tortured and killed!

Then Togura realised he was being ridiculous. There was no way the king could have got hold of an assassin so soon, even supposing that he had been made that angry; the stranger's appearance in this place was probably just idle coincidence.

Togura's analysis was correct.

Realising that the stranger was no danger to him, Togura was taken by the wild notion of following him and questioning him. Perhaps the swordmaster-assassin could use a road companion to carry his burdens and light his fires, to cook his food and to haggle for provisions in the marketplace. There was no harm in trying.

Enthusiastic about this idea, Togura set off in pursuit of the swift-striding man-killer, but lost him in a tangle of narrow streets crowded, suddenly and without warning, by a flock of sheep which were being driven through the town. He contemplated pursuing his quarry to the palace, but the thought of going anywhere near Slerma made him decide against it.

So it was that Togura Poulaan came within an ace of

becoming the road companion of Guest Gulkan. The fact that he failed probably saved his life, for the Emperor In Exile was on a dangerous quest which would in time decide the fate of powers, kingdoms and empires; there was horror behind him and peril ahead, and the life expectancy of anyone travelling with him would probably have been short.

The last of the sheep went by. Togura idly squished a knobbly dropping with his foot, chewed on another chestnut, and wondered what to do now.

As he was wondering, a small procession went by. It consisted of about twenty people dressed in mourning who were carrying amidst them a bier on which there reclined a man who was both very old and very sick. Togura, as a native of the district, knew enough to guess that the old man was going to be fed to the odex. He had never yet seen this process; as his meal had nourished his curiosity along with his other organs, he fell in behind the procession.

By and by, they came to the stronghold of the Wordsmiths. The original building, made of stone, had collapsed five years previously; the Wordsmiths had rebuilt in wood. The main gate in the stockade was open, but a grey-robed wordmaster halted the procession before they could enter. After a low-voiced argument, the leader of the procession signed his people to one side, and they sat down to wait.

Was it too early in the day? Or was the odex not hungry yet? Or was there an argument how much the people should pay to dispose of their sick old man? Togura did not know, and was not rude enough to ask. While waiting to see what would happen, he loitered beside an abandoned mine shaft, kicking occasional stones into the darkness, which fell straight and sheer to a pool of water far below.

From inside the stronghold of the Wordsmiths there came sounds of confusion. There was some banging and crashing and shouting, then three wordmasters sprinted through the open gate, running for their lives.

'Curiouser and curiouser,' said Togura.

Then there issued forth a monster, which came striding out of the gate on five or six of its seven or eight legs. It was not terribly imposing, as monsters go; it was scarcely twice the girth of a bull, and barely twice the height of a man; its grappling claws were hardly the size of a pair of shears.

Nevertheless, people screamed and ran.

Togura, amused, wondered why people were making so much fuss about the manifestations of an ilps. As it bent over the sick old man, he sauntered forward. The creature lifted its head and regarded him. Its skull was bald bone like that of a vulture. Its eyes were as green as gangrene, and its breath was fetid. Its skin was covered with warts and fents. The warts were a mixture of pink and grey; a few seemed to be purulent, while stark yellow pus oozed from the fents.

'Who are you?' said Togura, his voice loud and strong.

The creature blinked.

'Where do you come from?' he insisted.

It took no notice.

'I demand your nature!'

Losing interest in Togura, the creature bent down over the old man once more. And something terrible happened. As Togura screamed and screamed, the creature raised its head, slushed a mouthful of flesh and spat out a bone. Blood ran down its chin.

'Who?' screamed Togura. 'When? What?'

But the creature remained undamaged by his questions. Belatedly, he realised it was not an ilps at all. It was a genuine monster. As it forked, scrabbled and glutted, spraying the area with blood and offal, he turned and ran.

The creature roared and followed.

Blindly, Togura fled. The ground opened up in front of him. In a moment of sickening horror, he realised he had fallen into the mine shaft. He gasped for air as he fell. Then he went barrelling into the water, which went riveting up his nose. Stunned to find himself still alive, Togura struggled for the surface and looked around. In all directions were rock walls, dimly lit by wavering, splintered reflections of half-light from the water.

To his relief, he saw there was a ladder fastened to the side of the shaft. He swum across to it, took hold, and hauled himself out of the water. He had climbed to three times his own height when the wood, many years rotten, gave way, and sent him plummeting back into the sump.

'Help!' cried Togura, floundering.

He looked up and saw, far overhead, someone looking down at him.

'Help!' he cried. 'Help! For the love of Mothra, help me!'

Someone began to climb down. Too late, he realised it was not someone but something. The monster was coming to get him. Suddenly, it slipped, scrabbled then fell. He cowered against the side of the shaft. The monster shattered the water beside him. As it heaved up out of the depths, he took his only chance, and leapt onto its back.

Shoving his hands into two of the larger fents which disgraced the creature's hide, Togura hung on for dear life. The creature snapped and thrashed and shook and bucked. He thought it was urgently trying to get at him, but in fact it was urgently trying to save itself from drowning.

Finally, the monster got claw-hold on the flanks of the shaft and began to climb, slowly and painfully. Once it slipped, and almost went crashing back to disaster. But it struggled on, gaining, at last, the daylight. Togura, still back-riding, looked round and saw a small crowd watching from a distance.

A man advanced, bearing a meat cleaver.

As the man drew near, the monster attacked with a lurch and a slither. Its intended victim dropped his cleaver and fled. Exhausted, the monster collapsed. Togura, in danger of sliding off, shifted his weight. A mistake! Remembering his presence, the monster rolled over suddenly, almost crushing him. He fell off, leapt away from the grappling claw, ducked under the monster's scooping jaw and fell, almost on top of the meat cleaver.

Snatching the weapon by the handle, Togura slashed the next claw which tried for him. He lopped it off. The monster screamed and tried to scoop him with its jaw. He weaved and evaded, then hacked. His blade chopped into the monster's neck. In a frenzy, he slashed, stabbed, gouged and underthrust, fighting in a beserker fury. He never noticed when the monster died. Then, finally, one wild swipe took its head off entirely, and he realised it must be dead. Or, if not dead, then pretty sick.

Panting, sweating, swaying, Togura halted. He became aware of distant cheering, and realised it was for him. He felt dizzy and very distant.

A wordmaster advanced and clapped him on the shoulder.

'That was very well done, young man.'

'Thank you,' said Togura, good manners providing him with something to say.

'Come with me,' said the wordmaster.

'I must clean my blade,' said Togura, dimly remembering that it was something heroes were said to say after battle.

He tried wiping the bloodstained blade against the monster's flank, but succeeded only in getting it stained with yellow pus. He tried again, and failed. He was shaking. He was rapidly becoming tearful.

Realising the meat cleaver was causing his young charge some distress, the wordmaster wisely removed it from Togura's grasp and threw it to one side. Then he led Togura into the Wordsmiths' stronghold. As they walked along together, Togura tottering, and leaning on the older man for support, the crowd cheered once more.

'Who was that who just went in?' asked Baron Chan Poulaan, arriving on the scene.

'A young man. He killed the monster.'

'What kind of young man?' asked the baron, on the off chance. 'Do you know his name?'

'Oh yes, sir,' said a young milkmaid, who was more knowledgeable than her years might have suggested. 'He's Barak the Battleman.'

'And who might he be?'

'A visitor, sire,' said a woodcutter from Down Slopes. 'Assassin and swordfighter, they say. Escaped gladiator from the murk pits of Chi' ash-lan, if you ask me.'

And he pulled down one eyelid in a very suggestive gesture.

'Oh,' said the baron, losing interest.

He turned away, and set off for the Suets. He would

challenge them, and find out where they had hidden his son. If the Suets failed to yield up Togura, then there might be feuding about this.

CHAPTER SIX

Within the Wordsmiths' organisation the ranks, from lowest to highest, were:

1. servitor;
2. scribe;
3. translator;
4. wordmaster;
5. governor.

Brother Troop was a wordmaster. As befitted his rank, he wore a multicoloured harlequin robe and felt slippers. He was a short, bouncing, jovial man with a ready smile which showed him to be both pleased with himself and pleased with the world. He wore much of his worldly wealth beneath his skin, but Togura, after his recent encounter with Slerma, could not bring himself to describe the Brother as fat.

'So you're the hero,' said Brother Troop, rubbing his hands together.

'I suppose I am,' said Togura, with some surprise.

He had been given a change of clothes and the chance to cleanse himself of monster muck, but he was still a little disorientated.

'Ahaha!' said Brother Troop, not quite laughing and not quite not. 'You suppose you are. Of course you are ! The vigour of the very young. Amazing, isn't it?' And he touched his nose. 'Youth is a wonderful thing.'

'You're not so old yourself,' said Togura.

'Perhaps not, but I was never as wild as you. I was born sensible. And more's the pity! A great handicap, I think. All power to the brave and reckless, eh? Hey? Ahaha! Come, I'll show you around.'

'Well, really I'd—'

'Later, later,' said Brother Troop, giving him no chance to say that he'd really like a little to eat, a little to drink and a lot to sleep. Instead, the good Brother swept him away on a whirlwind tour which took him through kitchens — too quickly alas — sleeping quarters, lecture rooms, study rooms, dungeons and cloisters, and then to the main courtyard of the Wordsmiths' stronghold.

'Here's where it all happens,' said Brother Troop. 'And that, my son, is the odex.'

'That?'

'Believe me. You stand in the Presence.'

The odex was a thin grey disk; Togura could just have spanned its diameter with his outstretched arms. Seen side-on, it appeared to disappear entirely. Seen from an angle, it acted as a mirror, reflecting the surroundings.

'Stand in front of it,' said Brother Troop.

Togura moved round in front of the odex, which hung in the air, standing knee-high off the ground without any apparent means of support. As he came directly in front of it, the mirror surface broke up into discordant cascades of colour and light. These shimmered, swirled, stretched, contracted and pulsed.

'Is it angry?' said Togura warily.

At his words, a puff of red mist broke loose from the surface of the odex. It twirled lazily in the air.

'Who knows?' said Brother Troop.

At his question, the red mist broke apart with a sound like a breaking harp string; a dozen bubbles of bright light frolicked out of the odex and began chasing each other through the air. Similar manifestations and dispersions continued as the two spoke together.

'Where do these things come from?' said Togura.

'From the odex, of course. You can see that for yourself.'

'Is it dreaming?' asked Togura.

'No,' said Brother Troop, uncertainly; it had never occurred to him that the odex might dream. 'We don't think it dreams. We don't really think it's alive. After years of study, we've come to think that it's like a knife. It means neither good nor ill. If it cuts, that's due to our clumsiness. We don't think it dreams – or gets angry.'

'But it sent you the monster,' said Togura. 'Why did it do that?'

'It does nothing on its own,' said Brother Troop. 'Left to its own devices, it just sits there meditating. We speak. We summon. We call things out from its infinite resources.'

'Then how did you summon the monster?' said Togura.

'By accident.'

'Could you summon another?'

'Only by another acident. You see—'

A tangle of spiderweb came floating out of the odex. Brother Tropp knocked it aside with a casual sweep of his hand. It grabbed hold of him, battened onto his flesh and began to feed. It hurt. His senses demolished by pain, Brother Troop fell to the ground, flailing at the invader. Togura helped him destroy it. They succeeded, but there was a violent red rash on the wordmaster's hand where the web had been feeding.

'Look!' said Brother Troop.

Overhead floated an ilps. It was a large one, mostly teeth, horns and trailing tentacles. It had just escaped from the odex.

'Who are you?' shouted Brother Troop.

But the ilps was nimble. It floated fast and high, soaring up and over the roof and out of sight.

'Let's go inside,' said Brother Troop. 'We've endured the Presence quite enough for one day.'

At his words, there was a roar. Both of them jumped. But, fortunately, the odex had not generated another monster. Just the roar of a monster.

Inside, Togura asked a question:

'Why does questioning destroy an ilps?'

'Because every ilps is anomalous,' said Brother Troop. 'They don't belong in our world. We don't think they belong

47

anywhere. They're birthed at random by the odex every time we excite it. Make the anomalous question its own nature, and it destroys itself.'

'How do we excite the odex?'

'By the use of words, young man. You should have guessed that much from what you've seen today.'

'Then what words do what?'

'Different words do different things. That's for certain. But our real problem is that the same words also do different things every time they're used.'

'Hmmm.'

'Very much hmmm! Marry a woman who doesn't speak your language, and you'll be chatting away merrily in less than a year. Our conversations with the odex began in my father's day. We still don't know how to say hello.'

'At this rate, you never will,' said Togura. 'So why bother?'

'Because of the treasure, my boy. The treasure!'

Brother Troop took him to the treasury so he could see. A day's conversation with the odex would usually produce at least one real, solid, genuine piece of treasure.

By the time they reached the treasury, Togura was eagerly expecting to see miracles. He was bitterly disappointed at the motley assortment of oddments which was actually on view.

'This is it?' he said.

'Won with great pain, my boy,' said Brother Troop. 'Won with great pain.'

There were two lightweight diamond-shaped objects with holes in them – possibly buttons, and possibly not. There was a disk of thin metal stamped with concentric circles; it had jagged edges, and was rusting. There was a pale, slightly translucent object, very thin and sharp, about the length of a finger, which Togura was almost certain was a fishbone.

Next there was a curious square box, blue in colour, which was riddled with holes. Togura was about to explore the holes with his fingers when Brother Troop slapped his hand down.

'No, my boy, don't do that. Brother Dorban lost a finger to that little box.'

Togura stared into the holes and saw a wavering, ever-changing light inside. The box was humming.

'I'll tell you one thing for certain,' he said. 'You'll never find out what this is for.'

'Ah, my boy,' beamed Brother Troop. 'We know already. It's an insect trap. It lures them and kills them − or, at least, they go inside and they're never seen again. Fleas, flies, cockroaches − it doesn't discriminate. Leave your clothes by the box overnight, and they'll be free of lice by daybreak.'

There were more things. A pile of old rags. A curious stone globe which appeared to be filled with stars. Some objects made of lead which might have been said to imitate the shape of knucklebones. A length of strong, translucent green cord which appeared to be made all of one seamless piece; it was slippery, and difficult to knot. A stone adze, bearing cryptic markings in red paint. A friable, lumpy grey object which Togura was far too polite to identify as a rather old and shabby dog turd.

'All this comes from the odex?'

'Yes,' said Brother Troopm nodding. 'And other things, too dangerous to keep. Today's monster was a case in point. Come, I'll show you the reading room.'

They went to the reading room where there was a single very old and ancient book. Its cover, and its individual pages, were coated with a hard, transparent substance; thus protected, they did not seem to suffer decay.

'This is the Book of the Odex,' said Brother Troop. 'It was discovered together with the odex itself in the Old City in the Valley of Forgotten Dreams, in Penvash.'

'There's no such thing as the Old City,' said Togura. 'That's just a tale to frighten children with.'

The Brother shook his head.

'No. There really is a city. Men went there seeking wealth. Many died. Even before they got to the city, one was turned into a monster after a flower swallowed him; they killed him after he killed five.'

Togura nodded politely, though he scarcely believed a word of it, and the Brother continued.

'Of those who went, three returned alive. One was my father. They gained three things in the Old City: the Book, the odex, and their nightmares. Open the Book.'

Togura did so. The patterns within, splattered across the pages as if at random, made a bewildering maze of angles, corners and stunted lines.

'Can you read, boy?'

'A little. But not this.'

'That's scarcely surprising. It's written in two languages. Part is written in the Voice of Jade and Gold, which the scholars of former times used both before and after the Days of Wrath. A travelling wizard was able to translate it for my father. Thus he learnt that the odex was used in former times to store both knowledge and objects. There is vast wealth inside the odex, boy.'

'But you can't get it out.'

'Not unless we gain the index.'

'The index?'

'We summon things forth from the odex by talking to it. The ancients of former times used the index instead. The Book tells us that the index speaks in the Universal Language, whatever that might be. For want of an index, we've been trying to make our own Universal Language. That's why we've been gathering together all the world's languages, trying to make them one.'

'And does that promise you success?' asked Togura, unable to conceal his doubts.

'Nothing gives us any guarantee of success,' said Brother Troop. 'But! Knowledge! Wealth! Power! It's worth striving for, boy, it's worth striving for.'

'You said the Book was written in two languages.'

'That's right, my son. One's the Voice of Jade and Gold, which I've spoken of already. The other's the Cold Tongue, which even the wizards can't read. Back before the Devaluation, we paid the wizard of Drum to make the attempt, to see if he could succeed where others had failed. He couldn't. But he told us where we could find an index.'

'He did?'

'He did. After consulting his Catalogues, he told us where we could find a number of them. After the wizards became a power in the world, they discovered many things left over from the Days of Wrath; they didn't understand most of them, but kept them nevertheless, for thousands and thousands of years.'

'So where—'

'I'm coming to that, boy. Give me time, give me time. Over the years, the wizards acquired a number of small, flat boxes, each marked with the sign of a hand and a heart. They could never find out how to open them, or what was inside. Now, thanks to the Book of the Odex, we know. Each contains an index. Each will open on a Word. That Word is Sholabarakosh.'

'Shola—?'

'Later, boy. You'll have plenty of time to memorise it before we send you seeking.'

The Brother's words gave Togura something of a shock. They gave him a hint of what was in store for him. He thought of protesting, but held his tongue. As the old saying goes, it's best to hear out the bargain before you break it.

'Thanks to the wizard of Drum,' said the Brother. 'We know where to find these boxes. The nearest is in the bottom of a green bottle in Prince Comedo's Castle Vaunting, in Estar. A monster protects the bottle from those who would acquire it. The box itself lies at the very bottom of the bottle, and is Guarded.'

'Guarded?'

'I don't know what is meant by that, and neither did the wizard of Drum. However, his Catalogue says it, emphatically, which means there's death waiting nearby.'

'Charming,' murmured Togura.

'What's that?' said the Brother.

'I said, that would be a real challenge. Something I could get my teeth into.'

'Yes — or something which could get its teeth into you. Anyway, to continue. There's also a box in the Secret Store in Tormstarj Castle in the Ironband Mountains. That's south of Estar, as you know.'

'Yes,' said Togura, who didn't, but didn't like to say.

'There may possibly be a third box in the Castle of Controlling Power. There is definitely one in the possession of the Silver Emperor in Dalar ken Halvar. But that, of course, is a step and a way.'

'Yes,' said Togura, from habit.

'Galsh Ebrek may hold another box.'

'Who?'

'It is not a who, it's a where. It's the High City in Yestron. You know where Yestron is, of course.'

'Yes,' said Togura. 'It's west of here.'

'No! East! Beyond Argan. Beyond Ashmoles. Beyond Quilth. The west has nothing of interest, not to us. Unless there's a box in Chi' ash-lan, which is problematical. You know where Chi' ash-lan is, I hope.'

'Yes,' said Togura, who had a vague inkling.

He feared he had disappointed Brother Troop already, and that he would shortly have to disappoint the wordmaster again. For he suspected that he was about to be offered a job fit for a hero, and he had no intention whatsoever of accepting. He would rather stay alive.

'Well, boy,' said Brother Troop, beaming. 'I expect you know by now precisely what we want of you.'

'Yes,' said Togura. 'You want me to go to Estar to get the bottle which holds the box which holds the index.'

'Excellent!' said Brother Troop, slapping him on the back. 'I thought you'd accept. Let's celebrate with some bread and wine, hey?'

'Tai-ho!' said Togura, using a local idiom which meant something similar to 'whoa!', 'wait' or 'stop'.

'What is it?' said Brother Troop. 'You're not going to decline the honour of questing for the index, are you?'

Togura hesitated. He meant to say 'yes', but did not want to leave without indulging in the bread and wine he had been offered. With a swiftly-developing survivor's cunning, he equivocated:

'The question of payment arises.'

'Payment? But, my boy — the glory! Isn't that enough? No?

If not . . . no, this is neither the time nor the place. Come, let us eat and drink. The dinner table, my lad, is the civilised place for prolonged discussion.'

Togura was gratified by the success of his stratagem. Over their meal, he rewarded Brother Troop for his hospitality by showing an eager interest in the odex, the index and related matters.

Precisely what markings identified the box which held the index? Brother Troop sketched the heart and the hand for him.

What was that Word which opened the box? Brother Troop gave him the Word once more, and he memorised it: Sholabarakosh.

What did the index itself look like?

'Ahaha,' said Brother Troop. 'An astute question, truly. When you open the box, you'll know. Remember, it speaks the Universal Language.'

'Whatever that is.'

'Yes,' said Brother Troop, with an unfamiliar hint of sadness and defeat in his voice. 'Whatever that is.' Then, brightening: 'Ah, the chicken! They've brought us the chicken. Beautiful. Come on, eat, eat. You're not full already, are you?'

'No,' said Togura, who was, but thought it wise to stock up a little. He started on a chicken wing. 'What,' he said, 'happened to everyone else who went questing for the odex?'

'An interesting question.'

'Interesting indeed, as the chicken said to the chopper. Come on, I'll know the truth sooner or later. It might as well be now.'

'Then young man, since you insist, I must tell you that the truth is that we don't know. Five have been sent so far. None have returned.'

'Hmmm,' said Togura, thinking.

He was trying to calculate how many more meals he could get out of the Wordsmiths before they forced him to make a decision and commit himself.

'I see the quest takes your fancy, hey?' said Brother Troop.

'Your young blood boils with hot excitement. Horizons call you! Oh, you'll be a hit with the girls when you come back, young man. Every damsel loves a hero.'

'Give me a day to think it over,' said Togura.

And, after some further discussion, the good Brother did.

However, Togura did not get the chance to spend that day in rest, reflection and decision-making. Events were moving swiftly now; unbeknownst to him, he was well and truly embroiled in the world's turmoil. As he would soon find out.

CHAPTER SEVEN

Disturbed by the manifestation of the monster which had escaped from the odex, the City Council of Keep met in an emergency session at noon that very same day, and passed a Resolution Regarding Care And Confinement Appertaining To Monsters. Subsection 5(c) of Schedule 9 of Annex 5 attached to the Resolution stated that:

> Any organisation which does or can or may or might buy breed produce summon forth unearth uncover tempt call attract or otherwise obtain any demon fiend bog-crawler crocodile griffin dragon death-lizzard creature of the Swarms or related being or any similar or unsimilar scarth jinn brute beast or monster MUST protect the public security by obtaining the services of a suitably qualified and experienced hero sword-master death-dealer dragon-killer or similar.

Aware that the manifestation of the monster had excited a certain groundswell of public disfavour, the Wordsmiths sought to comply. They offered Togura the job on a temporary basis, while he decided whether he would quest for the index. He accepted, fully aware that only one real monster had emerged from the odex in more than three decades of operation.

The Wordsmiths then announced that they had recruited

the young monster-slaughterer Togura Poulaan, who had proved himself by killing a monster for them earlier in the day, in full view of the public. This announcement was met with derision by the citizenry, who were by now fully aware that the monster had been killed by Barak the Battleman, assassin and swordfighter, previously a gladiator in the murk pits of Chi'ash-lan.

'How many people in Keep know you to your face?' asked Brother Troop.

'A couple of dozen,' said Togura.

'Two dozen people can scarcely overturn the world's belief. From now on, till further notice, you're Barak the Battleman.'

'Agreed,' said Togura.

Armed with his new name, he stood taller and felt stronger; he began to walk with something of a swagger. The Wordsmiths equipped him with a sword, a stabbing knife and a helmet, and made an announcement correcting the name of their resident hero.

Togura, remembering his encounter earlier in the day with the swordmaster-assassin who had prior claim to the name of Barak the Battleman, wondered with some trepidation what would happen if that rough, burly swordsman of middle years heard that his name had been usurped.

The swordsman did hear.

And he shrugged, for it was nothing to him. He should have changed his name leagues ago in any case. That evening, as he set off east, his business with King Skan Askander completed, he decided that henceforth he would call himself Genu Vay Chanay. He would identify himself as a free-lance executioner.

Genu Vay Chanay gave no further thought to Keep or to its people or to the theft of his last roadname; he had plenty of things to worry about without troubling himself over trivialities like the use and abuse of his former name.

That very same evening, an invitation arrived at the Wordsmiths' stronghold for the Governor and the new monster-slaughterer to attend a Banquet of Celebration to be given by the Family Suet that very night. This gave Togura an attack of stage fright.

As Brother Troop was attempting to calm his nerves, the calm of the night was interrupted by a roar from the odex, followed by the manifestation of a dragon's head. Unfortunately, the head was very much alive. But, fortunately, it was not attached to any body, and consequently was soon dead.

'It's yours, boy,' said Brother Troop. 'Proof positive to all the world of your ability.'

'I can't claim it,' said Togura blushing. 'I cannot tell a lie.'

That in itself was a lie, or at least an exaggeration; he could easily tell a small lie, and often had and did, but he was unable to tell a lie on such an exaggerated scale.

'You needn't say anything about it at all,' said Brother Troop. 'We'll have it carried to the Banquet of Celebration. If anyone asks about it, then murmur politely and say it's beneath your dignity to discuss such trifles.'

'That's excellent advice,' said Togura, struck by the brilliance of this idea. 'It's very kind of you.'

'Not at all.' said Brother Troop, dismissing his thanks with a wave of his hand. 'It's us I'm thinking of. We have to have the confidence of the community we live amongst. You're a valuable asset to us, boy. Do us proud.'

So it was that Togura went to the Banquet of Celebration in triumph, together with the dragon's head, which took pride of place at the dinner, occupying a table all to itself.

Togura was rather miffed when he discovered that the banquet was not to celebrate his own success at monster killing. It was, instead, to celebrate the engagement of young Roly Suet to the king's daughter, Slerma, and to announce the launch of a new coinage in bronze, gold and silver. The coinage would bear the head of King Skan Askander but would be backed by the assets of the Family Suet.

However, Togura's ego was boosted by the fuss the young and beautiful Day Suet made of her hero. She was a little puzzled about his new name. He explained the misunderstanding which had forced it upon him. And, as he brought proof positive of his abilities in the form of the dragon's head, she could not doubt his courage.

'You're a real man,' she said, breathing admiration.

'I'm growing up,' Togura conceded.

'Your father was round here earlier today, real man,' she said. 'He was talking of spanking you.'

'I doubt that he'll get the chance,' said Togura, really cool and collected.

'Yes,' said Day Suet. 'But it would be interesting to watch one real man spank another.'

'Minx!' said Togura, swatting her.

She evaded him, and laughed.

And, before very long, she had persuaded him to laugh with her.

They ate.

They drank.

They danced.

The musicians, robust and virile men, laboured and belaboured their instruments, pumping, hammering, stretching, scraping and churning, till their faces went beetroot-red and the sweat poured down to their beards and their broad moustaches.

As Togura danced with Day, he dared, and she dared with him. Her breasts were soft. Her lips were hot and eager. Her eyes spoke just a little more than she would voice. His confidence grew. When he suggested they leave, she never asked him where. She led him to her room. As if in a trance, he stripped her to her skin. Her body, smooth and glabrous, glimmered in the light of a single candle. She closed with him, and gave him a drunken kiss. She smelt of sweat and musk, of perfume and spices, of hard liquor and youthful desire.

He undressed.

Standing before her, naked, he realised that now was the moment. Now he was really going to become a man. A real man. Initiated into the mysteries of the flesh. His desire was hard, urgent, swelling. He touched her thigh, lightly, finding it warm as new bread. Overwhelmed by her heat and aroma, he felt an irresistible imminence taking control of his flesh. Horror-struck, he tried to restrain himself.

He failed.

His male organ began to pump.

At the last possible moment, Togura clapped a hand to his cock, which pumped hot jism over his palm. That saved him from splattering Day from bosom to thigh with his semen. But the disaster was still absolute, unmitigated and irretrievable.

'Oh no!' he cried, in agony.

'What is it?' said Day.

Then, realising precisely what it was, she began to laugh. Blithe spirit that she was, she could not take this technical hitch seriously. She was puzzled when Togura began to ram himself into his clothes.

'Tog,' she said. 'No. Don't go. Tog, it's nothing. Talk to me, Tog. Tog. Wait!'

But, when she clutched at him, he broke free and fled, still fastening his garments. He was so embarrassed he could not endure her presence. He wanted to die. Or bury himself in a hole for half a thousand years.

He escaped to the autumn air and stalked through the streets, furious. Raging. Hating himself and the world and his own rebellious flesh. He had failed absolutely and miserably at a man's most important test. He was worse than nothing. He was disgraced. He would never be able to look Day in the face again. She knew!

When his half-brother Cromarty had accused him of being a day-dreaming masturbator, that had been bad enough. But he had been able to deny it with a straight face, even though it was true. After all, masturbation was furtively acknowledged or hinted at by many. But to fail with a woman!

Togura remembered Cromarty boasting about Toff the milkmaid:

'She was hot, boys. Hot, drunk and flat on her back. So I stuck it in to the hilt. Rammed it in. She loved it. She begged for more. I gave it.'

Everyone had their stories. Even Togura had his stories, though his were not true. (Could Cromarty's be untrue? He'd like to think so, but it was difficult. Cromarty was so brash, so arrogant, so confident.)

Brooding on his disaster, Togura grimly resolved that

tonight would be the night, no matter what. He could never face Day again, but he would find a way. He would lose his virginity by morning, or die in the attempt.

Thus resolved, he bent his footsteps toward the towerhouse of Melladona, one of the town's five whores, and rumoured to be the cheapest. She was awake and working; she had only lately discharged her last customer. He struck a bargain and paid.

He thought himself confident.

But when he actually saw her rancid flesh, her flaccid thighs, the fat veins snaking up her legs, the stale bruises and the odd blotched marks on her breasts, and the crinkling scar running from her neck to her navel, his courage failed. In her cold and narrow room, his worm disgraced him by shrinking to a cringing stump of flesh scarcely the size of his thumb.

He asked for his money back.

Melladona laughed, then, realising he was serious, attacked him. After he escaped into the street, she cursed him from her window. Trying to recover something from the debacle, he eased his ego by shouting a few well-chosen insults. Melladona responded promptly by emptying her chamber pot over his head.

Togura eventually washed himself off in someone's rain water barrel, then, sadder but not necessarily wiser, mooched through the night to the Wordsmiths' Stronghold. The gate was open, and someone, dressed in a winterweight coat and swaddled in a blanket, was sitting by the gate waiting for him.

'Togura Poulaan!' said Day Suet severely, standing up as he approached. 'So there you are at last. Well? Aren't you grateful to see me? Don't you realise you're lucky to see me at all? Running off into the night like that! Stupid fellow! Most girls would have given you away forever.'

'Day,' said Togura, not knowing what to say.

She had come for him. She was his. This must be true love! But, all the same, she was a source of mortification to him. She knew! Standing in the light of the gatelamp, he hesitated.

'Don't just stand there, stupid!' said Day, impatiently. 'Kiss me!'

Togura gathered her into his arms, and they kissed.

'Now take me inside,' said Day, 'And get me something to eat. It's cold out here, and I'm hungry.'

'I don't know if the brothers would approve,' said Togura.

Day kicked him in the shins, hard.

'I'm running out of patience, Togura Poulaan. You've used up most of your chances. You don't have many left.'

'My lady,' said Togura, the formality of romance coming to his rescue.

He took her hand in his and kissed it, gracefully. Then he led her inside. Unable to resist the opportunity to show off a little, he took her to the central courtyard to show her the odex. By night it was, when they stood in front of it, an amazement of brilliant colours, far brighter than the night lamps arrayed around the courtyard.

While they were standing watching, two figures dressed in black jumped down from the roof above and landed in the courtyard. Day squealed. The intruders drew swords. They were masked with darkness: only their eyes showed.

'We seek Togura Poulaan,' said one, speaking a foreign variety of Galish rather than the local patois.

'The swordmaster-assassin otherwise known as Barak the Battleman,' said the other.

'Here I am,' said Togura – and instantly wished he had held his tongue.

'Joke with us again and you're dead,' said one of the intruders, grabbing Day Suet by the throat. 'The girl dies, too. Now tell us where we find our quarry. We know he's here! The whole town knows. We know him to his face, so try no substitutes. We know the head required in Chi'ash-lan.'

Togura stood rooted to the spot, paralysed with terror. He had no weapons. Face to face with this twin death, what could he have done with weapons anyway?

'Tog,' gasped Day. 'He's hurting me!'

'Silence girl!' snarled the man holding her, looking around. For the first time he looked directly into the odex, and so, for the first time, he saw its ever-changing maze of kaleidoscopic colours. 'What,' he said, slightly startled, 'Is that?'

Day did not answer, but Togura found voice enough to say:

'A kind of Door.'

'You can go through it?'

'In a manner of speaking,' said Togura.

At that moment, they were interrupted by sounds of argument beyond the courtyard. Then in came the Baron Chan Poulaan with a squad of bowmen and spearmen. Two wordmasters were clinging to the baron, trying to restrain him.

'This place is forbidden by dark,' cried one.

But the baron advanced remorselessly.

'I'll have my son tonight,' he said. 'Or know the reason why. Ah, Togura! There you are! Come, boy. Heel!'

'Stay where you are,' hissed one of the men in black.

'Who are your funny friends?' said the baron, advancing, with his men behind him. 'Drawn swords, I see. Do we have a problem here?'

So speaking, the baron drew his own sword. He was by no means a master of the weapon, but he was strong, aggressive and enthusiastic. In Sung, he was regarded as fearsome.

The man holding Day in a throttle edged closer to the odex. His companion gave Togura a shove which sent him sprawling to the ground, then menaced the baron and his men.

'Back, rabble!' he said, speaking now in a loud, hard voice.

Baron Chan Poulaan was amused.

'There's at least seven of us and only two of you,' said the baron, reasonably. 'Throw down your weapons and surrender.'

'I,' said the man confronting him, 'am a ninth-grade adept of the Zenjingu fighting cult. I can kill all of you without thinking. Your very existence here is at your peril.'

'Your grammar suffers under stress,' said the baron, dryly.

'Out, vermin! Do you not know the dread doom which walks in the midnight black of Zenjingu fighters?'

'No,' said the baron, frankly.

He was essentially a provincial man who led a narrow and provincial life; he knew nothing whatsoever of the Zenjingu fighters, whose very name was terror in the lands around Chi'ash-lan.

'You have outlived your life,' snarled the Zenjingu fighter, raising his sword.

The baron snapped his fingers. An archer standing behind him unleashed an arrow. The Zenjingu fighter lurched, dropped his sword, threw up his arms, then waddled round in circles, gasping as he clutched at the arrow, which had pierced his throat.

'Thus we do in the highlands,' said the baron, striding forward with an easy gait.

As the Zenjingu fighter tottered, the baron hacked into the unruly fellow's head. On the third blow, the man dropped dead at his feet. Whistling tunelessly, the baron turned his attention to the remaining trespasser.

'Get back!' shouted the survivor. 'Get back, or I kill the girl.'

'The life of a female Suet is nothing to me,' said Baron Chan Poulaan, who saw no harm in telling the truth. 'Go ahead. Make my day.'

'No!' screamed Togura, launching himself at the Zenjingu fighter.

The fighter threw Day Suet into the odex, which had been described to him as a Door. Then jumped in after her. Both were briefly visible, then gone, disintegrating – with a jangle of music – into a storm of colours. An ilps, popping out of the odex, celebrated the occasion with hearty laughter.

'So much for that,' said the baron crisply, wiping his sword then sheathing it. 'Come along, Togura, we're going home. What is it, boy? Not crying, are we? Now now, don't be a baby.'

'I loved her,' said Togura wretchedly.

'I'm sure you did,' said the baron, unsympathetically. 'We all suffer these fevers in our youth. Stop snivelling, boy!'

'You killed her!' screamed Togura.

'She's gone into the odex,' said the baron. 'I've heard the Wordsmiths say that it stores whatever's fed into it. If that's so, then get them to unstore it. Or do it yourself. Or if it can't be done, forget about it. Suets copulate like ferrets. There's plenty more where that came from. Come come, there's no use crying over spilt milk.'

When Togura continued crying, the baron slapped him briskly. Togura clenched his fist and smashed him. His father fell unconscious at his feet, poleaxed. There was a murmur amongst the bowmen and spearmen.

'Take him,' said Togura, in a thick wet ugly voice. 'Him and his sword. Take him, and get him out of here!'

The men obeyed.

The two wordmasters who had tried to prevent Baron Chan Poulaan from entering their stronghold muttered to each other. Togura Poulaan, now of the Wordsmiths, had made war on the head of the Warguild: no good would come of this.

They had more to mutter about shortly, for Togura, bloodlust in his heart, began to attack the odex.

CHAPTER EIGHT

The night was cold, but Togura Poulaan was hot, feverish, burning. Armed with a sword which had recently graced the hand of a Zenjingu fighter, he was attacking the odex, hacking and slashing at its soft, yielding surface. It bled colour and music. As he fought, he became lost in a cloud of jangling rainbows, in a delusion of humming auras, in sprays of pealing orange and rumbling red, in veils of hissing mist and belching steam.

Finally, he stopped. He was panting harshly. His legs were shaking. Blisters had puffed up hard and ripe on the palms of his hands where the hard labour of battle had taken its toll on his innocence; he had never used a sword before, except in the occasional desultory half-hearted sparring match. The odex reformed and repaired itself, effortlessly, making itself perfect once more. The last free-floating colour died with a chord of music.

Togura hawked, and spat, and swore.

As he swore, an ilps jacked itself out of the odex and hoisted itself to the sky, smacking its bulbous lips, which were seven in number.

'Who are you?' cried Brother Troop, who had been standing to one side watching Togura's performance.

The ilps wavered.

'Where do you come from? Who owns you?'

Half of the ilps collapsed with a brief stench like twinge of silage; the rest escaped.

And Togura, having recoved his breath, began to attack the odex with his voice. Once started, he did not stop. Seeking the words which would recover Day Suet, he poured out the language of love, hate and obscenity, of eating and drinking, of battle and war, of farming and forestry; he cried out the names of birds, trees, mountains, rivers, seas, lakes, weapons, cities, people, pets, insects, stars and uncouth diseases; he called upon gods known and unknown, upon the powers of earth and sky, air and water, fire and stone.

Anything that served his purpose was pressed into use. He bawled out snatches of drinking songs and musical bawdry; he sung half-remembered phrases of love songs and madrigals, inventing his own words when memory failed him. And then, yielding to despair and fury, he poured out meaningless word-strings, shouting, demanding, pleading, screaming, commanding. As he excited it, the odex threw forth random assemblages with multiple heads, voices, smells, legs, arms, teeth, tentacles, manes, pseudopods, carapaces, eyes, ears, tongues and tails. As each ilps escaped, it drifted away, giggling, chuckling, snoring, roaring, swelling, pulsating, gleaming and shining, until the night sky above the stronghold of the Wordsmiths was cluttered with a positive fantasia of shapes and forms.

Sometimes, as Togura's words accidentally hit upon some transient code of retrieval, the odex sent real things out from its storehouse. Once it spat fire. Once it ejected a tiny corn-coloured disk which swelled in a couple of breaths to a huge wheel of hay the height of a man and girth of a bullock. Once a shower of coins blasted their way into the air, stinging and burning where they hit, for they were red-hot.

As the night wore on, an ever-changing audience watched Togura's frantic performance. Servitors, scribes, translators, wordmasters and even the governor himself joined the gathering crowd. Togura, scarcely aware of their presence, shouted, cursed, stormed, raged and pleaded, as if immune to all embarrassment.

Alerted by the plague of ilpses above the Wordsmiths' stronghold, the citizens of Keep began to wake; it would have

66

been hard for them to sleep, as all the dogs were howling and barking, for an ilps has the peculiar property of being very disturbing to dogs. Muttering imprecations, many hauled themselves out of bed and went to investigate. Picking their way through the night, wary of mineshafts and mad dogs, citizens began to gather outside the stronghold, a conclave of lanterns and speculations. Some infiltrated the stronghold to become astonished witnesses to an unprecedented scene.

They saw Togura, harsh and hoarse and sweating, berating the odex, threatening it and lashing it with the iron-edged fury of his tongue. As his non-stop attack continued, the odex no longer manifested one object or apparition for each of his assaults, but spat them out in twos or threes, and then a dozen at a time. More and more of its productions were real things rather than randomly-formed ilpses.

A little red snake, folded like a concertina, jumped out of the odex and hopped around on the ground, rupturing itself with a string of explosions. Then Togura was drenched and almost swept away by an onslaught of water, foam and spray in which a horde of fresh and saltwater fish kicked, thrashed and jumbled – pike, snapper, bream, bluefin, dogfish, cod, carp, smelts, dabs, haddock, lampreys, flounder, trout, salmon, catfish, whitebait, gurnet, mullet, groper, flying fish, mau mau, rays, eels, gudgeon and perch, all mixed in a slurry with sea slugs, sea urchins, crayfish, lobsters, gaplax, whelks and seaweed. While he was still thrashing round in the water, screaming and yelching and screeching and yelping, he was hit by a blast of vegetable scrapings.

Then a child fell bawling at his feet.

A newborn child, swaddled in a kind of soft white sheet.

A woman darted out of Togura's audience, snatched up the child and carried it off. As if a spell had been broken, people started to scrabble for the valuables ejected by the odex, and soon the central courtyard was filled with a turmoil of bodies and voices pushing, shoving, complaining, shouting, scratching, wrestling, pinching, pulling, Fish were torn apart or trampled underfoot or eaten raw on the spot before they could be snatched away. The courtyard, lit by the unearthly phosphorescent glow of more than a thousand ilpses, became a seething, pullulating mass of mud, bodies, greed, avarice, jealousy and outright violence.

Oblivious to the anarchy all around, Togura, sword in hand, continued to fight the odex. Now, excited not just by his voice but by the raging, screaming, shrieking crowd, it spat, pumped and ejected, spraying the crowd with parts of dead animals and mangled bits of human bodies, with lumps of gold and chunks of silver, with mine tailings by the bucket-load, with peaches, leeks and baby hedgehogs and then—

A monster!

Lurching out of the odex it came, a fearsome beast with scales of jacinth and claws like knives, with three snake-like heads on long and weaving necks. Togura swung with his sword and chopped off one of his heads. Fleeing from his death-bright blade, it ran straight into the clutches of a rabble of housewives, who swamped it, strangled it, tore it apart and crammed its separate pieces into their bargain bags.

The ilpses were now popping out from the odex in a never-ending stream. Togura, filthy, bloodstained, stinking, reeking, was shaken by a fit of riotous madness, and laughed. His laugh provoked an onslaught of birds which battered into the night sky. Some struck out for the darkness while others went looning around in the light of the ilpses, or fluttered here and there and everywhere, bewildered, shocked and disorientated. The air was a daze of feathers, a cacophony of screams, cries, chirrups and distress calls. Togura was lost in the swirling maelstrom of sparrows, thrushes, fan tails, gulls, gannets, petrels, budgerigars, huias, yodel birds, cockatoos and laughing owls, moreporks and dancing fins, ravens, jackdaws, crows, keas, sparrow hawks, skypes, mynahs, skylarks, starlings, strutting breckons, hens, wood pidgeons, nymphet skarks, muttonbirds and dark lartles.

The feather-storm cleared.

An egg fell out of the odex, bounced, and rolled to one side; it was hard-boiled. A penguin, very far from home, hobbled away as best it could. Togura cried in a hoarse, cracked voice:

'Give me Day Suet!'

A horde of ilpses stormed out of the odex. As he ducked and covered his head, the noise of the crowd of looters rose to a fresh peak. The odex responded with cheeses, showering one and all with a stream of weird, bizarre and alien concoctions — green mould and yellow stink, cheddar and kray, cantal, marolles, olivet, port-salut, livarot, limbourg, skwayjeg, soo, parmesan, brie, gournay, roquefort, troyes, romantours, brazlets and mont d'ors.

The air filled with screams of delight as the housewives packed into the cheeses.

Togura, hit, thumped, battered, plastered and knocked almost senseless by cheeses, fell to his knees and crawled away through the sour, dank, fetid reek of cheese. Soon the odex was buried in cheese, and Togura was adrift on a steadily-growing mound of cheese, which pulsed, twitched and billowed, forcing itself ever-upward.

Forced upward till he was level with the guttering, Togura hauled himself onto the roof and crawled upward to the roof-ridge. There, exhausted, he slumped down, collapsing under a sky now elbow to elbow with giggling ilpses, Eventually, he roused himself and looked downward.

The night was fading. It was growing light. The cheeses were no longer piling themselves up to the sky; the courtyard full of cheese began to empty rapidly thanks to a bucket brigade of citizens. It seemed that everyone in Keep who was not crippled or bed ridden, and several who were, had gathered in the stronghold or on its roof or in the surrounding streets or on the surrounding roofs. As the cheese-level fell, survivors were hauled out of the wreckage, choking and gasping or shocked and silent.

Suddenly cries of rage, fear and horror rose to Togura's ears. He saw that a tide of red was rising fiercely, swamping cheeses and people, The hot reek of blood rose to his nostrils.

Soon torrents of blood were pouring out of the courtyard, which was a swirling red maelstom. The blood swept out into the streets, drowning down into the mine shafts, flooding the cellars, racketing knee-deep through the alleyways, piling up at the squeezes and pinches, then shooting away into the gulf of air beyond the brink of Dead Man's Drop. The slow, the lame and the unwary were carried away down the streets, swept into mineshafts or, thrashing and screaming, tossed over Dead Man's Drop.

The blood-letting subsided, until finally the odex itself could be seen, standing in the courtyard. It was still pumping blood at a steady rate; a stream ankle-deep ran from the courtyard.

From the odex there then emerged a steady stream of clanking cantankerous machines and cute little stag fawns with ear tags of blue or green or gold. The stag fawns wandered out into the streets, picking their way through the blood and rubble and the litter of corpses with their delicate bloodstained feet. The machines, some taking to the air, others lumbering along the ground, began to fight each other.

As the machines fought, the air filled with the sullen cough of projectile weapons, the subilant hiss of energy beams, the hollow, booming thud of contact explosions, the thud of collisions and the high-pitched intolerable scream of despairing steel.

A light wind got up, sending the ilpses drifting away. The battle between the machines continued. Many of them sought refuge underground. The others followed, and the continuation of a very ancient war proceeded underfoot. The ground shook with muffled explosions.

The flow of blood diminished to a trickle. The last few stag fawns jumped out of the odex. The last thing to come forth was a female human dressed in silk. She slithered out of the odex and landed on her backside in the mud and muck.

'Day!' screamed Togura, with the very last of his voice.

Heedless of the danger, he raced down the roof and leapt into the courtyard. He landed, fell, and went sprawling into the soft, reeking squilg of blood and mud and water and bird droppings. As he hauled himself out of the ooze, the human female regarded him with distaste. She was, he saw, most definitely not Day Suet; she was taller, older and wore diamonds. Despite her muck-stained backside, she carried herself with all the hauteur of an empress.

'Help me,' said Togura, shambling through the mud toward her.

She took a tiny oddment from about her person and pointed it at him. The air sizzled. His limbs disco-ordinated and dropped him down in the filth. Slowly, cautiously, he raised his head, blinked, and peered at the woman. She asked him a question in a very foreign language.

'I don't understand,' said Togura, in a voice made of dry straw, sand, wood-shavings and iron filings.

The woman looked around, taking stock of the situation. She wrinkled her nose with distaste at the shambles around her. She had nothing but contempt for everything she saw. Picking up her skirts, she began to pick her way toward the nearest exit.

'Wait!' screeched Togura, wallowing through the filth on knees and elbows. 'You have to help us. Don't go!'

The woman turned, sneered, aimed her weapon again and fired, this time giving him a blast which knocked him unconscious for a day and a night. Then she turned on her heel and left, and was never seen again in Keep.

CHAPTER NINE

The servitor lanced one last blister. Clear fluid eased out, forming a painless tear which the servitor wiped away with a fleece-white dabbing cloth. Togura flexed his hand, which felt stiff and sore.

'Another time, bandage your hands before you fight,' said the servitor, a rough-bearded man with a strange accent. 'Until such time as your hands are battle-hardened.'

'Where did you learn that?' said Togura.

'In another place, another time.'

'Tell me about it.'

'Not today. No – don't get up. Rest. I'll be back soon with something good.'

'What?'

'Wait and see.'

The servitor departed. Togura lay back in bed, staring at the cobwebs sprawled across the timbers overhead, and listening to the fury of the autumn storm which raged without. The wilderness weather was scattering the ilpses far and wide across the land, or blowing them out to sea; it was killing or dispersing the mobs of birds; it was grounding most of those quarrelsome machines which had not yet run out of fuel. The war weather was dealing with the pests and enemies unleashed by the odex, bringing a kind of peace back to the city state of Keep.

The servitor returned, bearing a two-handled drinking jug filled with something hot and sweltering.

'Drink,' he said.

Togura did so. Warmth paunched in his belly and invaded his veins. His senses slurred. The colours of the darkened timbers overhead began to drift.

'Drink,' said the servitor, encouraging him.

Togura drank his fill. Though he was lying in bed, he felt that he was floating. He tried to ask a question. On the third attempt, he managed to curl his tongue round the words.

'What is it?'

'Quaffle,' said the servitor.

'And what's that?'

'A mixture of all good things. Alcohol, opium, hemlock, dark nightshade, the red-capped mushroom and the blue, a foreign herb called ginseng and a little oil of hashish. And honey, of course.'

'I could learn to like it.'

'You could learn too well,' said the servitor, with a laugh. 'But it's good for the sickness. Sleep now.'

And, at his command, Togura drifted off into silk-bosomed drug dreams which suckled him with nectar and fed him on honey-basted melody cats.

He woke, later, in darkness. The rain and the wind were still at work beyond the walls. He was alone, without the company of so much as a candle. Lying there in the darkness, he remembered Day Suet, in spring, cradling a tiny bird in her little hands, and laughing when it stained her fingers with a tiny bit of lime. Hot tears blistered his eyes.

He wept.

Later, in the darkness, he found the two-handled drinking jug. What was left in the bottom was cold to the touch. It sidled down his throat, cold as a snake, then transmuted itself to living fire. Sweating from the heat of that fire, and reeling from weariness, he allowed his bones to compose themselves once more for sleep.

When he woke, it was morning.

The servitor brought him mutton chops, swedes, rutabaga and water-cress. He ate, ravenously. For lunch, there was leek soup, venison and the brains of a pig, with a side-helping of

73

fried snails and pickled slugs. He devoured everything. In the evening, there was a slab of bread loaded down with beefsteak and a gill of milk, with blackbird pie to follow. He polished off the lot.

'Why am I so hungry?' said Togura.

'Good health makes you so,' said the servitor.

For days, as Togura recovered from the effects of the unkown weapon which the strange woman from the odex had used to knock him unconscious, the cold rains of autumn lashed the town, washing away dead fish, drowned rats and the smells of blood and cheese. While Togura ate and slept, while the days shortened and the rains pounded down, the townspeople counted the cost of their orgiastic session with the odex, and argued as to whether it was a blessing or a disaster.

'Of course it was a disaster, no question about it!' said Shock the Cobbleman, who had broken both legs on the Night.

But not everyone was quick to agree.

On the debit side, at least thirty-four people had been killed, fifty houses flooded, seventeen other properties damaged or demolished, and incredibile devastation wrought underground by war machines fighting to death in the mines. Through autumn and winter, the miners would be able to retrieve little gemstock; they would be too busy repairing and shoring up mineshafts.

On the credit side, three of the fighting machines, burrowing deep into the rock, had finally burst out into the daylight at the very bottom of Dead Man's Drop. Water was now cascading out of their escape tunnels. The problem of flooding in the mines, which had worsened as the miners delved deeper over the years, was now easing. This unexpected solution to the drainage problem meant that the total amount of gemstock available in the long term had greatly increased.

Bankers at banquet, gleaming with perspiration, toasted Togura Poulaan – also known as Barak the Battleman – with goblets of diluted ambrosia or strong mulled wine. The Gonderbrine mine, the largest in Keep, which had been threatening to default on its loans because assets underground had proved to be also underwater, had now negotiated a very satisfactory repayments schedule.

'To chaos,' went one of the more drunken toasts. 'To havoc.'

That was daring, but another toast capped it:

'To the unexpected.'

Now that, for a banker, was truly extraordinary.

While bankers celebrated, and while miners, though grumbling, admitted that they ultimately stood to benefit, a few dour, incorrigible pessimists argued that drainage would hasten subsidence, leading to a swifter collapse of the town. They were ignored.

Meanwhile, also on the credit side was the personal wealth so many had garnered. Many houses in Keep were now glutted with venison, and also with cheesestock, the name the people invented for the unholy mish-mash of half a hundred different cheeses which had resulted from the excessive generosity of the odex.

Others had gained birdmeat, fishmeat, gold, silver or interesting articles of metalwork. And many of those who had gained nothing had, nevertheless, abandoned themselves shamelessly on the Night; aware that they had fought and scrabbled and kicked and clawed, squabbling over the loot like so many carrion eaters, they were, for the most part, too ashamed to speak out and criticise the Wordsmiths, the odex or Togura Poulaan. Collective benefits and collective guilt served to nullify the chance of retribution.

Togura scarcely thought of the damage to the town and its people, but was deeply worried about the probable reaction of the Wordsmiths.

'Will I be punished?' he said.

'No, boy,' said the servitor. 'They're quite pleased with you, if anything.'

Indeed, within the ranks of the Wordsmiths there was general agreement that the Night had been a good thing. For more than three decades they had explored the odex in a slow, cautious, deferential fashion, learning little of its practical use.

Now, in one wild, rampaging Night, Togura Poulaan had taught them something very important about its use.

Brother Troop, the new Governor – the old one had died from an allergic reaction to an unfamiliar type of cheese – codified their new knowledge in Brother Troop's First Law Of Odex:-

The volume, variety and reality of production by the odex increases in proportion to the length of unbroken linguistic stimulation and the variety of linguistic excitement employed for that stimulation.'

In order words, a long shouting match with the odex, with plenty of people shouting, would lead to a great many things being produced, lots of those things being real objects instead of ilpses.

Brother Troop, pleased to be wearing the Governor's pink felt jacket and fur-lined codpiece, had his First Law Of Odex inscribed on a piece of the finest timber available. He ordered it to be done in letters of fire, by which he meant red paint; what he actually received was a fine example of poker-work, but he decided that his words looked splendid even when rendered in charcoal.

Now that he was head of his little empire, Brother Troop set about a little empire-building. Even though the Wordsmiths were having little success with the Universal Language they were trying to develop, there was still the possibility of recovering great wealth from the odex. However, as Keep might not take kindly to further frenetic experiments being conducted within city limits, a new location was in order.

Brother Troop sent scouts out into the surrounding countryside to search for a high, well-drained place where they could build a new stronghold, well away from inhabited places. A suitable spot was soon found on the estate of Baron Chan Poulaan, who objected violently to Brother Troop's proposal.

'My estate,' said the baron, 'is not uninhabited. Even if it was, I would not permit vermin to spawn and fester upon my freeholding. I demand the return of my son, the disbanding of the Wordsmiths and the destruction of the odex.'

Brother Troop thus became aware that his order now had an enemy. He decided that the baron was upset at the fame and acclaim his son had won by killing a monster, slaying a dragon and so on and so forth. That was true, but there was more to it than that.

Baron Chan Poulaan was worried about the forthcoming marriage between the king's daughter, Slerma, and the valiant Roly Suet. King Skan Asklander, on his own, was harmless, but the Suets were a wily breed – cunning, scheming and devious. And rich. And numerous.

The Suets had already taken the matter of the currency in hand, and now the baron's spies brought him unconfirmed rumours of plans for a praetorian guard, a police force, a small army of infantry, a poll tax, a mining tax, a road toll and a bridge toll, and, in addition to this, a special estate tax to be levied on barons.

It seemed that the wealth, power and energies of Keep were about to be harnessed and directed, undoubtedly with the idea of establishing a true kingdom which would end the privileges and freedoms of the barons. For his part, Baron Chan Poulaan was coming to see the Wordsmiths as part of an alliance of his enemies; he was sending horseback messengers across Sung, summoning a meeting of the Warguild.

This could mean civil war.

As Brother Troop refused to yield up Togura, Baron Chan Poulaan finally sent Cromarty to Keep to bring the errant lad to home and to heel. Cromarty, admitted to the Wordsmiths' stronghold, found Togura matching swords with a rough-bearded servitor. As Cromarty had arrived with no more than a boot-blade to his name, and with no bully boys to back him up, he had to attempt diplomacy; his wretched efforts in this direction excited laughter from the servitor and open contempt from Togura; Cromarty, to his shame, had to go home empty-handed.

Togura was training with the sword because he was preparing to go questing. His mission: to venture to Castle Vaunting in Estar, and there, hopefully with the permission of Prince Comedo, to contend against the monster guarding the green bottle, retrieve that bottle, recover the index, return to Sung, find out how to use the index, and rescue his true love from the clutches of the odex.

A jovial Suet had already told him that the loss of a daughter was of no account; there were plenty more in stock, and, if he wanted, he could marry one tomorrow.

'I have to save her,' said Togura. 'It's a matter of honour.'

It was a matter of many things. It would be one in the eye for his father, if he could rescue Day Suet from the odex. It would raise his status in Keep, confirming him as a hero. It would make him rich, because he had negotiated an agreement with Brother Troop which would guarantee him one per cent of the wealth generated by the odex. It would prove that he was a real man. It would make him famous. And, apart from all that, he was in love with Day. He thought.

So he trained with the sword, and received good advice from all quarters. The more he learnt, the easier his mission seemed to be. The chance of getting killed came to seem comfortably remote; he could not understand how other people had failed, and suspected that they were misfits who had not really gone questing, but had sneaked off into the never-never to start their lives afresh elsewhere.

After all, Estar was fairly close. Galish convoys went there all the time. Prince Comedo of Estar was, according to his reputation, not the nicest of men, but a promise of a percentage of the gains from the odex should sweeten his temper enough to bring him to let Togura have a crack at the monster guarding the green bottle.

The monster itself, he learnt, was a kind of disk-shaped slug known as a lopsloss; he could not imagine an overgrown slug giving him much trouble. He was startled when told that he would actually have to go inside the green bottle to get at the box holding the index; he doubted that this would be possible until the magic of bottle-rings was explained to him, at which point it came to seem easy.

In fact, he thought the whole thing was going to be a doddle. When he heard that Brother Troop was laying on an escort to take him to Estar, it seemed easier than ever. There was not a cloud on his horizon. Until he received his invitation to Slerma's wedding.

Then he panicked.

CHAPTER TEN

In the end, Togura Poulaan accepted the invitation to attend Slerma's wedding. As resident hero, he hardly had a choice. By declining, he would have offended both the Suets and the royal family, which would in turn have earnt him the disapproval of the Wordsmiths.

Because of the wedding, Togura's departure for Estar would be delayed by two days. He was not entirely unhappy with this. Though he had only been with the Wordsmiths for a short time, he felt at home in the Wordsmiths' stronghold; though his mission no longer seemed suicidal, he was not exactly enthusiastic about setting out.

For the wedding, Togura dressed in new breeches, new boots, a stout jerkin and a padded jacket; he wore a sword at his side and flaunted a feather in his cap.

'Etiquette does not permit swords at weddings,' said Brother Troop.

'For ordinary people, no,' said Togura. 'But certain things are expected of a hero.'

'You may be right my son, you may be right,' said Brother Troop, and let him go dressed as he pleased.

The wedding was scheduled to take place in the morning in the Suets' Grand Hall, a building which Togura had never visited before. Arriving early in bright autumn sunshine – a good omen, surely, as it had been unbroken rain for days previously – he found this immense wooden building almost empty except for workmen who were finishing off reinforcements to a section of the floor, and Suet women who were responsible for catering.

Togura walked through the building, strutting a little in his fine new clothes, and admiring all the good things to eat which had been provided in such profusion. Among other things, there were marvellous cakes created in the image of the new coinage.

The building echoed with bright, happy voices. Louder, ominously hollow echoes came from underfoot as people walked this way and that across the wooden floor. Togura walked across one spot where queasy floorboards sagged beneath his weight; he cleared the area quickly, then tapped the floor with his heel and toe, listening to the echoes.

'There's a mine shaft underneath us,' said a well-fleshed well-dressed elderly man.

'It must be a big one,' said Togura.

'One of the biggest. It was Shaft Suet, the richest gemstock sounding in all of Keep. It gave the family its start in life. By the time Shaft Suet was exhausted, the family was rich. Anyway, enough history. You're Barak the Battleman, aren't you?'

'I am. And you?'

'Name's Raznak the Golsh. I'm a Suet by birth and by breeding.'

They idled there for a while, talking of nothing in particular – weddings, cakes, music, the weather. But Togura sensed that Raznak the Golsh had a proposition for him. He was not wrong. Soon Raznak began to speak his mind:

'I hear you're soon to set off on your quest.'

'Very soon. Tomorrow, in fact.'

'What a pity. At the moment, we've got an opening which would just suit a fierce young warrior like yourself. We need a commander for the fighting force we're forming.'

'Honesty compels me to tell you that I'm not the fighter I'm cracked up to be,' said Togura. 'Besides, I'm too young. Few men would follow me.'

'We can use your reputation,' said Raznak. 'You'd grow into

the job. We've got people who can help you find your feet. You'd be a regular sword-slaughterer in a few short years.'

'I'm not the type,' said Togura, who had heard the rumours of civil war, and wanted nothing to do with it. 'I'll never have the fighting prowess.'

'Don't run yourself down. I was lucky enough to see you kill the monster which you rode up out of the mine pit. You've got what it takes, young man.'

'That was a fluke.'

'Perhaps. But your reputation's solid. So I'm making you an offer. Join us. Sung will soon be a proper kingdom. Soon enough, we'll be the royal family. Skan Askander won't live forever.'

And Raznak winked.

'I've got my duty to Day,' said Togura.

'You've been offered a daughter Suet before,' said Raznak. 'The offer still stands. It wasn't your fault that the little girl met her unfortunate end. Don't go throwing away your life on an impossible quest. I met some of those who went questing and were never seen again. Strong men. Brave men. Not a fool amongst them. They were strong, determined, capable. But they vanished, one and all.'

'All five of them.'

'Five! The Wordsmiths told you that? There's been fifty men go questing, if there's been one.'

This revelation shook Togura.

'Tell me you'll join us,' said Raznak the Golsh.

'I'll think about it,' said Togura.

'You do that, young man. You do that.'

And he most certainly did, pondering his options while the hall filled with guests. Fifty heroes, all missing in action! Could it be true? If it was, then Raznak's offer certainly had its temptations. So who could he trust? Who could he believe?

His troubled mind worried away at the problem until his cogitations were interrupted by the announcement of the arrival of Roly Suet. The young groom, fatter than most people but thin for a Suet, was dressed like a peacock. He looked calm — too calm. His eyes had a glazed, fixed expression. Togura suspected he had been drugged.

'Enter the sacrifice,' muttered a voice.

'The things people do for power!' said another.

Shortly after, the hum of conversation in the hall fell away to an absolute silence as Slerma entered. She was led into the hall and then seated by guides and helpers who made sure she kept strictly to the reinforced sections. At the sight of her, one tender young lady blanched and fainted. Two old ladies, a spinster and a relict, began to titter, and then, unable to help themselves, broke into frank and horrified laughter.

Slerma did not appear to hear. She stared around her, letting her eyes ooze slowly over the vast mounds of food which were on display.

'Slerma will eat well,' she said. 'This is good.'

Two female Suets with fixed smiles draped a veil over her countenance, but Slerma mauled it away from her face. She had gone to a lot of trouble with her appearance, and did not want her efforts to go to waste.

Slerma's make-up represented a unique experiment in abstract art. Stains of green and red were smeared across the flanks of her face, creating washes of gently undulating colour which swelled and contracted as she chewed her cud. She had applied mascara; dabs and dobs of black were scattered above her eyebrows, looking like the distant heads of soldiers peering over the brow of extensive earthworks.

Togura felt it rude to stare, yet could not help himself. He was not alone. Slerma was as huge as he had remembered – if anything, worse. A buxom girl could have been made from the flesh of each of her forearms, and a respectable whore from each of her thighs; her belly could have given birth to a regular conclave of washerwomen. Her fingers, as fat as sausages, looked deceptively soft and helpless; remembering the true strength of her bone-crushing hands, Togura shuddered. To think that he had almost been married to this!

Watched by a disbelieving audience, the wedding ceremony was conducted.

'If any man alleges prior claim to possession of this woman, let him speak now or for ever afterwards remain silent,' said the marriage celebrant, looking around sternly. No claims being forthcoming, he announced: 'I find, rule and declare that there are no prior claims on this woman.'

'What woman?' cried a wit.

Who was promptly suppressed, strenuously.

At the conclusion of the wedding ceremony, Slerma embraced Roly Suet, engulfing him in her arms. She held him close. She had decided to be very loving today. After a while, Roly began to make violent, animated movements with his arms and legs. It appeared he was suffocating. This was highly embarrassing! Senior Suets stood by, one openly wringing his hands, while people pushed and shoved to get a good view, standing on tiptoe and craning their necks. Gladiatorial sports were unknown in Sung, so they had never seen anything like it.

Finally, Slerma released her prey. He slid down to the ground and lay at her feet, limp but still breathing. Taking him by the hair, she hauled him onto her lap, where he lay like a rag doll, his face plastered with red and green and black; he had been kissed.

Someone cheered. Infected by an outbreak of mob hysteria, the others took up his theme; the hall rocked and resounded with applause. Slerma beamed. She was a success. She was glorious. She was beautiful. She was loved. Her happiness would have been complete if her father had been here to see her triumph, but unfortunately he was laid up with gout.

Determined music began; the cheering died away, and was replaced by a babble of talk, gossip and speculation. The festivities were underway.

As a skavamareen wailed along in the wake of a galloping thrum, Togura encountered a girl named Zona, who made it appear that she met him almost by accident.

'Are you a Suet?' he said.

'Yes. How did you guess?'

'What else would they send to seduce me?'

'The cheek of the animal!' she said.

'A kiss would be a good way to start,' said Togura.

She blushed, and Togura knew his suspicions were correct.

The Suets had sent one of their expendable females to romance him. He was flattered.

'Dance with me,' he said.

She yielded, so soon they were dancing the Dalataplash, kicking their heels and punching the air, whooping at the war-scream and shouting at the hoot, then embracing each other in the couple and the grind. She laughed a lot. She might have been sent, but she was willing. He was young, handsome and a hero, and a baron's son besides, heir to the estate if he killed his half-brother Cromarty. There was good meat on her bones; he knew himself lucky.

They danced then ate, danced then drank, then danced again. Togura cast occasional glances in the direction of young Roly Suet, who seemed to be making a remarkable recovery from his traumatic experience with Slerma. The royal couple were not dancing: Slerma was still eating, with Roly at her side feeding her choice morsels from a bucket.

'Would you marry me?' said Togura to Zona.

'Would I if what?'

'If I asked.'

'Ask.'

'That's no answer.'

'Still, it's the answer deserved. Are you a hero or aren't you?'

'I'll think about it,' said Togura. 'Come, the music's wasting. Let's dance.'

And dance they did. She was smooth, lithe, clean-limbed and lively. He wanted her. She was his answer to the urgency of the flesh. She was part of a contract for a fabulous future. In the face of such offers, what wisdom in questing? Fifty men missing, most probably dead? Where was the temptation in that?

It was many generations since Togura's ancestors had been sharp-bargaining Galish merchants, but, nevertheless, a trader's caution was still part of his heritage; he disliked unnecessary danger on principle, being entirely lacking in the kind of hang-devil recklessness which welcomes impossible odds.

But Day!

How could he forget about Day?

How could he just write her off like that?

He tried to bring her face to mind, but failed. He could not remember what she looked like! He tried, in a dutiful way, to fabricate feelings of regret and remorse, but failed.

'Kiss me,' said Zona.

And he could hardly decline.

As they danced, the music grew louder. An old-fashioned canterkade beat out a rythm in direct opposition to a new-fangled clay. A sklunk back-thumped, a chanter whined, a snot-pipe shrilled, then massed plea whistles hooted and honked, joining the screaming high pinions in a caterwauling fanfarade.

'So what's it to be?' said Zona, as the last of the music jogged down to nothing. 'Where will you sleep tonight and tomorrow? By some bone-rotting mountainside bog? Or elsewehere, far warmer?'

'Give me time to think,' said Togura, with a laugh of joy and triumph which he was unable to suppress.

Already he knew his answer. It was no contest. The people of Sung — even the young men — were essentially too sane and sober to make good questing heroes. They seemed wild enough, with their feuding and fighting, but such localised sports are essentially civilised in that they never take you more than a couple of days from your own warm bed and a hot-bread kitchen.

Though the Wordsmiths did not know it yet, Togura had just cancelled his quest for the index.

'Let's find a seat,' said Zona.

'Let's,' said Togura, coughing.

'It's rather smoky,' said Zona, waving a hand in front of her face.

'Rather,' said Togura, looking round to see who was smoking the acrid pipe.

He blinked. His eyes were stinging. People were starting to shout. Somebody screamed. Suddenly Togura realised there were clouds of smoke curling and coiling overhead. People were panicking, rushing for the exits. Togura drew his sword, then looked at it in astonishment. Why had he done that? He sheathed it hastily, before Zona noticed. Zona?

'Zona!' shouted Togura.

His voice was lost in the uproar. She was gone. She had fled. Somewhere, a loud voice boomed, roaring:

'Fire! Fire! Fire!'

Togura jumped on a table.

'Don't push!' he bawled. 'People will get crushed!'

But he was ignored. He coughed; the air was harsh with smoke. Looking round, he saw a disturbance. He saw part of a wall breaking down, admitting bright sunlight and a wedge of – masked men!

'We're under attack!' shouted Togura.

But nobody heard him.

He jumped down from the table and waded toward the attackers. With Suets and their guests crushing each other to death in the jam-packed exits, he figured that the break in the wall offered him his best chance of escape from a building now definitely burning.

He drew his sword again, and this time did not feel stupid for doing so.

CHAPTER ELEVEN

Togura, dizzy with smoke, fear and excitement, hung back as the masked men attacked. His drawn sword was strictly for self-defence. He saw them close in on Roly Suet, who fought as best he could, crowning one with a food bucket and kicking another in the privates. They overwhelmed him and carried him off.

'Give me back my man!' said a vast, slurred, grubbling voice.

It was Slerma. She was not pleased.

A man slashed at her with his sword. She threw up a forearm to defend herself. By rights, sword versus arm should lead to instant amputation. But the blade scarcely managed to cut deep enough into her blubber to reach the bone. Next moment she had seized the miscreant by neck and by ankles, and was tearing him apart. As Togura blinked, gaped and boggled, the man ruptured and split, spilling—.

Togura closed his eyes, feeling sick.

By now, others had realised what was going on. Suets and guests, arming themselves with tables, chairs, carving knives and roasting spits, gave battle. Those with no weapons flailed at the attackers with jackets, coats, cloaks and capes, seeking to entangle their swords or beat them down so they could close for a stranglehold. Roly's kidnappers were cut off from their escape route. Two sat on Roly, holding him down, while the others fought in the burning building.

Slerma, thinking the battle was going against her side, went to the rescue.

'No!' screamed Togura, seeing her bulking off the reinforced section of the floor.

But he was not heard or was not understood or was ignored. Slerma rumbled ahead, spitting and growling, ready to defend her true love with her life, ready to kill, crush, mutilate and mangle. Some of the masked intruders fled howling at her approach. Slerma advanced in triumph.

Then floorboards broke beneath her, precipitating her into the abandoned mine shaft below. The invaders raised a cheer, and began to prevail. Then a squad of musicians joined the affray, their instruments becoming weapons of war. As battle raged, huge bubbling roars came from underground. Slerma was still alive, and most indignant about her predicament. Two Suets, overwhelming an invader, tossed him into Slerma's pit. Shortly his pitiful screams maimed the air, then came a slubbering groan, and then − from him, at least − silence. The din of battle masked the sounds of feeding.

Togura, sword in hand, skirted round the outskirts of the brawl, making for the daylight. But a masked fighting man stepped forward to confront him.

'Who is it who dares to trifle with Barak the Battleman?' shouted Togura.

'Me!'

And the masked man tore away his disguise. It was Cromarty, claymore in hand.

'Crom!' cried Togura.

'None other,' said Cromarty, grinning with open delight. 'And what have we here? Why, why, it's little Tog-Tog. Gather round, boys. Now it's really party time!'

But there were no boys free to gather round.

'You're on your own this time,' said Togura.

'That's all right,' said Cromarty evenly. 'I'll manage.'

And, turning ferocious without further ado, he attacked.

Their war-blades clashed. Togura sliced Cromarty's thigh. Cromarty nicked his nose. Blooded, they broke apart, coughing and panting, their eyes stung with tears as smoke whirled about them. They began to circle, posing fiercely and talking tough.

'Come closer,' said Togura, 'and I'll slice you from pox to piles.'

'Not so hasty, salami minor, or you'll be eating your arsehole for breakfast.'

'Talk's cheap, you son of a slut.'

'A slut? Look who's talking. I raped your mother on the night she died.'

'Shut your filth and swallow it.'

'Believe me, Tog-tog. She loved it. She asked for more and more and more. She licked my—'

'Liar!'

A burning beam crashed down between them. A smaller timber fell, striking Cromarty, knocking him to the ground with a glancing blow. As the building broke up, the fight was breaking up. People were running for their lives. Togura started to scream a threat at Cromarty, but broke out into a fit of coughing instead. His half-brother was lost in the swirling smoke. Togura sheathed his blade. A man came blundering his way, blinded by blood streaming from a cut on his forehead. It was Roly Suet.

'This way!' shouted Togura, grabbing him.

Roly tried to fight him.

'It's me, stupid! Barak the Battleman, rescuing you!'

Togura hustled him out into the street. Smoke reeled up into the sky. Roly, coughing, tried to wipe the blood from his eyes. The street was filled with skirmishing fighters, rearing horses, screaming children and indignant citizens of all descriptions.

'Togura!' yelled a black-masked fighter standing at bay some distance up the street. 'Give us the boy!'

Togura knew that voice. It was his father. As Baron Chan Poulaan cut away the sundry Suets opposing him, Togura fought to control a frightened horse. He mounted up. The animal almost threw him, but he got control. He helped Roly up behind him. Cromarty came stumbling out of the building, still armed with his claymore.

'Cut him down, Crom!' roared the baron, wounded now, but still fighting his way toward them.

Half-blinded by smoke, Cromarty glanced round then attacked. Togura kicked him away, getting slashed on the calf in the process. He saw a gap in the scrabbling fight, and rode for it, with Roly hanging on for dear life. Behind him, the Suet's Grand Hall collapsed with a prolonged crash, sending burning debris sprawling across the street.

The baron was separated from his sons by a pile of burning wreckage. Gathering his wits, Cromarty ordered the nearest half dozen warriors to join him in pursuit. Seizing what horses they could, they did.

Togura rode for hell and high clappers, taking the road to the palace. When they came to the outskirts of the piggeries, he reined in the horse, thinking them safe. Then he looked round and saw the pursuit closing in behind.

'You should have stayed in the town!' yelled Roly. 'We would have lost them in the side streets.'

'Thanks for the good advice,' snapped Togura. 'It's brilliantly timed.'

He was tempted to push Roly off into the mud and the slother, but resisted the temptation. Roly was what Cromarty wanted. Togura was not going to let him have it that easily. Togura kicked the horse in the flanks, and they rode past palace and piggeries. The road, such as it was, soon plunged downward. They hastened down recklessly, making one of the fastest descents ever of that particular piece of track, which was known as the Slippery Skaddle. The pursuit followed remorselessly.

'Where are we going now?' cried Roly, as they started down a track between bogland and gorse.

'Ahead, unless you've got any better ideas,' said Togura.

He knew they were now on the Fen Route, a raggle-tag half-road picking its way across some of the worst country in all of Sung. The horse was close to failing, but before it could collapse they came to Skob Crossing, a festering marsh crossed by a disintegrating one-step bridgeway.

'Dismount,' snapped Togura, getting down.

When Roly hesitated, Togura gave him a push. As the Suet scrabbled up out of the muck, Togura, half-running, ventured the creaking bridgeway, which was green with moss and soggy with wetrot.

'Don't leave me!' cried the plaintive Suet.

Togura paused long enough to shout 'Follow!', then was off again. The Suet scuttled over the bridgeway behind him. Skidding, slipping and sliding, they panted down a rutted track. Behind them they could hear Cromarty and his mobsters baying at high hunt.

The track grew narrower, and became overgrown. They sprinted through nettles, yelping. Blackberry clawed at them. They shoved aside vines, hoping none were poison ivy. The gaunt trees overhead, their leaves a clatter of autumn, were drenched with draggle-moss, blighted by canker and pockled with fungus. Roly, glistening with sweat, was failing fast.

'I can't – keep – up,' he gasped.

'I'd guessed that much,' said Togura. 'Down! Take cover! I'll lead them off.'

And he shoved the Suet into a thicket of clox, kicking his backside when he hesitated. Then Togura ran on, holding his side, for he was getting the stitch. He blinked as sweat scabbed into his eyes, stinging fiercely. He could feel his strength failing. Behind him, the enemy cheered. They had him in sight now.

Togura slowed almost to a walk as he padded up the knoll ahead. On the far side was a narrow ribbon of swamp, just too wide to jump over. Togura sprinted down, tore a rotten pole tree from its foundations and swiftly probed the water, failing to find its depth. It was green with swamp grass; to the casual eye it could have been any depth from ankle onwards. Quickly, Togura nipped round the flank of the swamp, then used his snapped-off pole tree to thrust and stir, confusing the surface of the swamp so it looked as if he had sprinted straight through it.

Cromarty and his bounders came panting over the knoll. They saw Togura on the far side of the swamp, apparently untangling himself from some barbarian thorn.

'Have him, boys!' screamed Cromarty.

Whooping and hallooing, they charged down the slope and into the swamp, plunging in up to their noses. All except two. Who began to skirt the swamp as Togura turned and fled.

'You klech!' shouted Cromarty. 'You gan-sucking jid of veek-nucking ornskwun hellock! Come back here, you gamos-eating son of a toad-mother. Scalp him, boys! Cut his oysters and shaft him!'

Togura, labouring up another rise, stumbled. There were rocks underfoot. He picked up a large one, turned, and hurled it at his nearest pursuer. His victim flung out his hands. Snatching up one stone after another, Togura pelted them both. Battered, bruised and bleeding, they made a hasty retreat. Togura had no breath with which to celebrate his triumph.

Down below, the victims of his swamp-trap were extricating themselves from their predicament with some difficulty; the swamp did not have a quicksand bottom, but it was certainly soft. Togura managed a slight smile. Which vanished the next instant as reinforcements came over the knoll on the far side of the swamp-strip. They pointed, shouted, then joined the pursuit.

Togura turned and ran.

But he did not go far.

He ran a hundred paces, hit another rocky stretch which would show no footprints, leapt sideways, went down into a boggy wallow, crawled into a thicket of stilt trees, then hugged the ground and lay still. He waited. He did not have to wait for long. The pursuit panted past. As soon as he thought they were gone, Togura shuffled deeper into the stilt trees. Then, thinking himself out of sight of the track, he rose to a crouch and began to run, nipping from tree to tree, casting frequent looks backward.

He came to a stretch of swamp and plunged in heedlessly, going in up to his neck. He waded across, hauled himself up on the far side, and was off again. For a while he sometimes heard faint, distant shouts and cries, but after a while even these died away. He blundered on, losing track of place and time. Then, finally, he heard the far-off baying of hounds. It terrified him. Dogs! They were using dogs! He went crashing through the undergrowth, till he found a narrow, wending, slovenly stream snaking its way through sedge and mud.

Togura waded down his stream, determined to kill his scent so the dogs would be unable to follow. Unfortunately, he broke enough twigs, grasses and creepers for even the clumsiest tracker to follow, and splattered mud on vegetation that escaped his trampling feet. Fortunately, the dogs were not looking for him: they were seeking a member of the pursuit team, who, realising Togura had left the road, had ventured to search for him in the wilderness, and had become hopelessly lost. Unfortunately, Togura himself, by the time he stopped, was also hopelessly lost.

At first, Togura did not realise his predicament. What he did realise was that his dog-bewildering highway was full of leeches. He left hastily, and counted his assailants. There were seventeen of them, nine of them having battened onto his flesh where his calf had been slashed by Cromarty's sword. He had no fire with which he could burn off the leeches; he decided it was best to leave them to bloat themselves with blood, after which they would drop away of their own accord.

Still concerned about the dogs, he set off across country at the best pace he could manage. The predominant vegetation here was sickle trees, tall, thin and stringy, their shafts of autumn foliage closely clustered, soaring up into the sky above. As he went on, he became half-aware that the going was getting easier; the ground was getting firmer.

Then the sickle trees began to give way to some kind of vegetation he was unfamiliar with: tall, thick, scabrous grey trees set far apart, their foliage so dense that virtually nothing grew beneath them. These trees were covered with long, cruel, jagged hooks, barbs, spikes and claws; their leaves, when Togura was incautious to touch a few, snagged at him with myriads of tiny teeth. He decided they deserved the name claw trees.

Realising he was in a very strange neck of the woods, Togura stopped, and went no further. He decided it was time to orientate himself. He looked around for a landmark, but the thick-foliaged claw trees and the high, spindly sickle trees cut him down to hundred-pace horizons in all directions. He could see bits and pieces of the sky, which was now a diffuse, misty grey; the good weather which had graced the start of the day had failed. He could not climb the claw trees because they would cut him to pieces; the sickle trees, while harmless, would never support his weight. Without landmarks or sunlight, he could not judge his location or the time of day.

He sat down to think things over, and stood up immediately. The dead dried leaves of the claw trees, which littered the ground underfoot, retained their teeth even after they had littered down from their parental branches. Leaning against a couple of convenient sickle trees, Togura took stock of his situation.

He was lost.

He was tired.

He was hungry.

His clothes were damp and caked with mud.

He had no food, excepting half a dozen persistent leeches, which did not really count.

He had one sword, which by rights should now be cleaned, but which was not going to be because he couldn't be fagged.

He had no water.

He had a painful sword-cut on his nose; though only a tiny little piece of his nose appeared to be actually missing, this was not calculated to improve his beauty.

He had a more serious wound in his calf, which was not disabling – no tendons had been severed, and he did not think it was deep – but which was filthy with muck and mud and was now throbbing painfully.

The day was not getting any younger.

So what should he do?

He first tried to retrace his steps, but found himself rapidly getting lost amidst a featureless expanse of sickle trees. He managed to get back to the claw tree forest, then reconsidered his position. Whatever the dangers, he had no doubt that a return to Keep was his best option. But his chances of getting anywhere by blundering about the wilderness at random were slim.

The ground on which the claw tree forest grew appeared to be sloping steadily uphill. He decided to follow the rising incline, hoping to come to a prominence which would give him an all-round view, or, failing that, at least a prehensile tree capable of supporting his weight.

Togura set off, walking slowly, for he was weary; he limped, as his wounded leg was very sore. Remembering Cromarty floundering in the swamp-trap, he managed a slight smile. All in all, he could be proud of himself. He had kept his head in the burning building. He had matched Cromarty, blade against blade. Riding out of Keep, he should by rights have been able to shake off the pursuit; it was just bad luck that the enemy had managed to follow him through the streets and out of the town. Even then, hunted and outnumbered, he had scored a resounding success with his minor tactics. But that didn't alter the fact that he was lost.

Gradually, his little glow of self-satisfaction faded; he plodded onward, getting slower and slower. The day aged; the light faded; a little rain began to drizzle down through the trees. Eventually, he realised it was evening, and would soon be night.

The smart thing to do now would be to climb a tree, to be safe from wolves. Or find a cave, and barricade it. Or at least cut branches to make a lean-to shelter in which he could bivouac. Then eat, scavenging worms, snails, slugs and fungus. A country boy born and bred, he knew what he had to do. But the landscape was singularly unhelpful. He was surrounded by unclimbable claw trees; there was now no undergrowth at all, the ground below the trees being littered with sharp-toothed leaves; there were no helpful rocks or hollows; to the best of his recollection, he had not seen or heard any bird or insect since entering the claw tree forest, nor had he sighted any fungus, edible or otherwise.

He was in a cold, dead, evil place, barren of life and bare of water; the rain sifting down through the creaking, rheumatic branches was strong enough to chill and dampen him, yet insufficient to give him any hope of assuaging his thirst; a cold wind soughed through the leaves overhead, promising a bitter night.

Togura came to a decision.

What he had was nothing, but it was all he was going to get, so he had better make the most of it. Drawing his sword, he scraped away the leaves, clearing a space where he could lay his body down. Then it occurred to him that he could dig a shallow grave in which he could lie down out of the wind. Better still, he could dig a foxhole in which he could sleep with his knees drawn up to his chest to conserve warmth.

Eagerly, Togura set to work, but found the ground hard and unyielding, seamed and knotted with tangles of tough, fibrous roots. It was hopeless.

He ended up spending the night huddled on the bare ground, sleeping in snatches; whenever he fell asleep, he soon shivered himself awake again. By the time morning came, as unfriendly as a hangover, he was feverish. His wounded leg was almost too painful for him to walk on. The lymph node in his groin was swollen, hard and painful; he suspected that if he had been able to clean his wound and examine it, he would have discovered an angry red line running up his leg, denoting blood poisoning.

He had no food: even the last of his leeches had left him.

'On your feet, Togura Poulaan,' he said.

Rising, he sought for support, and tried to take hold of the branch of a claw tree. A mistake – and one that he immediately regretted.

CHAPTER TWELVE

'Zaan,' said the sun.

The ice-white light ran through his blood in splinters.

It was fading.

'Clouds,' he said.

A frog answered him. He spoke. It answered again. His teeth hurt. Then came the rain, drenching away the last of the sunlight. The skirling wind fladdered and scooped, outpacing his eyesight; it came in rents and buffets, sending the shimmy-shimmy leaves stappering and plattering from down to around. Some dead at his feet. He kicked them from ventral to dorsal.

'Tog,' he said.

Asking for someone.

He couldn't remember who.

His legs went balder-shalder-tok through the rain perhaps autumn or winter. His third leg was a gnarled unyielding strake padded with moss and wort where it jammed home to his armpit. The music of a flute cut closer than a knife; hard, high, unyielding, it lacerated his heart. He felt his pulse-beats bleeding through his body. The wind blew furnace hot; he shivered, his teeth tok-tok chin-cha-chattering.

'Hello,' he said.

A frog answered.

'Go away, frog.'

And then, again, hoping against hallucination:

'Hello?'

They didn't seem to notice him. Instead, they kept to their dance, tracing formalities between the green of green boughs and the red of red blood. He waved in their direction with what had once been a hand but which was now a club, a poisoned mass of striving darkness. The ground was rhythmic underfoot. A swathe of wind took him from behind and flattened him to an undug grave.

'Once I had a sword,' he said, or thought he said. 'But I lost it. Perhaps.'

She answered him in the cadence of birdsong, feeding him something which was honey and yet not honey.

'That is good,' he said.

'Sleep,' she said, or thought she said.

Then she was feeding him again, then hurting his hand; he tried to protest, but she fed him with even, placid spoonfuls which slurred and slubbered on his tongue. Her hands were diligent, the blankets very warm. Yet so uncomfortable.

His troubling fingers plucked bits of moss and lichen from the blankets. Dry. Tasteless. He spat them out. It occurred to him that perhaps he was not in a bed at all, but swallowed by some hole in the forest, chewing on moss and dreaming strange dreams while he eased his way toward death.

The rocks above looked solid, sullen, certain.

A cave, then.

The shiftless wind came shifting in through a cold square hole in the cave. Beyond lay a high harsh light which might have been daylight. Things clawed at the hole, scratching, scraping, grasping, gaping. They wanted him.

Frightened, he called for help.

She came to him. Her voice was half birds and half water. Or was it rainbow? Her eyes, dark. Her hands, slender. She fed him soup; he tried to hold the spoon, but found himself clumsy as a baby. She did not laugh.

The next time she came, she was shorter, heavier, and just a little bit sour. Her eyes had changed from dark to grey, her hair from black to fair. The blankets were still scratching him. He complained about them. This time, she said nothing.

99

Attempting diligence, he tried to remember her face, but it shifted with uncanny agility. As in a nightmare, he tried to stabilise his memories, only to have them prove incompetent each time she entered. Finally he thought:

– Different women tend me.

And knew his thought for truth.

He was healing.

He began to take stock of his situation.

The room was small. Square. Dark. One door. The door led through shadows to a coffin-lid dungeon of darkness. One window. From the bed, he could see the bare branches of a tree, grasping and clutching at the thriftless wind.

What was the room made of? Stone. Vast slovenly blocks of stone. No mortar. Above him, a single grey tombstone stretched from wall to wall. He thought of himself as a tiny huddle of flesh and sensation hunched up inside a dull, grey, senseless prison of dour mass, monotonous weight, inertia, and habitual oppression.

'I'm hungry,' he said.

She entered, matching none of his memories. By the windowlight, he saw she was dressed in bulky, padded clothes of woven bark. Tufts of moss and lichen peeked out between the warp and weft; perhaps, beneath that padding, she was as slender as a tree in sunlight. Or perhaps not. It occurred to him that, in any case, not all trees were slender. Not even in sunlight.

She did not frown or smile; though courteous, she was grave, restrained in her dealings with him.

She brought food.

He ate gruel, pap and watered bread.

It was all he could manage.

The bread was very strange. It was heavy and loamy, tasting sometimes of honey and sometimes of fish. Was it made from grain? Or from some kind of pasted root? Eating, he scented swamp. The bread was not to blame. The wind coming in through the window was bringing him the smells of marsh, bog and slough.

When she came again, he ate the soup without help; he

could sit up by himself. His blankets were the same woven bark as her clothes, padded with the same mosses and lichens. He resented their million million insect-creeping legs, claws and feelers.

'Wool makes better blankets,' he said.

She answered him with words which were half music, half ripening fruit. Which was strange, for it was the wrong season for ripening fruit. Unless he was mistaken, it was winter. So thinking, he spun down in a dizzy spiral, fainting.

When he woke, it was night.

The shutters had not been fastened properly; they creaked, groaned and laboured in the knock-kneed wind.

'Shutters,' he said, complaining.

And nothing answered no-one.

His head was light yet his limbs were death-heavy. His knee-joints were made of curdling milk. Hands alien. His throat was dry; he was thirsty. Perspiring, he reached the shutters; he could not remember getting out of bed. He found a cord which secured the shutters, tying one to the other. He pulled it free. The shutters swung apart.

He saw bright moonlight, broken buildings, and the titubant shadows of trees reeling in the violent, gusting wind. Banners of turbulent cloud streamed across the moon; when the clouds cleared, the moonlight showed him the dull, low-slung outline of a heavyweight wall which caught the moonlight in its open crescent. Set in the middle of that crescent, like a stump about to be reaped by a sickle, was a vast stone beehive, many times the height of a man. It had no windows, and only one door. Sullen fire glowed within.

– Where am I?

Leaves, thin scampering prey, fled before the wind. Others followed close behind, cruel scuttling predators which kept close to the ground as they moved on the kill. Then all the leaves were suddenly flung upward in turbulent spirals as the buffeting wind switched and turned.

The change in the wind brought Togura a whiff of something foul. It was not swamp or mud or wet water. It was the rot and decay of the flesh. It was a putrid, evil smell of degenerating nightmares, of soft fat becoming fungus, of bones riddled with worms, of eyeballs subsiding into dark pools of purulent liquid.

Togura was almost certain that the smell was coming from the beehive.

The wind changed. And the fire which he could see within the beehive was suddenly obscured, as if someone was walking down a passageway, blocking the view to the centre. Suddenly, terrified, Togura knew that he must not be caught here at the window, watching, witnessing.

He closed the shutters and secured the cords which held them against the wind. Returning to bed, he found himself unable to sleep. Yet when he opened his eyes again, it was morning. Feeding on soup and the meat of a small fresh-water turtle, he comforted himself with the thought that the wall, the beehive and the sudden stench must all have been part of a nightmare.

But when his recovering health allowed him to totter around at liberty, he found the window's daylight view the same as its night-time aspect. He had not been dreaming. Sometimes, indeed, the shifts of the wind brought him hints of something foul, and always he identified those hints with the beehive.

He did not know whether he was a guest, a slave or a prisoner, but when he was well enough to walk along a stone shaft as blind as darkness and make the turns which took him to the outer world, they put him to work.

It was most certainly winter now. His old clothes had disappeared, together with his leather boots; he wore clogs, and clothes of woven bark stuffed with mosses and lichens, and a great big ear-comforting flap-hat consisting, as far as he could tell, of several birds' nests held in a net of woven bark. His skin broke out into strange red rashes, which itched. But he endured.

They put him to work at first on the simplest of tasks. A woman took him to a fire which was burning outside a building inhabited by females. He had already once tried to enter that building, and had been prevented.

She pointed at the fire.

'Koo'-l'na-ve'e'e'esha,' she said, giving different musical values to each of her fleeting syllables, so that this, the simplest of her communications, became an intricate telestic pronouncement.

'What?' said Togura.

'Ko'laaskaa-n'esha-esa. Cha?'

'Ko?' he queried, trying to get her to repeat the phrase.

Impatiently, she slapped her elbow. He had seen these people use this gesture before. Sometimes it seemed to be employed as a form of negation, but in some people it seemed to be simply a kind of nervous tic. She showed him a cut-down hollowed-out gourd which was lined with clay. She took a stick and scraped red-hot coals into it. Shoved it into his hands.

'Ondolakon'n-puru-sodarasonsee. Cha?'

'Cha,' he said, experimentally.

She slapped his face.

'Why did you do that?' he said, sharp tears pricking his eyes.

She made no answer, but went into the females' building which was forbidden to him, returning shortly with a long stick which had a hook at one end. She spoke sharply, then set off. He followed, holding the clay-lined gourd, breathing in the heat which ascended from the coals.

Their clogs clicked down a broad, deserted street flanked by dull, squat, pyramidal buildings, The street ended abruptly in swamp. They crossed a series of rickety bridges between swamp trees and swamp islands. Here and there, occasional bits of masonry obtruded from the chilly waters – a single column, or a bit of wall, or a stairway to nowhere. He blew on the coals to keep them alive. They glowed hot and red, relishing the life fed to them by his breath. He was glad that at least something in this cold, desolate universe appreciated his existence.

In the grey waters, he caught sight of their reflections. Dressed in their gross, bulking clothes of bark and moss and lichen, crowned with their swollen, shrouded headgear, they looked like strange, deformed insects. The bridges ended. They had reached a place half swamp, half city. Huge, decayed buildings hulked up out of the grey waters. Paths and roads walked variously above and below water. The buildings were drenched in winter-withered vines; he saw that the dead vegetation was poison ivy.

'Lora-ko-lara-sss-daz'n'n'boro,' she said, kicking together a few fragments of stick.

He guessed her purpose, and helped build a fire. They lit it with one of the hot coals from the gourd. Then, using the hooked stick, she raked down some dead poison ivy. When it was heaped on the ground, she set it alight. She passed him the stick. He did the same, keeping well clear of the ivy, for he knew better than to handle it, for all that it was dead.

'Shor-nash-n'esha-esha-ala'n-cha,' she said.

Then clicked her tongue and walked away, heading back the way they had come. When he followed, she turned on him, screaming. She gave him a push. He retreated. She kicked the stick. He picked it up and began to pull down poison ivy. She clicked her tongue once more, slapped her elbow, then left him.

He worked all day. In the evening, another woman came and led him back to the settlement. There was a meal waiting, of sorts; it was prepared by women, it was served by women, and he ate amongst the women,

This, for a time, was the pattern of his days. He was woken at first light and served a solitary breakfast. Then he was led along the bridges to his place of work. He was never trusted to go alone. The person who took him would wait until he had a fire going and had started on the poison ivy, and would then depart. He once returned of his own accord, and was severely beaten; after that, he knew that he was not supposed to go home until he was fetched.

He worked, all day, alone, eating a communal meal with the women in the evening.

And sleeping alone.

He was bored and lonely.

And hungry.

And puzzled.

He saw old men, who held themselves apart from the rest of the community; there seemed to be about thirty of them, living in the massive stone beehive. But where were the old women? And where were all the people of middle years? Some of the young women were pregnant, but where were their husbands?

For the most part, work appeared to be done by children of both sexes, who began to toil away from the earliest age, and by young women. Togura saw a few young men; he guessed their number at half a dozen in a community of perhaps three hundred people. The young men were always silent and withdrawn; they seemed to be sleep-walking. As far as he could tell, they never spoke.

In the evenings, the women talked at Togura readily, but he could never make sense of anything they said. He found it impossible to learn their names; they, for their part, seemed to think that he was concealing his own identity. He named himself first as Togura and then as Togura Poulaan; they memorised that with no trouble at all, but never seemed satisfied with it. His own attempts to come to grips with their half-sung names were disastrous; his efforts provoked frowns, shock, pain, dismay or open contempt. Nobody laughed. These people did not seem to know what laughter was.

Togura came to suspect that these people changed their names according to the time of day, or swapped and traded their names between each other, or identified themselves with one form of a name yet expected to be addressed in an entirely different fashion. He was baffled, frustrated by his failure to unravel the tantalising mystery of their liquid, ever-singing language.

Not that he had all that much time for philological research. For many days, that evening meal was his one link with the rest of humanity; for the rest of the time, he was as solitary as a hermit, enduring the long cold nights spent in his small stone cell, or working alone in his own quadrant of the city.

As the days grew shorter and colder, and the weather grew worse and worse, he did less and less work. Sometimes he spent all day huddled by a tapering fire lit in a mute stone room in the mute stone ruins, listening to a storm howling outside and watching for cracks in the sky.

The numb days of isolation, one much the same as the next,

105

seemed to run together to become one single, endless day. Exiled from all effective community, he began to hallucinate. The stones mumbled to him. His ears sang with high, distant voices. He watched the sky twist into yellow flame then bleed with purple. Trees stirred and shifted at the periphery of his field of vision, though he was never able to actually catch them in the act of walking.

The days hardened to ice. The storms died away, giving him brittle, frosty mornings of absolute silence. He worked hard on those days, for it became a pleasure to see the swift, passionate flames leaping to the sky, to hear the wing-beating roar of the burning as incendiary passions consumed his tangled ivy, and to warm himself by that energy treasured up from the long-gone sun.

Yet, though he worked to the best of his ability, he did not get all that terribly much done. The food was meagre now. He realised that he was very weak. He had boils and chilblains; his gums bled. He feared scurvy.

Once, in a thaw, he inspected his reflection in the waters of the swamp, and did not recognise what he saw. Was this Togura Poulaan, this thing with long hair, dull sunken eyes, a notched nose and vast birds' nest excrescences? How could these thin legs, these cold aching hands, these clog-clad feet, belong to the son of the strong, powerful and well-fleshed Baron Poulaan, that brave, stout-hearted fighting man who commanded all the Warguild?

'I am Togura Poulaan,' he said.

But his words carried no conviction. He was no longer certain of his own identity. Who was he then? And what? He was something cold and hungry which lived in a cold, unsmiling place where the people spoke like birds and wind and water. He examined the livid purple scar where the wound on his leg had healed. He tried to remember Cromarty's steel cutting home, but could not focus on his memories. His recollections of people and places seemed blurred, dim, unreal.

Perhaps he had always lived here amidst these ruins in the swamp. Perhaps the whole world without and beyond was nothing more than an idle half-formed fantasy he had conjured into being to give himself some solace in his misery. He tried to dismiss the thought, believing himself, apart from anything else, to be incapable of inventing the language he used to think in, which was certainly not the tongue of the community he now endured.

Nevertheless, his hold on his own identity grew steadily weaker and weaker until, on a day which was suddenly warm, and which startled him with the sight of fresh green growth, he saw one of the old men was wearing his jacket.

'Hey grandad!' cried Togura, without thinking. 'What are you doing with my jacket?'

And he approached the ancient. Who looked at him with a gaze of such implacable contempt and disdain that Togura, frightened, retreated.

That evening, Togura became aware of a number of old men regarding him from a distance. He had the impression that they were discussing him. And now, frightened, he could no longer suppress his knowledge of the full gravity of his situation. He was trapped in an alien city ruled – he was sure of it now – by a coven of evil old men who exercised sufficient terror and power to keep every man, woman and child from ever smiling or laughing.

He could only guess at the cause of the noticeable dearth of young men of his own age. He knew nothing of what happened inside the beehive where the old men held court; any conclusions he came to regarding the nameless abominations practised within must be pure speculation. He could not say who impregnated the young women of the community. He could not say for sure why no women survived their youth.

Yet, while all his knowledge was based on guesswork and speculation, lacking any hard evidence, and lacking all possibility of conclusive proof, he was, nevertheless, certain of one thing – if he wanted to live to be much older, then he had to escape.

That spring, he dedicated himself to the pursuit of life and liberty. His life, and his liberty.

It proved very difficult.

He did not know where he was, and he did not know how he had come to be there. Possibly he had walked in over the hills; alternatively, he might have been salvaged from the wilderness and carried here while his mind was still blurred with fever. His memories of his wanderings were vague and fragmentary; some, indeed, were frankly hallucinatory.

His memories could not help him escape, so what he needed to do was to explore. This, unfortunately, was easier said than done.

Now that spring was here, and the poison ivy was spreading its brisk fresh green over the buildings he had cleared during the winter, he was taken off his incendiary detail and made to turn his hand to many different kinds of work. He worked all through the day with the women, who instructed him by example.

In the swamps of the half-sunken city, which was ringed round by steep, forest-covered hills, he drew water, cleared fish traps and used a dull, stone-bladed axe to fell lean, stringy swamp-trees for firewood. He helped make tools, grinding away at bits of the city stone with powdered grit. He worked on the fragile punts used for getting around the swamps. He helped repair bridges, and was taught how to weave ropes and cordage from human hair.

When he found a little free time in the evenings, he never managed to go far. Whichever direction he took led him to despairing bogs and quicksands, swamps deeper than drowning, or dry ground hopelessly infested with poison ivy and barbarian thorn.

In the end, he decided that the only way to escape would be to steal a punt and set out by water.

He made his plans accordingly.

CHAPTER THIRTEEN

Spring performed its ritual poetry. Flowers budded and bloomed. Eggs hatched in hidden nests. Togura Poulaan in the manner of the young, lusted hopelessly after a certain set of thighs; rebuffed and forced to retreat – at knifepoint – he celebrated the allure of that flesh by secret acts of onanism in musty corners of the darkness.

He was very lonely.

Once, Togura caught a duck-billed fledgeling with webbed feet. It had been running on the loose, skittering through the undergrowth with an urgent peep-peep-peep. Once in his hands, it struggled at first, then lay still. He stroked its yellow-brown plumage. He wished that he could keep it to be his friend, but he did not know what he could feed it on. Besides, other people would probably think of it as food, and act accordingly.

He kissed the little bird, and then released it. The earnest little creature ran off, once more going peep-peep-peep; he watched it until it was out of sight, hoping it knew where it was going. For days afterwards, he wondered just what had become of it.

The flowers aged, curled into senescence, withered and died. The birds, growing to maturity, left their nests. The swamps hummed with a delirium of insects. Togura Poulaan cut a wisdom tooth, which made a slow painful passage through the gum. He invented fantasies in which he saved Day

Suet from the odex, and lived with her in splendour. With great care, he designed her undressing and conjured her in heat.

As day followed day, his fantasies became more and more elaborate, dulling the reality of the world he lived in. He still thought that he was diligently planning his escape, but in fact he was doing nothing of the sort. Stealing away in the evenings, after work, he would make tentative little forays into the wilderness, but would always retreat when he got muddy, or when some insect stung him, or when he found the way barred by open water or poison ivy, or by impenetrable screed-growths of swamp-plants reminiscent of bulrushes but much taller.

Thwarted by the swamps, he concentrated on the preliminaries necessary for escape. He would need a store of food. He explored as many of the city's buildings as he could, finding spiderweb passages and darkened stairs which led him to the silent chambers within, and, sometimes, to the roof tops. He found places where he could cache food, but there was never any food to cache; on the rare occasions when he had a surplus, he ate it regardless, finding himself unwilling to leave good food in the dark, where scavenging rats might claim it.

Escape, then, was no more than a hobby which complemented his idle fantasies. Settling into the routines of his working days, he had become slow, idle, lethargic, complacent. His diet, which was poor, undermined his ambitions; he had no conspirators to support and encourage his hopes of escape; he was not entirely certain that the outside world existed to escape to. It would have taken a real shock to his system to overcome his inertia and finally force him to decamp.

At the height of summer, he got such a shock when the community tortured a child to death.

Togura Poulaan was so appalled that he refused to believe what he was seeing. Because he did not believe it was happening, he watched from start to finish. It took from dawn to dusk; it was a regular holiday. Belief finally came to him in

110

a dream. He woke from nightmares, screaming, and knew that he had to flee. Immediately.

In fact, it was three days before he departed. He left at twilight, stealing a punt and poling it away through the swamps. He had no certain idea of where he was going. He had hoped to be helped by the moon, which should have been almost full, but he had no such luck. The stars were soon bedimmed by clouds; by the time moonrise was due, the clouds had ceiled the sky. The night was warm, but black.

He went on through a darkness that was alive with singing insects. Progress became difficult; the punt was slowed, delayed and then halted by a shoal of water lilies. He was not surprised to find that he was lost. Maybe it would have been better to run away in the daytime. But, somehow, he doubted that he would have had the nerve to slip away in broad daylight.

He curled up as best he could on the bottom of the punt and tried to sleep. He was not very successful. Inquisitive insects tasted him, and, finding his flesh acceptable, they spread the word. Something bumped into the punt from underneath, spent some time gnawing at it, then, disheartened, left. An animal went flipperty-flopperty through the blacked-out swamps with a blood-curdling chuckling scream.

Togura several times considered punting on, but, knowing that he would only succeed in getting himself more lost than he was, he stayed put. Dreams claimed him briefly, then nightmares woke him; he found it was early morning.

Sunlight slouched through the swamp. A dawdling insect lumbered through the air amidst nearby osiers, lulling him with his dull, lethargic drone. Though it was still the cool of the early morning, his limbs were heavy with a siesta-sun weariness. He wanted to lie down and sleep. Now that it was daylight, he thought he would sleep quite well.

Resisting temptation, Togura poled his way through the waters, habitat of eel and ewt. Slowly, he negotiated the hazards of the swamp. Occasionally, bubbles stirring on the surface hinted at the direction of a current which might lead him to an outlet from the swamp. He followed one hint after another, only to find that the current dispersed and disappeared, or that the way ahead was an impossible acreage of sedge, or a morass of oozing mud where his punting pole could not find the bottom.

Often the punt ran aground on a slop, a stinking mudflat riddled with wormholes. Then he had to back it off and try some other avenue. He wished – though there was no use in wishing – that he had tried to escape in spring, when the water level would have been higher. He was now more tired than ever. He passed a low-hanging tree, the largest he had seen in the swamp; he was sorely tempted to make camp, and let one of its ergonomically-designed branches nurse him to sleep.

He forced himself onward, driving the punt over a splodge-shaped fresh-water nettle-fish. The day was now alive with the steady hum and blur of insects. The sun had ascended to the heights. High, willowy swamp-trees arched overhead; sunlight, warm and heavy, settled down through a fantasia of branches and foliage. Little scraps of blue sky were mixed into that dense green soup of bough and leaf. In the wake of the punt, which left scarcely a ripple on the waters, tipsy reflections wavered momentarily, then composed themselves. It was now a long time since Togura had seen any hint of a current.

He blinked against the heavy lull of the sun. He tried to convince himself that he was a hunted fugitive, running for his life. But it was impossible. Everything was slow, heavy, lazy. The leisurely rhythms of punting refused to support his claims to urgency.

As he eased the punt down hidden channels between overhanging trees, he slapped away an overhanging branch. Irritated, it retreated: it was a snake. He felt no sense of alarm. Everything was too lazy to consider hurting him. Violence was impossible.

He halted, for water weed and water lilies barred the way ahead. He could go no further. The gnarled voices of frogs, in concord with the droning insects, were persuading him toward sleep. Then, excited, he saw signs of a current in the water. Looking closer, he saw it was a rat swimming, nosing its way between intolerably bright sun-dapple reflections. The waters congealed behind it.

A gaudy dragonfly, child of the sun's pleroma, hovered above the humid waters. As Togura watched, a free-floating rainbow cascaded away from its colours. He blinked, and the hallucination was gone. He decided he had better rest, at least for a few moments. There were trees around him and branches overhead; he was well concealed. A little sleep would do no harm. He curled up in the bottom of the punt, heedless of its discomforts, and was soon lost in slumber.

Togura slept, dreaming of Day Suet asleep in a bed of turquoise, jacinth and ligure. She woke, a sultry melon-light glimmering in her eyes. Giff-gaff, said an insect, eating her nose. He tested her jymolds. She was hot. He was swollen. A sheep pushed him to one side. He plucked mint and ate it, gnawing the sheep. He watched his mother, now perissodactyl, walk across the water lilies. I raped her, said Cromarty. Not so, said Togura; you're just saying that because this is a dream. He closed with Cromarty. His swelling spat. Hot. As birdsong sang.

Togura woke and heard the birdsong. There was something wrong with it. True birdsong should not be like that. He was hearing people talking. They were hunting him. Hunting me, said Togura. His words took flight, becoming shovels of goldleaf; with relief, he realised he was still dreaming. Sleep on, said Togura to Togura. He did, but his dream soon became a nightmare.

Togura Poulaan dreamt of the gaping mouth of a child, which sweated blood. He heard the heavyweight thud of a waterlogged club. White bone splintered through ruptured skin. A woman pulled out a tooth, licked the bloody stump, then swallowed it. The sun licked down, licking his face, stripping away the skin as it did so.

Then something shaded out the sun.

Togura woke for real, and opened his eyes.

In the trees above him, something lurched and giggled. And moved. Sunlight stabbed downwards. He flinched, blinked, and shaded his eyes. He saw bright eyes staring down at him. He leapt to his feet, almost strangling himself. Clawing at his throat, he fell back to the floor of the punt. Someone had looped a noose round his throat as he slept.

They attacked him then, swarming down out of the trees. It was the young women who had hunted him and found him. They beat him, punched him, pinched him, scratched him. The punt, of course, got swamped in the process. They ducked him, forced him underwater and held him there until he almost drowned.

He cried out, his words gashing the air with incoherent fear. The noose was still round his neck. As he floundered in the water, the other end of it was passed up to someone in the trees, who held it while the punt was bailed out.

Then they started off for the city.

Some of the women waded through the swamp on long, high stilts, which he had never seen before. Others rode in punts. Togura was dragged the whole distance behind one of the punts. As his clothes caught on underwater obstacles, the bark was slowly torn to pieces; he left a trail of waterlogged moss and lichen behind him. He had already lost his clogs. By the end of their journey, he was cold, muddy, exhausted and entirely naked.

They imprisoned him in a wickerwork cage hung in a half-submerged hall on the outskirts of the inhabited area of the city. They left him there overnight, without food or water. In his misery, he thought that they were going to starve him to death, so he was most relieved when a woman came early in the morning, opened a hatch which was too small for him to escape through, and passed him a gourd filled with potable water, and a wooden bowl filled with a steaming pot-pourri of turtle meat, snake meat, bird meat, boiled vegetables, steamed herbs and caterpillars.

She watched while he ate the lot, then she took back the bowl, gestured for him to drink, took back the gourd, and then, to his surprise, slipped him a tiny ornamental knife. She slashed a finger across the side of her neck in a swift, emphatic gesture. He understood. She was counselling him to commit suicide. That was what the knife was for.

She left.

He contemplated the knife, which was scarcely the length of his little finger. The diminutive handle was of nacreous mother-of-pearl; the blade, catching a gleam of light in that gloomy place, was of a kind of steel which was brittle yet would take a keen edge.

'I will not die,' said Togura, slowly.

He refused to kill himself. There were so many things he had to do! He heard voices; people were coming into the hall. He had to hide the knife. But how? He had no clothes and no clogs. The blade was razor sharp — he could hardly secrete it in a body orifice. Deciding swiftly, he knotted it into his thick, straggling hair, which had not been cut for more than half a year.

He barely had time to finish the job before his handlers were upon him. They took him from the cage and soon brought him before the stone beehive. Out in the open air, the old men of the community were sitting in state on ornately carved benches which must have been brought out especially for the occasion.

Togura, naked, stood facing the old men. He was aware that the rest of the community, perhaps three hundred people in all, was gathered behind him, keeping at a cautious distance. He was cold. The sun, withdrawing from the scene, consoled itself with its celsitude. Togura coughed. He wondered if he was coming down with a chill. He coughed again. The old men glared at him;

'I can't help coughing,' he mumbled.

Someone screamed at him.

He tried to hold himself rigid, as if that would suppress his coughing. His fingers made small, meaningless, involuntary movements. The old men sat like statues, saying nothing. There was not a sound from the crowd gathered behind him. He felt unearthly, unreal. Dizzy. The light staggered. He swayed. Then the light ebbed away entirely, and he fainted.

When Togura came to, he found himself lying in a crumpled heap on the ground. One of his elbows was hurting badly, but, rising to a half-sitting position, he found the joint was still functional. A long and entirely unintelligible speech was in progress. It was being given by a wart-faced little man, an undershapen gnomish figure who clapped his hands repeatedly to emphasise the points he was making. Somewhere, a drum was beating.

Togura, sitting up properly, tried to work out what was going on. He nursed his elbow, which made it a little more comfortable, which in turn made him realise just how much of the rest of his body was sore and aching. He felt a little bit feverish. The dwarf, an old, old man whom Togura had never seen before, continued his speech, assaulting the air with his high, harsh, glittering voice. On and on he went, evidently tireless, incapable of being bored by his own words. In the background, the monotonous thung-thung-thung of the drum continued relentlessly.

'Shabana loy, zerd-nek,' muttered Togura, thus giving voice to the worst obscenities available to him in his native patois.

A scream menaced him. He doubted that anyone had understood what he had just said – if they had, they would have torn him to pieces – but they were giving clear warning that they were not prepared to tolerate any noise from him at all.

'Well up yours,' said Togura, hauling himself to his feet. 'You can't push me about forever,' he said. His voice, half anger, half anguish, rose to a shout. 'I am Togura Poulaan!' His voice hurt his throat. The rusty sound it made was so strange that it almost frightened him to silence. But he kept going. 'You hear me? I! I am Togura Poulaan. I! I am the son of Baron Chan Poulaan! I! I! I!'

The dwarf, enraged, screamed at him. Togura continued regardless.

'You have brought me here without my consent. You hold me here now against my will. I demand – I demand! – to be returned to my own home immediately. Failing that—'

He was taken from behind by two strong women. As the dwarf capered, dancing out his anger, gesticulating wildly as he shrieked and shrilled in his high-pitched voice, Togura was marched toward the beehive. He struggled all the way.

116

When they reached the doorway, Togura's resistance intensified. The two women responded by lifting him off the ground and ramming his head into the stone roof. Stunned, with thick blood trickling down from a cut on his scalp, he stopped fighting. He made himself a limp deadweight, pinning his hopes on passive resistance. It was useless. They womanhandled him down the hallway without any trouble at all. His feet, bumping over the stone floor, were getting hurt. He had just decided it would be better to co-operate when, without any warning, they let him go. He fell face first to the stone floor.

He was in a hot, close room which stank of rot, filth, slime and decay. A roaring fire was cackling-clakling in the centre of the room. The old men came crowding into the room; the women, as if dismissed, departed. A door was thrown open on the far side of the room. A strange door, for it was small and circular. Half a dozen of the old men grabbed burning brands from the fire and menaced Togura. Warily, he eased himself round the room, forced toward the circular door by the threatening flames. The old men shouted to each other in high, excited voices. Their eyes gleamed with unhallowed joy.

Togura knew there was something terrible beyond the circular door. It was the source of the stench which filled the room. Reaching the door, he glanced inside. He saw a circular room with a stone ledge running round the wall and—

With a shout, the old men came hustling forward, jabbing at him with their burning brands. Togura leapt through the door and almost went hurtling into the pit which lay beyond. He scrabbled for balance on the narrow stone ledge, slipped, saved himself, was jabbed by a burning brand, crawled along the stone ledge circling the room, then, when out of reach of the old men, stopped to take stock of his situation.

Some of the old men came crowding in through the circular door to watch. One or two of them threw their burning brands into the pit; something in the pit creaked or groaned with a noise half owl, half pig. Togura looked down.

On looking down, Togura saw a stinking confusion of rubbish crowding the pit below. The reek was appalling; it

117

stormed his senses and laid siege to his sanity, slapping his naked body in hot, wet, putrid waves, cramming his nostrils with its intolerable unclean insinuations, clambering into his lungs and making him want to vomit. He screamed at the smell, but it did not go away.

The old men bellowed and cheered. Another threw his burning brand into the pit, stirring up more noise down there. Quite apart from the burning brands, the pit was lit, toward the bottom, by its own clear, harsh, unwavering light; despite the illumination, Togura could not make much sense of its jumbled contents.

Togura looked around, examining the massive stone-block walls, which had been built without mortar. The circular walls rose sheer toward the sky. Peering upwards, he saw that the room was open to the sky. If he had to, he should be able to climb the wall, if these old men would go away and leave him in peace.

As Togura was so thinking, he looked down again, and saw what seemed to be a snake. It was in amongst the rubbish. It was weaving slowly. But it was too hard and bright to be a snake. And too long. It seemed to be some kind of tentacle. And it seemed to be made of metal. A metal tentacle?

Yes.

Having made sense of that detail, he slowly began to make sense of the others. And began to realise just what he was looking at. Down in the pit, those dark-stained filthy bubbling things, crusted with scabs and writhing with degenerating fluids . . . they were not random assemblages of rubbish. They were bodies. Human bodies. Gleaming, convoluted metal penetrated their flesh. The metal hummed softly.

As Togura watched, one of the slowly-weaving metal tentacles kissed a body and tasted it. The body flinched. Somewhere in the degenerating mass, an eye closed. Then opened.

'They're still alive!' screamed Togura.

Hearing his scream, the old men began to laugh. They cackled with unconcealed glee, jeering at him and at their victims, who endured a slow, agonised death of endless torment, decaying while still alive.

Then they left, scrambling out through the circular door. They closed it behind them. Togura crept along the stone ledge, reached the door, and hammered against its unyielding timbers, crying for mercy.

It did no good.

Nobody answered.

Nobody came.

He was on his own.

Shuddering, he yielded to urgent necessity, and voided his bowels, adding marginally to the stench which pervaded the room. He moved to a cleaner spot and sat down to think. One last drop of blood fell from his bleeding scalp to the stones, which were scalloped and sculpted in a most peculiar way.

What now? He decided he should think, and rest, then try to escape. Rest! It was easy to say, but almost impossible to do. His body was trembling uncontrollably. He could not keep himself from looking down into the pit. Remembering how he had almost fallen into it on first entering the room, he could not keep himself from imagining his own body already pierced to a scream and beyond by hard metal shafting into his armpit, his omphalos, his . . . his . . .

Overcome by his fear, by the stench, by the pitiless horror, he vomited. And felt better, as if he had purged his body of some kind of poison. He felt calmer. He could deliberate, analyse and plan. He wished he knew how all those people had got into the pit. Had they been thrown in? Or had they chosen to consign themselves to the pit rather than die of thirst and hunger. And, quite apart from all that, how had the pit come into existence in the first place?

Looking down into the pit with a cold, clinical eye, Togura decided it must be an ancient device for torture and punishment dating back to the ages before the Days of Wrath. As he studied it, one steel tentacle slowly reared upward and started questing in his direction. It searched toward him, slowly but surely. It knew he was here! And it wanted him!

He could not break the door down. The walls were solid, as

far as he knew. There was only one way out: straight up to the open sky. But that was too easy. Too obvious. Peering upward, he caught a glimpse of something sharp. There were blades or knives embedded in the walls. That, then, was part of the torment: to see a way of escape, to climb with a growing sense of triumph, and then to be slashed, gouged and mutilated by the waiting blades, and finally to fall screaming to the waiting pit.

The metal tentacle drew nearer. He edged away. It tasted the blood which had spilt to the stone, then, with a convulsive thrust, it skewered its way into the rock, seeking the source of the blood. Finding nothing, it withdrew, leaving a fresh scar in the stone. It started hunting again. Out of the corner of his eye, Togura saw another tentacle rising from the pit.

They were hunting him, and him alone. If only there had been someone else! Some other source of hot blood! If the tentacles had been forced to hunt two people simultaneously, he might have had at least the shadow of a chance. But there was nobody else. No other source of blood. Just him.

Blood! That was it! The answer! As the tentacle swerved toward him, Togura skipped sideways and tore away the knife which was knotted in his hair. It came free, together with a hunk of hair. He slashed his arm.

A bright pulse of arterial blood pumped from Togura's wound. He let it splatter across the wall, directing it deep into the cracks between the mortar-free blocks of stone. Slowly, he walked along the wall, wounding the architecture with his blood. Then, feeling light-headed, he crushed the bleeding down to nothing with the heel of his hand.

By now, a dozen tentacles were in pursuit of him. They savaged their way into the cracks between the masonry, striving for the source of the blood. Huge blocks of stone shifted, grated and cracked. A trickle of rubble went clobber-sklabber-klop as it rattled down into the pit.

Then one massive block of solid rock, attacked by half a dozen tentacles at once, splintered, burst and collapsed. The whole wall shifted. It began to fall. With a roar, an avalanche of stone pounded down into the pit. Steel screamed in agony.

A fine yellow spray hissed from ruptured tubing. The light from the pit blinked, wavered, then abruptly died.

Togura, trembling, realised he was still alive. A block of stone nudged him, hinting. He scampered away, gaining a position on the rubble-slide. The bit of wall he had been crouching by promptly collapsed; if he had stayed where he was, he would have been killed.

The air was heavy with rock-dust. Togura coughed, then coughed again, then spat. He could hear confused shouting. High, over-excited voices squalled in fear and panic.

Something came questing up out of the rubble.

A metal tentacle!

Togura went scampering up the new-born scree slope, and found himself in the room with the fire burning in the centre. A lot of rock had spilt into the room, crushing some of the old men; he could hear someone moaning under the rubble. All the survivors had fled, but for one — the speechmaking dwarf, who, incoherent with rage, grappled with him.

Togura smashed him.

Then picked him up and threw him in the fire.

The dwarf writhed and screamed, his agony rising to a frenzy as the brisk flames licked away his skin. Togura picked up chunks of rock and hurled them at his victim shouting with unholy joy. Then, as the dwarf subsided, unconscious or dead, Togura snatched up a burning brand and strode down the corridor to the outer world.

Outside, to his astonishment, he found a revolution in progress. The sight of the old men panicking out of the wrecked beehive, many of them cut, bruised and bleeding, had been enough to trigger off an uprising. The balance of power had changed more swiftly than the weather.

Togura, who had no experience of revolutionary politics, was amazed at the transformation of the people. He knew them only as sullen but reliable servants of the ruling regime. Now they had gone berserk. Before his very eyes, the young women who had so diligently hunted him down in the swamps were mobbing the old men to death. Children of both sexes, giving vent to high, hysterical, manic laughter, were helping with the slaughter. The community's handful of young men, no longer sleep walking, had crippled one greybeard and were now kicking him to pulp.

'This is excessive,' said Togura. 'This is insane.'

He was rapidly becoming experienced in the more bloodthirsty aspects of revolution. Despite hunger, fatigue, shock and terror, his mind was still acute enough to realise that there might be a lot to be said for the idea of getting out of town – and fast. The crowd would soon run out of old men to murder, but their bloodlust would still be running high and hot, and there was no telling what they might do then.

Togura padded through a mixture of blood and brains to the nearest doorway, which led to female quarters he had never entered. They were empty, as everyone had joined the slaughter. He bound up his self-inflicted wound with a bit of bark and some cordage, found a set of clothes and clogs and dressed himself, then exited the building through a door on the far side, well away from the administration of revolutionary justice.

As the screams of hate and agony faded away behind him, he walked click-clock through deserted streets to the swamp. There he stole a punt and poled away.

As Togura poled through the swamp, his wound started bleeding again, despite his attempt to bandage it. He tore away his makeshift dressing, salvaged some spiderweb from some swamp vegetation, and used that on the wound. It stopped the bleeding. When he halted toward evening, he felt very weak, perhaps as a consequence of losing so much blood. But he knew he would live.

CHAPTER FOURTEEN

It took Togura three days to get out of the swamp. He never once relaxed during those whole three days. He would sleep, but only lightly, waking for any unusual sound. Finally, he found himself on a stream, which became a creek, which he followed down to the sea.

By the sea was a tiny hamlet housing thirty-two fisherfolk. When they saw him approaching in his clothes of moss and bark and lichen, wearing his birds' nest headgear, they fled screaming; perhaps they were not entirely unaware of the abominations practised until so recently in the swamps of the hinterland.

Togura looted their houses shamelessly, dressing himself in sealskin clothes, and loading what food he could carry into baskets of woven flax. Then he left, hurrying off before they could gather their courage and come back to kill him.

He had not been able to steal any proper shoes, but the clogs he wore were hateful to him, contaminated as they were with bad dreams and claustrophobic memories. Two days along the coast, he tossed them into the sea. They bobbed up and down in the waves; he imagined he heard them over the thunder of the surf, walking the waters with a steady tromp-chop-tromp; he watched until they were out of sight, floating away, perhaps, to the smudged, hazy distances where the horizon was burdened with cloud, or by an island, or by, perhaps, the coast of the continent of Argan.

Then he marched on, barefoot.

CHAPTER FIFTEEN

In his early childhood, Togura Poulaan had once visited the coast in the company of his parents. They must have gone there on business connected with the Warguild, for the baron would seldom stir from his estate for any other reason. Or perhaps that had been the year of the plague, and they had fled to the coast for their health. That was long, long ago, back in the days before his mother had gone mad and died, back in the days before his little brother Stoat had died of rabies.

From that visit of long ago, Togura had dim, distant memories of a quayside clatter and of a hot, clamorous harbour where boats like broken insects sculled to the leering hulks floating in a stifling calm. On that hot, hot summer's day, the harbour had been filled with simmering sewage; he had spent an entire afternoon on the quayside, stoning helpless turds to death.

That was how he remembered the coast.

Here, however, there were no close-shouldering houses loud with voices and barking dogs; there were no cobblestone streets reeking of fish nets and onions; there were no vendors offering cockles, whelks and whitebait for sale; there was no putrefying mass of enclosed harbour waters, quiescent as a jellyfish.

Instead, there were open shores of rock and sand; there were cliffs, headlands, inlets and bays; there were creeks, streams, and rifts of coastal marshland alive with herons, shags and

124

nameless stilt-legged birds; there were sheltered dells, fragrant with herbs, lumberous with bees, swamped with heat in the noonday summer sun; there were rolling hillsides and uprearing cliffs, a mix of stunted trees, wild roses and impoverished coastal grasslands; there were wide, wild vistas, bare of habitation, where even the slightest summer breeze hinted at the possibility of summer storm.

And there was the wide-shouldering sea, booming in from the far-flung horizons. The sea! The sea, the ultimate cuspidor, here running clean and empty, bare leagues of weather-water where the white-whip winds scoured away to the distance. Togura was fascinated, watching blue rolling upon green upon grey as the lumbering billows swayed switch-back onto the shore to break – break! – with a coruscating roar of turbulent thunder, a roar swiftly dissolving to a clattering rush of baubling light shimmering over pebble, sand and rock, ending with a final hiss, that hiss itself annunciating the start of the sea suck which would haul back all in an incoherent jumble of rock-sliding shale and snake-sliding light.

The sound of the sea was always with him as he tramped along the coast for day upon day. At nights, sometimes he slept in caves high above the sealskin rocks, or laid himself down beneath a fallen log, or rested beneath the open sky on a patch of pebbly sand on a scrubbly beach nestled between high-pitched headlands.

He was almost alarmed to find himself free.

For the time being, his march along the coast provided him with necessities which liberated him from the problems of free will. Dealing with the demands of the march, and the day to day difficulties of survival, he did not have to trouble his head about the probable political situation in Keep, or about where he stood in the conflict between his father and the Suets, or about what, if anything, he should do about the quest he had promised to undertake for the Wordsmiths.

He was at peace.

His peace was interrupted when he sighted a tower on a promontory in the distance. He approached with circumspection, and, drawing near, he laid himself down in the sea-heather while he puzzled out his next move. The tower was of white stone which dazzled in the sealight. It appeared to be octagonal. Concluding that it was deserted, Togura approached, and walked round the tower.

Each side was pierced by a single doorway. As there were no doors to bar the way, he entered. Inside, the stone floor was bare but for a few broken snail shales; there were no windows, but it was bright with doorlight and skylight.

Togura looked up — and up — and up — and saw above him an octagon of day. This building had no roof. He was reminded of another place which had had no roof. Remembering the torture pit inside the stone beehive, he imagined that he smelt an intolerable stench of decay. Half-singing voices yakkered and laughed. A tentacle clutched for him.

He staggered outside, fleeing from the tower, screaming as he ran. Then, panting, he stopped. He shuddered, and looked back. The tower rose, high, white and graceful, gleaming in the bright, clean light. He could see through one door and out through another. It was an open place which could imprision nothing. He shook his head at his own foolishness.

Then, to give himself time to recover completely, he sat himself down on a convenient rock, breathed slowly and deeply, and watched the thick brown slubbery kelp rising and falling in the sea surge. Waves came billowing in, drenching over the rocks, flinging spray to the sky. When the waves withdrew, bright fish scales of sunlight glittered on the rocks; pebbles, momentarily gemstones, gleamed with smooth satisfaction. Out across the ocean, two gulls tangled in the sky, contending for possession of a fish.

'This is a good place,' said Togura.

Calmed, he returned to the tower, and laid his cheek against the dry skin of its whitework masonry. The rock underfoot was warm, but the tower was cool.

'Forgive me,' he said.

Then he entered its hospitality. With eight open doorways and no roof, it hardly offered him much shelter against bad weather, but he was minded to stay. It had frightened him at first, but he was starting to realise that for a long time a great many inconsequential things might alarm him.

'I will be happy here,' he said, coming to a decision.

And, with his flight along the coast at an end, he explored the promontory and the hinterland beyond, singing makeshift little songs to himself, peculiar melodies which he invented on the spur of the moment, thinking himself very musical.

Deep in the hinterland, amidst thickets of conifers loud with clicketing insects, he found a dry, deep cave half-concealed by tumbledown rocks. It was not very dark, for flaws in the roof admitted shafts of daylight. They would also admit rain, in season, and the cave would be draughty. Nevertheless, someone had once lived here for many years, carving a stone sleeping platform out of one side of the cave. On a stone shelf, there were half a dozen stone jars, in which were the blackened husks of some food now many years dead.

'I will stay here,' said Togura.

He lived there for many days. He made snares to catch rabbits and birds and traps to catch fish. The sea gave him the rotting wreck of a whale; it was foul beyond eating, but he salvaged bones which he later sharpened against rock. He made a stabbing spear, a bow, and arrows without fletching. He plaited the intestines of animals to make cordage. He ate seaweeds, frogs and butterflies, raw fish, raw meats, wild mushrooms, limpets gathered from the rocks, snails, grassland grubs and incautious beetles.

He repeatedly tried to make fire, rubbing sticks together, trying to build a fire drill, and, finally, trying to conjure wood to flame by force of will alone. Although he failed, he was not unhappy. He cut fish and flesh to thin strips and dried it in the summer sun, arranging black rocks in a sheltered spot to form a suntrap. When he got bored, he found a cliff which was difficult but not quite suicidal, and climbed it, or swam in the surf, coming out shuddering from the cold of the summer sea.

But he was not often bored, for he had so many things to do. They were things which properly belong to childhood, yet he did them shamelessly, for there was no-one to disparage his

127

play. He investigated the close-coiling shells of the sea, the articulation of the claws of the crab, the quill-pen feathers of the gull. He built a sand castle, and thought it an original invention. He sorted sand from pebbles and sifted it through his hands, letting it drift down to make patterns on flat black rocks.

As the days went by, he had fewer nightmares.

Sometimes, he saw sails in the distance, but he had no desire to join their journeys.

'Time is my journey,' he said.

And, having said it, wondered if he would become a philosophical hermit living out his days amidst wind and rocks.

A day later, he was sunbathing when something shadowed out the sun. Opening his eyes, he saw a stranger standing over him. A man. Black hat, black beard, black cloak. Weapons? A dagger. Black strides, black boots, black bootlaces. A weatherbeaten face.

'Hello,' said the stranger, in a barbarous accent.

'Greetings,' said Togura.

Then closed his eyes, to make the hallucination go away. When he opened his eyes again, the hallucination was still waiting patiently.

'Are you real?' said Togura.

He meant the words to mean what they meant in his native patois: do you truly exist? But the stranger interpreted them to mean what they meant in mainsteam Galish, which was, literally, 'Is your presence sincere?', and implied 'Do you really wish to make a bargain?'

'Boy, I've said nothing of trade,' said the stranger.

'Neither have I,' said Togura.

'Where is your keeper, boy?'

'What do you mean by that?' said Togura, speaking slowly, and with some difficulty; he had fallen out of the habit of language.

'Have you no keeper then?'

'What would I need a keeper for? Do you think I'm simple or something?'

128

'If you're not simple, then how else do you explain yourself?'

'I don't explain myself at all to nameless earth-walkers,' said Togura. 'Name yourself.'

'My name is Jotun,' said the stranger, meaning 'dwarf'.

'That's a strange name for a fellow of your height,' said Togura, for the man was the same size as he was.

'Truth to tell, I guard my name amidst strangers. But whatever you are or aren't, you look honest enough to me. So I'll give you my true name, which is Soy Doja. I'm a healer by trade; I'm on this coast to look for the plant they call Moonbeam. Very rare. Do you know it?'

'No,' said Togura, who had never heard of it. He felt it was now time to name himself, but, since the other had lied about his name – and was, incidentally, still lying – Togura decided not to trust him with the truth. 'I'm Parax Gemenis myself,' said Togura. 'I'm a fisherman from many leagues along the coast. There's a feud in my village which threatens my life, which is why I'm here.'

After telling each other a great many more elaborate lies, and exchanging a considerable amount of deliberate and accidental misinformation, they did a little trading. Togura sold the traveller some sun-dried fish, accepting in payment a small coin which bore the head of Skan Askander.

The traveller stayed the night in Togura's cave. He had a tinder box, so they had a fire; when the traveller moved on the next day, Togura kept the fire burning. He would need it in the winter.

Now that he had fire, he should have been happier still, but he was not. He was restless all day. Brooding. That evening, he sat by the fire, turning the coin over in his fingers. Part of the new coinage minted by the Suets, it brought back memories of the wedding feast in Keep. Of the cakes baked in the shape of coins. And of Slerma, who must surely be dead by now.

Overwhelmed by homesickness, he remembered, with an intolerable sense of longing, the pleasures of his former life. Drinking, jokes and conversation. Real shoes. Horses which would carry you over the league-roads and eat out of your hand. Hot meals cooked by women. Women themselves, their eyes alive with temptation, their breasts hot and swollen beneath their clothes, their reception waiting. Real blankets. The welcome of friends. Lying in bed in the morning, dozing. Spending days being utterly idle. Eating real bread. Shutting out the wind at night. Cock fighting.

Togura knew what he had to do. He had to return home. He would be reconciled with his father. He would beg his father's forgiveness, and would become a true brother to Cromarty. They would live together happily ever after.

Enthused, animated and excited, he could hardly sleep. He rose at first light, tied his bow, spears and arrows into a bundle he could carry over one shoulder, ate the little bit of dried food he had left after dealing with the traveller, knotted the traveller's coin in a bit of bark then knotted the bark to his wrist, and was ready to go.

'Goodbye cave,' he said. 'Goodbye rocks. Goodbye tower.'

He spent some time sentimentalising in this manner, then turned his back on the place and trudged along the coast, heading in the direction his itinerant stranger had come from.

He was making for D'Waith.

CHAPTER SIXTEEN

The weather broke up; Togura Poulaan travelled through storm, wind and rain, enduring the worst which summer could bring. Once, the night caught him out in the open; he huddled in the lee of the largest rock he could find, and shivered there, sleepless, until dawn. Once he slept in a sea cave, and was washed out of it by the high tide. The next evening, harried over a hill by an electrical storm, he was close to despair when he surmounted the summit and saw, on a clifftop at the bottom of the hill, a ruinous cottage near an ancient horned cairn.

Togura went bounding down the hill and went burrowing in through the door of the cottage. It was cold inside, with rain dripping through rotting thatch, the wind blowing in through windows now without shutters, and turbulence playing piffero in the chimney. Nevertheless, it was a vast improvement on the world outside, where thunder exploded across the sky, and forked lightening – hot as molten silver and as bright as sunrise – stabbed down through the slashing rain to the laundering sea.

'Hello house,' said Togura.

'Hello, Togura Poulaan,' said the house – not by means of voice, for it had none, but by embracing him with a load of rotten thatch.

'Pleased to make your acquaintance,' said Togura, brushing thatch from his hair, neck, eyes and ears; he sneezed, expelling it from his nose.

'Gronnammadammadamyata,' said the thunder, shattering the sky with a blast which shook the cottage, or what was left of it.

'That too,' said Togura, vaguely, not sure what he meant by his own words; he was exhausted, and very close to collapse.

But, in a way, happy. For the cottage helped prove the existence of the world he remembered, which was the world he belonged to. He was approaching civilisation; soon he would be back in the society of men — and women, too — and his disfellowship would be at an end.

He moved to the driest spot he could find, and very shortly was asleep. And dreaming. Outside, as the thunder slowly blundered away into the distance, and the rain eased, the last of the light subsided to the sea, and was gone. Swift-moving clouds rucked across a sky of absolute darkness. At the foot of the cliff, sullen waves heaped themselves against the rocks of the Ravlish Lands, pounding home with a beat too deep, heavy and protracted for any drum to match it. Togura, accustomed to that sound, did not notice it; the surf did not figure in his dreams.

Instead, Togura Poulaan dreamt of Day Suet. Her breasts winked at him lewdly through holes cut in the dolman which fell weeping to her feet; her eyes and her lips were smiling. She stretched out her arms to him, but he found himself floating in a meditative sea, watching the underwater world. A fish went by, hideously maimed, crabbing through the sea with blood and clear fluids scuppering out of old, old, ulcerated wounds in its flanks.

'Kill it for pity,' said Day.

'We can negotiate,' said Togura.

Then woke, and wondered what he had meant by that. Then, alarmed, wondered who was touching his neck with such a cold, cold bony hand. He looked around, started, tumbled head over heels like an acrobat, reached the safety of the furthest corner of the cottage, then picked up a heavy stone which he could use as a weapon. His hair, if it had not been so crabbed, knotted and dirty, would have been standing on end.

'Who are you?' hissed Togura, menacing the glimmering, skeletal figure which confronted him.

It addressed him in a foreign tongue. Its voice was old and watery. He could see through its pearl-white armour, through the shadowy outlines of its flesh, through the harder white of its bones, and out to the walls of the cottage beyond.

'What are you?' said Togura, attacking this phosphorescent manifestation with questions. 'Where do you come from? What are you saying? How? Why?'

The phosphorescent apparition did not flinch, diminish or withdraw. It was not an ilps. It might well be a ghost.

'Vara vinklet venvindaanaas telyauga zon makovara,' said the spirit-thing.

'Up yours too,' said Togura, recklessly.

The spirit-thing beckoned to him. He could see, quite clearly the bones of its hand articulating within its spectral flesh.

'No,' said Togura. 'I'm not going with you. So cut it off and pickle it.'

The spirit-thing did not seem to understand his refusal, or his gratuitous obscenity. Its voice became louder and more demanding. It took a step toward him.

'Okay, okay,' said Togura. 'I'm coming.'

He discarded the stone, chose a short stabbing spear from his meagre bundle of possessions, and followed the phantom out of the cottage and into the night.

The sky was pitchblende black, but for the light, as cold and pallid as the frigid starshine of glow-worms, which flickered around the horned cairn. That ancient burial mound, a barrow raised by forgotten peoples in the long ago – time out of mind! – seemed to be burning with cold, cold flames, which failed to consume its substance.

A door had opened in the nearest flank of that cold-burning tumulus. Togura could see down a curving gem-bright hallway, leading down into unknown depths. He caught a whiff of roasting rotch, heard the chimes of an uncanny music, and the shouts of bright brave voices glittering with laughter.

The phantom entered the hallway then paused, and gestured with a hand now positively imperious.

'Come!' said that gesture.

And Togura Poulaan knew he was confronted with a challenge fit for a hero. To dare the unknown! To brave the perils of the land of death or faery! To rouse great warriors from their sleep!

Or, perhaps — and this was experience talking — to be slaughtered without warning, and eaten.

The phantom, growing impatient, advanced to claim Togura. He hurled his spear at it, saw it miss, then turned and fled to the night. He ran till exhaustion checked him, and then, unable to run any more, he walked. Dawn came, but he did not stop; he walked through the day to dusk, and into the night beyond.

During the course of his flight he lost his one and only coin. He was now penniless, but that, for the moment, was the least of his worries.

CHAPTER SEVENTEEN

Togura Poulaan was cold, wet and hungry, but his spirits were high, for he could see D'Waith in the distance. It was a small walled city set on a hill about half a league from the sea. He could not make a beeline for it, as swathes of barbarian thorn blocked the most direct route; instead, he was forced to follow the coastline.

The weather was the worse he had seen so far on his journey. He was astonished to see a boat on the sea, and was not surprised, shortly afterwards, not to see it. He stumbled forward through the wind, which hazed and harassed him. He was cold to his bone marrow.

'Civilisation,' he said, promising himself a hot fire, a mug of ale and a meal of something good and nourishing.

Hope kept him going.

As he staggered on, buffeted by the wind, he passed an old herbalist who was gathering gypsywort, horehound, vetch, chickweed, bistort, bracken and sea-cranny. The old man bent to his work, regardless of the weather, ignoring him.

'He must be mad,' said Togura.

This clinical judgment, though made by a rank amateur, was entirely accurate.

The weather, if anything, was getting worse. The tumbled sea was wrought into great spumes and fraughts by the gale. The avalanching waters, afroth with yellowish foam, sent sleets of water spuming over Togura's shore path.

Ahead, Togura could see D'Waith's marginal harbour, where seven ships were rocking at anchor, a beleaguered hebdomad which, until a disaster earlier in the day, had been an octet. The waves were roaring in over the mole which attempted to guard the anchorage: the tides were even threatening some of the low-slung buildings scattered around the foreshore. There would — surely — be a road from here to the city on the hill.

'If I'd built D'Waith, I'd have built it by the harbour,' muttered Togura.

This being so, it was fortunate that he had not built D'Waith, as the boggy ground would have swallowed it. He found out just how boggy it was as he sank to his waist in the marshy ground. He struggled to firmer ground and plugged on relentlessly until he came to the nearest building. A wave from the sea foamed around the building and tugged eagerly at his ankles.

Soaking wet, shivering, stung by the pelting rain and driven by the wind, Togura hobbled to the door. He opened it. The door swung inwards, opening to a roar of conversation, laughter and thumping tankards. Togura, peering into the gloom of beards, voices and storm lanterns, wondered if he was hallucinating. Three fires were blazing in three separate fireplaces; three rousing drinking songs were competing against each other; gusts of noise, heat and communal stench billowed out, together with smells of drink and food which set him reeling with giddy hunger.

'Come in!' roared the landlord, who had the head and the horns of a bull.

Embarrassed, Togura hesitated. He could imagine what he looked like, soaking wet from head to toe, mud from waist to foot, his hair in tangled dreadlocks, his body clad in mouldy old sealskins, an unkempt feathery moustache clinging to his upper lip just beneath his notched nose, and an unkempt straggly growth — a body's excuse for a beard — sprouting from his chin.

'Come in before I break you in half,' bellowed the landlord. 'In boy, and shut the door.'

A wave, chasing round Togura's feet, swarmed through the door to join the waters inside, which were already knee-deep. He went in, closed the door with effort, descended a couple of steps to the floor level, and stood there in the knee-deep water, gawping.

'Here!' yelled the landlord, thumping the bar. 'You paralysed, boy?'

Togura waded to the bar, which was a vast slab of battle-scarred oak. Behind it stood the landlord, a towering figure who really did have the body of a man but the head of a bull. His eyes were fierce, burning, red. His horns, their ivory polished to the brightness of the moon, grazed the ceiling. There was a heavy gold ring in his nose. Ranked up behind him were casks, barrels, stone jars, stone bottles, wineskins and tobacco holders. Helping the landlord at the bar was a motherly woman of middle years who looked perfectly normal except that her hands were the paws of a cat.

As Togura reached the bar, a drunk, bleeding badly from a recent knife fight, embraced him and gave him a kiss. Togura shook him off. The drunk fell backwards to the water, where he floated with a seraphic smile on his face, singing incoherently.

'Here we have us a hungry little man,' said the landlord to Togura. 'Hungry! Pinched, even. Yet honest, all the same. I pick you for an honest man.'

'How can you tell?' said Togura.

'I can't,' said the landlord. 'But I was born and raised politely.' This, apparently, was a joke, for he laughed uproariously, his merriment deafening the storm. The patrons took no notice; they were used to it. 'Come on now, boy. Will you eat? Answer me!'

'I won't deny my hunger,' said Togura. 'But I have no money. Have you any work that needs doing?'

'None, but there's plenty in town. Here, have a bowl of polenta,' said the landlord, shovelling great gollops of steaming porridge into a huge wooden bowl.

'At what obligation?'

'None.'

137

'What do you mean, none?'

'I mean this is free, gratis, given for nothing. Come on, boy, don't look so startled. Eat! Eat! It's hot. It's good. Oatmeal, maize, chestnuts, barley. Here, have some hot milk with it. Now eat. No, not with your fingers! Were you born in a barn?'

'Yes,' said Togura, in all honesty.

'Then here's a spoon regardless. No slobbering fingers here. This is a respectable house, you know. We have standards to maintain.'

And the landlord laughed again.

'Well thank you,' said Togura, sampling the food.

It was hot, it was good, it tasted like youth and wild honey, like nectar and sunlight, like hot bread and kisses, like pollen and potatoes, like the strength of life itself. The first mouthful cleared his head; the second mouthful warmed him; he took a third, then remembered his own manners.

'Thank you,' said Togura. 'Thank you.'

'Thank me later, boy. Thank me when you come swaggering back to town with gold in your pockets and silver in your socks.'

'That may be never.'

'What a dirge! Come. boy, why so grim? Have you not arms and legs and balls and a cock the girls will greed on? Have you not eyes and ears and nose − well, nose of a sort − and a good stout stomach within?'

'I've had a hard time,' said Togura, a little offended to find this stranger dismissing his rightful claims to pessimism without even hearing them out. 'I've suffered.'

'Suffered? Piffle!'

'I tell you—'

'Don't tell me, boy, eat. Slop down the food, it's good for you. Priorities, boy, priorities! Food first then friends. And a drink withal. That's the making. Dox! Dox, my good man. Buy the young man a drink. A drink for a boy born in a barn, and, by the looks of him, not recovered from the shock. Dox! Don't pretend you can't hear me. You hear me all right, you cheese-faced stoat-shagging tobaccanalian. Come on, Dox, you idle son of a shit-shoving whoremaster, bring out your silver.'

A disfigured man with a clay pipe wedged between his naked gums waded to the counter. He smelt heavily, but not unpleasantly, of tobacco.

'Cold potato twice,' he said, laying his bronze on the counter.

'Hard spirit for you, Dox,' said the landlord, passing him a beaker of a clear and odourless fluid, 'but ale for the boy.'

And he drew a tankard of thick, nourishing dark-stained ale and passed it to Togura. It was cold; Togura preferred his beer warm – preferably at blood temperature – but he accepted it with a good grace nevertheless.

'Come,' said Dox.

Togura, food and drink in hand, followed him to a crowded table, where they found buttock-space on a creaking bench jammed with men in rags, furs, flax raincoats, fighting leathers, feather capes, canvas coveralls or businesslike sea gear. While men eyed him and summed him, Togura ate and drank, bewildered by the landlord's hospitality, which was so unlike what he had learnt to expect from the world.

'Who are you?' said Dox, suddenly, without any preliminaries.

Dox, the toothless pipe smoker, had a hoarse and rasping voice, and had an ulcer the size of a fist on one side of his face. He was missing his ears and his nose. Togura, disconcerted by his appearance, and even more disconcerted by the free food and drink, concealed his own identity with an untruth of some cunning.

'They call me the Forester,' he said. 'Before certain misfortunes, I was part of a party searching for Barak the Battleman, also known as Togura Poulaan.'

'Ah! After the reward, no doubt. But you have no sword about you. So how would you take him?'

'I have my hands,' said Togura, restraining his astonishment.

'Hands, yes. Lovely things! Strangulation, hey? Yes, of course. That's the story! Squeeze them till their eyes pop. I love it. Take him when he's sleeping, eh boy? But find him first. The reward's worth having, nay-so? Did you hear Cromel's doubled it?'

'His name isn't Cromel,' said another man, a hard-faced villain with pietra-dura eyes. 'It's Cromdarlarty.'

'No,' said a third, a sallow-faced consumptive windlestraw with a thin, piping voice. 'Cromarty, that's the name. I met him face to face in Keep myself. We argued belly to belly. He told me himself, the reward's now set at a hundred crowns. A hundred crowns for the head.'

'That head's probably done and deep rotted by now,' said another voice, slurring out of an alewashed face which was one part tattoos, one part scars, one part burns and one part syphilis sores.

'What do you mean?' said a big, brawn-voiced one-eyed man with a beard dyed green and yellow.

'I mean that the oath-breaking father-killer is probably dead and buried. What do you think, Forester?'

Togura, spooning down his polenta, said nothing, waiting for Forester to answer.

'Forester!' said Dox, seizing his elbow and banging it on the table. 'Are you deaf?'

'Somewhat,' said Togura, remembering, as he rubbed his elbow, that he was Forester. 'What was the question?'

'He claimed a death for Barak. You agree?'

'The last rumour that came my way,' said Togura, lying as sweetly as a poet, 'held that Barak had been to Estar and back. Lately he happened on the road for Chi'ash-lan, or so it was told, but then I met a man who swore he'd turned for D'Waith.'

'That's wrong,' said a hoar-skinned fellow with sausage-shaped lugs of ulcerated flesh spilling down his cheeks and his neck. 'He's at Larbster Bay for certain. What do you think—'

The rest of the question was drowned as a huge wave, larger than all the rest, pounded into the building. The storm lanterns hanging from the roof beams were set to swaying. As see-saw shadows and gutteral light swung back and forth across the haggling card games, the helpless drunks, the boozing syndicates, the wrist-wrestling bravos and a gaggle of pipe-smoking ancients, an even larger wave slammed against the seaward wall, bursting shutters open. A torrent of water poured inside, scattering a game of dragon chess. The participants shouted in dismay, but the rest of the tavern broke into drunken cheering.

As hands laboured the shutters home to close out the wind, the door was flung open and a woman entered. She was tall, she was blonde and she was built like a butcher's block. The cry went up:

'Mary!' 'It's Mary!' 'Why bless your heart and spit on it!' 'Mary, my doxy, come kiss me quick.'

'Silence,' she roared.

The building shook with her voice, which could have shouted the landlord himself right down to nothing. Every jargoning mouth in the whole building quailed down to zero. Even the sea seemed muted.

'That's better,' said Mary. 'Now stay your cheek and rattle your pins. There's pirates wrecked on the coast. West of us, three leagues. Get up off your shit and get moving.'

With a roar and a whoop, the tavern emptied to the howling storm. Togura, only half understanding, swilled down the last of his polenta in three and a half desperate gulps, drained his tankard, then allowed himself to be carried along with the others. As they staggered through the brawny weather, he saw that other buildings were also emptying. The mob, a rough and raggedy beast if ever there was one, slouched and stumbled through the storm, heading for the west.

CHAPTER EIGHTEEN

Togura Poulaan was once more cold, wet and hungry. As he made his way back to the tavern, the thought of its warmth, its drink and its food was increasingly appealing. Nevertheless, he had his misgivings. It was dusk, and Togura did not think the tavern a good place to be at nightfall, even though he was no longer alone.

Togura's new companion was Gelzeda Zurdok, a merchant from Androlmarphos, which was a distant city in the south of Argan, one of those fabulous foreign places which Sung knew only by rumour. Togura and his new acquaintance made an odd couple, for Togura was still in his barefoot rags, while Zurdok, on the other hand, was a mature, bearded man, richly dressed from his swaggering seaboots upwards.

Whistling lightly, Zurdok led the way. Togura was still unarmed, but Zurdok wore an ornate swordbelt which sustained a cutlass, a throwing knife, a dirk and an apple corer.

'Why did they let you keep your weapons?' said Togura.

It was a question which had only just occurred to him.

'I was on parole,' said Zurdok. 'We merchants of Androlmarphos have the highest reputation when it comes to probity. When I told the pirates I'd make no trouble, they took me at my word.'

'That was kind of them.'

'I'm rich. The ransom was going to make their kindness worth their while. Believe me, they knew it, too. Every pirate

142

on the twenty-seven seas knows the wealth of Tezelja Burnok.'

'I thought you said your name was Gelzeda Zurdok,' said Togura.

'So it is, my son. Gelzeda Zurdok. A good name, too, isn't it? My credit's good from Androlmarphos to Selzirk. And beyond.'

'But just now you called yourself—'

'What?'

'I can't remember.'

'No, boy, I don't think I called myself that. Gelzeda Zurdok's the name, always has been, always will. If you start hearing different, wash the wind out of your ears. That's the tavern, I take it?'

'That's right,' said Togura. 'That's the tavern.'

Bending his steps toward it, Zurdok resumed his whistling. The wind, which had weakened dramatically, was blathering away in the background; the rain had eased to a drizzle, and the sea to a sullen chop. Occasionally a wave larger than the rest sent a little bit of water slouching up to the tavern walls, but it seemed the storm was over.

As they neared the tavern, picking their way with care between the boggier bits of ground, a blue-feathered mocking gull, a bird of ill omen, went caterwauling overhead. Togura spat, and made a warding gesture in the direction of the retreating gull, but Zurdok did not seem to notice. Togura had already tried to dissuade Zurdok from seeking refuge in the tavern. He had failed, but now he tried again.

'I don't know that the tavern is quite the place for us,' said Togura.

'Why not?'

'It's full of thieves, pimps, card sharps and drunks.'

'Low types like us,' joked Zurdok. 'They'll make us feel at home.'

'They'll more likely draw cuts for the privilege of slicing and dicing us. It was bad enough by day. It's no place to venture at nightfall.'

'It's not dark yet, boy,' said Zurdok. 'So we'll risk a look at the place, at least.'

For a man who had recently come close to death, Zurdok was in exceptionally high spirits, all smiles and whistles. Then, as they approached the tavern from the blind side, the whistling abruptly stopped. They heard hoarse shouts and a cry of pain. A duel? A brawl?

'This may be one of those times,' said Togura, 'when it's best to leave before arriving.'

'Gather your courage,' said Zurdok. 'And follow me.'

They ducked round to the doorway side of the tavern. The first thing Togura saw was a man lying dead on the ground. The landlord was being held at bay by half a dozen masked men armed with staves, flails and hatchets. He was armed with a whip and a pitchfork. His horns were stained with bright fresh blood.

'Back, you braggarts!' roared the landlord. 'Back, before I scupper the lot of you.'

'You're the one who's scuppered,' shouted a bald man with golden roses tattooed on his naked pate. 'Here's reinforcements!' He appealed to Togura and Zurdok: 'Will you join us for the monster's gold? His death's a fortune for each of us. Will you join us?'

'Yes,' said Zurdok, striding forward.

'Good,' said the man of the golden roses.

And Zurdok booted him in the crutch then wrecked him with three well-placed blows too swift for Togura to follow. As the others gasped alarm, Zurdok's fingers flickered. A man went down with a throwing knife in his throat. The landlord hurled his pitchfork and slashed away with his whip. Zurdok drew his cutlass and laid about him. Closing with his nearest victim, the landlord gored him through the heart.

And suddenly there were four men freshly dead and two men running for their lives. The action had been so swift that Togura had scarcely had time to realise it had started. The landlord shook himself free from the body of the man he had gored.

'You!' said the landlord, in surprise.

'Me!' said Zurdok.

And the two embraced.

'I thought you'd setsko and amanacain,' said the landlord.

'Me? Log Jaris, you'd fana-ma-skote.'

There was a lot more of this swift, jabbering argot, which Togura found impossible to follow. The language the two men were speaking was basically Galish, but it was so full of slang and foreign lingo that he found it incomprehensible.

'Well,' said the landlord at last, breaking off the conversation, 'I'm sure we can bed down a boy and a pirate. So come in, the two of you.'

'Pirate?' said Togura, looking round.

'He's the pirate!' said the landlord, laughing as he pointed to Zurdok.

'He's no pirate,' protested Togura. 'He's Gelzeda Zurdok, merchant of Androlmarphos. He was being held prisoner on the pirate ship which was wrecked.'

'And you helped him escape from the frenzied mob.'

'Yes!' said Togura, who was proud of his effort, which had taken a lot of quick thinking and a nimble bit of bluff.

'Well, well,' said the landlord. 'What a brave little boy. Come on, let's no more linger. Inside!'.

And in they went.

The landlord's woman, she of the cat's paws, was standing behind the bar, mopping the counter. She greeted them with a placid smile, then carried on sponging up the blood which had been spilt so liberally on the counter. There were at least five sodden bodies floating in the water.

'Love,' said the landlord to the woman. 'Fetch us two bailing boys from the Nun's Backside. And send a messenger to old Karold; tell him there's butcher's meat here for the taking.'

'Shall I set up first for the evening trade?' asked the woman, her voice smooth and mellow.

'There'll be no evening trade tonight,' said the landlord. 'They'll be whooping it up at the wreck, burning their prisoners alive. Come, boys, let's have an ale.'

The three sat themselves down at a table with bread and tankards, then the landlord talked ninety to the dozen with Gelzeda Zurdok. Togura, unable to follow their quick-weaving cant, felt excluded and insulted. Finally he could stand it no more.

'What's that language you're talking?' he demanded.

'Galish,' said the landlord easily. 'Galish as she is spoke in the Greater Teeth.'

'The Greater Teeth? But only pirates live there!'

'Then what else would we be? I told you already, the man you saved from the wreck is a pirate. No – don't give me that merchant nonsense again. What merchant from Androlmarphos would walk with a sea swagger as he does? Besides, boy, if you knew your Androlmarphos you'd know that the men there have a fashion for clean shaving. They walk their lives beardless – not like Draven here.'

'Draven?' said Togura, staring at the man he knew as Gelzeda Zurdok. He'd heard that name before. The more notable sea bandits were known by name even in the households of Keep. 'Draven the Womanrider?'

'No, boy!' shouted Gelzeda Zurdok, slamming the table with the flat of his hand. 'Do I look like him? Do I speak like him? Do I stink like him? No and no, and again no. Don't confuse me with the most notorious coward of the twenty-seven seas. I'm not the Womanrider. I'm not Draven the leper, either, or Battleaxe Draven. I'm Bluewater Draven, and you'd better remember it.'

'Peace,' said the landlord, with a smile. 'Peace, the pair of you.'

'I wasn't arguing!' said Togura.

'Then peace regardless,' said the landlord. 'He tells the truth. An unusual experience for him, but he tells it. He is, in truth, Bluewater Draven of the Greater Teeth. His ship, which was wrecked today, was one of three on passage to Ork, an island far distant which you're not likely to have heard of. They were on a mission which does not bear naming at the moment.'

'How do you know all this?' said Togura.

'We've been talking, haven't we? Why so fierce, youngster?'

'Because I've been cheated and tricked and lied to. Because I risked my life to save him and because I thought him an honest stranger. Because he conned me and duped me and gives me no thanks. Look at him smirking!'

'Thanks is not in his nature,' said the landlord, 'but he can surely redeem his debt to you all the same. As I was telling you, his ship was one of three. They had a rendezvous point for gathering in case they were separated in the Penvash Channel – which is that body of water at our doorstep, in case you didn't know.'

'I know,' said Togura, who hadn't until that moment.

'If one or both remaining ships survive, they'll search for Draven's vessel. In all probability, they'll put a boat ashore to make discretions in D'Waith.'

'Discretions?'

'They'll ask after the lotch, but carefully,' said the landlord patiently.

'The lotch?'

'The missing one, the retarded one, the latecomer,' said the landlord, supplying the meaning of the cant word. 'If they varry—'

'Varry?'

'Enough of this language lesson!' said Draven impatiently. 'Come on, let's pay off the boy.'

'I don't want to be paid off, I want an apology,' said Togura.

'What an innocent little mannikin,' said the landlord, with a laugh which – and this was unusual for him – had something of a jeer about it. 'Apologies? From a pirate? You'd be searching! There now, don't take it hard. You saved a life. That's something for a day's work. You've got Bluewater Draven in your debt, so take what's offering. Take his gold or his services. He can ship you to Ork, if you're wanting.'

'Can I think about it?' said Togura, seeing that argument was going to get him nowhere.

'Thinking's free,' said Draven. 'But have a decision by tomorrow's daylight.'

At that moment two boys arrived, with buckets, and began to bail out the tavern. Shortly afterwards, a butcher from D'Waith arrived to take away the dead bodies to be made into sausage meat. Then some jubilant wreckers entered, bearing trophies — the heads of five sea rovers — and pirate gold. As the tavern began to get lively, despite the landlord's expectations, talk of sensitive matters ended.

From the tavern talk, Togura was able to complete his picture of what had happened while he had been absent from civilization. On the day on which the Warguild had attacked the wedding at the Suet's Grand Hall, Baron Chan Poulaan had gone missing. Rumour had it that Togura Poulaan, also known as Barak the Battleman, had pitched his father into a mining pit, thus murdering him.

Togura's half brother, Cromarty, had assumed control of the family estate near Keep, and had offered a reward for Togura's head. Rumour held that Togura, aka Barak, had been sighted in fifty different places during the time he had been hunted — which was now almost a year. He was credited with five rapes, two murders and several acts of vandalism and arson; most recently, or so rumour had it, he had attacked a homestead in the mountains, routing the seven men who tried to defend the place against his depredations.

'Ay, I can credit that,' said a one-legged card sharp, and proceeded to give a vivid eyewitness account of how he had confronted Barak half a year ago. 'Chewed off my leg, he did. Turned himself into a great black manul, leapt, fanged me, bit, chewed, swallowed — kneecap, ankle, shin, he ate the lot.'

'Give over, Doss,' said an onlooker. 'You lost that leg ten years ago if it was a day.'

'No,' insisted the card sharp. 'That's not true. Listen, it was up in the mountains. A cold day. I challenged him. One moment he was standing there, as clear as I see you — a great big unruly fellow with a spiked club in his hand — and the next moment he'd turned himself into this gory great cat, as big as a horse if it was larger than a mouse.'

His eyes shone with sincerity; his voice carried the tones of impeccable conviction; it was clear that more than a few believed him.

These being the rumours that Togura did hear — and in a single night, at that — he could only guess at those he didn't hear. Offering a reward for a man's head was a foreign practice previously almost unheard of in Keep; the reward made this manhunt a novelty, and the recent increase in the amount of the reward had made it a topical novelty at that.

With his dreams of retiring into his father's home now shattered, Togura had to think of his own safety. There were no portraits or sketches of him in circulation, so few people outside Keep would know what he looked like. Nevertheless, it would be safest to get out of Sung until this trouble blew over.

By morning, Togura had come to a decision. He asked Draven to take him to Larbster Bay; from there, he would make his way along the Salt Road to Estar. Once he reached Estar, he would be faced with another decision. There were two possibilities. Either he could stay in Estar and work at some honest trade, hoping for Cromarty to get himself killed in a duel or a feud, thus opening the way for Togura to return home; or, alternatively, he could approach Prince Comedo of Estar and ask for permission to dare the terrors of the monster which guarded the bottle which contained the box which contained the index which spoke the Universal Language which would give him control of the odex.

'Can you take me to Larbster Bay?' said Togura to Draven.

'Nothing easier,' said Draven. 'Once a ship calls for us. It's on the way to Ork. Perhaps, of course, there'll be no ship. If so, I'll buy us a passage with the next Galish convoy travelling from D'Waith to Larbster Bay. We'll get you on your journey, youngster. Trust Draven. Thousands do – and no man ever regretted it.'

Togura, judging Draven to be sincere, ate well, drank well, slept well, helped the landlord tend the bar, and waited until they could start their journey.

CHAPTER NINETEEN

The seas at the end of summer were in full flood. The tall ship strode the ocean, riding over the scalloping light, urged by a brisk wind which drove it through the dalloping dolloping waves.

The name of the ship was the Warwolf, but her figurehead was no wolf but a dragon. She had been built by the best shipwrights of the Greater Teeth. Her timbers were of winter oak and cedar, but for the masts, which were of kauri from Quilth, and the deck, which had been made of a chance load of mahogany alleged to have originated in Yestron. She had three masts, and sails of green canvas.

Togura Poulaan, taking his ease on a sunny yet sheltered part of the deck, surveyed the work going on near at hand and thanked his stars — which were the two green ones known as the Cat's Eyes — that he was not a pirate. From this vantage point, it looked too much like hard work.

Taking advantage of the fine weather, the weapons muqaddam was supervising the overhaul of armaments and muniments. He was a broad-fisted man with shoulders like an ox and a shadow like a menhir. He was bald but for a little floccus scabbing the centre of his skull. His eyes, squinting out of a sun-weathered face, were as sharp as caltrops. His tongue was as rough as pumice, and he used it industriously.

Glad to be a passenger, Togura closed his eyes and leisured out at full length on the deck. Then cloud quenched the sun; a

150

crisp whippet of wind came cleaning around him, and, chilled and annoyed, he sat up again.

'Come back sun,' said Togura. 'Go away wind.'

The wind, obedient to his commands, veered away to vanishing. But the sun remained hidden by a sulk of cloud. In the sea, something hinted through the waters. Seal? Dolphin? Whale? Rock? Togura narrowed his eyes, trying to see it more clearly. But it had gone. Perhaps it had been nothing to start with, or a chance bit of driftwood or float-stone now smothered by a wave.

Togura closed his eyes again, but was abruptly jolted into full alertness when a fight began. Looking round, he saw it was only two young pirates sparring with a lot of brag and paraffle. The weapons muqaddam, seeing their footwork looked sloppy, screamed abuse at them. They took heed, stopped fooling around and became more businesslike. They were rather good.

Togura had alway imagined pirates as being lazy, leisurely beasts, loafing through the idle seas, amusing themselves with wine and women until the opportunity for pillage aroused them from their sport. Now, after only a brief acquaintance with the breed, he knew the reality was altogether different.

There was wine aboard, true, but it was rationed – a gill per man per day, which was next to nothing. There were women somewhere below deck – not that Togura had seen them – but the woman ration was stricter still. Most of the day was spent in work, maintenance, exercise and training. The Warwolf was a taut, sober, workmanlike ship, captained by the stern, ascetic Jon Arabin; there was no layabout nonsense here.

If Togura had ever had the misfortune to sail on Draven's ship, the Tusk, then he would have found a state of affairs rather closer to his imaginings – which was the main reason why the Tusk had been smashed on the coast of Sung, the crew butchered by the local populace and the wreckage looted, while the Warwolf rode out the storm with matchless aplomb.

As the sun came out again, Togura dozed down to the deck and relaxed. For the moment, he had no worries. This ship, its mission urgent, had no time to call at Larbster Bay on this leg of its journey. Instead, it would take him all the way to the distant island of Ork, then drop him at Larbster on the return voyage. For the time being, all he had to do was eat, sleep, and enjoy the sun at the end of summer.

With all his difficulties thus comfortably postponed, it was pleasing to toy with the idea of being a questing hero. Once he finally got from Larbster Bay to Estar, he would most certainly have a look at the monster in Prince Comedo's Castle Vaunting. He would then be able to decide whether he should attempt to recover the box which held the index.

He remembered back to the days when he had lived in the stronghold of the Wordsmiths in Keep. Brother Troop had talked about the box, which held the index which could control the odex. Asked what the index looked like, he had answered:

'When you open the box, you'll know. Remember, it speaks the Universal Language.'

Togura, daydreaming, imagined himself performing desperate heroics and recovering the vital box. It would open at a Word. And that Word was?

– Konanabarok?
– Yaradoshek?
– Slonshenamenel?

No, it was nothing like that. It was something else, but, for the life of him, he could not remember what. For a moment, he panicked. Then he relaexed. There was no need for him to remember how to command the box. All he had to do was get it to Keep. The Wordsmiths would do the rest.

It would be easy.

Or would it?

After all, there was not just Castle Vaunting's monster to deal with. If he slew the monster, that in itself would not be enough to give him the box which held the index, for the box was at the bottom of a bottle. Togura tried to remember Brother Troop's instructions for getting into the bottle, but could not. All he could remember was Brother Troop saying:

'The box itself lies at the very bottom of the bottle, and is

Guarded . . . which means there's death waiting nearby.'

Remembering this talk of death made Togura once more doubt the wisdom of being a questing hero. He decided to procrastinate his decision until he reached Estar, which would not be for many days yet: there was no hurry.

A shadow blocked out the sun. Togura opened his eyes and saw a fair-haired young pirate looking down at him. The pirate, who was unarmed, was wearing a woollen shepherd's rig and rope-soled shoes.

'What are you staring at?' said Togura.

'Nothing that catches my fancy,' said the youth. 'They told me you were a manhunter, so I thought you'd be something special. But you're not.'

Togura wondered whether to take offence, then decided against it. The doughty little pirate was a tough, nuggety piece of work; Togura might have trouble handling him if it came to a scuffle.

'Tell me, for you're the expert,' said Togura, venturing a little flattery, 'what's that island over there?'

And he pointed at a high-rising island some distance off. Its coast was 'walled around with bronze,' as the pirate idiom had it – that is to say, it had a rugged, iron-bound coast.

'That?' said the youth. 'We name him Drum. That's—'

He broke off as the ship shuddered as if something had struck it. There was instant alarm on board. Men rushed to the side and peered overboard. Shouts rang out as deck queried crow's-nest.

'What was it?' said Togura.

'Sharbly we grounded a whale,' came the laconic answer. 'No worry. It's gone, and us, we're not drinking.'

At that moment, the ship lurched hideously. Togura was sent sliding. As he clung to the deck rail, he saw something rising up out of the sea. Up, up it came, ascending in blue-green coils.

'Snake!' said the pirate.

Its jaws leered toward them, as if it would strike, then it dipped down into the sea again. It was indeed like a snake, except that it was three times the length of the ship and had the girth of a bullock.

153

'There's another!' cried Togura.

There were two — no, three . . . four! five! . . . there were six sea serpents in the waters around them. Togura heard Jon Arabin, the ship's captain, bellowing orders. Shortly he heard wails and screams as the ship girls were brought on deck. Fighting and biting, they were dragged to the stern and thrown overboard. They thrashed round in the water, screaming. Blood foamed on the waves as the sea serpents ravaged them.

'That's murder!' said Togura, shocked.

The young pirate gave a twisted grin.

'Them or us,' he said. 'Which would you prefer?'

'Well . . . '

It was indeed a difficult question.

Jon Arabin gave another order. And the weapons muqaddam grabbed Togura and started to drag him to the edge of the deck.

'This is a joke, yes?' said Togura.

The weapons muqaddam made no answer.

'A joke? Understand?' said Togura desperately. 'A joke?'

They were now very close to the edge.

'Draven!' screamed Togura.

And started to kick, scratch, struggle and bite. It did him no good. He was hauled to the very edge.

'Draven!' shouted Togura, sighting his friend at last. 'Stop him!'

'Sorry, boy,' said Draven, advancing at a casual saunter. 'This isn't my ship. I've no authority here. So enjoy your swim.'

'I can't swim!' screamed Togura.

A lie — but he thought it worth trying.

He locked his hands round the stern rail, and, struggling vigorously, managed to kick the weapons muqaddam in the guts. His enemy did not even grunt.

'Did you hear me?' screamed Togura. 'I can't swim!'

'Bait doesn't have to swim,' said Draven, grabbing hold of Togura's flailing feet. 'Give my regards to the chiefest of serpents.'

'Don't do it. Please!' begged Togura, as he lost his hold on the stern rail. 'Draven, help me!'

'Heave ho!' said Draven, cheerfully.

They gave him the old heave ho, and over he went. Arms and legs flailing, he tumbled through the air. He hit the sea awkwardly with a crash, a shock of cold water, and a blunt, ugly pain, as if someone had rammed his rectum with an iron bar. The impact drove him deep.

Momentarily stunned, lost to all knowledge of his place, time and name, he struggled for the light. Breaking the surface, he gasped for air. A slip-slop wave slapped him in the face. He remembered what was happening. A shrill whinny of terror escaped him. He thrashed at the water as if having a fit.

'No no no,' moaned Togura, drawing his legs up to try and stop anything from biting them.

Another wave slapped him harshly, cutting off his moans. Blinking away the stinging salt of the sea, squeezing a web of water from his eyes, he dared to look around. He could see no women. No sea serpents.

The big seas hoisted him up then slopped him down again. The Warwolf, bulking away from him, heeled in the wind. He saw its lower timbers were foul with weed, barnacles and sea squirts; it was overdue for careening. Draven waved to him from the stern, then shouted something; the wind blurred away the sense of his words.

'What?' shouted Togura.

Draven shouted more unintelligible words, then pointed at something. What? Trying to see, Togura forgot all about keeping his legs up. They drifted down. The next moment, Togura felt something firm underfoot. Ah, ground! A miracle!

The ground began to rise.

Oh no!

Togura began to cry out with short, panting, uncontrollable, hysterical screams. Up came the green surge in a smooth, hypnotic flow, riding up between his legs and lofting him into the sky. He found himself straddling a sea serpent, which was racing through the sea toward the ship. He began to slip. He grabbed for a handhold, finding nothing but a few barnacles clinging to battle-scarred scales. Taking his weight, the old scales themselves started to scab away, revealing fresh, gleaming, frictionless scales beneath.

As the sea serpent raced toward the ship, Togura slid sideways. He scrabbled desperately for purchase. He had a brief, hallucinatory glimpse of the deck of the ship. It was below him. Men were scattering in all directions. Then the sea serpent crunched down. The stern splintered. Timbers smashed. Togura was thrown through the air.

Togura, bruised to the deck, rolled to his feet in an instant. He stood there, swaying. The ship lurched, the deck canted, and down he went again. He saw a scream wailing between the sea serpent's jaws. Then the scream was gone. The jaws were turning toward him.

Togura accelerated from a crawl to a sprint in one and a half paces. Then he collided with a pirate. Both went down. The sea serpent slavered above them. Blood dripped from its jaws. Togura, paralysed with fear, mewled weakly with terror. But the pirate bravely struggled to his feet, drawing his cutlass. A mistake. The monster snacked on the cold steel, then munched down on the pirate. Togura slithered away, then got to his feet and ran with a blind, lurching gait.

Knocked to the deck by the ship's next ungainly movement, Togura turned to see half a dozen pirates charging the sea serpent, using a spare spar as a battering ram. Wood splintered, bones crunched, and Togura went humbling up the ratlines, climbing for dear life or cheap, life at any price, there was no time for bargaining.

He climbed and climbed until he could climb no more, and then, at a dizzy height, he hooked his arms through rope netting and slumped there, exhausted. The ship, struck by another sea serpent, heeled alarmingly then righted itself; the motion, amplified by the mast, did sickening things to his stomach.

'Enjoy your swim?' said a laconic voice beside him.

Togura opened his eyes to look at his neighbour. It was the fair-haired young pirate he had conversed with earlier in the day.

'You're a murderous pack of unprincipled bastards,' said Togura savagely.

The youth laughed.

'What did you expect?' he said. 'We're pirates! You got off lucky, though. Bait can be cut, blinded, tortured. Or ship-raped, my hearty. If there's time. This time there wasn't.'

'Does that mean I was bait all along? Did you expect to meet—'

'Not so angry, man. Settle, settle! You, you were our much loved, honoured, respected passenger until we met the monsters. Stall it, man, don't say it — of course we weren't expecting them. None in their right minds — or out of them, for that matter — would sail to a monster's jaws full knowing. My name's Drake. And yours?'

'Togura,' mumbled Togura, his strength for anger fading.

'What?'

'Forester,' said Togura, speaking up loudly, amending his name as he remembered who he was masquerading as.

'Welcome, Forester. Do you—'

The mast lurched alarmingly.

'Dahz!' exclaimed the pirate Drake, using a foreign obscenity.

Togura realised a sea serpent had coiled itself around the base of the mast. Even as he watched, the mast, very slowly, began to bend. Then, with a sudden shatter-crack, it snapped.

They fell.

Togura screamed.

The sea roared up and smashed them.

Engulfed in green, harassed by rope, choking and breathless, Togura struggled for air and daylight. Breaking to the surface of the sea, he snorted water, sucked air, was floundered over by a wave, ducked by another, hauled down by a third, rolled over and over by a fourth, then lifted up by a fifth to an eminence from which he saw the Warwolf, encumbered by a trio of sea serpents, crabbing away through the sea with its broken mast trailing.

'Swim!' yelled a voice.

It was Drake.

Togura saw his young pirate friend, still clinging to the mast. What was better? To cling to the mast until the sea serpents were ready for dessert? Or drown in the bottomless ocean?

'Swim! Now!' shouted Drake, wind and distance rapidly eroding his voice.

Togura struck out for the mast and the ship, but it was hopeless. The sea was rough; a strong, fast current was sweeping him away from the ship. Finally he gave up and trod water, watching the ship, listing badly, dragging itself away from him, still in the grip of three implacable monsters.

Seeing a stray spar surfing through the water, Togura swam for it, reached it, latched on and clung to it for dear life. One end was all munched, crunched and splintered; he shuddered. The ship was now too distant for him to make out any detail of what was happening on board, but he saw black billows of smoke beginning to rise from the vessel. Soon one of the remaining masts was on fire; it was Togura's guess that the ship was doomed.

'Drown down, you buck-rat bastards,' he muttered, cursing the ship and its crew.

By now he was very, very cold; he began to shiver violently and continuously. He would be chilled down to his death unless he could get to land. But there was no land anywhere near. Or was there? The island of Drum was now much closer. The current was taking him toward the shore.

The current was swift, but, even so, it seemed a long time before he could cast off from the spar and strike out for the shore. He swam very slowly. Caught in the surf, he almost drowned, surviving by luck alone. The waves tumbled him onto a pebbly beach. He struggled up the beach and across the driftwood line at high tide mark, then shuffled into a cave and collapsed, exhausted.

CHAPTER 20

Waves thrashed, humped and slubbered, mounted and surmounted, gashed themselves recklessly against the rocks of Drum, sifted through seaweed, chopped each other into foam, then hurled themselves against the beach, tumbling stones, sheals and crab claws over and over in a bounteous explosion of spray. The daylight slowly weathered away.

Exhausted, defeated and badly frightened, Togura Poulaan lay in his cave in a state of collapse. At the beginning of the day, buoyant with confidence, he had been a warm, brave, well-fed questing hero, riding a ship on his way to high adventure. Now he was a cold, hungry, shivering vagrant, a helpless waif of a gadling, marooned on the island of Drum, home of the notorious wizard of Drum, an ill-tempered necromancer known to have the unpleasant habit of feeding strangers to his household dragons.

Togura wanted, very very much, to be home on his father's estate. In bed. With a cup of something hot to warm and cheer him. He did not like it here. He was too cold, too wet, too lonely. It was dangerous. Things would hurt him. He would never get off the island alive. Recovering a little strength, he used it to produce hot tears of grief and regret.

He was eventually roused from his blubbering self-pity by a strange clinking crunching slithering sound which he could hear even above the rouse, souse, suck, slap and gurgitation of the sea. It sounded like four or five men dragging a log across

159

stones. Or, perhaps, like a large animal of peculiar construction making its way across the beach.

Sitting up, Togura faced the cave mouth. The strange noise stopped. A beast peered inside, then withdrew.

– A dragon?

Togura was almost certain he had seen a dragon. He did not know whether to scream, to run, to freeze, or to pick up a stick and a stone so as to be prepared to fight for his life.

In the event, he froze.

There was a hiatus, in which Togura heard his own pounding pulse and the sea doing leisurely break-falls on the beach. Then the dragon looked in again. It gave a prolonged gurgling cough as it cleared its throat, then it spoke.

'Hello,' said the dragon, in Galish; the word was clear and distinct, marred only by a superfluous bark at the end of it.

'Piss off!' screamed Togura, hurling a rock.

Fortunately, he missed.

'That's not very polite, you know,' said the dragon, mildly. 'Come outside. Let's have a look at you.'

The cave was large enough to admit the dragon, so Togura saw no percentage in disobeying. Reluctantly, expecting at any moment to be incinerated, he quit the cave. As no immediate disaster befell him, he was able to take stock of the dragon. Entirely green except for its eyes – which were red, with yellow pupils – it stood about as tall as a pony but was three times the length. It had short, stubby wings which were folded against the side of its body.

'You look cold,' said the dragon. 'You need a fire. I'll give you one. I'm an excellent pyrotechnist.'

'A what?' said Togura.

'Watch,' said the dragon.

It clawed together some driftwood then breathed out flames which were delicate shades of blue, yellow and green. The wood scorched, charred and flamed. Togura squatted down by the fire.

'Thank you,' he said, belatedly remembering his manners.

'It was nothing,' said the dragon, in a voice which managed

to hint that it was really quite something. 'We sea dragons are very talented, you know.'

'I'm sure you are,' said Togura, hoping that he was engaging in a real conversation and not just being subjected to a before-dinner speech.

'Sea dragons are characterised by versatile genius,' said the dragon, encouraged. 'Not like those ignorant hulking land monsters we are so often confounded with. We are not primitive brutes like the land dragons. No! A thousand times no! Sea dragons are the true lords of the intellect, noted for their wit, intelligence, grace, charm, sagacity and fashion sense, for their matchless command of all the philosophies, for their eloquence, good humour and comradeship, for their surpassing physical beauty, their wise counsel, their profound logic and their highly developed artistic sensitivity.'

'And for their modesty?' asked Togura — and instantly wished he had bitten off his tongue.

'That too,' acknowledged the sea dragon, failing to realise that his comment was somewhat barbed. 'Considering the true extent of our genius, considering the power of our swift-speeding inquiring minds armoured by their world-famous panoply of knowledge, we're remarkably modest, believe you me.'

'I do, I do,' said Togura, earnestly.

'Now warm yourself by the fire, young human,' said the sea dragon, 'while I go off to get instructions. Don't worry! I won't be long!'

It waddled down the beach, its tail dragging across the shingle, then spread its wings — which, as it was a sea dragon, were water wings, not capable of flight — and plunged into the water. Swimming swiftly and gracefully through the lumbering seas, it rounded a headland and was lost from sight.

It had gone to report to its master — the wizard of Drum!

Togura knew what he had to do. He did it. He made himself scarce, and, for the next five days, used all his native cunning — plus a lot which had been grafted on in recent months — to avoid and evade his pursuers. But, in the end, he was cornered by a number of dragons — all very pleased with themselves, and saying so at great length — and, after a lot of spurious speechifying, the dragons led him off to the grim, castellated stronghold of the wizard of Drum.

CHAPTER 21

As Togura Poulaan was marched into the shadows of the castle of the wizard of Drum, the iron-clad gates creaked open. Yawning darkness hid the nameless horrors beyond.

'Come on,' said the leading dragon, as Togura hesitated.

The command ended with a short bark, followed by a hiss of smoke, steam and pulsating flame. Reluctantly, Togura shuffled forward. He was sure his death awaited him.

Darkness gave way to the daylight of a big, bare, high-walled courtyard.

'Stand here,' said the leading dragon.

Togura obeyed. The dragons formed a circle, with Togura in the middle. They looked eager. Expectant. Something was about to happen. Togura closed his eyes. One of the dragons started to sharpen its claws against the courtyard stones with a slick, evil, sizzling sound which reminded him unpleasantly of a butcher's shop. The leading dragon cleared its throat.

'This,' it said, 'is the dragon hof. Here we gather each evening to eat, drink and recite poetry.'

There was a pause. Togura opened his eyes. All the dragons were watching him, as if they expected something from him.

'That sounds very nice,' said Togura cautiously. 'Very civilised. Dragons do seem to be very civilised.' This was going down well, so he elaborated. 'I only wish I had time to know you better. Time to appreciate your full conquest of the higher intellectual dimensions.'

'Time to hear some of my poetry, perhaps?' said the leading dragon, eagerly.

'That too,' said Togura.

'Then we shall oblige.'

And, to Togura's dismay and astonishment, the leading dragon began to recite its poetry. At great length. It was windy, ostentatious and stunningly boring. Nevertheless, he applauded politely.

The other dragons, jealous of the applause, demanded to be given their own chances to recite. Togura, faint with hunger, listened to their angry, arrogant, hogen-mogen voices disputing precedence. Each wanted to be first to recite. They barked, snapped, spat smoke, and suddenly fell to fighting. Togura, ringed round with fighting dragons, screamed at them:

'Stop! Stop! Stop!'

It did no good whatsoever.

Then a voice roared:

'Begenoth!'

The quarrelling dragons instantly quailed down to silence.

'Shavaunt!' shouted the voice.

And the dragons turned and fled.

Togura was alone.

'Now then,' said the dragon commander, entering the courtyard. 'What started all that off?'

The dragon commander was an old, old man with a dirty grey beard, who walked with the aid of a shepherd's crook. Despite his age, his eyes were bright, his voice was firm, and he looked fit and healthy.

'Well, boy?' asked the dragon commander.

'I . . . I asked if I could hear some of their poetry.'

'You what!?'

'Only some poetry, that's all. I just said I wished I had time to hear some.'

'No, boy, no, a thousand times no, that is one thing you must never ever do when you're face to face with a sea dragon. You must never ever – not on any account – encourage their artistic pretensions. Art, you see, is purely their excuse for

164

being the most lazy, idle, shiftless, foolish, irresponsible, degenerate pack of gluttonous sex-obsessed drunkards this side of the east ditch of Galsh Ebrek.'

'I'm sorry, sir, I didn't know.'

'This time, you're excused,' said the dragon commander. 'Come this way, boy.'

And he led Togura along halls and passageways, up and down staircases, through doors, gates and gloomy portals, past statues, weapon racks and antiquated skeletons, and, at last, into a comfortable room with wall-to-wall carpeting, leather furniture, two cats, a hubble-bubble pipe and large leaded windows where the glass was patterned in circles, squares and diamonds.

'Sit, boy, sit,' said the dragon commander, motioning Togura to a chair. 'Good. Now tell me what you've been doing with yourself since you left Sung.'

'Sung?'

'Your homeland, boy. To be specific, Keep.'

'How did you know that?' said Togura, in amazement.

'I met you there. I introduced myself, didn't I?'

'Did you?'

'Of course I did. I distinctly remember giving you my name – Hostaja Torsen Sken-Pitilkin, wizard of Drum. Well, boy? Why are you so blank? Senility, is it? Losing your memory already? And you so young? A tragic case!'

'I really don't think—'

'You don't think! Confession time, is it? I'm sure you don't think. I only hope the condition isn't permanent. What did they call you? Let me think. The girl called you Tog. Yet the rumbustical boy called you Spunk Togura. Or did he call you Chids? Anyway, the man – the man called you Master Togura. That's for certain. That was before he bedded me down in that shacklety old building – a garrow, I think he called it.'

'Well ... '

'Come on, boy! Surely you remember. There was a dreadful noise. I complained. I remember that distinctly. You called it music – a mistake, I thought, but I didn't object. I was tired. I'd just flown in from Chi'ash-lan.'

'Ah!' said Togura, suddenly enlightened. 'You were the old man with the bundle of sticks. A great big clutter of sticks like a huge bird's nest. You called it a ship.'

'Yes, boy, and if you'd roused yourself from your slumbers in the early morning, you'd have seen me fly away in it. Why didn't you remember my name? I always introduce myself. I did so then, I'm certain of it. Or was that in the morning? Perhaps I introduced myself in the kitchen, when I scavenged the breakfast that nobody thought to offer me. I had a long argument with the cook. She was drunk.'

'That would be Salomie,' said Togura.

'That's the name! And what are you, boy? Tog, Spunk, Chids? Speak up, boy!'

'Togura Poulaan, if you please. Son of Baron Chan Poulaan.'

'Ah so! You're the one they call Barak the Battleman. There's a price on your head. I could use it. What say you give me your head, boy? I'll split the reward with you. Straight down the middle.'

Togura blanched.

'Come now, boy,' said the wizard of Drum. 'Can't you tell when someone's joking? I wouldn't dismember a guest. Come now, don't say you believe all that slander spawned by King Skan Askander? All that nonsense about using people as dragon-chop and such-such? Boy, you're looking quite faint. When did you last eat?'

'I don't remember,' said Togura.

'Then sit there quietly and I'll get you something. You're looking as bad as I do after a long trip by air. Relax, boy, relax! You're safe on Drum.'

Togura did not feel safe, but he relaxed all the same. In fact, he closed his eyes and went straight off to sleep. The wizard woke him to eat, and, as he ate, his spirits began to revive.

He realised that he had reached a place of refuge.

CHAPTER 22

In the days that followed, Togura gave the wizard a long account of his adventures, which, despite several evasions and a certain amount of exaggeration, was generally truthful. The one big lie in the whole account was Togura's claim that he was dedicated to questing for the index.

'You're very brave,' said the wizard.

'It's my duty, sir.'

'Don't call me sir, call me Hostaja,' said Hostaja Torsen Sken-Pitilkin. 'Tell me, what are you being offered for success? Hmmm? Exactly what do the Wordsmiths propose to pay you?'

'One per cent of everything won from the odex.'

'One per cent? That's scandalous. Young man, you've been done! Diddled and cheated! Ten per cent is a minimum, that's what I say. You need an agent.'

'But I've made an agreement already. It's a little late to change now.'

'Not so,' said the wizard. 'I'll fly to Sung myself, later in the year. I'll have a word with Brother Troop. We'll sort it out.'

'What's in it for you, then?'

'Don't worry your head about that. Whatever I get will be from the Wordsmiths, not from you. I'll be adequately remunerated, you can be sure of that.'

Togura was no longer a beggarly castaway. Instead, he was a valuable commercial property. The wizard of Drum, who had sworn never to set foot in Sung again — he still had painful memories of a certain game of Stone the Leper and of the devaluation of the punt — had changed his mind entirely now that profit beckoned.

Togura had certainly guaranteed his immediate survival. But there was a penalty for his deceit — he must now play the part of a death-dealing questing hero, at least while he was on Drum.

'You should set out in spring,' said Hostaja. 'I'll take you to Estar myself.'

'In spring!' said Togura, alarmed at the prospect of being on Drum for so long. 'I'm ready to leave now!'

'You can't leave before we've renegotiated your agreement with the Wordsmiths,' said Hostaja. 'Risking your neck for one per cent? That's lunacy!'

'But, really—'

'I have spoken. You're staying here till spring. That way, I'll be able to teach you something. The young are always over-confident, it's the ruling characteristic of the breed.'

'I don't need any training.'

'I see. You don't need any training. You know everything about everything, is that it? Well, boy, tell me this — what's the Word you need to open the box which holds the index?'

'That's a secret.'

'Fiddlesticks! The truth is, you've forgotten, if you ever knew. Don't think there's anything secret from me, boy. Do you know the history of the Book of the Odex?'

'Brother Troop found it.'

'No! Nonsense! Brother Troop wasn't even born at the time! Troop's father helped find it. There was an expedition to the Old City in the Valley of Forgotton Dreams, in Penvash. There were three survivors. Troop's father was one of them. They brought back the odex and the Book of the Odex. They were lucky to bring back their own lives, if you ask me.'

'Why? What's so terrible about the Old City?'

'Most of the people who have gone there to find out have never come back,' said Hostaja. 'Some of those unfortunates were wizards far more powerful than me. Consequently, I

168

know better than to investigate. The Melski stay out of the whole valley, and, to my mind, that's the wisest thing to do. Anyway. Tell me. Who translated the Book of the Odex?'

'Brother Troop?' said Togura uncertainly.

'No! No! A thousand times no! It was me! Troop's father brought the book here more than a generation ago. I've laboured heartily since. Ah, but what thanks do I get for it?'

'I think . . . perhaps Brother Troop did mention your name.'

'A passing mention, perhaps! I know those people. They play down my role the best they can. It's the scholarly ego, my boy! A terrible thing, a terrrible thing. I tell you – no, I'd better not. There's nothing to be gained from rehearsing these old, old quarrels. Just remember that I know as much about the odex as Brother Troop – no, more! – and what he knows, I taught him.'

'I understand, sir.'

'The word you need to open the box is Sholabarakosh. You'll know it as well as you know your own name, by the time you leave here. And more, besides. It's death to teach some of the things I've a mind to teach you, but the confederation of Wizards has sentenced me to death five times already, with no visible effect.'

'Why would they do something like that?'

'Internal politics, boy! I can explain it, if you've got a month to spare – but you've got better things to learn. Tell me, boy, what have they taught you about the ancient wizard castles?'

'Well, I've seen this one, so—'

'Boy, this is a pirate castle. It was built by the sea raiders a thousand years ago, when Drum was the centre of piracy. Barring my own occupation, it's got nothing to do with wizards. But when you get to Estar you'll find a true power stronghold. Prince Comedo of Estar lives in Castle Vaunting, which was built by wizards. Tell me, how many towers does it have?'

Togura guessed one, then guessed fifty. Despite the instruction he had had from Brother Troop, he had never known a great deal about the quest he was on; what he had known had been mostly forgotten during the course of his traumatic adventures.

'When you dare your indigestion on this quest,' said Hostaja, 'Ignorance is death. I'll do my best to instruct you, boy, though I suspect it'll be painful for the both of us.'

And lessons began that very same day.

Togura Poulaan studied through autumn, learning more than he really wanted to know about the eight orders of wizards, the Confederation of Wizards, the nature of magic and the history of the troubled continent of Argan. Autumn turned to winter. Bleak winds scoured the island, bringing cold, slate-grey rain, which hammered against the windows while Togura laboured to memorise Words of power and command.

As the weather grew colder, the sea dragons, having gorged themselves on pine needles, retreated to a deep, dank dungeon to sleep. When Togura went down to have a look, he found them all reciting poetry in their sleep. The wizard of Drum, told of this, laughed:

'The pretentious little brats are only shamming. When they're really asleep, they snore.'

And, indeed, when Togura went down a few days later to have another look, the dungeon was a sonorous slother of snoring dragons. At first, they woke up every few days, and would come stumbling up the stairs for meat and drink. They were no longer the lively, argumentative creatures he had met at the end of summer; winter made them slow, sluggish and dim-witted. As the days shortened, they woke no more, but hibernated, while fleas bit them with impunity. The cats, which had fleas of their own kept to the fireside, also sleeping.

Between study sessions, which increasingly bored him, Togura did a lot of sleeping himself. He also cleaned and sharpened old blades he found about the castle, then practised solitary swordplay in echoing halls and cloisters. The great outdoors, a wasteland of rock, wind and tumbled sea, held no attraction for him.

Togura, as befitted his student status, did the cooking. They lived on salt beef, pickled octopus, boiled abalone, fried turnip, pig weed, sea anemone soup, garlic, onions and a noxious substance which Hostaja named siege dust. After meals, Hostaja would smoke a litle opium, pick his nose with a golden spoon, sandpaper his false teeth — which were made of metal — or fall asleep in his chair to dream of whatever it is that old men dream of.

Hostaja also spent a great deal of time closeted in a private room which was secured against intrusion by a green door which was locked and bolted. He claimed that he spent the time meditating, though Togura had no way to verify this; his teacher still found plenty of time to scold Togura for his lackadaisical attitude to his studies, and to exhort him to greater efforts.

Toward the end of winter, when the winds were quiet for once, and the dragons still deep in hibernation, the wizard of Drum flew to Sung to confer with Brother Troop. Togura desperately wanted to go with him — to go to Sung, and stay there — but did not dare ask for the privilege. Hostaja, having spent so much time and effort on Togura's education, would be enraged if his hero reneged just because he was homesick. The time to back out would be later, when he got to Estar; if he was ever questioned, he could always say that Johan Meryl Comedo, prince of Estar, had refused him access to Castle Vaunting — it would be most unlikely that anyone would check.

Before going away, the wizard of Drum warned Togura that he was not to open the green door into the wizard's private room.

'Understand?' said Hostaja. 'You will not, may not, must not open that door. No matter what! Not even if the door smokes, screams, or dances a split polka.'

'Is it likely to do that?' asked Togura anxiously.

'With that door,' said Hostaja, grimly, 'anything can happen.'

Then he levitated his ship of sticks, and flew away to Sung. He expected to be gone three days, but a storm broke out, and he did not return for thirty. On his return, he seemed disappointed to find that the green door had not been tampered with.

'Why didn't you open the door, boy?' he demanded.

'You told me not to!'

'Since when did the words of the old carry weight with the young?'

'I've adventures enough ahead of me without seeking them here. Who cares what's behind the green door? It might be something which wants to eat me!'

'So it might, boy, so it might,' said Hostaja, sounding troubled. 'But where's your spirit? You're a bit of a disappointment to me, boy.'

'I've killed a monster,' said Togura. 'I've matched my skills against Zenjingu fighters. I've fought against the Warguild. I've started a revolution. I've survived the treachery of pirates. I've ridden a sea serpent — you don't believe me, but I swear it. Now if that doesn't make me a hero, what does?'

The wizard of Drum shook his head.

'Boy,' he said. 'You've had your accidents and you've scraped your way out of them, but I've got my doubts about you all the same.'

Now Togura understood. The green door had been a test, and he had failed. He felt crushed. But the news from Sung helped revive his spirits. The wizard of Drum, a seasoned negotiator, had extracted formidable concessions from the Wordsmiths. Togura Poulaan was appointed to the rank of wordmaster, with seniority backdated one year; when he brought the index to Keep, he would be guaranteed eleven percent of the returns from the odex, plus a minimum payment of one hundred crowns; the Wordsmiths would persuade, bribe or coerce Cromarty into withdrawing the reward he had offered for Togura's head.

'With all that on offer,' said Hostaja, 'I hope you start to take your responsibilities seriously. Study hard. We don't have very much time.'

Togura did study hard, and found they didn't have much time. Soon winter was at an end, and they were on their way to the east in the wizard's flying ship. The journey was a nightmare; the ship thrashed about in the air turbulence, plummeted, dropped, spun, twisted, raced and decelerated, making Togura sick, dizzy and terrified. He was throroughly glad when they grounded in a clearing in Looming Forest, somewhere east of Lorp and north of Estar.

As the wizard had already explained, he had no wish to fly any closer to Lorford because of the danger posed by the dragon Zenphos, which lived in Estar in a cave in the mountain of Maf.

'Are you sure you know where you go from here?' asked Hostaja.

'I go east,' said Togura, 'and pick up the Hollern River, which flows south. I follow it south. Just before it reaches Lorford, it turns west. I'll know when I get to Lorford because there'll be a bridge, a town and a castle on a hill.'

'Right.'

'I've had a thought,' said Togura. 'Why don't I walk south? Then I could pick up the Hollern River as it flows toward the Central Ocean, and follow it upstream, toward the east, and get to Lorford that way.'

'You could do that,' said Hostaja, 'but it wouldn't be wise. In Lorford, they're used to people coming down the Hollern River. It's part of the Salt Road, after all. But someone coming out of the west, from the sea, is a different proposition altogether. They might take you for a pirate scout, which would be unfortunate, to say the least. Yours wouldn't be the first head to decorate Prince Comedo's walls.'

'Is he very dangerous then, this Prince Comedo?'

'Courage, boy! He's a coward and a fool. If he menaces you, then menace him back in my name. Here − here's a parting gift for you. A letter of introduction from the Wordsmiths, written by Brother Troop in his capacity as governor. Another letter, also introducing you, which is written in my own fair hand. One last caution − never let any wizard know you've been associating with me. It could be the death of you. The Confederation is strong, boy, and ruthless, and is sworn to destroy me and all my works.'

'Thank you, sir,' said Togura, and bowed.

'Call me Hostaja,' said the wizard of Drum, not for the first time. 'When we meet again, you with the index and destined to be much richer, call me Hostaja.'

And Hostaja Torsen Sken-Pitilkin, wizard of Drum, no longer Sung's most bitter and implacable critic — money is a great sweetener! — levitated his flying ship and was gone.

Togura was alone in Looming Forest, but, for once, he was properly prepared for the task at hand. He had weather-worthy clothes and boots, a couple of knives, a sword, a bow, a quiver of arrows, five spare bowstrings, a big leather pack, a sheepskin sleeping bag, plenty of salt beef, a tinder box, enough rope to allow him to scale a respectable mountain, his two letters of introduction, a little money and a pot of boot grease.

Togura, who felt that the wizard of Drum had over-equipped him in every respect but money, threw away the boot grease, the rope, half the salt beef and a great hulking lump of driftwood which he found at the bottom of his pack — perhaps one of the sea dragons had put it there as a joke — and started walking east. Soon, to his pleasure, he encountered an eastward-running stream. He knew that it would take him, without fail, to the Hollern River.

This time, he could not get lost.

And as for this business of being a hero? Well, there would be plenty of time to make a decision on that after he got to Lorford. But before he made any decision about hero-work, he would undertake a far more urgent project: he would find one of Lorford's cheaper whores and finally cure himself of his virginity.

CHAPTER 23

The trees of Looming Forest were unfamiliar to Togura. The first time he made a fire, the wood was damp, and reluctant to start; when it finally kindled, it burnt with bleak, blue-grey flames, unlike anything he had ever seen before. Disturbed, he wondered if it was a bad omen.

That first night, he hardly slept, but lay awake listening to a mournful, night-foundered wind wandering through the trees. He was further from home than he had ever been before; he had left the Ravlish Lands, had crossed the Penvash Channel, and was now in the continent of Argan.

His fire went out.

A large animal went crunching through the undergrowth.

Togura sat up in his sleeping bag, huddled against a tree and drew his sword, prepared to fight to the death if need be. The animal crunched away, and he did not hear it again. But he listened for it. Dawn found him tired, ragged and irritable, but he told himself the first night was always the hardest. He was sure things would improve.

But they did not.

Togura did not relish being back in the wilderness. Indeed, it was something of a shock to him. He had forgotten the cold of the night, the immense height of the stars, and the enormity of darkside shadows and noises; after that first night in the open, he dearly wished he was back in the safe, comfortable castle on Drum. But wishing failed to help him, and renewed

175

familiarity failed to make the nights less cold and dark.

The winter spent slouching around the castle had softened him. The days marched his heels into blisters. Each night, slumping to sleep, he had rheumatic nightmares in which his swollen joints stumbled down forest paths at a crawling pace. He would wake from these dreams to hear heavy-footed noises hunting each other through the darkness; he would keep a silent vigil until they departed, permitting him to sleep. Each morning, when he woke, he found his body still aching from the rigours of the day before.

On waking, he would eat some salt beef, drink from the stream he was following toward the east, break camp, shoulder his pack, then tramp on through the forest. His pack, heavy and invincible, oppressed him every step of the way. Unaccustomed to marching under load, Togura suffered. The shoulder straps restricted circulation, making veins in his hands swell; his burden constantly tried to drag him backwards, so he finished each day with an aching back and aching shoulders.

Reaching the point of mutiny, Togura hurled his pack at a tree, then tried to kick it to death. It was indifferent to this treatment. To kill it properly, he would have to burn it alive. But he was not reckless enough to do that. He needed his pack to carry, among other things, the salt beef he needed to stay alive. But he was sick of salt beef! He longed, with fervent nostalgia, for some pickled octopus − or even some sea anemone soup.

As he drew nearer to the Hollern River, Togura kept an eager lookout for any sign of human beings. He longed for human voices, proper food, fireside companionship, laughter, jokes, songs, music, and the beauty of women.

The first sign which looked hopeful was a fresh, deep-ploughed scuffling track, as if something of great weight had been dragged through the trees. The track approached the stream then veered away from it. It had certainly not been made by any animal. Whatever burden had been dragged through the forest had flattened undergrowth and small trees; from the way the vegetation had been crushed down, the direction of the track was clear, and Togura followed.

He had not gone far when he saw a stone standing in the forest at the end of the track. It was a large stone — twice his own height. It was covered with dirt, mud, pulped vegetation, filth and muck. Togura could only presume that it had been abandoned there. But some of the mud was still damp. Those who had dragged this enormous chunk of rock to this place — strange that he could see no sign of footsteps — could not have gone far.

'Hello?' called Togura.

The rock quivered, moved, and fell over on one side. Are falling rocks back luck? Togura was not sure, but, just in case, he touched wood, which was a protection against many kinds of misfortune.

'Is anyone here?' cried Togura.

His voice quavered disagreeably. He was ashamed of himself. He gathered his strength and gave a great shout:

'Hey! Is anyone here?'

The rock got up.

'I did not see that rock get up,' said Togura, in a slow, deliberate voice.

But the great mass of dirt-stained stone was now most definitely upright.

'Rocks, perhaps, sometimes fall upward,' said Togura.

But he knew this was not true. The world has its habits, and never deviates from them. The sky is always up; the earth is always down. The rock must have —

'Gongaragon,' growled the rock, shadows shaping to a vortex which appeared to be its mouth.

'I did not hear a rock speak,' said Togura, in a level, even voice. 'I am tired. I am over-stressed. I am starting to hallucinate. This is not unusual for an isolated solo traveller.'

The rock took a step toward him.

'I did not see that rock move,' said Togura. 'I did not —'

The rock launched itself toward him on full attack. Without a moment's hesitation, Togura turned and fled. He had no time to drop his pack. He went sprinting back the way he had come with the rock roaring behind him. Togura reached the stream. He leapt across it. Then ran straight slap-bang into a tree.

Stunned, dizzy, he spun round and confronted the rock, which had stalled on the far side of the stream. It stood there, roaring at him. Togura wiped his nose, which was bleeding copiously.

'It cannot cross water,' he said, hopefully.

As the rock continued to roar impotently, he convinced himself that it must be true. The thing had no way to cross water. Drunk with relief, he started to hurl abuse at it:

'Muck-eater! Flat foot! You mud-screwing hump of a scallion! Pig-stuffing whoreson scab! Go eat yourself! Gamos!'

The rock backed off, then charged at a tree. Axed down in an instant, the tree fell dead, chopping across the stream. The rock slammed down another tree right next to it. And then it began to cross.

'No!' screamed Togura, his voice a high-pitched wail.

He fled.

The stone, lurching, swaying, smashing its way through branches, came after him. Togura doubled back and leapt across the stream. He ran a few paces further then stopped, panting violently, and turned, knowing that the stream would stop the stone.

What he knew was not what happened.

The stone charged straight through the stream. It screamed when it hit the water, but it kept on coming. Half-crippled by the water, its movements wild and erratic, its stumped toward him.

'No no no!' screamed Togura.

Then ran.

It was gaining on him.

Ahead, he saw something through the trees. The river! He charged toward it, summoned all his strength for one last spring, hit the bank and jumped. With a crash, he hit the water. His pack promptly dragged him under. As he struggled to free himself from the pack, the obdurate leather seemed to grow arms and tentacles. It was hauling him down, holding him, clutching him, strangling him.

Then he was free.

Free!

He shot to the surface, swifter than a bubble, gasped for air then looked around. A current was swiftly carrying him downstream. Upstream, he saw the rock. It was lying half-submerged in the water. He hoped it was dead.

His pack!

Togura struck out for the shore, gained the bank and hauled himself onto dry land. Just upstream, a little swirl of muddy water, swiftly dissipating, marked — he hoped — the place where he had discarded his pack. He made his way to the place on the bank closest to the muddy swirl — now a memory only, for the water was running clean again — and marked it with a broken stick.

Then he went to check on the rock.

It was really dead.

And Togura, giving vent to an outbreak of hysterical anger, hammered the rock with a stick, jumped on it, swore at it and threw mud at its corpse. Then, exhausted, sat down and wept. It was really all too much. He had been prepared to meet dragons in Argan, and bears, and hostile wizards, and Castle Vaunting's monster, but nobody had ever told him anything about walking stones.

It was intolerable.

'This is intolerable,' he said, later, at evening, after a lot of hard diving had allowed him to recover his pack.

His clothes were wet, his weapons were wet, his pack was soaked, his sleeping bag was completely sodden, his tinder box was saturated, and his salt beef had not been improved by being immersed in the river.

'I'll probably die in the night,' said Togura, bitterly.

But he didn't, so, when morning came, he had to pull himself together, and decide what to do now.

'At least I've reached the river. That's something,' he told himself. 'A little southing will take me to Lorford.'

Unfortunately, his letters of introduction addressed to Prince Comedo of Estar were now, after their bath in the river, illegible. When he reached Lorford, he would have to go to

179

Castle Vaunting and introduce himself without any assistance.

'I don't have much luck,' said Togura.

So many things had gone wrong. Was he unlucky? Was he cursed? Was there an inescapable doom upon him? Back in the old days, when he had lived on his father's estate in Sung, he had never paid any attention at all to signs, omens, portents, or the traditional prognosticating indications – bad dreams, flecks of white in the fingernails, unexpected encounters with two cats keeping company and so forth – but in recent days he had found himself becoming increasingly superstitious.

'Give me the day,' said Togura , using a traditional formula for addressing the sun.

And, so saying, he bowed four times to that luminary, a practice which, or so he had heard, would bring good luck.

It didn't.

He had followed the riverbank south for scarcely half a day when he became aware that someone was following him. Stopping to listen, he realised there was someone in the trees alongside him. He hastened along the bank – and two men, armed and in armour, stepped out in front of him.

Togura drew his sword.

'Wah-Warguild!' shouted Togura, using one of his father's old battlecries.

The two men drew their own weapons.

'On the other hand,' muttered Togura, looking around, and seeing that another two men had stepped out of the forest behind him, 'maybe we could negotiate . . . '

And, so saying, he threw his sword in the river – an action which may have saved his life, but did not save his dignity, for the armoured men promptly crowded in, looted him and made him prisoner.

'This is not my lucky day,' said Togura.

And, on that score, he was quite right.

– I could have jumped in the river.

So thought Togura, after he had finished lamenting his bad luck.

Then he had second thoughts:

– No. The river would only have carried me down to Lorford. These must be Prince Comedo's soldiers. They would have taken me in Lorford if they hadn't taken me here.

A little later, he had third thoughts:

– If these are Comedo's soldiers, their behaviour's very odd.

But, even though he later had fourth and fifth thoughts, he was unable to work out who or what the soldiers were. They had no permanent camp, but slept rough. They risked small, bright, smokeless fires by day, but would not have a fire by night. As they moved from place to place, they sometimes met other groups of soldiers carrying the same weapons and wearing the same armour, occasions which would lead to long, earnest, low-voiced conferences. Every one of these soldiers wore, slung round his neck on a cord, a strangely decorated oval ceramic tile.

Togura, their captive, was made to carry a great weight of gear like a beast of burden, to scrape out primitive latrine pits, to gather firewood, light fires and tend fires. This he endured; there was no point in complaining, as he had no language in common with these strange foreigners. But what he really resented, more than anything else, was that they refused to share their rations with him, making him eat his own salt beef.

And Togura made one solemn resolution:

– If I get out of this alive, I'll never eat salt beef again in all my life.

That was for certain.

CHAPTER 24

Togura woke from unpleasant dreams about salt beef to find that it was night. Without surprise, he noted that it was cold and wet. The night was full of shadows and pattering rain. His clothes were damp; his knees were aching; his flesh felt thin. Cold rainwater — very wet rainwater, by the feel of it — was dripping down his neck.

Perhaps this was the night he would escape. Yes! He would run away into the forest. He would make for the north, for home. Home! Warm beds, warm honey, friendly voices. Once he got home, he would stay there, and never stir again. As for this idea of being a hero — piss on it!

Comforted by thoughts of escape, Togura began to slip back into sleep. He was jerked wide awake as a shift in the wind brought him sounds of fighting. Rain, wind and distance hashed the sounds together; he could not say how far away the combat was, or how many people were involved. Someone muttered; another voice spoke, curtly, in a tone of command. Togura realised the soldiers were all wide and awake, straining to hear the noise of the distant alarm.

The sounds of combat rumoured away to nothing, leaving only sea-soughing wind and the tap-rapper rain coming skittery-skit through spring leaves. Wind, rain and leaves were all the colour of night. As were the low-pitched voices of the soldiers, who, now that the noise of battle had died away, were

182

evidently discussing it. While they were still talking, Togura quietly dropped off to sleep.

At first, Togura dreamed of darkness. Of pitch. Charcoal. Midnight. The colour of silence. Eclipse. Throttling fingers. Dead echoes. Shadows mating with stone. Mud underwater. The true ideology of the worm. And then, hearing, in his dreams, the high, cruel note of a flute, he began to dream of brightness, of rainbows, of turbulence, of heat.

He dreamed of a flesh-eating rat in a teakwood beaufet, gnawing on a diamond tiara. Of a cat, demolishing a boiled entomostracan. Of a whirlpool, in which the island of Drum span round and round, its resident sea dragons prating poetry while they slipped toward destruction. Of a padma bouquet, in the middle of which was a frog. Of Day Suet, a sausage between her lips. The sausage became a – well, it became something which made Togura positively blink.

'This dream,' said his dream, 'signifies that you are asleep.'

Togura blinked again, and, blinking, woke. Blinking once more, he realised it was morning. Rain was falling steadily. He wished he could have slept longer, but knew he was expected to get himself moving. Cold and hungry, he quit the makeshift lean-to which had kept him alive – but not dry – during the night. Hunched against the rain, he tried to light a fire. It was hopeless. Yesterday's ashes were sodden, the tinder was damp, the wood was wet – nobody could have done it. But he got kicked for his troubles all the same.

Sullen and resentful, Togura breakfasted on salt beef. Reluctant and weary, he once more shouldered the weight of the heavy pack loaded down with other people's gear. He hated the brusque daylight. He hated salt beef. He hated mud, rain, wet, cold, damp, and the prospect of another day spent marching from here to there with no apparent purpose. This was lunacy!

As they marched off through the cold and the wet, Togura longed for a shot of quaffle or bub, anything to put some warmth in his limbs. Marching under load warmed him soon enough. Indeed, it made him too warm. He was sweating when, unexpectedly, they paused. There were men in the forest up ahead.

The men, a dozen in number, were allies. Togura, conticent and uncomprehending, listened while they talked away merrily. The men of Togura's party, who had been dour, sour and despondent over the last few days – they were low on rations, for one thing – grew cheerful and animated. One of them did a little dance in the pelting rain, while the others cheered. There was a lot of backslapping and ready laughter.

Then the two groups parted. The dozen men went north. Togura's party went south, with their lead scout setting a vicious pace. Togura, bowed down by the weight of the pack, went slip-slop through the mud. He had no breath to spare on curses. They took no rest breaks and did not stop for lunch, but made all the southing they could with all speed they could.

After a march which seemed almost endless, Togura heard axes at work up ahead, then the crash of a falling tree. His party went past a forestry work gang, and exchanged jubilant, shouted greetings. Then Togura heard the sound of a river, and, distantly, the tumultous sound of many men, of voices shouting, of horses neighing.

They burst out of the forest and into the open daylight. They saw before them a clear stretch of land, a river with a bridge across it, and, beyond the river, an amazing array of men, carts and animals, and, beyond that, a castle on a hill. Togura was stunned by the size of the castle. Downstream lay the smouldering ruins of a town.

'Where am I?' said Togura.

But there was no-one who could give him an answer.

As his party trooped across the bridge, Togura tried to figure out where all these thousands and thousands of men had come from. Seemingly oblivious to the rain, they were raising tents, digging pits in the ground, excavating trenches, shouting and arguing. He had never seen so many people before in his life. He could scarcely credit the existence of so many people. Most of the men he saw were accoutred as soldiers. This was an army! Comedo's army? Or an army of invasion?

The army could scarcely be Comedo's. Estar, from what Togura knew of it, was poor and sparsely populated, its wealth and population both depleted by the dragon Zenphos, lord of the heights of Maf. So this army had to come from foreign lands.

But Togura, though his grasp of geography was sketchy, was convinced that there was no country within marching distance which was rich enough and strong enough – and mad enough – to dare an army of this size into Estar. There was nowhere all these men could have come from. There was no reasonable explanation for their presence. With a growing sense of dread, he realised that the whole thing must be part of a nightmare incarnated for the sole and special purpose of persecuting him.

'What have I done?' wailed Togura.

Again, there was nobody who could give him an answer.

They were now tramping through the encampment. The ground underfoot was churned into mud. They were challenged; there was an argument; Togura was made to drop the pack he was carrying. Near at hand, there were a whole lot of men gathered in a circle. Togura had the impression that a fight was taking place in the middle of that circle, but he did not get the chance to investigate. A squad of spearmen took him in charge and marched him away.

'Do you speak Galish?' said Togura, hopefully. 'I'm Togura Poulaan, also known as Barak the Battleman, or, if you prefer, as Forester. Do you recruit mercenaries? I'm a trained soldier, you know. My father's head of the Warguild in Sung.'

Nobody answered him. And, belatedly, he remembered that his father, Baron Chan Poulaan, was missing, and probably dead. The spearmen were arguing with each other in their foreign jabber. Coming to a decision, they forced Togura into a tent. He was just getting his bearings – there was a monster in one corner of the tent, and someone huddled on the ground – when he was dragged out of that tent and forced into another, which was crammed with all kinds of people – men, women and children – shouting, coughing, crying, bleeding, snotting in public and eating it, or babbling their foreign nonsense.

Togura was just about to ask if anyone spoke Galish when

two soldiers claimed him from the tent and marched him away elsewhere. By this time he was confused, disorientated, bewildered and positively dizzy. Then, as they marched along, he thought he saw a familiar face. It was Draven the pirate, ambling along looking sleek and well-fed, if a trifle rain-wet.

'Draven!' he cried.

'Do I know you?' said the pirate, pausing.

'It's me, me, Togura Poulaan. You know!'

'No, I don't know. Oh — snatch on, I remember! Yes, it's Forester.'

One of the soldiers snarled at Togura and thumped him with a spear butt. He held his ground.

'Forester, that's right. I saved your life, remember? At D'Waith. I saved your life!'

'Thank you kindly for the courtesy,' said Draven. 'And, while I think of it — welcome to Lorford.'

And with that, Draven turned and walked away.

'Draven, help me! What's going on? Who are these people? What's happened?'

But Draven walked on.

'Draven!'

The pirate turned, gave a parting wave, and called:

'Sorry, can't stay! Busy, you know!'

And he disappeared from sight amidst a crowd of soldiers. Togura tried to follow, but was restrained. He was forced into a tent — which was empty — and left there. While he waited to be moved yet again, he tried to make sense of his meeting with Draven. The pirate was happy, cheerful, free, and evidently doing well for himself. So were all these people pirates? They couldn't be pirates, otherwise they'd know Galish. Foreign pirates, from the distant island of Ork, perhaps? What did he know of Ork? He knew, in a word, nothing.

Scattering rain was falling on the tent. Through the tent fly, Togura could see the legs of a soldier standing guard outside. The soldier was singing softly to himself; he swayed from time to time, giving Togura the impression he was drunk. Togura was hungry. And thirsty. He could have done with something to eat. Even, at a pinch, a bit of salt beef. As time went by, he started to get quite nostalgic about salt beef. He stuck his head out of the tent fly.

'Hey,' he said. 'I have to—'

He ducked back inside swiftly, as the guard tried to clout him with the butt of a spear. Well, so much for that. Now what? With a bit of stick, Togura dug a little hole that he could piss in and bog in. Digging, he found a worm, which he ate. A little water dripping through a hole in the roof of the tent allowed him to moisten his mouth.

Now what?

Now nothing.

Togura waited, while rain washed the day away. When it was dark, he saw a fire burning outside; half a dozen soldiers were sitting round the fire, talking. This was enough to make him forget all thoughts of escaping. He was tired; he wanted to sleep. He laid himself down on the dirt, and, by now inured to the cold and the damp, he slept.

Togura had odd dreams, in which thunder brangled with earthquake. When he woke, the night was just about to capitulate to the dawn; the ground underfoot was shaking, and a dull, thunderous roar dominated the background. What on earth was going on?

His mouth was dry. He was parched, and more hungry than ever. He was most relieved when a surly soldier entered the tent and handed him a bowl of mash made from bran, turnips and water. He was used to such a lean diet by now that it quite satisfied his hunger; it also helped slake his thirst, though he could have done with a proper drink. He would also have preferred the mash to have been hot rather than cold.

Much, much later, the soldier returned and ordered him to his feet with a gesture. Then, with another gesture, ordered him to follow. More tents had gone up all around, cutting off the view in all directions. Togura, longing to satisfy his curiosity, was irritated. What he wanted most of all was to find someone who spoke Galish.

'Draven?' said Togura.

The soldier ignored his query, perhaps not understanding it. He pushed Togura into a tent which was filled with the smells of food, of drink, of pipe smoke, of opium. Half a dozen men were inside, singing, making a terrible drunken charivari. Razorblade laughter broke out as he entered. One man pinched his cheeks, one pawed his buttocks. One kissed him, then pushed him to another, who grabbed him, and rammed his own finger into Togura's mouth. Togura, shocked, disgusted, frightened, felt sick. He did not dare to bite. He was released, and shoved into the centre of the tent. Commanded by a gesture, he sat.

The men started to roll dice. Their noise died down; gambling made them serious. Togura, appalled, suspected that he was going to lose his virginity – but not in the way he had intended. He knew that he should have tried to escape in the forest. Or should have tried to escape the night before. He swore to himself that he would take his very next chance of escape. But by that time—

One of the men giggled.

The world wavered.

'Sharskar?' asked Togura.

He did not understand himself.

'Day?' he said, seeing Day Suet in front of him.

She took him in her arms and kissed him.

'Oh, Day,' he said. 'Oh help me.'

He breathed in. The air tasted of marzipan. Day Suet disappeared. Togura shivered, and rubbed his eyes.

What had happened?

In the tent, there was a dead man at his feet. He had been knifed. Two men broke off fighting; they had been trying to strangle each other. One was sitting in a daze; another was vomiting. One was screaming: and no wonder, for he had just clawed his eyes out.

'What's happening?' screamed Togura, in a mixture of terror and frustration.

He blundered to the door of the tent, and exited. One of the men pursued him, and grabbed him. Then the outline of the world stumbled. The sun became five suns, which blinked green then purple. The clouds rolled across the sky with terrifying speeds, shaping themselves into the form of a dragon.

Then the world snapped back into its usual focus. Togura found himself sitting in the mud. He got up and staggered off. A soldier pursued him. Togura turned and smashed him in the face with a bunch of fives, cutting his knuckles against teeth. The soldier went down.

Through a gap between two tents, Togura saw a riderless horse, fully equipped with saddle, harness and saddle bags. He sprinted for the horse, mounted up, and was off in an instant. Taking the line of least resistance, he rode hell for leather, seeking to get out and away as fast as possible.

When the horse, lathered and exhausted, refused to gallop any further, Togura started to calm down. Looking around, he realised his flight had taken him south of the army, the castle and the ruins of the town. Near at hand was a battered, badly maintained stone-paved highway, which must surely be the Salt Road if it was anything at all.

Looming Forest lay to the north. That way was home, shelter, safety. But an entire army lay between him and the forest.

'South, then,' muttered Togura.

He was still very badly frightened. He could not, for the life of him, work out what had happened back there. Why had he imagined that he had seen Day Suet? Why had a man gouged out his own eyes? Why had he seen those terrifying hallucinations — five suns in the sky, and the clouds breeding themselves into a dragon? How had the horse lost its rider?

'Get out,' said Togura. 'While you're still alive.'

It was good advice. He took it.

The horse, urged by his knees, advanced down the Salt Road at a steady trot, thus advancing Togura on what, obviously, was going to be a new adventure.

'A pox on adventures,' said Togura. 'A pox on all the world.'

He said it, and meant it.

Later, he realised it was getting dark. And, moreover, he realised that the mountain on the left-hand side of the road, which had been getting nearer and nearer all the time, was, in all probability, the mountain of Maf, where the dragon Zenphos had his lair.

'A pox on dragons, too,' said Togura.

He spoke bravely, but was very much afraid, for Zenphos was a true dragon, strong, ferocious, air-worthy and ravenous in appetite. While sea dragons were virtually harmless if handled properly, a true dragon like Zenphos was the stuff that nightmares were made of; even the wizard of Drum acknowledged as much.

It was going to be, obviously, an uncomfortable night.

CHAPTER 25

The dragon Zenphos, lord of the mountain of Maf, made no move against Togura Poulaan. This was scarcely surprising, as the said dragon was dead and rotting, having been killed at the end of winter. Togura, nevertheless, went in fear of it, for he had no way to know of its demise.

As Togura made his days down the Salt Road, Maf, guarding the road behind him, was demoted from mountain to hill, then to a wart; as the flesh of his horse grew thinner, a range of mountains steadily escalated the southern horizon. Behind him, Maf was whittled away to nothing.

Another day brought another evening. Togura hobbled the horse and rummaged some food from a saddle bag – some hard yellow cheese and some pemmican. Many leagues north, he had thrown away some appalling, stinking stuff which reminded him of rotten milk; now, with his rations bottoming out to nothing, he was beginning to regret his fastidiousness.

Togura chose the tree he was going to sleep under, and named it home. The name failed to convince him. As the last sunlight was fawning on the horizon, he kindled a fire with another man's tinder box, part of the loot from the saddle bags. The horizons swallowed the last reminders of the sun.

'Firelight, burning bright, keep the sun alight tonight,' chanted Togura.

The little incantation was an old, old children's rhyme from Sung, his true home and homeland. Togura fell asleep by the fire, and dreamt of children's songs, of children's jokes, and of a voice which might, perhaps, have been the voice of his mother.

When he woke, it was still dark. What had roused him from his sleep? There was a contingent of horsemen on the road, going south. They were passing by so close to where he lay that he could almost have reached out and touched them. He heard the clotter-clopper of iron-shod hooves, the painful wheezing of a rider with asthma or bronchitis, the fluid-filled cough of a man who then hawked loudly and spat, and a strange scraping sound which he could not identify. He saw the silhouettes of men, of horses, of lances.

One, riding past Togura, suddenly called out. With a certain amount of noise and cursing, the whole convoy reined in and halted. Togura smelt men, many days unwashed, and horses. Could they smell him? They would smell his fire! It was long dead, but there had been no rain to kill the lingering odours of ash and smoke. Togura, not daring to move, stared at the shroud-dark outline of the man who had called the convoy to a halt.

The man jumped down from his horse. His boots slurred over the ground. He was walking shuffle-foot, sliding his feet from step to step so he would get warning of a hole or a ditch. He found the remains of the fire, the cold ash mortuary, and kicked it apart. A scattering of ashes sifted through the night. Togura lay rigid, as silent as his bones.

The man spoke in his foreign language, then took another step forward. He trod on Togura's hair. Then, finding Togura's head with his boot, he kicked it experimentally. Then cried out aloud, for, concentrating on what was under his feet, he had walked into a spiked branch. Swearing to himself, he backed off.

From the head of the convoy came an imperative shout. Togura's unwitting assailant mounted up, and the convoy moved on. The last of the horses was dragging a burden of some kind which scraped over the road. Togura guessed that it was a sledge, possibly heavily loaded. He got to his hands and knees, momentarily considering pursuing the sledge and trying to scuffle off some equipment, then thought better of it.

The sky slowly lightened to sunrise. Togura hunted the bogland round about for his hobbled horse, and found it grazing by a lochan a hundred paces from the road. If it had neighed when the convoy had been passing, the men would probably have mounted a search for it. He had been fearfully lucky.

Togura was just about to lead the horse back to the road when he heard the sound of hoofbeats coming from the south. Leaving the horse down by the water's edge, he gained a small rise and watched the road. Four cavalrymen were riding north along the Salt Road at a steady trot.

As they went past, Togura came to a decision. He would abandon the road. He did not want to chance another meeting with soldiers who might celebrate his physical beauty – such as it was – by raping him, or who might kill him out of hand as a horse thief. Ignoring the road, which ran due south, he would make for the south-east, and find his own path across the mountains.

Togura had a vague idea that Selzirk, capital of the Harvest Plains, was somewhere to the south-east. He had made so much southing already that he was sure he must be nearly there; it was probably just over the mountains up ahead. Selzirk was said to be a civilised place; once there, he should be able to find his way to the port of Androlmarphos, and seek a passage to Sung.

With such optimistic thoughts in mind, Togura set off overland, making for the south-east. Unfortunately, his geography was faulty, to say the least. He had yet to realise the true size of the world. Having come so far, with so many dangers and hardships, he felt as if he had travelled almost to the end of eternity, whereas, in point of fact, he had scarcely left his local neighbourhood.

Selzirk was still far, far to the south, several horizons away. The range he was approaching was the Ironband Mountains; crossing it, he would find himself in the Lezconcarnau Plains, a wild tract of backwater country inhabited by wild backwater people.

Once, on his journey to the Ironband Mountains, Togura seriously considered crosssing another range which he could see lying due east. Fortunately, he decided against such an adventure; that range was the Spine Mountains, and any crossing of them would have taken him into the hostile interior of the continent of Argan, where his survival would have been problematical.

When Togura began his climb, he soon found that it was going to be almost impossible to cross the mountains with a horse. Simultaneously, he exhausted his rations. That left him with two problems. With one masterstroke, he solved both of them: he murdered the horse. He ate some of the meat then and there, glutting himself on big, barbecued steaks with plenty of blood in them. He camped for five days, eating well; then, labouring uphill under the weight of a saddlebag crammed with smoked horse meat, he headed deeper into the mountains.

He looked forward, with some pleasure, to the thought of a warm bed and a warm ale once he reached the fabled city of Selzirk, pride of the Harvest Plains.

CHAPTER 26

Faced by the daily challenges posed by this wilderness of mountains, Togura was not dismayed. He liked to climb; he had no fear of heights; he welcomed the difficulties posed by his chosen route, for every difficulty diminished the chance of an unpleasant encounter with other human beings.

The views afforded by altitude, which grew daily more extensive, were proof of his accomplishments. At the end of each day, with more and more of the world at his feet, he was able to congratulate himself on an undeniable achievement. Having survived all kinds of terror, he was convinced that the worst was over. His living nightmares were over. He was free. He was full of confidence. He was happy.

He drank fresh, clear water from tumbling mountain streams. At night, he built huge, raging fires; roaring with exuberant delight, he danced beside these shameless beacons, rousing distant echoes with raucous drinking songs. He had nothing to drink but water; it was unmitigated freedom which made him feel drunk.

He woke early, always filled with eagerness for the day ahead. Every day brought him new challenges, new delights. Wild mountain flowers, the like of which he had never seen before, as few flowers grew in Sung. Elegant rock crystals, some sunlight white, others delicately tinged with violet. The sight of mountain hawks and eagles, sliding effortlessly through the air as they hunted the echoing skies.

In bad weather, his journey could have been a dreary saga of suffering and torment. But chance favoured him. The sky, a perfect ascension of blue, breathed fair winds only; the sun, miraculous, constant luminary, lazed from the eastern quadrant of the sky to the west, bright as a promise of perfection.

Togura, shaking off a certain world weariness which sometimes afflicts the very young, indulged himself, daring his life on difficult climbs when an easy ridge would have allowed him a more sober ascent, then — sometimes with a memory of rotten rock rattling away to disaster beneath him — celebrating his triumph with a shout:

'Three cheers for Togura!'

Free from the irrational conflicts of human affairs, he forgot all about the superstitious notions which had formerly begun to take possession of him. In the mountains, he trusted to his own balance, timing, judgment and strength. His universe yielded to his mastery. The nights, lit by his carefree fires, held no terror for him. He saw nothing which made him afraid, even though he once exchanged discourtesies with a wild-cat at close range.

Possessed by the unmitigated sanity of the mountains, Togura rapidly began to doubt the reality of many of his own memories. Had he really fought against his half-brother Cromarty, matching blade against blade? Had he really seen torture, death and revolution in a ruined city in the swamps of Sung? Had he really met a man in D'Waith who had the head and horns of a bull? He could not credit any of it.

Indeed, he thought all of human history increasingly improbable. Possessed of the perfection of his own health, joy and freedom, he could no longer believe in the incestuous rages, the narrow hatreds, the jealous lusts, the uncouth slanders and the muddy, scuffling wars which constituted the annals of human enterprise.

'I declare a Golden Age,' said Togura, greeting yet another dew-bright sunrise. 'We are born perfect to a perfect world, therefore perfection is our nature, truth and destiny.'

The sanity of the mountains had made him, within the terms of the world he had escaped from, quite mad.

Togura the Prophet, bearer of an uncommonly optimistic Revelation, gained the uppermost heights of the Ironband Mountains. It was noon, on a clear, bright day, with the sun at its zenith and somewhat to the south; despite the sunlight, it was cold, for at this height there still remained patches of snow and slush, the last debris of winter. Togura surveyed the view, and gave himself three cheers − one for initiative, one for effort and one for success.

Then, in a moment of arrogance quite contrary to the tenor of his Revelation, he declared:

'I, Togura Poulaan, lord of all I survey, name this summit Mount Togura. I name these uplands the Togura Heights, claiming all for me and mine for all eternity.'

Having thus annexed his territory, he then had the problem of whether to call himself baron, earl, duke, prince, king or emperor.

'Lord Emperor Togura,' he said, announcing his choice aloud. 'Master of All the Mountains, their Surrounds and Surrounding Oceans.'

That had a nice ring to it. He celebrated his bloodless imperial conquest by eating a little smoked horsemeat, chewing it slowly while he admired the view. At his rear, to the north, lay the lowlands of Estar. On his right, to the west, in the distance, the Central Ocean. On his left, more mountains. And to the south? Ahead of him, to the south, there were lowlands of some kind. The Harvest Plains, he hoped.

As Togura gazed down at the southern lowlands, which were in fact the Lezconcarnau Plains, the wind started to get up. It was cold; shivering, he started downhill. By late afternoon, the sky had clouded over; by evening, a grey, persistent drizzle was dampening down his spirits. Nevertheless, he was not despondent. He found a scratch of a cave which would give him a dry night, and, with the competence of a seasoned traveller, lit a fire, and made a brilliant blood-warming blaze from damp wood.

The next few days were difficult.

Going was very slow. The southern side of the mountain range proved to be steep, dangerous and heavily wooded.

Where he could, he followed wandering animals tracks through the trees, as the undergrowth, surfeited with nettles and brambles, proved uncommonly inhospitable. Once he sighted a wild pig, a monstrous wild-haired razorback boar; prudently, he climbed a tree. Finding a rotten log which had been torn open, apparently by heavy-duty claws, he suspected the presence of bear. He found deer tracks, and then paw marks like those of a wild-cat, only much larger.

Though this should by rights have been the sunnier side of the range, the heavy vegetation made it cold, dank and shadowed. Often, stooping down a deer track with crowding branches overhead, he would go for half a day through unbroken twilight. Then the trees would end with a burst of sunlight, revealing the gash of a gorge, the looming depths of a massive sink hole, or a sheer cliff plummeting down to bone-breaking rocks.

Running into such obstacles, Togura had to sidetrack and backtrack. Every day gave him at least five good reasons for sticking to the Salt Road. Still, he was here, now – he had to find a way to the south, or starve. He cut his rations down to almost nothing, and persisted.

Finally, to his delight, he found a small river with a track running alongside it. The track was overgrown, as if nobody had come this way for a season or so, but, with the help of a stout stick with which he could beat down the more unruly outcrops of nettles, he could follow it. He did so, for the river ran south.

Early on the second day downriver, he rounded a riverbend, eager to get a clear view of a massive red brick edifice which he had glimpsed through the trees. He was rewarded by the sight of the river running downstream for half a league or so until it disappeared into a gap in one wall of a castle.

The castle, a massive pentagon of red brick, many times taller than the surrounding trees, was surmounted by a pyramid, also built of red brick. There was no sight or sign of any gate or door; only slit windows pierced the brickwork. Togura gawked at it – then realised he could be seen from those slit windows.

He ducked down out of sight behind some shrubbery, but, after a moment, rose to his feet again. The surrounds were so overgrown that the castle could scarcely be inhabited. He had seen no huntsmen or herdsmen, no farms or fields, no charcoal burners, no woodcutter clearings, no beggars or wandering lunatics; he had seen no roads and no woodsmoke, and no paths barring the single overgrown rivertrail he was following; the area was, as far as he could tell, a deserted wilderness.

Boldly, Togura set off down the riverpath. He was half way to the castle when an arrow thunked into a tree just beside his head. Togura had scarcely had time to react when half a dozen men downriver broke cover. They were a bunch of hairy individuals with bows, spears and wildskin clothes. As they shouted at him, he turned and fled. They pursued, gaining on him easily. Their laughter came scarpering after him.

Another arrow slammed into a spindly tree-trunk just in front of him. Togura dropped his baggage, but still they gained on him. Whooping ferociously, they closed in for what sounded very much like the kill. Despairing of escape uphill, Togura jumped into the river. It was cold, swift and deep. It swept him away toward the castle.

Floating in the water, Togura saw his pursuers turn and start to trudge down the riverpath. They seemed in no hurry. He wondered why. Looking downriver, he saw the castle was much, much closer. Its walls blocked up the sky ahead of him. Suddenly he did not like the look of the gaping black hole in the castle wall which was swallowing the river. It looked cold, dangerous and nasty.

Togura struck out for the riverbank. But the current was too strong for him. Momentarily, he gained a hold on a slimy rock near the water's edge. Then the current plucked him away and channelled him into the darkness. The daylight rapidly slid away from him. Hearing a thunderous water-rumble up ahead, he guessed that there was a weir or waterfall waiting for him. Desperately, he struck out for the bank, fearing that it would be a wall of sheer rock.

His fears had no foundation. He found the bank, which was low, was made of something spongy which tore, broke and crumbled as he kicked and clawed, fighting free from the water. Once on the bank, cold, shivering and dripping wet, he tore away another handful of the spongy substance underfoot and held it up to the light. The diminished illumination showed him something looking grey, unpleasant and unhealthy; he dropped it.

Togura did not know it, but he was standing on a vast, lethal, carnivorous fungus. By now he had kicked several holes in it, and had torn away chunks of its substance. Usually, it did not take kindly to such cavalier treatment; in the usual course of events, it would have eaten away his legs by now, and would have just been making a start on his testicles. However, this was one of its rare periods of dormancy, which lasted for twelve days and occurred once in every three hundred and thirty-three years. So, for the moment, he was safe.

Walking upstream, Togura was met by a solid wall running flush with the river. Going downstream, he met the same. He realised he was standing on a kind of landing bay. There was no path by the river. He could trust himself to the water, which thrashed into thunder in the darkness ahead, but he suspected that that would be suicide − or at least a severe form of masochism. The alternative was to see if there was a tunnel, stairway, chimney or sump leading away from the landing bay.

Togura wandered about in the dark, bumping into things, swearing, shouting to test the echoes, and falling into holes. One of the larger holes dropped him down so sharply that he almost broke his leg. He got off with a sprained ankle. Hobbling about, swearing more viciously than ever, he found, at last, a stairway, which he climbed.

The stairway led into a maze of passages dimly lit by strips of green illumination running along the ceilings − a kind of lighting unlike anything Togura had ever seen before. The passageways, which were hazy with spiderwebs, were thick with dust and littered with junk − shards of pottery, empty stone jars, petrified bones, snail shells, drifts of ironsand, broken glass of truly amazing quality, containers of a light and fragile metal which did not seem to rust, buttons and other oddments.

At regular intervals, the floor was punctured by bright sunlight streaming in through slit windows. Peering out through one of these windows, Togura found himself looking to the south; the river exited from the castle below him. Two men on the bank were patiently watching the river. Much wandering later, he found himself able to get a view to the north. The view here was graced by the presence of a man squatting by a riverside fire, apparently roasting something on a spit.

Togura was – this did not surprise him, for he was used to being in this situation – both hungry and thirsty. He was not yet seriously worried. However, after having lost himself and found himself several times, he realised that he was going round in circles. His clothes were still damp, his boots were still sodden, and he was getting very tired from walking on the hard, unyielding floor.

'It'll take a miracle to get out of here,' said Togura, in one of the moments of despair which he had thought he had outgrown.

A miracle – or magic.

Of course! Why not try magic? There was nothing to say that wizards had built this place, but, on the other hand, there was nothing to say that they hadn't. Togura promptly tried some of the tricks which the wizard of Drum had taught him, in defiance of all the laws, rules and regulations of the Confederation of Wizards. He tried a Word of Opening, a Word of Closing, then three or four Words which were supposed to do something, though he could not for the life of him remember what.

Nothing happened.

The brick remained brick, the dust remained dust, the glass remained glass, the bones remained bones. In frustration, Togura shouted aloud a Word of Ultimate Destruction, which he had been warned never ever to use except in the direst emergencies. Again, nothing happened. If wizards had left any power in this place, he had failed to find the right Words to activate that power.

What else could he try?

'Onamonagonamonth!' chanted Togura.

It was a Word of Location.

It worked!

In the distance, a ringing note, like that from a bell, sounded loud and clear, then died away to nothing. An artefact of power lay in that direction. Togura took a few paces, then spoke his Word of Location again. The bell-bright note ignited once again. In this manner, he led himself through the maze, reaching, at last, a big, high-vaulted hall where the ringing note was almost overwhelming.

'It's here,' muttered Togura, as the note once more died away.

But where?

The hall was cluttered with the most appalling jumble of antiquated lumber, spinning wheels, mirrors of startling brightness, decayed paintings, broken tiles, weapon racks, body armour, spokeless wheels of a black substance which was hard yet flexible, and assorted lumps of rust which perhaps had once been something functional, together with old leather-bound books in indecipherable scripts, stone tablets, graven images of bronze and jade, coins made of lead and bits of seamless lightweight piping.

'Onamonagonamonth!' cried Togura.

The ringing note almost deafened him. As far as he could tell, it seemed to come from one particular corner. As the sound died away, he waded toward it, barking his shins on an ironbound chest, which served to diminish his enthusiasm. He cautioned himself not to get over-excited. When he found the whatever-it-was, he might find it incomprehensible. Or useless. It might be a wizard-made device for skinning onions by enchantment, a magic funnel for desalinating the sea, a novel weapon specifically designed for killing dragons, or any other of a thousand million unhelpful devices.

Once he reached the corner, he rummaged through various kinds of junk — more rocks, more bones, a crown made of a heavy metal which was possibly gold, a box decorated with a design of a heart and a hand, a couple of dirty stone jars, a feather cloak which fell to pieces when he picked it up, a lump of rock-heavy swamp kauri and a ship in a bottle.

The only thing which looked like it might be magic was the ship in the bottle, for it was a thing which was, on the face of it, an impossibility. Togura hated to break a piece of glass so large, so finely wrought and so rare, but, yielding to necessity, he smashed the bottle. Then, for good measure, dismantled the ship. Finding nothing. He ran through his Words again. There was only one he had failed to use, so now he used it on principle:

'Sholabarakosh!'

There was a sharp click.

And, in the dust, something moved.

CHAPTER 27

What had moved?

As far as Togura could see, nothing had changed.

Then he noticed that the casket bearing the design of a heart and a hand was ajar. For some reason, the decorations on the lid of the box seemed familiar. Of course! Now he remembered! Long ago, in the Wordsmiths' stronghold in Keep, Brother Troop had sketched that identical design for him. Later, the wizard of Drum had drawn the same. At his feet was the box which held the index!

Or so he hoped.

Togura stooped to secure the box. As he lifted the casket, the lid snapped shut. He could not pry it loose by any exercise of brute force.

'Sholabarakosh!' said Togura.

Raising the lid, he saw within a very curious device, which he removed, discarding the box. This device was, he presumed, the index which he had been questing for – on and off, with varying degrees of resolve – for so long.

It looked rather like three miniature harps stuck together, each harp string ending in a pearl-white button. The three layers of buttons, corresponding to the three layers of strings, were stepped, so they did not obscure each other. There were also a dozen multicoloured buttons which were not attached to any strings.

Cautiously, Togura plucked a harp string with one of his

black-rimmed broken fingernails. It did not respond. Then he touched one of the buttons. A pure, clear note, sweeter than birdsong, sounded through the hall. Other buttons raised other notes, some low, some high. Togura was at first entranced, then disappointed. This could hardly be the index, for it did not speak. It was no more than a musical plaything from the days of antiquity – charming, but ultimately useless.

He tossed it aside.

Then sat down in the dust, feeling despondent.

He must have been crazy to think that he had found the index. The index, as he knew full well, was at the bottom of a bottle guarded by a monster in Castle Vaunting, at Lorford, now many leagues to the north. So it could hardly be here. There was, after all, only one index.

Or was there?

Togura tried to remember precisely what he had been told about the index, but it was difficult. He lacked the scholarly impulse; if he was honest with himself, he would have to admit that he had never given his full attention either to Brother Troop of the Wordsmiths or to the wizard of Drum. His chaotic lifestyle, full of death, horror, disaster and sundry shocks to the system – sea serpents! walking rocks! – had not improved matters. It was hard to spare much thought for scholarly revision when one was starving to the bone in a foreign land, or being hunted through the wilds by assorted rapists and butchers.

Nevertheless, after some concentrated thought, Togura did manage to remember something of the lectures he had endured. The wizard of Drum, Hostaja Torsen Sken-Pitilkin, had talked about the index in connection with the Old City of Penvash. Or was that the odex he had been talking about? Brother Troop had mentioned that there might be another index in Chi'ash-lan – or was it Galsh Ebrek? There had been some mention of other places, too. Androlmarphos? No. But some place in the south.

'Let's be honest,' said Togura, speaking aloud. 'To tell the truth, I've forgotten.'

His voice sounded so forlorn and lonely in that old, dusty

hall that he wished he had not spoken. He gave the musical instrument a little kick. He was tempted to break it, but his mercantile instincts restrained him. In context, the triple-harp was a useless piece of junk, but in a cultured city like Selzirk it might well be worth a fortune. Togura put the triple-harp back in its casket. Harp and box were light and easy to carry.

'On your way, Togura Poulaan,' said Togura.

He left the hall by way of a high, arched doorway. The floor beneath was paved, not by bricks but by huge slabs of stone.

'Curious,' said Togura.

He advanced boldly down the passageway, then stopped when one of the huge slabs of stone seemed to shift underfoot.

'Curiouser still,' said Togura, sweating a little.

Cautiously, he started to retreat back the way he had come. But he had taken only two steps when the stone slab pivoted, flipped, and precipitated him into the darkness below. Screaming, Togura fell through the darkness toward a roar of thunder.

206

CHAPTER 28

Togura Poulaan, alive and still kicking, floated into the sunlight on the southern side of the castle. He dragged himself ashore and collapsed at someone's feet. Someone's boot nudged him, so he raised himself to a sitting position and looked around.

A fierce young man in wildskin clothes was standing over him. Another man similarly dressed was wading in the river in pursuit of something bobbing away downstream.

'Togura,' said Togura, pointing at himself.

'Kogo,' said the stranger, slapping his heart.

'Do you speak Galish, Kogo?' asked Togura.

Kogo didn't.

Kogo's friend came wading out of the river, bearing his trophy, which was the casket which could only be unlocked by a Word. Togura, after plunging through darkness into the river, had forgotten all about it.

'Togura,' said Togura, slapping his heart – he was learning fast.

'Satari,' said the stranger, introducing himself. 'Seki Natabari Satari.'

'Do you speak Galish?'

Satari didn't.

'Another dormant bunch of ignorant savages,' said Togura, who felt that life would be a lot simpler if everyone had the decency to learn some Galish.

Satari, failing to open the enchanted casket he had retrieved from the river, passed it to Kogo, who tried to pry it open with a knife, then passed it to Togura.

'Sholabarakosh,' said Togura, eager to appease these strangers who, he strongly suspected, regarded themselves as his captors.

The casket opened. He took out the triple-harp, played a few notes to demonstrate its use, then offered it to the two men. They laughed uproariously, and, with air-slapping gestures, declined.

'I'm not a trained musician,' said Togura, offended, thinking they mocked his failure to produce a melody.

Still, he was glad that they made it clear he was to keep the triple-harp. He was still thinking of the money it would bring in Selzirk. One of the men scouted away, and before long returned with the rest of the savages. The savages now totalled up to six. The newcomers insisted on hearing Togura play the triple-harp, which he did, provoking copious laughter.

'I still don't see what's funny,' said Togura. 'I can't be that bad.'

The language barrier prevented anyone from enlightening him. For as long as he could remember, he had known that Galish was spoken everywhere, by everyone; it was the universal trading language, the lingua franca of all the world. He had done a lot of unlearning since then.

'When I get back to Sung,' said Togura, 'I'll teach them a thing or two.'

His optimism surprised him. But then, the savages, with their easy laughter, seemed friendly enough.

There was still plenty of daylight, but the savages were in no hurry to go anywhere. They camped by the castle that night; Togura, gaining confidence with the triple-harp, played to them by firelight. The next day, slowed by Togura's sprained ankle, they tramped downriver; toward evening, they reached a larger encampment on the edge of rough, rolling lowlands. At this larger camp, there were horses.

As there were no women and children, Togura guessed that the savages were still a long way from home. Without surprise, he found himself put to work gathering firewood, gutting fish, skinning animals, stretching hides to dry, gathering particular types of bark for a use which could not be explained to him, and cooking food. He was also called upon to play music every evening, and to cut hair. He doubted his own competence as a barber, but nobody objected to the rough and ready hairshaves he managed with a sharpened knife; nobody even laughed.

After a number of days — it could have been as many as twenty, though he could not say, for he soon lost count — they broke camp and moved south on horseback with loads of meat and skins.

Riding south, the savages became tense. They travelled with scouts ahead and a rearguard behind, posted sentries at night and kept their weapons at the ready. Twice they encountered the tracks of other riders, which occasioned excited, animated discussion, and led to increased vigilance. Togura did not have to be psychic to realise that they were riding through enemy territory.

At last they saw a stockade ahead, and, raising whoops and cheers, they charged. Togura at first thought he had been caught up in an episode of tribal warfare, but the gates of the stockade swung open, the citizens within greeted them rapturously, and he realised that this, for the savages, was home.

Very shortly, as he became acquainted with that home, he began to realise the big mistake he had made — and the nature of his present predicament.

CHAPTER 29

The village, though it was out on the open plains, was a crowded, noisy, smelly place. Lean yellow mongrel curs scavenged, fought and mated in the mud-paved alleyways between the mud-walled huts. Chickens, voicing a persistent chok-chok-chok, strutted about underfoot, their heads bobbing forwards as they walked. Cats and rats played games of pursuit and evasion by day and by night.

Worst were the children. Togura, coming from a remarkably small family, had never had much to do with them. Here they were in abundance. They were everywhere. They screamed, squabbled, shouted, chased the chickens, harassed the cats, made excavations in the mud walls, scratched obscene drawings on the ground, played with dung, pulled each other's hair, stole food, told lies, committed acts of arson, and experimented, with no sense of shame whatsoever, in gang warfare, sex and torture.

By day, the place was largely left to the women, the children and the old people. The men kept to the open plains, hunting, racing horses, and tending the horse herds which were the wealth of the village. Some of the men stayed out for days at a time, guarding the herds or riding their territory on long, military-style patrols, but most retired to the village in the evening, gathering in the village meeting hall to eat, drink, tell jokes, wrist wrestle, throw food at each other, experiment with strange drugs, show off their jewellery — which was only worn indoors – or boast about their weapons and their kills.

Togura slept in a small, windowless annexe to the meeting hall, and nightly attended these gatherings. Nevertheless, he had no place in the society of men. His place was with the women, and the triple-harp, an instrument now hateful to him, was the cause of his exile from masculine affairs.

In Sung, the making of music was stout, hearty, heroic work. At feasts and banquets, sweating, beer-swilling men belaboured the krymbol or blew on the kloo; ancient warriors, bearing the scars from many honourable feuds, tortured the air with the skavamareen; battle stalwarts with walnut-crunching fingers manhandled the thrums. Music making, like drinking, fighting, gambling and rampant fornication, was one of the marks of manhood.

In the land of the savages, however, the status of music was reversed. The younger, thinner women with the least status were tasked with the job of music making. They rattled husky gourds, blew on plaintive bone flutes, beat horsehide drums with little whips, provided a supplementary background rhythm by shaking clickety-clackety multi-jointed sticks, hit racks of little bells with human thigh bones, and sang wailing little songs. Togura, with his triple-harp, fitted in as best he could; his first beating had persuaded him it was best to show willing, and his second had convinced him he must succeed or die.

The evening entertainment ran right through the month except on the night of the full moon, when the men – exclusive of Togura – barred the hall against all comers and did something within which involved a lot of shouting, stamping and chorus singing, and the occasional scream. On all other nights, Togura sat with the women, making music. He was always seated directly behind the headman, a lean, alcoholic old gentleman with a wart raising its monticulus in the middle of his bad pate; Togura grew very familiar with that wart. He was less familiar with the headman's face, which he saw less often, and which always came as a shock to him. The headman had a hare lip, one good eye and a deeply-seamed inflamed red scar channelling into his face where his left eye should have been.

During the day, Togura was not left in peace to practise with his triple-harp. Instead, he was put to work with the women. Those of the highest status were, in this village, tall, wide and hearty. And immensely strong. If he displeased them, they slapped him about with hands which could have killed an ox by accident; he was terrified of them.

All the women felt free to express their contempt for him, but for one alone. She was plainer than some, but slimmer than most. She was a little thick in the waist all the same, and a little square-shouldered, but she was still, in his opinion, the most womanly woman of them all. Her name was Namaji. She was a little bit prissy and very, very vain.

Togura courted Namaji as best he could, though he had to be careful. If the other women caught Namaji exchanging endearments with Togura, then both the young lovers would get slapped about severely. There was precious little privacy in the village. Togura was sure he could have got himself laid if there had been any long grass to lie in, but there wasn't. He was still a virgin.

He was also an overworked virgin. A woman's work is never done, and Togura now had a share − and more than a fair share, in his opinion − of that unending labour. Could he escape? No. Given a chance to venture the open plains on horseback, he might have tried to break away. But he only got beyond the village walls when he was compelled to go to the nearest stream to draw water, or to spend an afternoon at the horse corral, milking the mares in the company of stalwart amazons who would have killed him without blinking if he had tried to steal a horse.

The sun whiled away the last of the spring and began on the summer. Togura grew desperate.

− These are my golden years. I have my life to lead. I can't stay here!

He didn't have much choice. Those horses used for riding and for the village milk supply were corralled at night under guard; sentries watched from the village walls; foot patrols roamed through the darkness, checking and double-checking; dogs barked at strangers in the night.

So he stayed.

Really, he should have counted his blessings. He should have been happy. He was integrated into a closely-knit society living a properly balanced life in harmony with the local ecology and the surrounding environment. It was one of those traditional societies where, or so we are told, servitude is painless because a rigid hierarchical structure leaves people with no choices. The village had its own rich, unique culture, complete with song, dance, music, myth and legend.

The people deployed efficient population control, without recourse to unnatural practices such as chastity or abortion, by a simple and healthy expedient – they strangled unwanted infants and ate them. They practised warfare, of course, but mostly by way of sport and ritual. War helped release unhealthy aggressions, and helped bind the community together, particularly on those festive occasions when they had prisoners they could torture to death.

It could be said that they had no concept of land ownership; unlike the greedy, depraved peoples of other civilisations, they did not build fences, dykes, ditches or walls to mark off little fields and gardens as 'mine' and 'yours'. Instead, they had a healthy, spiritual attitude toward the land, which they regarded as a communal heritage; they celebrated this healthy, spiritual attitude by butchering anyone caught trespassing on their territory, and by making such incompetent trespassers the main course at cannibal feasts.

The children, products of a largely peer-based education system, grew up without any unhealthy neuroses; they did not repress their basic urges, but delighted in expressing a full and frank physical and emotional response to their natural and cultural environment.

In contrast to the rich, complex tapestry of village culture, the daily life of Sung could be seen as what it was: a thin, distorted parody of what life could be and should be. The economy of Sung, heavily dependent on mining and organised trade, was not properly integrated with the local ecology; the people of Sung, their lives perverted by mercantile greed, did not have a spiritual attitude toward land and the environment.

213

Togura, as one of the unhealthy products of what is known in some quarters as 'civilisation', should have welcomed the opportunity to immerse himself in the multi-faceted, communal and so-called 'primitive' lifestyle. He should have welcomed the opportunity to integrate himself with the natural environment in a timeless, sustainable, communal mode.

But he didn't.

He hated it.

As far as he was concerned, he was living in a stinking hole in the mud in a stinking dungheap village filled with stinking jabbering savages who were making life hell for him.

Namaji was his only comfort.

It was Namaji who started to teach him the native language. Togura found this heavy-going. For a start, he was no linguist. Galish was all he spoke, and Galish was a coarse, brutal creole, its grammar simplified by much use and abuse along the trade routes. The villagers, on the other hand, spoke a subtle, reflexive dialect full of difficult tenses, and using, as part of its daily vocabulary, references to the local religion, which was entirely unknown to him.

One day, under a hot, blazing summer sun, Togura sat streamside with his true love, Namaji, trying to work out whether 'shomana shomo' meant 'blue sky', 'sun at zenith' or 'clear horizon'; his difficulties were due to the fact that the words actually meant 'God (is) manifest', and were said, for good luck, at times when the sky was blue, the sun at zenith and the horizon cloudless.

The stream was running low, slow and sluggish. Namaji and Togura were supposed to be drawing water from it. Nearby, some fierce boy children were playing. They daubed their faces with clay, scratched their wrists with thorns, mingled their blood, then split into teams and went hunting. Shortly, they caught a frog. With much shouting, they broke its legs, one by one. They embedded it in the earth, with only its head showing. Then there was an argument. Togura suspected that one faction wanted to bury their victim alive while the other side wanted to stone it to death.

Namaji nuzzled his neck.

He shivered with pleasure. He wanted her. She was so close, so warm, so yielding.

The boys saw what Namaji was doing. They started to jeer. Then they began to throw things – clods of dried earth, handfuls of water, sharp little stones.

'Stop that!' shouted Togura.

One of the boys hauled the quadriplegic frog out of the earth and threw it slap-bang! into Namaji's face. She began to wail. Togura, to his shame, retreated. What else could he have done? He could think of nothing, short of breaking a few skulls, which would not have endeared him to the parents.

He began to contemplate suicide.

The summer days shortened to autumn. Togura thought of several ways of killing himself, but could not bring himself to take the final step. Planning suicide, in fact, made life easier, for at least it gave him a hobby of sorts.

One autumn afternoon, while helping the women to make felt from horse hair, Togura realised it was now two years since he had left Keep, that friendly, familiar mining town far away in the land of Sung, where, according to his memories, he had been very happy. His beard was stronger now, a hairy little tuft at his chin, which he did not trim.

Winter came, and, for him at least, it was a bitter season. His growing competence with the triple-harp was no consolation. He found out how to use its twelve multicoloured buttons to sustain chords, to raise and lower the volume, to add vibrato, or to generate percussion, woodwind or brasswind effects. But music could not make him a man. It could only make him a more competent woman.

At mid-winter, he got a real shock to his system when he was made to tend the fire in a hut where a woman was in labour. Right from the start, he felt uneasy, feeling he should not be there – but the women, delighting in his embarrassment, forced him to stay. The labour lasted a day and a night. No man visited the woman in question; it was Togura's impression that the men of the village shunned all contact with pregnant women.

The birth itself terrified him. So much pain! So much blood! And the child, when it was born, so ugly! Covered with blood and mucus and something that looked like a layer of white fat, and might well have been. And the mother took that horrible disgusting slime-covered animal to her breast, and smiled as it suckled. And then, when he thought it was all over, something obscene happened. A great lump of the woman's guts followed the baby out of her body! Togura vomited, straight into the fire, there being no other place available; realising the cause of his distress, all the women howled with laughter.

The birth, from their point of view, was a victory.

The female who had given birth was up and about the very next day, apparently none the worse for losing a great big chunk of her guts. But Togura did not get over it for days. Though he was a country boy, he had never done farm work; he had never seen an animal give birth, let alone a human being.

And, while he had always known, vaguely, that a baby grows in its mother's belly, he had never thought about where it comes out, and had never been told. At an early age, his father had instructed him on how a man impregnates a woman; that stage he found intensely interesting, but he had never troubled himself much about what comes afterwards, having no curiosity about the private mysteries of women.

Now that he knew the truth, it quite put him off the thought of sex. For practical purposes, that made no difference one way or the other; however, considering his sensitivities, it was probably just as well that he had not yet had a chance to learn about menstruation, as that might have quite blighted his steadily developing romance with Namaji.

CHAPTER 30

In spring, the men daubed themselves with clay, as had the frog-hunting boys of the previous summer, then rode off to take a slap at someone beyond the horizon. They came back a few days later, some wounded, a couple missing, and one, slung over the back of a horse, most definitely dead. The men had a roistering feast; as part of their celebrations, they honoured their dead comrade by eating him.

As a great concession, even Togura was honoured with a bit of human flesh, which over-roasted, tasted mostly of charcoal. He ate it eagerly, for it gave him at least a momentary association with the world of men, which is the world of swordblade legends and conquering heroes; Togura was living in the world of women, and he hated it.

The human flesh concession was a once-only indulgence. It changed nothing. Togura, in the eyes of the men, was a nominal woman, which made him almost invisible. They might give him a kick if he got in the way, or get rid of a bit of rubbish by throwing it at him, but generally they scarcely seemed aware that he existed, except when they came to have their hair cut. He had no knife, his blades having been confiscated long ago, so the men provided their own. Often he was tempted to cut a throat or two, but never managed to nerve himself to the act.

Togura did not know it, but his readiness to cut hair had lowered his status to about that of a dog. In terms of the local religion, hair, once separated from the body, was regarded as a particularly unpleasant form of dead and death-inducing matter; Togura, as hairdresser, was ritually unclean. He had compounded his uncleanness by stockpiling a great heap of hair in the annexe in which he slept, intending one day to stuff a mattress with it. This stockpile was now the subject of many jokes which were, in their local context, obscene.

Namaji, however, did not mind. Namaji thought Togura was beautiful. Namaji longed for him. Namaji worshipped him. Togura, having outgrown his brief-lived horror of female flesh − he had by now convinced himself that the birth he had seen was a tragic medical freak, and that most babies probably exited to the outside world by way of a woman's navel − was once more being tormented by his unappeased lusts. Given half a chance, he would appease them with Namaji.

That spring, a stranger arrived, bearing a green bough, which was perhaps a sign of peace, for he was admitted, even though he was not of the village. He smelt differently. His hair was elaborately styled, tied into ornate knots in front, plaited into three pigtails behind, in stark contrast to the men of the village, many of whom, thanks to Togura Poulaan's latest contribution to the world of fashion, were wearing their hair shaven close to the skull in front, and wild and woolly behind. The lobes of the stranger's ears were tattooed with blue, black and red, which, for reasons unknown to Togura, made many of the women giggle.

After a day of public palaver, in which the stranger made several speeches which were very well received, the men of the village fêted the stranger in the meeting hall. Togura was there, sitting on a three-legged stool just behind the headman, playing his triple-harp.

It was a wild night. The men got drunk on fermented mare's milk heavily laced with a juice extracted from a special kind of toadstool. This potentially lethal brew was forbidden to women, and to untouchables like Togura, so he could only watch, stone cold sober, while the men got legless to the tune of his music.

At the height of the festivities, when most of the men were

flat on their backs, the visiting stranger suddenly drew a knife and advanced on the headman. Togura at first thought it was a joke. Then a warrior, staggering on uncertain legs, tried to intercept the stranger, and was stabbed with three swift, professional blows. Nobody else was fit to stand.

As the women screamed, Togura picked up his three-legged stool and hurled it at the stranger. It clipped him on the head. Momentarily stunned, he wavered. Togura closed with him. And down they went, fighting for control of the knife. The women started to shout, stamp and applaud.

'Don't just stand there!' yelled Togura. 'Hit him!'

But nobody understood his Galish.

The stranger was a strong, tough, wiry warrior, experienced in battle. But he had drunk a little of the night's brew, so as to appear sociable. Togura had drunk nothing. He, too, was tough, strong and wiry, capable of spending entire days lugging around heavy pots of water, milking mares or making felt. He found a stranglehold, and made good use of it.

Togura, with the stranger dead, stood up.

The stranger started to stir – he was not dead at all. Togura tried to finish him off, but the women restrained him. Since the would-be assassin was not dead, they would have the pleasure of skinning him alive.

The next day, terrible things happened to the captive. In public. He clung stubbornly to life; he was not a pretty sight by the time he died. Togura watched it all, without emotion. He had seen worse. The body lay in state while everyone filed past to give the corpse a good hearty kick, which helped tenderise the meat; Togura gave it the hardest kick of all. The corpse was then demolished; some small boys began a tug of war with the intestines, while the women sizzled chunks of flesh on a barbecue.

'Togura!' said the headman, when the first steaks were cooked.

At first, Togura did not realise he was being addressed, for the headman's hare lip made the name slurred and distorted. Everytime Togura heard the headman speak, he was reminded

219

of Slerma, who also used to have a strange, slurred voice; he still had occasional nightmares about her.

'Togura!' said the headman again.

This time, Togura realised who was being spoken to. He got such a shock that he almost jumped out of his skin. He advanced, with some hesitation. The headman embraced him, then presented him with a prime piece of rump steak. He was flattered. He ate heartily. Excellent! But this was not the end of his reward, for, after several long speeches, all the unmarried women of the village formed a line. The headman thumped Togura on the chest, then indicated the women.

Slowly, he began to understand.

A miraculous future revealed itself.

By triumphing over the assassin, he had saved the headman's life; he had proved himself as a man and a warrior. He was going to be allowed to marry into the tribe. He would have weapons and a horse. Riding off to battle with the other men, he would prove himself as a great war leader. In time, he would become chief, an honoured patriarch revered at home, and feared abroad for his cunning, his sagacity, his reckless violence on the field of battle.

He looked the women over. He could see which ones fancied themselves – those who were tallest and widest. Well, bugger that for a joke! There was no way he was going to get himself hitched to a woman he couldn't beat up if it came to the crunch. There was only one choice for him, and he knew it. He picked Namaji.

Incredulous laughter greeted his choice. The headman laughed until tears of mirth came blubbering down his cheeks. Little boys rolled about on the ground, chortling, kicking their heels as if they were being strangled. Togura dearly wished to have a go at a few of them. Namaji, embarrassed beyond endurance, broke down and cried. Togura comforted her bravely.

Finally the headman recovered himself, and made a short speech which set the people stamping and cheering. Namaji managed a small smile, and Togura knew everything was going to be all right.

The marriage took place the next day. The ceremony started at dawn and ended at sunset. There was a lot of singing, dancing and eating; Togura, for once, took no part in the music-making. During the ceremony, a horse was tortured to death as part of the festivities. Togura couldn't help noticing that it was a rather old horse, which had been lame to start with. He felt slightly insulted by this, feeling that he deserved the best.

At sunset, all the men escorted Togura and Namaji to a hut which had been made ready for them. He found himself trembling as he closed the door on the outside world.

'Namaji.'

'Togura.'

They found each other in the darkness. Togura, his hands shaking, laid rough hands on Namaji. In his haste, he stripped her more swiftly than he should have; he heard a little rip as fabric gave. Urgently, he grappled with her, sliding a hand straight to her privacy, and finding—

Togura screamed.

'No no no no!' he shouted.

Outside the hut, there was a chorus of cruel, knowing laughter. The men were out there. They knew! And what they knew was that his 'she' was a 'he'. Namaji touched Togura with small, gentle, seducing hands. He slapped them away. Namaji wept.

'Togura,' said Namaji, pleading.

'No,' said Togura. 'It's no good. I don't want a make-believe woman. I want the real thing.'

He desperately wanted, needed, lusted for the real thing, so he could rut it under, taking what other men wanted, thus proving his strength, sagacity, wisdom, superiority and manhood. His ego lusted for status as much as his body lusted for flesh.

He opened the door to the night, finding the men without. Gleefully, they bundled him back inside. He slammed the door on them, and swore.

'Togura?' said Namaji, tremulously.

'No!' roared Togura. 'No! Forget it!'

He threw himself down in a corner and lay there, sulking. When Namaji lay down beside him, he did not have the heart to push her away. Nevertheless, he lay there stiffly, rejecting her with his silence. She touched him again.

'Namaji,' said Togura, removing her hand. 'It wouldn't work.'

'Togura?' she said hopefully, not understanding his Galish.

'No,' he said. And then, using the local word: 'Kal.'

Understanding, she began to cry again. And Togura felt ashamed with himself, and sorry for her, and, at the same time, disgusted by her, and hated himself for being so narrow and cruel as to be disgusted, and felt bitter, angry and outraged at being forced into a position where he had — he felt this strongly — just had to be narrow and cruel to be true to himself. And—

But there is no need to elaborate. Suffice to say that he felt very mixed up, his emotions flickering like a chameleon trapped in a kaleidoscope, making his mind an agony of confusion.

He should be loyal to Namaji. But she had tricked him, so he shouldn't be. But maybe she thought he knew all along. And, after all, a warm body was a warm body. But nobody else in the village wanted this body! But he had known that all along. But he had not known why. But—

'Sod it sod it sod it,' said Togura, biting his arm viciously, trying to relieve his agony by hurting himself.

And he started to weep.

Outside the hut, the men started to sing a loud, vigorous song which was probably obscene; maybe they had made it up especially to mock him. He wished he could kill them all. Kill them and castrate them. Rape their women one by one and burn their village down to nothing.

Why were people so vicious?

Why was life so cruel?

'Why was I ever born?' said Togura.

Whatever the reason for his birth, he was sure he was not fulfilling it by lying in a mud hut weeping for the amuse-

ment of a bunch of jabbering savages. As his sorrow began to
ease, it was replaced by a fierce, furious determination.

'Live free or die,' said Togura.

And he started making a hole in the roof.

CHAPTER 31

When Togura Poulaan finally punched through to the starlight, he heard men outside, talking in low voices, their conversation punctuated occasionally by laughter. Supposing that they would eventually get bored and go away, he waited. Namaji, exhausted by emotional trauma, fell asleep, snoring loudly. Waiting in the darkness, Togura did mental revision, working through all the ways he knew of killing people. He concluded, with regret, that his repertoire was rather limited.

He heard some men saying their goodbyes, and, after that, no voices, no laughter. He enlarged his hole, then hauled himself out onto the roof and dropped down into the darkness. He stood there, listening. He heard insects cricketing away, frogs croaking in the distance, a few muffled snores, and, far away, a horse neighing. It was a dark, cold night, lit by starlight; there was, as yet, no moon. He could have wished for some wind; the night was very still.

Togura began to slip between the hulking shadows of the mud huts, moving lightfoot-brightfoot through the night. Without warning, a cock crowed close at hand and close at ear:

'Co co rico! Co co rico!'

The noise was as loud as a slap on the ear. Togura started, as if someone had sheathed a blade in his heart. The cock crowed again.

'Who will rid me of this turbulent rooster?' muttered Togura.

He should have known better than to speak. His voice was low, but it set a dog to barking. Other dogs roused to the challenge. As they barked, furiously, sleepers awakened. Mobbed by angry shouts, Togura sprinted for the village wall. He went over it, ran into the darkness and lay flat.

Togura knew there was no point in escaping without a horse, for the village men would quarter the country and ride him down by daylight. He had to have a mount. But there was no point in making immediately for the horse corral, because it was guarded; no doubt the guard would soon be reinforced. He lay quiet and still, a shadow lost in the shadows.

A furious search was soon going on. Togura heard sounds of fighting, then cries of pain from a man. He speculated that a sentry who should have been patrolling the wall had been caught sleeping. He heard a lot of noise from the horse corral. Men with burning brands searched the area near the corral; someone seemed to be searching in amongst the horses. Soon a number of mounted men were circling the village.

Togura, though he was shivering in the cold night air, did not move until all the fuss and excitement had died down a little. Then he crept back to the village wall and followed it round to the gates. Some men, dismounted, were standing there by their horses, arguing. A dog barked loudly as Togura approached; a man cursed it and kicked it to silence. Someone was urinating noisily in the darkness.

As humble as a cockroach, Togura went sneaking to the nearest horsy shadow. Closing with the animal, he ran his hands along its back, locating the saddle. He found the nearside stirrup and got his foot in it. He found the reins, took them in hand, then mounted.

'Wah-Warguild!' screamed Togura, kicking the horse.

His mount reared. A man grabbed Togura's leg. Togura kicked, and was free. Screaming, he urged the horse to a gallop. A warrior threw a spear, which missed. Still screaming, Togura galloped away into the night. His screams, as he had intended, had scattered the other horses, giving him a decent head start.

Navigating by the stars, he headed north. Once he reached

the hills, he would kill the horse then trek over the mountains back to Estar. With dismay, he realised the moon was rising.

Sooner than he had thought, the village men managed to secure their horses and join the pursuit. He heard their shouts and hoofbeats behind him. The rising moon betrayed him to all the night.

'Ride, beauty,' urged Togura, slapping the horse.

He galloped the horse until it could gallop no more; fortunately, the riders behind him were having similar problems with their own mounts. The chase continued at a steady trot.

Suddenly, to his dismay, Togura realised there were riders ahead of him. How had that happened?

He was still trying to work out what to do next when the riders up ahead dispersed. They disappeared into a little bit of hummocked land off to his left. He blinked, wondering if they were ghosts, or if he had imagined them all along. No matter. The way ahead was clear.

But behind him he heard hastening hoofbeats, and realised the village warriors were once more trying to close the distance. He urged his horse as best he could, but it faltered, stumbled, then fell, throwing him. He picked himself up and remounted, but by then it was too late. The village riders, fierce, eager, shouting closed in around him.

'Togura!' shouted the headman.

The name was slurred, but Togura knew it for his own. The next moment, the headman slapped him, almost knocking him off the horse. Then there was an argument. Six riders had made the distance. Some, perhaps, wanted to butcher Togura on the spot. The headman finally mastered them to silence, then began to lead the way south. The horses, after all this hard treatment, could only manage a walking pace; they were not bred or fed to ride so far and so fast.

'Perhaps I'd better tell you,' said Togura. 'I saw some other horsemen back there.'

The headman, who did not understand his Galish, swore at him, and slapped him again. Togura, his nose gently bleeding, did not speak again. He had not been on horseback for ages; as a consequence, he was now saddle-sore.

They were some way back toward the village when shadows on shadow horses came screaming out of some hunchbacked wasteland. Arrows sang through the air. Lances rode home. Horses screamed, flailing down to their death. Togura urged his horse away. An enemy rode up alongside him, jumped, grabbed him round the neck, and took him crashing down to the ground. Togura felt a sickening pain in his right leg. The enemy drew a knife and tried to stab him. Togura fought with all his strength. The knife moved steadily, inexorably, toward his throat.

If Togura had been made of sterner stuff, he would have devoted all his energies to the struggle, and consequently would have died upon the spot. However, he didn't. He panicked instead, and screamed:

'Help help help!'

An enemy, whirling out of a skirmish, heard Togura's voice, and hurled a spear in his general direction. The spear slammed home, taking Togura's attacker fair and square between the shoulder blades. Killed by his own side, the attacker collapsed on Togura, who, thinking him still alive, damaged him dreadfully. Togura had just realised the man was dead when a horse, mortally wounded, collapsed on top of him. Suffocating, he fought it. By now he had a knife in his hand. The horse rolled away, staggered to its feet, managed a few steps, then dropped again, and died – this time falling clear of Togura.

He breathed the sweet cool night air in lurching gulps, sweating with effort, trembling with adrenalin, his heart still doing a decathlon. Somewhere out in the night, someone was being killed, and the sound was not pleasant. Someone, close at hand, was groaning hideously. Togura tried to get to his feet. An agonising pain in his right leg persuaded him against such foolishness. After a little experimentation, he realised the leg was broken.

'Things are not improving,' muttered Togura.

Then he heard someone walking through the night with a strange, shuffling gait. He decided it was best to play dead. He lay there with his eyes tightly shut, listening intently. Shuffle-foot wandered, paused, wandered, then fell heavily, and did not move again. Slowly, Togura opened his eyes.

Old Scar Face, the moon, floated above him, cool and remote. Somewhere close at hand, someone was crying bitterly. Togura listened, carefully, and ascertained that it wasn't him. Despite his current predicament he was, for once, dry-eyed and clear-headed.

Out in the night, some unknown animal cried.

Togura was still trembling – but now it was not adrenalin which was responsible, but the cold.

He could see that it was going to be another one of those long, long nights.

CHAPTER 32

Togura slept fitfully, dreaming that he was lying out under the sun with a broken leg. He woke to find it was true. The morning was still young, but already the day was dominated by unseasonable heat. His mouth was hot, dry, dusty. Flies picked their way over his face. He shook them off.

The air was loud with the buzz of flies. Dead men, dead horses, discarded weapons, a confusion of tracks and bloodstains marked the scene of battle. Togura, careful not to disturb his broken leg, looked around. He counted five dead horses, a dozen dead men, the bodies being spread over quite a considerable area.

Who won?

There was no telling.

Carefully, he examined his broken leg. It was the shin bone which was sore. He slit his trews below the knee so he could examine the break. To his relief, he found the bone had not forced its way through the skin. The area was very, very painful, but there was not much swelling. As broken legs went, this one was not very serious. But there was still no way he could walk on it.

'Togura,' said a familiar, slurred voice.

It was a bit early in the piece to be having hallucinations, so Togura looked around. One of the bodies had moved. It was the village headman, who was lying on the ground a dozen paces away, both wrists bent at a strange angle. Togura could

229

only presume that the headman had broken both wrists in a fall.

'Come and help me,' said Togura, though there was not much hope that the headman would understand his Galish.

The headman, urging himself forward on his elbows, moved half a pace forward then stopped, his face a mask of pain. Obviously he hadn't just broken his wrists. Something else was smashed. Leg? Legs? Pelvis? Spine?

'Togura,' said the headman. 'Dosh.'

'What did 'dosh' mean? It meant 'go'. Togura knew that much.

'I can't,' he said, hurt by this totally unreasonable order. 'I've got a broken leg.'

The headman repeated himself.

There was, or so Togura supposed, some sense in the order. The attackers, to judge from their dead, were of the same tribe as the assassin who had tried to kill the headman – Togura could tell that by their hairstyles. They might have been a scouting party, or they might have been part of a much larger war party. If any had got away alive – and quite possibly the enemy had had the better of the battle – then they might come back with reinforcements. The area was unhealthy.

'If I had half a chance of getting anywhere,' said Togura, 'then I'd go. As it is, I'm staying.'

'Dosh,' said the headman, thrusting one of his broken wrists in the direction of the south.

'What do you mean, dosh?' yelled Togura, angry now. 'You're crazy.'

The answer was the same.

'Dosh yourself!' said Togura.

'Togura,' said the headman, his voice intimate, urgent, commanding. 'Togura, dosh.'

They could go on like this all day. It was very frustrating arguing with someone who didn't speak your language.

'All right then!' shouted Togura. 'Dosh dosh dosh dosh!'

His throat was sore. He wished he hadn't shouted so loudly. He saw the headman smile.

'Ssh-schaa,' said the headman; Togura recognised that as an expression of satisfaction.

'This is crazy,' said Togura.

But, despite his reservations, he looked around for something he could use to splint his leg. The nearest suitable object was a spear sticking out of the back of one of the enemy dead. Togura wrenched it out, disturbing a hubbub of flies in the process. Using a knife which was his by right of combat, he cut it down to size. He cut into the flesh of a dead horse; he used lumps of horsemeat as padding, and strips of horsehide to tie the splint in place.

He ate some horsemeat, raw, then, as an afterthought, threw a dollop at the headman; it hit his nose and fell to the dust. The headman salvaged it with his mouth, tasted the dust and spat it out.

'Choosy,' said Togura. 'Beggars can't be choosers, you know.'

'Donz-m'dola,' said the headman.

That little phrase had something to do with the idea of getting bigger, or increasing. Togura had a hazy notion that in some contexts it was obscene, but that could hardly be the case here. Realising what the headman meant, Togura cut a sizeable chunk of meat and tossed it so that it fell within mouthreach.

'Zon,' said the headman.

Which meant more.

Togura provided. He ate some more, feeding methodically. When he could eat no more, he decided it was time to go. To give his broken shinbone the smoothest possible ride, he was constrained to travel on his back. He started off, using his hands and his good leg. Raising his buttocks from the ground sent pains shooting along his right leg; his saddle-sick buttocks would have to drag along in the dust.

'Gjonga,' said the headman.

The word, a very formal form of 'goodbye', was unknown to Togura. He did not answer, but concentrated on the task at hand. He scraped along, clumsy as a broken insect. Under the pitiless sun. Under the pitiless sky. Flies were already festering on his horsemeat padding. His broken leg, even though it was splinted, nagged him constantly.

It was hot work. The meat ripened as the sun lazed through the sky. He started to feel nauseous, perhaps from the burden of horsemeat in his stomach, or from the stench of rotting meat wrapped round his leg, or from the constant twinges of pain from the leg – pain which was sharp, stabbing, unrelenting, worse than toothache.

– Pain is the worst thing.

The battlefield was distant now. He could just make out a small clump of shadows far away on the open plain. Carrion birds circled overhead.

– Courage, Togura.

His hands hurt. His buttocks hurt. His legs hurt. Thirst, like a jagged spatula, scraped at the back of his throat. Familiar muscles began to cramp; unfamiliar muscles ached and protested. He was starting to get backache. He was a crippled skeleton. An insect man, a freak of nature. A damaged organism.

The skin was wearing away from his buttocks. And from the palms of his hands. He should have padded himself with something. Strips of horsehide, perhaps. From time to time he had little dizzy spells in which the world blurred and darkened. Drops of sweat crept down from his forehead.

He needed water. So what was he going to do about it? Dig a well? Do a rain dance? He laughed, hurting himself. He tried to generate saliva, so he could ease the scraping thirst in his throat. No joy. He should have brought some horse meat with him. He could have sucked on it. Before setting out, he should have dragged himself round the dead men and the dead horses, looking for a water skin. Surely there would have been at least one. He was an experienced survivor. He had no excuse for not thinking of these things.

He halted, to take a rest. High overhead, a skylark was singing. He listened intently to its attenuated song. It carried him up, up, up, higher and higher into the dizzy sky. Then vanished, dropping him away to nothing.

He fainted.

He woke when something hurt his leg. Opening his eyes, he saw a big bald-headed bird gashing into his horsemeat splint padding. He waved an arm. It went scuffling into the air, then settled on the ground. Its beady eyes considered him. Then it hopped forward. He dragged himself away, thinking unpleasant thoughts about the carrion birds he had seen circling over the battlefield, and about the headman lying there, utterly defenceless, with two broken wrists. Well, at least the headman would be able to jerk his head around; that would probably be enough to dissuade the birds, at least while they had plenty of quiescent carcases to feed on.

— Onward, Togura.

He dragged himself on, chafing away the last of the clothing protecting his buttocks. The skin began to rub away. He endured.

— Pain is life.

Night came, bringing unrelenting cold. Togura slept a little, then dragged himself on. When the pain was at its worst, he cried out with high, harsh, half-singing exclamations, which sounded almost like broken snatches of song. He allowed himself a little sleep, dreaming of pain only to wake to pain.

— Worse things happen at sea.

He kept the stars of the north dead ahead of him, knowing that the south lay behind his head. The moon rose, making shadowed craters out of the hoof-marks of horses. He was on the right track.

Towards morning, he heard dogs barking in the distance.

— Strength, Togura, strength.

He was taking his journey a step at a time. Pause. Brace. Push. Scrape. Endure the pain. Rest. Think out the next move. Gather courage. Brace. Push. Scrape.

— This is your test.

Rest. And brace. And now — strength! — push. Scrape. Rest. Endure. And once more, Togura, once more. Brace! Push! Scrape!

— And once more.

The night slowly lightened. The sun rose. His blood, pulsing through his ears, sang to him. He felt the steady thud

233

of his heart in his chest. He pushed himself along. Relentlessly. He was a master torturer now, absolutely without pity for the broken organism he was punishing. Brace — push — scrape—

— And rest . . .

Resting, he heard hoofbeats. They came closer and closer, then the horse wheeled, riding in to halt beside him. Looking up he saw, hazily, a man in the saddle. Togura recognised him by his haircut. He was from the home village.

'Dosh,' croaked Togura, pointing north. Then, louder: 'Dosh!'

Then he fainted.

CHAPTER 33

Togura's arrival back at the village was a source of some surprise to the inhabitants. Unbeknownst to him, one of the village men who had survived the fight in the night had come riding back, wounded, to say that the pursuit party had been slaughtered by half a thousand of the enemy. As Togura's return cast doubt on this story, a rescue party went north, eventually retrieving the headman from the open plains. Apart from his broken wrists, there was nothing wrong with him but a slipped disc, which was put back into place by skilled manipulation.

As for Togura, his leg was properly splinted. With time, the bone healed, as bones will. The skin he had lost grew back, or was replaced with scar tissue. By the time he was able to walk again, his muscles were badly wasted. He found his tendons had shortened because of his long, idle days in bed without any exercise; his legs were stiff. But the headman, who took a personal interest in his case, showed him, by sign and example — Togura's language skills had not improved — how to build up his strength and regain his flexibility.

Togura found that his right leg ached in damp weather. But there was not much damp weather for it to ache in; spring was at an end, and summer had begun.

Soon after he was up and about, there was a big festival, with much eating and drinking. And music making, which he took no part in. He did not sit behind the headman, as he was accustomed to, but beside him, in a place of honour. The next day, all the unmarried women — Namaji this time being excluded from their ranks — were lined up in front of Togura.

He hesitated.

Someone said something, and all the women laughed. The headman silenced them, then pointed to one of the taller, wider women and gave her an order. To shouts, applause and the stamping of feet, the woman stripped, proudly. She was not what he was looking for, not exactly — she was stronger than he was, and taller — but there was no doubt that she was a real woman. He smiled.

The headman laughed, slapped him on the shoulder, then drew thirteen crescent moons in the dust. He pointed first to the moons, then to Togura, then to the woman.

'A year?' said Togura in dismay.

The woman was already getting dressed again. It seemed he would have to endure his virginity for another year. But he was tough. He would survive.

And life, in the days that followed, was sweeter than it had been.

Togura had a hut of his own now. And a knife, a spear, a bow, arrows, saddles and harness. And a horse, given to him by the headman. He wished he had a stallion which could have challenged the wind. Instead, he had a scrubby little gelding with a hard mouth and an evil disposition; he vowed that as soon as success in battle gave him something better, he would volunteer the gelding for sacrifice.

Early that summer, when Togura had just about finished cataloguing the defects of his present mount, some strangers arrived in the village. They were clean-shaven foreigners in long robes, who brought with them bearded, heavily tattooed tribesmen who acted as interpreters. The strangers spoke at a public meeting; each man of the village then had his say at length. Togura wondered if all this palaver had anything to do with him, but nobody was discussing the life and fate of Togura Poulaan.

What they were talking about was war.

The very next day, all the men began to pack. They were

taking all the food, weapons and clothing they could muster, so this was not likely to be a casual, overnight raid. Not knowing what the future might hold, Togura packed the magic casket holding his triple-harp, stuffing it down to the bottom of one of his saddlebags. He hated the very sight of it, but knew it would be valuable if they ever reached civilisation.

Once packed, they rode south. A day along their journey, they fell in with another group. To Togura's surprise, those in the other group had their hair knotted in front and tied in three pigtails behind; he recognised them as enemies. But everyone got on very well, singing, joking, laughing, and, in the evening, engaging in friendly wrestling matches. So where were they going? What superior power had made them allies?

As they rode south, the places they passed were more substantial. The villages became little towns. They picked up a track, which became a road. At one of the larger towns, there were negotiations with a blacksmith, after which many of their unshod horses were shod for the first time in their lives.

At that town, another foreigner in long robes handed out a little bronze coinage to everyone, including Togura; he had to sign for it by inking his thumb then pressing it on a piece of paper against some foreign writing. It was the first piece of paper he had seen for months. He regarded this little ceremony as proof positive of his involvement in a great adventure – and found it increasingly disconcerting not to know where he was going, and why.

They began to travel through farmland under cultivation; the fields of grain by the roadside had been badly damaged by trampling horses, as if a great body of mounted men had passed this way, and had found the road too narrow for their numbers. Those fields which had survived intact were badly in need of weeding, suggesting a labour shortage.

Their journey through cultivated land lasted a day. Late in the afternoon, they surmounted a rise and saw before them the sea, which occasioned many great shouts of amazement. They came to the water's edge in the early evening. Men tasted the water, and exclaimed in delight or dismay; much money changed hands. There had obviously been heavy betting on the question of whether the sea was really salty. One man rode his horse right into it, then returned, grinning, and claimed some money from a sceptic who had refused to believe in the existence of such a vast amount of water.

The next morning, they rode into a huge harbourside city. It was larger than Keep, D'Waith and the ruins of Lorford all rolled into one. A foreigner in long robes did a roll call. Togura was delighted to find that his name was on the roll. He was Someone now – he only wished he knew what. A little more money was doled out to each person in turn. They housed their mounts in vast, empty stables; they were shown to a great, gaunt, empty barrack building where they could sleep.

And now what?

Now the men began drifting off in ones or twos; Togura gathered that they had a free day. He wandered off on his own, careful to take good note of his route, so he could find his way back. The city was almost depopulated, the streets filled with sunlight and silence. It stank, but only in a half-hearted way. Togura saw some children, some old women, and a few legless beggars propped up against walls. No whores accosted him, their bodies hot for his money, though he lived in hope.

Walking down one narrow street, past some buildings which had been looted and burnt out, Togura heard Galish voices. Turning a corner, he saw two Galish merchants in conversation.

'Please, please,' he said, running to them.

His voice sounded hoarse, febrile, over-loud. He was in a panic in case these miraculous people suddenly disappeared. They did not. But they looked as if they wouldn't mind him vanishing.

'Run away, beggarman,' said one.

'Oh, please, I have to talk to someone, where am I?'

'On your two feet, by the looks of you.'

'Is this Selzirk?'

The men laughed.

'No, seriously,' said Togura. 'Where am I?'

'Away with the bats in the darkness,' said one, meaning that he was crazy.

They began to stroll away. When he went pestering after them, they first ignored him, then turned on him with knives drawn.

'I've got a magic harp I can sell you!' cried Togura, desperate to keep in conversation with them.

'Yes, and a sister, for sure. Go back to your lunatic kennel! Leave us alone!'

He did not think it wise to risk his life just to find out where he was; he let them escape. Now that he had met two people who spoke Galish, he was sure he would find others. But he did not. He had a long, hungry day wandering the city; there was little food for sale, and what there was was high-priced. Using sign language, he bartered for some fish; he was almost certain that the fishmonger knew Galish, yet could not persuade the man to converse with him.

Towards the end of the day he managed to buy a considerable amount of garlic, which he ate raw, hoping to rid himself of the worms which had been troubling him of late. He bought some more in case his war band moved on without warning.

They did.

The very next day, they boarded a ship, one of the few vessels in the harbour. It had been modified to take horses; ramps led from the deck to the reeking darkness down below, and it was a devil of a job to get the horses down it. They then sailed south. The ship, a big-bellied two-masted trader, trudged along through the big blue oceans, rolling heavily. The journey seemed to last forever, as Togura had nothing to do but complete his worm cure – which had partial success, though he resolved to obtain a proper vermifuge when he could – and to watch off-duty crew members fishing for fish and for seagulls.

For this coasting voyage, they had the western shores of the continent of Argan on their left hand side. The land was flat; much of it was marshy. They were four days south when the winds turned against them. The ship, almost as broad as it was long could not tack against the wind with its big square sails; the crew, used to long, leisurely voyages, cheerfully anchored.

239

The next few days were very hard work. A raft was made from barrels and spars; a horse-hoist was improvised with ropes, pulleys and big leather slings; the horses were lowered onto the raft and rowed ashore so they could exercise and pasture on the bitter salt shore grasses as best they could.

Two horses drowned; a crew member was kicked in the head and died; Togura's mount, the first time he exercised it, stumbled and dropped dead under him, possibly from old age. The dead horses were all recovered, cooked and eaten; the dead crewman was stuffed into a barrel of brine, to be taken back to his family.

Togura, horseless, helped gather mud snails from the marshes; boiled up, they made a hearty dish to supplement increasingly meagre rations. He looked out to sea, often, longing for the wind to change; as he was a landsman, he did not trouble himself over what would happen if the wind started blowing onshore and the anchor started to drag.

Finally, graced with favourable winds, they sailed on south. The headman had a bad stroke, and died a day later; they tossed his corpse overboard, and watched the seagulls mob it as it floated inshore with the tide. Togura felt desolated by this death; he had come to feel that he could trust the headman, and did not know how he would fare in that worthy's absence.

The next day, they made landfall at a rivermouth city. With the help of boats and ropes, their ship was muscled into a harbour protected by a mole. The harbour was crowded with ships, and every ship was crammed with men.

A bureaucrat arrived in long robes, accompanied by an interpreter who spoke Savage. They were given a harbourside sail loft to sleep in, though they had to park their horses in the street. Both men and horses got fed and watered, after a fashion.

Togura never got to explore this new city, for, soon after arrival, he fell sick. Perhaps the riverwater was to blame; in any case, he was soon down with dysentery. A bureaucrat came and inspected him, and he was shifted out of the sail loft and into a hospital – the hospital being a ship in which dozens of people in a similar condition lay in the darkness between decks. Body handlers came round daily, to see which of the filthy, stinking bodies had become corpses overnight; other workers served up soup and water at noon each day.

Togura fully expected to die, and was soon past caring. He was marinated in filth, embraced by the stench of filth, jostled by the moaning, groaning darkness. Rats scampered across him, occasionally testing his powers of resistance with their teeth. Lice, fleas and bedbugs hit him. Cockroaches set up house beneath his shadows.

This, he was certain, was his end.

Nevertheless, though he was sick, suffering, humiliated by his predicament — no chance to get from here to the topdeck jakes, and no such thing as a chamber pot on hand — he retained enough cunning to protect his prospects as best he could. He put his triple-harp, his most valuable possession, in a small pouch, which he hid beneath his clothes, knotted round his waist on a piece of rope; everything else, including the last of his garlic, stayed in a saddle bag which he used to pillow his head.

The saddle bag got stolen while he was sleeping, and he once woke and kicked away a villain who was trying to remove his boots, but the triple-harp stayed with him.

CHAPTER 34

Heat oppressed him.

Footsteps click-clocked back and forth, treading on timbers overhead. He did not know whether the sunlit air lay above him, or whether there were more layers of death and suffering between him and the daylight. He did not know, but it would not be true to say that he did not care, for today he felt stronger – strong enough, in fact, to be appalled by his physical weakness and his degraded condition.

A couple of body handlers clomped by, dragging a corpse which they had shuffled into a canvas removal bag. When they were gone, there were the usual moans and groans, but apart from that it was strangely quiet. It was daylight, certainly; a little blade of sunlight had prised apart the timbers not far away, giving Togura a proof of the sun. Usually, by day, the harbour was loud with shouts, swearing, battle drills and the constant clamour of woodwork and repairs. Today, nothing. Except, somewhere, a gull crying: claw-claw-claw.

Togura tried to sit up. He impressed himself by accomplishing this feat. He impressed himself less by promptly fainting. When he roused himself again, it was soup time. He drank greedily from the serving bowl; it was good.

He rested, then nerved himself to attempt a heroic project: namely, making his way to the upper deck. He found himself too weak for the task; exhausted, he slept. He woke to find the darkness alive with activity. Men, some screaming with pain, were being carried down to join him. A chop-surgeon wearing a blood-bespattered leather apron prowled up and down with a lantern, looking for mutilated limbs he could hack off. He eyed Togura hopefully, then, disappointed, moved on.

Very shortly, he found a suitable victim. Togura, with a little bit of hell now visible by lantern light, watched. And soon saw enough to make him faint dead away.

When he recovered himself, he was being dragged along in darkness. Something heavy and dark shrouded him. He screamed, and punched at the darkness with his fists. The dragging stopped. Daylight opened at his eyes; a face peered in. Two men conferred, then, without ceremony, tipped him out of their canvas removal bag. He lay on the open deck of the ship, blinking at the sunlight. A sailor grabbed him by the armpits, hauled him into the shade of a tarpaulin which sheltered twenty wounded men, and left him there.

From where he was lying, Togura could see cremation fires burning on the quayside; he suspected he was lucky not to have been incinerated.

'Do you speak Galish?' he said to his nearest neighbour.

But the man was zombie-silent, his eyes staring into the distance. Togura could get no response from him.

'What about you?' he said to the next-nearest man.

'Shrrr-shrrr,' said the man, his breath muttering in and out between stubbly yellow teeth.

'Sure,' said Togura, heartlessly. 'And what's your name and all? Hey?'

'Shrrr . . . ' said the man.

And said no more, for he was dead. Togura was disconcerted by this unexpected development, and felt a little bit guilty at his heartlessness.

A man came round with soup and water; Togura took his second soup-share of the day. He eyed the dead man. A chest wound had ruined his jerkin, but his trews looked stout enough. But Togura was not bold enough to strip him by daylight, and soon corpse men dragged him away.

Togura was now feeling well enough to be disgusted by his own mired, filthy body and his dungbath reeking rags, which

243

were softly seething with vermin. He swore that he would get the next set of clothes which were going. But, each time the opportunity arose, his courage failed him, When evening fell, he was still in the same rags.

He woke in the darkness to find distant sounds of battle carrying through the still night air; there was fire inland, to the east. He was cold.

He slept again, waking before dawn because of the cold. The rising sun found him stripping a corpse for its clothes; nobody raised an eyebrow. Later in the day, he managed to draw up a bucket full of harbour water which was marginally less disgusting than he was; he washed himself, after a fashion.

There was a lot of coming and going and gossiping. He heard many people talking in Galish, but was too sick and shy to dare their disfavour and ask his basic questions; their gossip, apart from their commonplace complaints, was unintelligible because he did not know its context. Then, late in the afternoon, as he was tottering about the deck, exercising his shadow, he came upon a man he thought he knew. It was Draven, flushed, sweating and feverish.

'Draven!' cried Togura, in amazement.

The pirate, who had been dozing, opened his eyes and surveyed Togura. At first, Togura thought he was too sick to speak, but speak he did, and his voice sounded strong enough.

'Who would you be, young man? No — don't tell me. Yes! Forester! Or should I say, Togura Poulaan? Isn't that how you introduced yourself in Lorford?'

'I did,' said Togura.

'You gave me quite a shock, turning up like that. I'm sorry I couldn't have stopped for a word — it would've been more than my life was worth.'

'Why?' said Togura, remembering his desperate efforts to make contact with Draven at Lorford.

'Because,' said Draven.

That was all the explanation he was ready to give; Togura suspected that if he pushed for more, he would only get an elaborate series of lies, so he let the matter drop. He was so glad to see a familiar face and hear a familiar voice that he didn't chastise Draven for the disgraceful episode on the Warwolf, when Draven had helped throw Togura to the sea serpents.

'So,' said Draven. 'You're the man with the price on his head.'

'Yes,' said Togura, claiming this identity with something close to joy, even though it might expose him to danger. 'That's me. Togura Poulaan, also known as Barak the Battleman, a veteran of many wars and battles.'

'Including, now, the battle of Androlmarphos. We're lucky to still be alive, wouldn't you say?'

'Androlmarphos?' said Togura, blankly.

'Yes, yes, Androlmarphos.'

'Where's that?'

'Where's that? What's wrong with you? Did you just fall out of the sky? What do you mean, where's that? Androlmarphos is here. Around us. Under us. To the left of us, the right of us. It's where we are. We — tattoo this on your skin, in case you forget — we are now, and have been for some days, in Androlmarphos. The main port of the Harvest Plains, in case you didn't know. This thing we're sitting on is called a ship. That—'

'All right, all right,' said Togura. 'I get the picture. Don't be so hard on me. I've had a very difficult time.'

'So have I,' said Draven. 'Right now, I'm dying of fever.'

'You have my sympathies,' said Togura, without any sympathy; Draven looked too sick to fight or ride, but the vigour of his conversation proved him to be a very long way from death.

'Apart from the fever,' said Draven, stung by Togura's obvious lack of concern, 'I've been to Gendormargensis and back. I've been tortured. I've been killed.'

'For sure,' said Togura. 'For sure. May I stretch out my bones right here? I feel faint.'

'Stretch away,' said Draven. 'Stretch away.'

Both of them were in fact rather ill, and both had over-excited themselves with too much talking. Draven roused later in the evening, to listen to gossip about someone called Menator, who had been parlaying with the enemy, and had been murdered.

'This is very bad news,' said Draven.

'Why?' asked Togura. 'Was this Menator a friend of yours?'

'No, my enemy,' said Draven. 'I swore to kill him and eat his liver. The first part of the vow is now impossible, and the second, in this heat, is probably already over-ripe.'

'What have you got against him?'

'I'll tell you,' said Draven.

And he did, in detail. But Togura found pirate politics too complex to follow, and fell asleep in the middle of the explanation.

The next day, just after soup, Draven resumed his tale of his trip to Gendormargensis and back.

'Gendormargensis is in Tameran,' said Draven. 'It's so far to the north that it's cold all year, so they make buildings out of ice. They freeze the heads of their enemies in blocks of the stuff. Wherever you walk in the streets, there's dead eyes staring at you.'

'If the buildings are made of ice, then what happens when they light a fire?'

'They don't have proper fires, not in Gendormargensis,' said Draven. 'What they have is the heads of dead dragons. They shove their food between the jaws, and it cooks. They have live dragons, too. Hundreds of them. Armies of them. It was outside the dragon stables that they killed me.'

'They killed you?!'

'Killed me dead. Then hacked me apart. Split me from stem to stern. Chopped me into dogmeat.'

'You look healthy enough to me!'

'Ay. I was resurrected. A dralkosh it was which did the deed.'

'A dralkosh?'

'A woman of evil,' said Draven, with a shudder. 'Her name was Ampadara. Yes, that was the name. Yen Olass Ampadara. She was chief torturer for the Lord Emperor of Tameran, the man they call Khmar. She had me cut to pieces, starting with my testicles.'

Togura at first had his doubts, but Draven backed up his tale with so much detail that it surely had to be true. Draven was eloquent about the terrors of the Collosnon Empire which dominated the continent of Temeran.

'The women have the rule of it,' said Draven. 'That's the worst part. The rule of women is a fearful evil.'

He told of the streets of Gendormargensis, which were paved with layers of ice-covered skulls; of the Yolantarath River, which ran red with the blood of human sacrifices; of the Lord Emperor Khmar, a huge giant of a man with three arms, who went about naked, butchering babies and eating their livers raw; of the evil Ampadara, mistress of the knife, an ugly hag with a voice as vicious as a whip.

'She laughed as she cut me,' said Draven. 'A foul laughter, ay, like a bird of prey gone rabid.'

He told, in agonising detail, the story of his death and resurrection.

'It was that Ampadara who raised me from the dead,' said Draven. 'She meant to make me her slave. But I escaped. When all's said and done, a man's a match for any woman — though in this case it was a near thing.'

'But what were you doing in Lorford?' asked Togura.

'Oh,' said Draven. 'That's another story.'

'It's one I wouldn't mind hearing,' said Togura, who felt much stronger today, and was not going to be put off as easily as he had been the day before. 'You owe me an explanation. You owe me quite a lot, for throwing me off the Warwolf.'

'Throwing you off?' said Draven, astonished. 'I did no such thing! You jumped!'

'I did not!' said Togura, indignantly.

'But yes — I was there. I remember. You were fooling around at the stern, watching the women get slaughtered. I told you to watch your footing. You remember — come now, don't tell me no. I even grabbed a hold when the sea lurched you over. But you slid from my grip, no helping it.'

'That's not true!'

'Well . . . perhaps I misremember a detail or two. But the main sighting's there. I wasn't to blame.'

'You threw me over!'

'That's a lie. I distinctly remember the weapons muqaddam

247

had you in his grips. Throwing you or saving you, I'm not to know, but he had you. Didn't he?'

'Well, yes, but—'

'There you are then,' said Draven, triumphantly. 'You say I threw you over and now you admit I didn't. Memory's a funny thing, young man, I tell you that. Don't trust yourself too far.'

Togura was about to protest further, but at that moment something strange was heard from the east. He could not see what it was; ships at anchor and harbourside buildings allowed him no vistas inland. There was a heavy grinding, growling sound, like ice breaking up, perhaps. He heard much shouting and screaming in the city, then an incoherent roaring, loud as breaking surf, or louder.

'What is it?' said Togura.

'We're under attack,' said Draven, with fear in his voice. 'We're under attack.'

248

CHAPTER 35

They heard a huge, discordant roaring, the crash of buildings being demolished, the rending of timbers, screams and alarums.

'What's happening now?' said Togura.

'If you're so honey-sniffing curious,' said Draven, 'go and see for yourself.'

Togura wasn't tempted.

Somewhere in the city, a fire started; smoke billowed upwards. Men, disorganised, running in panic, stumbling, falling, pushing each other, came hustling out of the streets and onto the quayside. They began swarming onto the ships. On Togura's ship, nobody was giving orders; the captain was not in evidence.

'Well,' said Draven. 'So much for all that octopus-talk' – he meant hype – 'about conquering the world. We've lost.'

'Lost what?'

'The battle. The war.'

'Which war?'

'The war we're fighting in, little loon,' said Draven. 'Hell's blood! Where's the captain?'

'What do you want him for?'

'So I can bugger his boots with a jack-knife! What the hell do you think I want him for? So we can get the ship the hell out of here, that's what for.'

'I think,' said Togura, 'you'd better take charge yourself.'

'This isn't my ship!' said Draven. Then, looking around at

the scrummage on deck: 'On the other hand — maybe you've got a point.'

And Draven started roaring out orders.

'Avast there, salts and gobblers!' screamed Draven. 'Listen for your lives! Brazen the spazjits! Lubber the lee! Untrice the hawsers!' Nobody paid any attention. 'Come on, you rat-scum whore-rapists! Drop the scurfs in the brine! Get the plugs run-hauling!'

It was useless.

'Draven,' said Togura, urgently. 'Grab that man there. The big one, with the dragon tattoo. Talk him into your crew.'

'Oh knot off,' said Draven, pushing him away. Then, to the milling mob: 'Plug up your gobs, you mouse-cocked chicken-shaggers! Hear out my orders!'

While Draven screamed himself hoarse to no avail, Togura spoke to the dragon-tattoo man with an eloquence inspired by fear of death. Triumphant, he led his recruit back to Draven.

'Captain Draven,' said the man, giving a clenched-fist salute. 'I'm Ratbite Jakes, at your service.'

'Good man!' said Draven, slapping him on the shoulder. Then, seeing Togura's strategy, and seeing now that it would work, he adopted it as his own. 'Jakes,' he said, pointing. 'Grab that fellow over there! The one with red hair! We need him!'

On the quayside, a battle royal was raging. No enemy was yet in sight, but men were fighting each other to get aboard the ships. Something in the city was roaring — it sounded like a huge animal. There was a cacophony of wreckage and rupture. It sounded as if all hell was marching toward them.

Draven, having gathered up half a dozen big, husky, capable-looking men, spoke to them swiftly, giving his orders. Then they dispersed, shouting their orders, press-ganging men as they went. Togura, Jakes and Draven, a three-man hunting pack, began to recruit a second echelon of group-leaders.

Soon, Draven was getting control.

Half a dozen rowing boats were pirated from the harbourside. They began to lug the ship toward the harbour mouth. Togura, still weak, sick and dizzy, got booted upstairs, and found himself in the rigging, floundering amidst the canvas.

The ship was slow, slow, slow to move.

'Hell's grief,' said a man, in shocked disbelief.

'What?' said Togura, trying to steady himself in the rigging and tie knots at the same time.

'Look!'

Togura looked.

A rock was smashing its way out through the harbourside buildings. Roaring, it charged. Men ran, screaming. The rock crunched into them, corpsing them, pulping their bodies to strawberry jam. Togura, stunned, sickened, appalled, almost fainted and fell.

'Steady yourself!' said his comrade, grabbing him with a most welcome supporting hand.

The rock smashed its way to the quayside and charged their ship. It crashed into the gap between the ship and the sea, plunged down to the water, screamed, and was drowned down under. Draven, on the deck below Togura, shouted at the oarsmen to haul harder.

Togura closed his eyes.

He shuddered.

Togura had once had a clash with a walking rock in Looming Forest, north of Lorford, but had later dismissed the whole incident as a hallucination. But it seemed walking rocks were real! Hell's grief, indeed!

'Work on,' said his comrade, shaking him.

'Yes,' said Togura. 'Yes.'

The rowing boats lugged them clear of the harbour mouth. The wash of an outgoing river helped push them west, into the Central Ocean. As men did battle on the quayside with invading rocks and soldiers, other ships cleared the harbour.

Draven's ship picked up its rowing-boat men and began to sail with all canvas set. Five ships got free from the harbour. Togura clambered down to the deck, sweating, exhausted, his arms and legs quivering. His recent illness had left him weak as a butter-doll.

251

'Hello, Forester,' said a friendly voice.

Togura turned, and found himself looking at a fair-haired young pirate with a raw straw beard.

'Who are you?' said Togura, sure he had never set eyes on the fellow before in his life.

'Come now! You remember me!'

'From where?' said Togura.

'From the time we were married, lover. No, jokes aside – I'm your old shipmate Drake. What's with the cuttlefish head?'

'Cuttlefish?' said Togura, bewildered. 'What kind of fish is that?'

'No kind of fish at all,' said the pirate Drake.

It was, in fact, a type of cephalopod, and 'cuttlefish head' was, in pirate argot, a term for amnesia.

Togura found his legs folding up under him. He folded up after them. Shadows danced in front of his eyes like demented mosquitoes.

'If you don't remember me,' said Drake, sitting down beside him, 'I suppose it's the beard that's to blame. I didn't have it last time we met. Aboard the Warwolf, remember? Jon Arabin's ship. We lost you in the Penvash Channel, near the island of Drum.'

'Oh,' said Togura.

'Not very talkative, are we?' said Drake. 'Got a hangover, have we? Better pull ourselves together, I think. We might have fighting soon.'

'How so?'

'Look back to the harbour, man.'

Togura looked, and saw another ship setting out to sea.

'So some more of us have got away,' he said.

'That's not ours!' said Drake. 'That's enemy!'

'How can you tell?'

'The sails, man, the sails! That gap-toothed raggage was never set by pirates! There's landsmen aboard that ship. In pursuit of us, my friend. Lusting for our eyeballs. Hearty for our gizzards. They'll cuttle us down and under, unless we're careful.'

'Yes, well,' said Togura. 'Tell us when it's fighting time. I'm going to sleep.'

He snoozed for a while. When he woke, eight enemy ships were in pursuit.

'Eight against five,' said Togura.

'As odds go,' said Drake, 'it's not exactly picnic time. But never fear – I think we're hauling away on them. Griefs, they're still having trouble getting their canvas up!'

'Tell me if anything changes,' said Togura.

And closed his eyes.

The sun was warm, the motion of the ship was easy, and he was very, very tired. He drifted off to sleep again, and was soon dreaming confused dreams in which blue-green sea serpents tangled their way through piles of chicken feathers which were swarming with baby turtles. In his dream, he found his way into a woman's thighs, and was just about to apologise when she clouted him on the head.

He woke.

'What?' he cried, dazed by a mix of sleep and sunlight.

The ship lurched.

Something smashed into the vessel with a blow which was felt from keel to masthead.

'Sea serpents!' screamed Togura.

'No, whales!' shouted someone, looking overboard.

And whales there were. Big ones. Sperm whales, each more than twenty paces long. Water-surging cetacean wrath, charging the ship and battering it.

'Let's find ourselves a swim, and quick,' said Drake.

'A swim?'

'Something to float us,' said Drake.

The ship, struck again, staggered, listed. It was holed. It was sinking. Togura was knocked to the ground as men brawled for possession of a choice 'swim', a well-founded barrel. He lost sight of Drake.

The deck canted. The seas surged up. Togura staggered upright. Water boiled around him. He struck out, trying to swim clear, lest the descending rigging snag him and drown him under. Clearing the ship, he floundered round, turning in the water. He caught a glimpse of fully-rigged masts and canvas plunging under.

The water was cold and turbulent. The waves smashed down the screams of drowning men. The blue sky billowed above. Everywhere, pirates were going under. With a shock, Togura realised that hardly any of them could swim.

Then, with a greater shock, he realised another ship was sinking. And a third was in trouble. Big trouble! As he watched, it suddenly turned turtle and plunged down out of sight, quick as gasping.

Another ship was riding through the waves toward him, closing the distance steadily. It looked as if it would ride him down. He saw men busy at its deckrail. Boarding nets were being lowered. Big, slow and stately, the ship ploughed through the seas toward him. He could make out its figurehead: a green-haired girl with three breasts and five nipples.

Closer still it came, till he could see the name of the ship painted on its bow. He could see it, but he could not read it: it was scripted in arcane foreign ideograms he had never seen before in his life. Looking up, he saw the canvas being furled; the ship was losing headway.

'Swim, boy!' shouted someone.

It was Draven, floundering toward the ship.

'Come on, Forester!' yelled another voice. 'Don't just float around wallowing! You're not in the bath, you know!'

That was Drake.

Togura struck out for the ship. As it yawed, he saw the black tar of its undersides. It plunged down again, rolling toward him. He grabbed the rough hemp of the boarding net.

'Climb, you lazy whoreson dog!' shouted Draven, already half way to the deckrail.

But Togura could not. He clung there, shivering, exhausted. Someone climbed down to him. It was Drake. Who grabbed his hair.

'Up,' said Drake, yanking.

He was merciless.

Togura managed to claw his way up a bit. Drake helped him.

Bit by bit they scavenged their way up, while the rolling seas tried to batter them to death against the ship's indigo topsides.

They gained the deck, and Togura promptly fainted.

When he recovered, Drake told him the news. The enemy, for reasons unknown, had turned back for Androlmarphos. And the whales had gone.

They were, for the moment, safe.

CHAPTER 36

Togura lay dreaming wild, chaotic dreams. Waves went stumbling-tumbling through his memories, stirring up fragmented images which bit, raged, swore, hummed, pulsed, sweated, stank, sang, sundered and bifurcated.

Ants clambered out of his navel.

He was giving birth.

While the ants swam through his fluids, feeding on his milk, Slerma ate Zona. The moon burnt blue. Guta pulled a hatchet from his head then wrestled with a sea serpent, his sex striving.

'Shunk your cho,' said Day Suet, running her eager little golls over Togura's body as he savoured the curves of her bum.

Her woollen chemise tore open and a wave rolled out of it, swamping him down to green anemone depths where turtles spun out lofty poetry in the accents of sea dragons. He swam downwards, breaking his way through mounds of salt beef, fighting through to the sun.

'Zaan,' said the sun.

Its light washed over him, scoured away his skin, hollowed his bones, dragged his brain out through his nostrils then washed his guts in rosepetal water. He fell through a hollow tower, pursued by the music of a kloo, a krymbol and a skavamareen.

'Unlike yours,' said someone, 'my floors are not knee-deep in pigshit.'

'Who said that?' said Togura.

And was so curious to discover the truth that he chased his question over the edge of Dead Man's Drop and fell screaming to the pinnacles below. They shattered his body, killing him.

The shock woke him.

Waking from his dreams, Togura blinked at the sun. He was lying on the deck of the ship; it was so crowded with refugee pirates that there was no hope whatsoever of finding accommodation below.

'Zaan,' said Togura, looking at the sun, then looking away, blinking at purple after-images.

Togura remembered that the Wordsmiths had given him the rank of Wordmaster. He thought his chances of getting back to Sung were now remarkably good, yet it seemed that, having failed to find the index, he would be returning empty-handed. Perhaps he could at least bring back another language.

Yes. He could see what he should do. Invent a language, claim that it was spoken on one of the smaller islands of the Greater Teeth, and thus gain kudos for making a valuable contribution to the Wordsmiths' quest to discover or invent the Universal Language. He would call his invented language Pirate Pure. Togura thought he could assemble Pirate Pure easily enough, using Orfus pirate argot, bits and pieces of Savage as spoken on the Lezconcarnau Plains, and his own made-up words.

'Zaan', in Pirate Pure, could be a name for the sun.

This scheme was, no doubt, dishonest, but it was, really, no more daft than any of the other mad projects the Wordsmiths were engaged upon. As far as Togura could remember, one Wordmaster, noting that all men swear, had been attempting to create a Universal Language made entirely from insults and obscenities, from the 'rat-rapist' of Estar to the 'lawyer's clerk' of Ashmolean bandits. Another had claimed that the Universal Language was that of love, and, on the strength of this theory, had left to do practical research in foreign brothels.

Togura had also heard of a scholar who, thinking the Universal Language might in fact be the Eparget of the northern horse tribes of Tameran, had gone to the Collosnon Empire to research it. Perhaps his grasp of foreign etiquette had been faulty, for he had returned as a jar of pickled pieces. (More accurately, part of him had returned — even bulked out with some spare dogmeat, he had made a pretty slim coffin-corpse.)

In Togura's considered opinion, the Wordsmiths were a bunch of ignorant nerks. But they did have the odex. Which gave them a source of income. And, if he could cut himself a slice of that income ... well, that would at least solve the purely practical problem of scraping a living for himself.

'Hi, Forester,' said Drake, bragging along the deck with a little swagger; his face had taken a knuckling, so he had obviously been in a fight, but, from the look of him, it would appear he had won.

'What've you been fighting over?'

'A woman,' said Drake. 'A most beautiful bitch with red hair thick in her armpits. Her name's Ju-jai.'

'Where is she?' said Togura, looking around.

'Not so eager,' said Drake, laughing. 'She's on the Greater Teeth. A scrumpy little bit, though. Hot meat, well worth kettling. How's yourself today? Feeling better?'

'Much,' said Togura.

Drake sat himself down, and they began to talk. Drake boasted of the way he had first deflowered the virginal Ju-jai, some three years ago; Togura, for his part, narrated the intimate details of his sexual exploits with admiring women like Day Suet and the slim and elegant Zona.

'Have you children, then?' said Drake.

'Oh, a few bastards here and there,' said Togura. 'That's why I had to leave Sung. Jealous husbands, raging fathers, murderous boyfriends ... '

'Aye,' said Drake, sagely. 'I know the score.'

At that moment, they were interrupted by a wounded man who had been slowly making the rounds of the deck, talking to each and every pirate. The man had his arm in a sling, a little dead blood staining the sling-cloth. He had black hair and a square-cut black beard; his clothes, now battle-stained, had once been elegant. His demeanour was proud, haughty, arrogant — yet his voice was friendly enough:

'How are you, boys?'

'Hearty, sir,' said Drake.

'Except,' said Togura, 'we've been a precious long time away from women.'

The stranger laughed.

'Youth,' he said, 'is a wonderful thing. Now listen, boys — there'll be a ration of hardtack and water at sunset. Not much — but we'll be on short commons till we reach Runcorn.'

'Runcorn?' said Togura. 'Where's that?'

'It's a city on the coast to the north,' said the stranger. 'Where do you come from, boy?'

'Sung,' said Togura.

'Ah. One of our bowmen. I thought we lost you all in the fighting.'

'I'm hard to kill,' said Togura manfully.

'Good,' said the stranger, with a touch of amusement in his voice. 'That's what I like to see.'

'Excuse me,' said Togura. 'But when do we reach Runcorn?'

'That,' said the stranger, again amused, 'depends on the wind. But it'll be some time within our lifetimes, that I guarantee. Any other questions?'

'No, sir,' said Drake, speaking for both of them before Togura could ask any of the hundreds of supplementary questions boiling in his head.

The stranger nodded and moved on down the deck to a little group of gambling pirates, who laid down their cards to attend to him.

'He's a happy fellow,' said Togura.

'Man, that's his style,' said Drake. 'Since we lost, he's probably bleeding to death inside. But he wouldn't let us see that, no way.'

'Who is he then?'

'Elkor Alish, of course.'

'Who?' said Togura.

'Have you just fallen out of an egg or something?' said Drake. 'Who do you think he is?'

'Well, a sea captain, I suppose,' said Togura.

'What?' said Drake. 'Like Jon Arabin?'

'Who's Jon Arabin?'

'Man, your head's got as many holes as a pirate's wet-dream! You'll be forgetting your own name next!'

Togura, who sometimes found it hard to keep track of his aliases, could hardly disagree. He shrugged off the criticism and tried again for an answer:

'Well then, who is this Elkor Alish?'

'You really don't know? Okay then. Elkor Alish used to be the ruler of Chi'ash-lan. He made himself famous by working a law so every woman had to serve out a year in the public brothels, starting from when she was blooded.'

'Blooded?' said Togura.

'You know,' said Drake. 'From when her months began.'

'Oh,' said Togura.

He was puzzled, as he hadn't a clue what Drake was talking about. Blooded? Months? It meant nothing to him. But he didn't want to appear more ignorant than he had already, so didn't question further.

'Anyway,' said Drake. 'For a while he got really rich.'

At this point, Drake's story — which was, incidentally, pure invention — was interrupted as Draven came strolling along. He was rattling some dice in his fist.

'Hello there,' said Draven. 'Care to roll for this evening's rations?'

'I hear your dice talking,' said Drake. 'And I can already hear them telling lies. Don't roll with him, friend Forester, for he'll have you rolling for your spleen unless you're careful.'

'Sure,' said Togura. 'I know how far I can trust him. He threw me overboard once.'

'I did no such thing!' protested Draven. 'That's slander! We settled it out already, remember? You misremembered.'

'Our friend Forester is a bit shaky in the head,' said Drake. 'He'll butterfinger his own name unless he's careful.'

'Yes, but,' said Togura, 'I was thrown overboard. To the sea serpents! You remember, Drake. You were there. Draven chucked me over, isn't that so?'

'Why, no,' said Drake, blandly. 'You were such a brave little sword-cock you insisted on challenging the sea serpents, hand to hand. You were that keen on jumping we couldn't restrain you.'

'That's a lie!' said Togura.

'Such heat and fury,' said Draven, laughing. 'Stoke you up on a cold day, and and we'd be warm in no time.'

'You don't know what you put me through,' said Togura bitterly. 'You don't know what I suffered.'

'We all suffer,' said Draven. 'Why, I've done my share of suffering myself. Like when the torture-rats bit off my nose in Gendormargensis.'

'That was your lower nose, I suppose,' said Drake. 'For your snout's still as big and ugly as ever.'

'No, no,' said Draven. 'It's not my snorter I'm talking about, it's my sniffer. Let me tell you . . . '

And he was off again, launched on one of his tales of the terrors of Tameran and the evils of the dralkosh Yen Olass Ampadara, she of the blood-red teeth, the man-demolishing stare, the stone-shattering laughter.

At sunset, hardtack and water were handed out, with the ration-handlers putting a daub of red paint on the left hand of every man (or the left cheek of amputees) so none could claim rations twice. The next day, it was some indigo paint on the right hand, and the day after that it was some black on the forehead.

Elkor Alish proclaimed stern laws against gambling for food and water, and enforced them by making everyone eat and drink under the eyes of hand-picked manhandlers. The first two people caught infringing the regulations were thrown overboard and left to drown, after which there was no further disobedience.

By a combination of fair dealing, ruthless discipline and punctilious organisation, Elkor Alish eventually brought his ship safely to Runcorn with its multitudinous refugees in reasonably good shape.

Togura, who had waited eagerly for his first sight of this new city, found, to his disappointment, that he had been here before. Runcorn was the place where he and the Lezconcarnau villagers had first taken ship for Androlmarphos. A deserted, depopulated place with no women to speak of — and certainly no whores, as far as he could see.

CHAPTER 37

Amongst the Korugatu philosophers of Chi'ash-lan, there were perennial debates about the role of the individual in history. Are all people shaped and controlled by historical forces? Or can an exceptional person shape history? Some supported the view that human beings are like chips of wood floating in the flood of a great river, unable to control their destiny; others held that certain world historical individuals are like master engineers, able to dam, divert or indeed reverse the river of history.

By the time of the batle of Androlmarphos, the debate had been going on for half a millenium, and, far from being exhausted, was growing steadily more complicated; the matter of the role of the individual in history now involved questions of free will versus predestination, and, most recently, fractious deliberations about the very meaning of the word 'history'.

Some argued that history is 'a sequence of events'. Others insisted that it is 'events determining culture'. But then, in that case – what is culture? (To that supplementary question, at least twenty-seven different answers were proposed – and that was only in a single day's debate.) One philosopher – Klen Klo, a noted drunkard and kleptomaniac – argued that 'History is everything which happens apart from the weather.' This satisfied many people for almost as long as half a day, until one of his rivals – Shomo Shamo Shah, a one-time gladiator – refuted Klen Klo's assertion by noting that

'Whoever could change the weather would be a world historical figure, therefore the unchanging of the weather is a historical event.'

Shomo Shamo Shah, intoxicated by what he liked to think of as his own cleverness, went on to claim that unevents – such as the non-changing of the weather – are also part of history. In the terms of this definition, any uneventful life which failed to change anything at all could be seen as world historical. The world, said Shomo Shamo Shah, might be full of world historical figures – such as Klen Klo.

Whereupon Klen Klo, also intoxicated – though alcohol was the villain in his case – promptly punched Shomo Shamo Shah in the nose, thereby sparking off a battle between philosophers which was, at least in one of the more mundane and generally accepted meanings of the word, a historical event.

None of this directly affected Togura Poulaan, who was a long, long way from Chi'ash-lan, and who never got to hear of the punch up between Klen Klo and Shomo Shamo Shah, let alone the debate about the role of the individual in history. Accordingly, questions of what Togura might or would or could have thought about the debate must remain strictly theoretical; he did not do much spontaneous philosophical thinking, apart from wondering, not infrequently, 'Why am I here?', 'What's going on?' and 'Why do these things always happen to me?'

Nevertheless, it is possible that Togura might – if given the opportunity to participate in the debate in Chi'ash-lan – have made a certain contribution. One cannot imagine it being made with much style, as he was no orator; being young, he would undoubtedly have had to speak through an interpreter. In the manner of the inexperienced, he might well have been long-winded as well; however, assuming this fault to have been cured, he might have come up with something like this:

'History is what we understand. The rest is a waking nightmare. History is the explanation of who holds the knife. Without that explanation, all we understand is the pain.'

His remarks, of course, would have left the major questions

unanswered, but, unlike some of the frivolities ventured by the philosophers, they would have been heartfelt truths discovered by experience. If challenged to justify his own position, Togura could have easily supported it with material drawn from his own life.

It was in Runcorn that he finally managed to get a reliable account of events which had been, until then, unexplained nightmares. A mild-mannered pirate with designs on his virginity (which, in the end, came to nothing) spent a whole day talking with him in a bar. They were sober the whole time, as, thanks to strict rationing, they had to while away the whole day with a single mug of ale apiece.

Togura learnt that rocks could be wakened to life by a magic artefact known as a death-stone. That explained the walking rock which had chased him through Looming Forest so long ago. As Draven had told him, the troops Togura had met at Lorford, in Estar, had been Collosnon soldiers in the service of the Lord Emperor Khmar of Tameran.

It seemed that the warrior Elkor Alish had defeated Khmar's army of invasion, with, perhaps, a little help from certain wizards. Later, Alish had gone hunting for a death-stone. Finding one, he had made an alliance with a pirate chief, Menator, and had set out to conquer the world. Recruiters had scavenged even the Lezconcarnau Plains, enlisting mercenaries, which was how Togura and the villagers had, belatedly, come to join Alish's conquering army in the city of Androlmarphos.

Alish had lost a great battle on the plains to the east of Androlmarphos; Togura, fortunately, had been ill with dysentery at the time. Subsequently, the enemy – who had come into possession of the death-stone, stealing it from Alish – had stormed Androlmarphos with the help of animated rocks.

All was much clearer.

With the help of a rough and ready map (drawn on a tabletop with someone else's spilt beer) Togura was even able to make an estimate of the route he had travelled after leaving Estar. He had crossed the Ironband Mountains – he remembered, distinctly, a mad moment when he had claimed part of the mountains as his empire – and, descending those mountains, had reached the northern part of the Lezconcarnau Plains, there to be captured by a roving band of villagers.

Thanks to that tutorial session in Runcorn (he was offered another kind of tutorial, too, but declined), his nightmare became history.

This, of course, does not answer the original question: does history dictate to the individual or vice versa? Some philosophers – Lunter Hojo, for instance, the notorious lunatic who was almost killed in a kite-crash – hold that 'both possibilities are true'; in the case of Togura Poulaan, however, it could be asserted, on the basis of what he had endured until reaching Runcorn, that 'both possibilities are untrue'.

Togura had been severely buffeted by the turbulence on the fringes of great events, but those events had not created a destiny for him – they had simply kicked him until he was dizzy. And he had never yet been in a position where he could personally influence the world's affairs. Using Togura as an example, it is possible to argue that 'some of our lives are random' – though anyone unwilling to become embroiled in the tiresome disputes of Korugatu philosophers would do best to ignore the subject altogether.

Certainly Togura's first chance to put the theory to the test, and to attempt to become a world historical figure – or to be forced, by the thrust of events, to accept that destiny – came at Runcorn. Though there were few people in the city, there were many plans, plots, cabals, schemes and conspiracies. Little hives of intrigue were abuzz with low-voiced diplomacies, threats, promises, oaths of allegiance and wild speculations.

Men were planning to murder their defeated leader, Elkor Alish. Others were hoping to steal the death-stone back from the opposition, and ensure that Elkor Alish did become world conqueror after all. Some were for over-running one of the small mountain kingdoms on the coast to the north of

Runcorn – the choice was either Chorst or Dybra. A few were for setting up a kingdom in Estar. Many held that, with their depleted numbers, the only sensible thing to do was to retire to the Greater Teeth.

On one hot summer's day, the fair-haired young pirate by the name of Drake made Togura an offer. They had just collected the day's ration of rice and vivda (which was issued together with a single metal token good for a mug of beer in any tavern in town) and were sitting eating when Drake made his proposition.

'I'm going with an embassy to Selzirk,' said Drake.

'Selzirk?'

'Don't tell me you don't know where Selzirk is,' said Drake. 'I'd have thought even you'd know that.'

'I do,' said Togura, with dignity. 'Selzirk's the capital of the Harvest Plains. The capital of the people who defeated us at Androlmarphos. I wouldn't have thought it'd be a healthy place for a pirate to venture just now.'

'We go as an embassy,' said Drake, patiently. 'We'll be safe enough. They're civilised, you see.'

'I think maybe you're bloating the fish a bit,' said Togura, using a bit of idiomatic pirate-talk. 'Ambassadors don't come so short in the tooth.'

'Oh, I'm just going along as a pair of ears,' said Drake. 'I was born in Selzirk, see, so I speak the local lingo. I've got authority to take a companion. Do you want to come?'

'No thanks.'

'Have you got enemies in Selzirk, then?'

'No,' said Togura. 'But I've a home in Sung.'

'Man, home is a place for old men to die in. We're young! Come! We're leaving tomorow!'

'I'll think about it,' said Togura.

It was his chance, perhaps, to venture to the heart of the action, to dare all and become a world historical figure, a hero, a giant bestriding the world of events. In the event, however, he turned it down, and Drake left without him.

Finding that Bluewater Draven was sailing for the Greater Teeth on a courier cutter, Togura begged a ride; from the beer-table map, he knew the Greater Teeth were a step closer to home, so he quit Runcorn, leaving, without regret, the melancholy, mostly deserted city, and his best chance of proving or disproving certain theories of history.

CHAPTER 38

As the courier cutter coursed for the Greater Teeth, Draven did his best to dispel the prevailing gloom aboard, a gloom which was consequent on defeat behind and an uncertain future ahead. He organised sing-songs, joke-telling sessions and a fishing competition.

Togura, who won the fishing by catching a small thresher shark, was dismayed to find that first prize was being thrown overboard. Second prize was the chance to command the courier cutter for a man overboard exercise; fortunately, the man with the second-best fish was a competent seaman, and Togura, very angry and very wet, was rescued from the waters of the deep.

Third prize was a choice between getting keel hauled or eating the thresher shark, raw, bones and all. Shark-eating proved to be an amusing spectator sport; the man playing gourmet vomited twenty-seven times before he finally mouthed down the very last of the fish.

'Fourth prize,' said Draven jovially, 'is getting skinned alive.'

However, as only three people had caught fish, fourth prize was not awarded.

Draven also organised a tug-of-war, a rat-fighting competition and a knuckleskull league, knuckleskull being a pirate game which is played with cudgels, and tends to lead to bad headaches or worse. Then there was the game of 'Quivliv

Quoo', which means, literally, 'Slippery Octopus'. One person ties another up; the captive, if he can escape, gets the chance to throw a bucket of water over the person who did up the knots. There was, once, a drinking race; they did not have enough liquor on board for a second session.

They also played the traditional pirate game of 'First Off', which, though it was obscene and improper in the extreme, did not lead to Togura losing his virginity.

Then there was story telling.

Draven told the best stories, for he had been to that weird and wonderful place, the continent of Tameran. Most of his stories were about the evil dralkosh, Yen Olass Ampadara, who had tortured him, killed him, then resurrected him.

'A one-woman brothel, she was,' said Draven. 'She took on the whole army once, out in the open sun. I was there. I saw it. Even when they were exhausted, she still hadn't had enough.'

And Draven told the story of how, thanks to his wisdom, his cunning, his sagacity, his strength and his courage, he had finally been able to outwit the Ampadara woman and escape, returning, in the end, to his beloved Greater Teeth.

'That Ampadara woman,' said Draven. 'She was the most monstrous bundle of female sin I've ever clapped eyes on. In her own person, she was argument enough for the rule of men over women. Her every act was designed to break me — she couldn't bear to see a man live free.'

'She might tell it different,' said Togura, still displeased about having been thrown overboard from the cutter.

'Ay,' said Draven. 'So she might. But then, she was the most wily liar in all of creation.'

'What happened to her then?' asked Togura.

'That,' said Draven, 'is another story. I'll save it for tomorrow's night watch.'

But Togura never got to hear that story, for when dawn broke the next day, they found themselves closing with the islands of the Greater Teeth, notorious lair of the Orfus pirates, of whom Draven was one.

In former days, many generations ago, the island of Drum had been the centre of piracy. Then the sea dragons had arrived. In theory, pirates and sea dragons could have co-existed. In practice, the pirates had failed to conceal their contempt for sea dragon artistry; outraged sea dragon poets, philosophers, orators, rock gardeners, punsters and pyrotechnists had responded by slaughtering their critics. The surviving pirates had retreated to the Greater Teeth.

Since then, the sea dragon population of Drum had sharply declined, thanks largely to their promiscuous sexual habits, which had helped spread disastrous venereal diseases through their ranks. Indeed, over the last couple of generations, an epidemic of a viral disease causing an acquired immune deficiency syndrome had almost driven the sea dragons to extinction.

However, the pirates, being creatures of habit like everyone else, had not returned to Drum; they had stayed on the Greater Teeth.

As a small boy, hearing idle adult talk of pirates living on the Greater Teeth, Togura had imagined rows and rows of huge molars – perhaps twice the height of a man – with one or two pirates squatting on top of each. He had imagined the pirates dressed in beggarman rags; in his fancy, the molars had been set in the middle of butterfly meadows.

Traces of this boyhood misapprehension remained in his mind, so he was surprised, at first, to see gaunt skerries thrusting up from the surf, and, beyond those skerries, towering rock ramparts crowned with trees.

'Where are we?' he asked.

'This is Knock,' said Draven. 'We'll berth at the Inner Sleeve, which is my home harbour. You'd best stay at my home for the time; you've nowhere else to go.'

'Why thank you,' said Togura.

'You look surprised. Don't be so. I may be rough, but I've got my honour, like any other man. I pay my debts.'

This was said with such sincerity that Togura, for a moment, actually believed it; in any case, whatever he thought of Draven's honour, he did need somewhere to stay, so Draven's invitation was welcome.

The coastline of Knock was forbidding. Rocks awash with

water jutted from the waves; other rocks lurked beneath the surface.

'Is this dangerous?' said Togura.

'Naw,' said Draven. 'We all of us know these waters as well as we know our toenails.'

A moment later, the courier cutter scraped on the bottom, suggesting that none of them knew their toenails terribly well. They got off without damage, but Togura became increasingly jittery, watching the sea swashbuckle against the pitiless cliffs.

A big skerry slipped past, giving him a view of a new stretch of cliff. At first, in a moment of dreamlike dismay, he thought he was looking at a vast expanse of black cloth seething with lice, and that the lice were screaming at him. Then he realised that the entire cloud-challenging cliff was one huge bird rookery, and that what he was hearing was the cries of a million sea birds.

Ahead was a clutter of skerries, with a narrow sealane between them and the cliff. The courier cutter sailed into the sealane and promptly lost the wind. Men began to furl the sails.

'Well then,' said Draven. 'How do you like it?'

'How do I like what?' said Togura.

'My home.'

'Your home? Where?'

'There, of course,' said Draven, pointing at one of the larger skerries. 'Can't you tell a house rock when you see one? Look, don't you see the handholds cut in the side?'

'You mean we have to climb up there!'

'Yes, and pull the ship up after us,' said Draven, deadpan.

'Oh, bullshit,' said Togura, realising he was being conned.

'Not so,' said Draven. 'There's no bulls in the Greater Teeth. Though fishshit makes a handy meal when the famines come.'

'The famines?'

'Every tenth year they come,' said Draven, solemnly. 'All the little stones come to life. They crawl up from the sea. Feeding. You can hardly walk, for they're shifting under your

272

feet. They'll eat the leather from your boots, the snot from your nose. If you're not careful, they'll crawl up your arse and eat—'

'Give it a rest,' said Togura. 'That's a story on stilts if ever I heard one. You won't get me believing a dreamscript like that – I'm not a child, you know.'

'No?' said Draven. 'You could've fooled me.'

At that moment, they were hailed by a boat rowing out from a cleft in the cliff. Their courier cutter had been sighted by a lookout; soon more oar-boats came to meet them, and they were towed into the cleft, which was larger than it seemed at first blush. The cliff-cleft opened onto a small, rock-locked harbour, where they docked.

After a dockside conference at which news was exchanged – many of the women and children who had come to meet the cutter were soon weeping, for the cutter brought news of many deaths – some of the men set out in smaller boats to spread the news throughout the Greater Teeth. But Draven set off home. Togura went with him.

They travelled through long, gloomy tunnels, reaching, at last, a cave home which had light shafts piercing through a seaward cliff face, and a waste shaft delved down sheer to the black night of a seafilled cave. In an inner chamber lit by smoky seal-oil lamps, Draven and Togura ate, feeding on crabs, fish paste, whelks, edible seaweeds, pickled onions and mushrooms.

Two of Draven's women served them. The women wore their hair in the leading fashion of the Greater Teeth: grown long, it was tied in a multitude of plaits evenly arranged around the head, so that some plaits, falling directly over the face, served as a veil of sorts. After the meal, the women – who did not speak to the men – served small cups of a hot, dark fluid which Togura took to be liquid mud.

'This is coffee,' said Draven.

'Coffee?'

'Foreign stuff. We get it by way of loot, but seldom. It's rare, so drink – you'll not get it elsewhere.'

Out of courtesy, Togura drank. He decided that he would

273

not care if he never got it elsewhere. All things considered, he'd rather have an ale.

Togura supposed that he would get the chance of an ale soon enough, for there would surely be a homecoming feast of some kind. But he was wrong. There was no feast – only a gathering of sombre, serious men who came to talk politics with Draven. Who was forthright in his views:

'I said for starters we'd no business whoring after foreign wars. The sea's a steady business, we'd no need for speculation. This empire talk's no good for us.'

'Many men,' said a pirate, 'support this Elkor Alish. They say he's got an army coming from Rovac.'

'Ay, walking the water no doubt. Many men say this, and many men say that, but I tell you one thing for certain – many men are in their graves thanks to this empire nonsense. You speak of support for Alish. I say: here's a blade. Good steel, this. A length of it can unsupport a hero, if need be.'

'Walk softly, friend Draven. Some would call that treason.'

'Would they? And are we not free men? Since when did a pirate hold his tongue, under the sun or out of it? Treason, you say! What kind of lubber-lawyer talk is that? What next? A law of libel and a court of defamations? Come, friends, what's this talk of treason? This Elkor Alish weighs upon the earth like an emperor, yet his empire non-exists. Non-existing, how does it dare to claim our freedoms? All our gain is loss. We've had not a whit-jot benefit from these foreign wars, yet many men breathe earth or water thanks to this foolishness. I say: finish it. Elkor Alish can lord it over Runcorn with those who wish to be lorded over. But we: we lord it over ourselves. I say: if Elkor Alish ventures here, we'll feed him steel to breathe. This steel. With my own hand I'll do it.'

Thus spoke Draven. Then turning to Togura:

'Did you hear what we were talking of?'

'Me?' said Togura. 'I'm stone deaf.'

'Ay, and mute, too, if you're wise. Now, enough of this dirging! I'm home from the wars. I'll not talk blood and burial all night. Let's have a bit of sparking, hey? Deaf-mute, sing us a song.'

Togura hesitated.

'What, silence?' said Draven. 'Is this how you repay hospitality?'

Togura knew, by now, something of the nature of pirate fun. It could well be that he was in the most fearful danger. What if they didn't like his singing? They might cut out his tongue! What if they did like it? They might reward him by cutting his testicles off – he had heard vague rumours of such things happening to favoured singers in far-off Chi'ash-lan.

Coming to a decision, Togura hauled out the casket which held his triple-harp.

'Sholabarakosh,' said Togura.

'What kind of a song is that?' said Draven.

'It's not a song, it's the name of my harp,' said Togura, taking the triple-harp from the box, which had now opened.

Shyly, he struck up a note. Then conjured up some percussion. Then suddenly, without warning, roused the air with trumpets louder than elephants. One man sat up so fast he knocked himself out against an overhang.

'That's something!' said Draven. 'Can you pick up this tune?'

And he sang the tune of 'The Pirate's Homecoming', the words of which begin like this:

'Her thighs were hot, her thighs were wide,
And ready she was waiting.'

After a little bit of difficulty, Togura managed to pick up the tune. Soon he was embellishing it. Truly, as has been Written (in Golosh IV, magna 7, script 2, verse xii): Music hath Powers. Soon all the pirates, though they had no liquor inside them, were singing, clapping and slapping their thighs; and Togura, no longer in fear of death or demolition, was learning what it was like to be popular.

275

CHAPTER 39

The seas at the end of summer mourned onto the rocks of Togura's island of exile. He cast a chip of wood adrift. Watching it wash away in the waves, he wished himself home.

Elsewhere on the island, Draven was campaigning. The last leader of the pirates was dead, killed at Androlmarphos. Draven said that Elkor Alish, who had led them since then, had no claim to their loyalty:

'After all, he's never had to face a vote in a free election. Remember that, boys. We all know that elections are the only way to get government of the pirates, by the pirates, for the pirates.'

'But,' said someone, 'Elkor Alish is the world's greatest warleader. We need an alliance with him. He can make us rich.'

'Rich?' said Draven. 'All the profit so far has gone to the earth, enriched with our blood and bones. I can't see that changing. If I could, of course I'd make an alliance for income – the pirate trade is thin at times, no doubting. But to make an alliance for the privilege of losing my liver? Now that's another story.'

So spoke Draven.

But Togura, of course, never heard him.

Togura was far away, trying to decipher the weather-worn inscription of an ancient seashore tomb. Giving up, he sat down on a rock and looked out to sea. The sun was burning down into the Central Ocean. Soon it would be night.

Elsewhere, Draven was still at work.

Ten days later, he was still hard at it.

'I'm an honest man,' said Draven, making politics to pirates. 'You don't believe it? No doubt you've been listening to that fool Mellicks, a drunken sod of a sot with a barnacle backside, a liar since birth, like his whore-beefing father before him. Now listen here . . . '

The days weathered away.

While Draven politicked, Togura, on his lonesome, explored paths, tunnels and stairways, the legacy of generations of stoneworking. He discovered the stoneworkers of the Greater Teeth: a dwarvish undercast of untouchables, an inbred people with stunted noses, heart defects and bad teeth. He heard the melancholy melodies of their pan pipes, then tried, without success, to reproduce those melodies on his triple-harp.

'Hark to me,' said Draven, addressing a pirate gathering. 'Harken up. You – yes, you, the woman in the corner – fart off! You men now – hear me out. What do we want from life? Two ships for riding – one made of wood, the other made of woman. We've got that. So why so many of us killed for no good purpose, tideline wreckage on a foreign shore . . . ?'

While Draven preached and debated, Togura, elsewhere, investigated sea caves – some, half-flooded by the tides, used as harbours or as dry docks. He met the shipwrights of the Greater Teeth, who were slaves but proud regardless, for they were masters of their craft; he heard stories of their strange and distant lands, and, in return, played them music, the like of which they had never heard before.

'How can I get a passage to Sung?' he asked.

'Nobody sails for Sung,' he was told. 'Some, though, sail on the now and then for the Lesser Teeth.'

'How so?' he asked.

'Because the Greater have the rule of the Lesser.'

Exploring this half-hope of getting at least half-way home, Togura learnt that under the rule of the pirate chief Menator – now dead – the pirates had conquered the sand-shore fishing islands known as the Lesser Teeth. They now maintained a shipboard garrison in Brennan Harbour, the only half-decent port in the Lesser Teth, and exacted tribute from the populace.

Precisely two and a half days after Togura learnt of this, a few pirates arrived in the Greater Teeth, having come south from the Lesser in an open boat. They brought a tale of terror. On a dark night of hard and driving wind, the people of Brennnan had rowed out to cut the anchor ropes of the three garrison ships, which had been driven ashore and wrecked. The crews had been slaughtered.

'We set out to get an empire,' said Draven, darkly, to all the pirates who would listen. 'At this rate, we'll be lucky to keep our bones.'

Togura, despairing of any swift return to Sung, accepted an invitation to tour the Outer Rocks, the most barren part of the Greater Teeth. There, he played music for sealing parties. Sealing was an important part of the economy of the Greater Teeth, which could not be sustained by loot alone. Oil for lamps, furs for clothes, meat for the pot − all this the seals provided. Seal blubber was eaten by all; being an excellent antiscorbutic, it helped keep them healthy.

While Togura was playing music on the Outer Rocks, Draven, still on the island of Knock, was calling out his main rival for the pirate leadership:

'Your father had no cock. He used a sausage instead. So that's what you were born with. But your mother bit it off at birth. Draw, you cockless hunk of shit-ballast, draw!'

They drew, and fought, blade against blade. Draven killed his rival. Thanks to his diligent campaigning and the eloquence of his steel, Draven's triumph over the imperialists was complete; having convinced his peers of the futility of fighting wars of aggression in foreign lands, he was elected as leader.

'What now?' asked someone.

'What now? Why, get your cocks out, boys, and breed, boys, breed. We're down a generation, so let's make up for it.'

This programme of action − simple, cheap and practical − proved suitably popular.

Togura, sitting alone on the shores of the Outer Rocks, brooded about the news of the breeding programme. He could not participate, for he had no woman of his own. He played his triple-harp to the wind, the gulls, the seals alive and dead, and the heaping surf of the flotsam-jetsam waves; homesick, he longed for Sung, and mourned for the loss of his true love, Day Suet. He remembered the voice of Day Suet, the warmth of Day Suet, the naked thighs of Day Suet, and the night when she had almost made him a man.

Day Suet was gone forever, for an evil Zenjingu fighter had thrown her into the odex, and had then jumped in after her. Togura had gone questing for the index which spoke the Universal Language, and which would have allowed him to rescue Day, but he had failed to find it. All he had was a magic casket − it would, he supposed, make a good tinder box − and this stupid triple-harp.

'At least I tried,' said Togura.

And comforted himself by telling himself how very hard he had tried.

A message came from Draven, brought by word of mouth:

'Come back. We need you to play at a banquet.'

Togura supposed that the banquet was to celebrate Draven's accession to the leadership of the pirates of the Greater Teeth − as indeed it was, at least initially. But by the time Togura got back to Knock, which was a few days later, the purpose of the banquet had changed dramatically. It was now to honour the warrior Elkor Alish and the mercenary army which had lately arrived from the far-off islands of Rovac to serve under his war banner.

'A week,' said Togura, sagely, 'is a long time in politics.'

Elkor Alish, who had been defeated at Androlmarphos, had now recovered the death stone and two magic bottles besides. It was a mystery how Alish had managed to steal these things away from the enemy, but there was no doubt about what they signified. They meant power, glory, victory. War fever swept the Greater Teeth. Loud-mouthed imperialists once more boasted about how they would be princes, kings, lords of pomp and circumstance in a world-conquering empire.

And Draven?

He cheered for conquest with the rest.

The soldiers of the mercenary army from the islands of Rovac had come, for the most part, in trading ships chartered in the west, though a few had arrived in Rovac longships – slim, beautiful, shallow-draught vessels which Togura would have thought too fragile to dare the open ocean. He could only guess what hardship the longship crews had suffered on their long journey east.

Elkor Alish had brought five longships and two hundred Rovac warriors to the Greater Teeth; most of the Rovac and most of their ships were at Runcorn. The Rovac were the proudest, hardest, most humourless men Togura had ever seen; they frightened him, for it seemed that a grim, relentless Purpose possessed them.

Elkor Alish spoke to a general meeting of all the fighting men in the Great Hall of Knock (which should by rights have been called the Great Cave). He spoke partly in Rovac, partly in Galish. He was entirely changed from the relaxed, genial man Togura had met after the defeat at Androlmarphos.

Now that Alish once more had the chance of victory, he too had become hard, humourless, driving. When he spoke, his voice rang out, a thundering challenge in which even Togura could hear the underlying notes of remorseless fanaticism. Alish spoke of war, conquest, glory, vengeance. And men cheered, shouted, stamped their feet, roared out their absolute approval. Even Togura found himself, for a moment, excited by the prospect of war, loot, slaughter, arson, rape.

At the banquet which followed, pirates and Rovac warriors got drunk together, drinking away as if their leading ambition in life was to die of alcoholic poisoning or cirrhosis of the liver. While mostly everyone got legless, Togura, promising himself a dram or two later, played his triple-harp to general acclaim.

There was no confrontation between Alish and Draven, for Draven knew when he was defeated. At the height of the banquet, he stood and freely pledged himself to the world conqueror:

'I, Bluewater Draven, speak to you, Elkor Alish, that all men

280

may hear and know. Harken! By my heartbeat's blood, I swear, with all my honour, to love you as my brother, to obey you as my captain, to accept you as my king, to follow your wars to the hilt of my sword and the last of my leather. I ask nothing in return; to serve is enough.'

It was handsomely said. There were cheers. The banqueting men guzzled down drink after drink and got raucous. The Rovac roared out drunken poetry in their own language. Togura noted that neither Draven nor Elkor Alish drank much; they spent a lot of time conferring together, their voices masked by the uproar all around.

Finally Draven sent one of this sidekicks to Togura with a message:

'Elkor Alish and myself are removing our enjoyments to my own home. Follow, with your harp.'

Togura obeyed.

CHAPTER 40

In Draven's cave home, Togura played a little light music, but Alish and Draven scarcely listened. They were talking business. It was Alish who took the initiatives.

Togura, listening, was amazed at the range of subjects they covered. Alish discussed the rule of the Greater Teeth, the appointment of a judge to resolve any disputes between Rovac warriors and pirates, a revised ration scale, a programme of weapons training, the provisioning of Runcorn . . .

In the end, Togura listened no more, but played; Alish's bodyguards dozed. Draven served a little wine. Togura was not offered any. The bodyguards refused; they had their orders from Alish. Draven himself did not drink, saying he had had enough.

But Alish drank.

And, having drunk, grew sleepy.

'We'll talk on tomorrow,' he said.

Then tried to stand, and stumbled.

'Strike!' roared Draven, in a bellow so loud it hurt Togura's ears.

Alish's bodyguards were instantly on the alert. They drew weapons, preparing to fight to the death. One of them made as if to attack Draven.

'No, no,' said the pirate, making a warding gesture with his hands. 'There's nothing wrong. I was only calling my slave, Strike. That's his name. Strike. Understand?'

One of the Rovac warriors checked the tunnel leading from Draven's cave home.

'It's all clear,' he said.

Yet Draven's shout had made the bodyguards suspicious, hostile, aggressive. In this foreign place they were quick to take alarm, and slow to relax.

'Please,' said Togura, wishing to avoid an incident in which his head might get lopped off by accident. 'He's drunk. I've seen him like this before. His brain's half-rotted. Waking nightmares attack him, then he screams.'

The bodyguards, mollified, withdrew, taking Alish – who was now totally insensible – with them. Once they were well and truly gone, Draven began to swear, viciously. His anger needed an audience; he poured out his heart to Togura. Despite his speech at the banquet, Draven wanted nothing more to do with the mad adventures planned by Elkor Alish.

' . . . so I arranged for twenty of the best to be here tonight,' said Draven. 'On the word 'Strike!' they were to do just that. Alish should be dead by now, by rights. We should have this death-stone which gives him his power. We should have his magic bottles, too, and the rings which command them.'

Thus spoke Draven. And, after enlarging for some time on the habits, appearance and ancestry of the twenty cowards who had broken their word to him, he turned on Togura:

'So now you'll have to do the job.'

'Me?'

'Yes, you. Get into his sleeping quarters. Kill him. Steal the death-stone. While you're about it, steal the rings and the magic bottles. There's one red, one green.'

'Green and red rings?'

'No, fool! Green and red bottles. The rings are on his fingers. You'd have seen them there tonight, if you'd been watching.'

'This is madness,' said Togura.

'Twenty men have let me down tonight,' said Draven. 'How do I know who they're talking to now? Any of twenty might betray us to the Rovac.'

'Us?'

'Yes, us. You and me. You're known as my associate. Do you think they'll think you're innocent? Take your harp. Bluff your way to Alish's bedside. Then knife him. Take what we need.'

'This,' said Togura, 'is crazy.'

'It's our only hope!'

And, shortly, Togura was on his way to Alish's quarters. Draven halted at the last tunnel-turning.

'I'll wait here,' said Draven. 'Be swift. Be sure. Be certain.'

'But he might wake and kill me!'

'He won't wake. Not tonight. That last wine I fed him was drugged. You're safe. I guarantee it.'

Trembling, Togura set off down the tunnel, harp in one hand, and oil lamp in the other. Eight guards were on duty outside Alish's quarters. When he drew near, they challenged him in their own native tongue, which he did not understand.

'Peace,' said Togura, speaking in a low, even tone; he didn't want anyone getting over-excited and attacking him. 'My name's Togura Poulaan. I'm here to tell you about a plot to kill Elkor Alish. It's Draven who wants to kill him. Draven's waiting close at hand. You can grab him now. Chop his head off – that's what I'd do. Do you understand?'

The Rovac warriors didn't seem to. The bodyguards who had carried Alish away from Draven's cave house had gone off duty; this was a new set of guards, and it seemed none of them spoke Galish.

'This is very very important,' said Togura, speaking urgently. 'Elkor Alish, understand? Killing. Chop chop!'

The guards looked at each other, and conferred in their alien tongue. They saw the harp; a couple of them recognised Togura from the banquet. Finally one of them gestured: he was free to enter Alish's quarters.

'No, no,' said Togura. 'That's not what I want! I want—'

The guard grew impatient, and gave him a push.

He went sprawling, losing his grip on harp and oil lamp. The lamp went out. One of the guards, a bit of a bully, gave him a kick in the backside. Togura snatched up his harp and went bundling through some heavy door hangings, entering Alish's quarters.

The first room, a windowless cube hewn out of solid rock, was lit by a single long-burning candle. It was a living room; there were some sheepskin rugs on the floor, a couple of leather-padded chairs, a couch, some cushions, a couple of low-slung tables, and, set in niches around the walls, a collection of tobacco-coloured shrunken heads.

More heavy door hangings barred the way into the next room. Togura, breathing heavily, made his mind up. He would wake Elkor Alish. If Alish was too heavily drugged to wake, then he would sit up – all night, if necessary – until Alish did wake. Alish spoke Galish. Alish would have Draven's head chopped off.

That was the only reasonable thing to do. Togura, after his near-drownings, his illnesses, his bone breakages, his captivities and his throat-shaving escapes, was acutely aware of the fragility of his own existence. The Rovac warriors frightened him from nerve ends to bone marrow; the very last thing he wanted was to bring down the wrath of the Rovac nation on his own head.

Boldly, he went through into the inner chamber.

Elkor Alish was sleeping in a narrow bed, his body covered with a wolf skin.

'Alish,' said Togura, trembling, stepping toward him.

Then someone touched him from behind. Shocked, he whirled, slamming an uppercut into his assailant's jaw. His attacker fell, knocked unconscious. It was a she! And she was naked!

Now what had he done?

He had over-reacted, knocking out Alish's bedtime playmate.

There was a grunt from the bed.

Togura turned to see Alish throwing aside the wolf skin. He had been put to bed armed and fully dressed. He started lugging his sword out of its sheath.

Togura snatched up a small table. As Alish lurched toward him, he threw it. Smashed by the table, the Rovac warrior went down.

Togura felt sick.

What a mess!

Was Alish dead?

No — despite the drug Draven had fed him, and a heavy blow from the table, he was still breathing. But he had taken a hard crack on the head. Exploring the warrior's skull, Togura's fingers detected a massive bruise already forming.

He was horrified.

Should he wait, and see if Alish recovered consciousness? A nice idea indeed — one of the guards outside might come in to check on his leader. And then what would happen? It would be head-in-lap time for Togura Poulaan.

He had to get away.

He had to get out of here. And off the island. He would have to ask Draven to help him. But Draven would be after his blood when he came back without the death-stone. And the rings. And the bottles.

Togura looked around, desperately. He saw a small bottle decorated with green glaze. That must be one of the magic bottles which people spoke about — bottles in which an army could hide. Now — the rings. He looked at Alish's hands. Finding one ring only. Where was the other one? Where was the red bottle? And where was the death-stone?

He searched, swiftly, but did not find what he sought. One ring, then. He took it off Alish's hand, with difficulty, for it was a tight fit. A ring and a bottle. How was he going to get them out of here?

He stuffed the bottle under his clothing, but it made an obscene, bulbous lump. There was no way to crush it down so it would lie flat and inconspicuous. In the end he hid it under his clothes, but jammed up into his armpit. That was where it was least conspicuous, though he had to keep an arm in close to his body to hold it in place. Now — the ring. Simple! He popped it into his mouth for safe keeping.

Then left, harp in hand, bottle under arm.

From the inner chamber he went to the outer chamber, and from the outer chamber he went to the tunnel beyond. There, the guards grabbed him. He was so startled that he swallowed the ring.

One of the Rovac guards, speaking incomprehensible foreign words, asked him something.

'Do you want me to explain myself all over again?' asked Togura, catching the note of interrogation in the man's words. 'Well, the long and the short of it is that I've raided Elkor Alish's quarters. I've taken a bash at his resident sex toy. I've smashed the man himself – he'll possibly die tonight. I've taken his green bottle, which is this goiterous lump under my arm which I hope none of you are looking at. And I've just swallowed the magic ring which commands that bottle. That was your fault. You startled me. Now let me go!'

And he pulled himself free.

One of the guards grunted, and gave him a kick, and he set off down the tunnel at a sedate walk.

Draven met him.

'Did you get the goodies?'

'One bottle only,' said Togura. 'No death-stone. No rings.'

'Did you search his clothing? His bedding?'

'No, but—'

'Fool! He'll have them in bed with him, or next to his skin. Give me that bottle! Give it! That's better. Now go back for the rest. Now! This instant!'

'But—'

'No buts, or my slice will unsplice you. Back! Back!'

Togura took a few hesitant steps back the way he had come. Then he heard shouts of anger, rage and alarm coming from the direction of Alish's chamber.

'Draven,' he said, 'I think we're in trouble.'

And they fled.

CHAPTER 41

Draven and Togura escaped from the wrath of the Rovac by putting to sea in a dinghy. They didn't go far. Dawn found them in a sheltered cliff-walled inlet.

'Strip!' said Draven.

'What?'

'Take your clothes off.'

'Are you mad?'

'Do what I say!'

Togura, reluctantly, obeyed. Draven searched him and his clothes minutely.

'So you haven't got it,' said Draven, disappointed.

'I haven't got what?'

'The death-stone. What else? You let me down, you useless heap of turdshit. You failed me. After all I've done for you! We could have ruled the universe. I should cut you up for sharkmeat.'

Draven, angry, thwarted and vengeful, seemed to be working himself up to a killing rage. Togura, eager to make amends for his failings, almost blurted out the truth about the missing ring to command the green bottle. Then restrained himself, suspecting that Draven might cut to his gut to be sure of getting his hands on it. As Draven drew his knife, Togura cried:

'It's the dralkosh! Yen Olass Ampadara! The evil one! She's making you do this! You're still under her spell!'

288

'What?' cried Draven, amazed.

'Yes,' said Togura, desperately. 'You told me all about her. She killed you. She chopped you up. She resurrected you.'

'Oh . . . that,' said Draven.

The pirate was, for some reason, suddenly acutely embarrassed. All the rant and rage drained out of him; looking rather shamefaced, he sheathed his knife.

'Get dressed,' said Draven, speaking roughly, as if harsh words could dispell his embarrassment. Then, in a more conciliatory tone: 'I was wrong to draw on you. That was my failing. You were right to remind me of the Ampadara woman. But speak no more of it – the subject is painful.'

'I'll never mention it again,' said Togura, dressing.

Conjuring with the name of Ampadara had been a desperate ploy. It had worked. So there really had been a woman in Tameran by the name of Ampadara, who had had dealings with Draven. Togura was starting to suspect that the history of Draven and Ampadara was not quite as the pirate had told it, but he also suspected that he would never be sure of the truth, and that the matter of Ampadara would be an unsolved mystery for as long as he lived – which, if the Rovac caught up with him, would not be long.

By this time, the sinking tides had unwatered a fraction of a deep-tunnelling cave. Draven pointed to it.

'That's where we're going to hide.'

'In there?'

'That's what I said.'

'Well . . . hadn't we better wait for the water to go down a bit more?'

'This is as low as it gets.'

It was impossible to row into the cave, for the edges of the rock almost scraped the edges of the dinghy. Togura and Draven had to lie flat on their backs in the oar-boat, and walk it into the cave, bracing against the roof with their boots.

Within, the cave opened up into a vast chasm, half water, half air. Flaws in the rock above pierced upward to the sky, but the wan light which filtered through those flaws was scarcely as strong as starlight.

'My father found this cave,' said Draven. 'He never told a soul, save me and my brothers.'

'What if your brothers betray you?'

'One drowned when diving for gaplax. One fell off a cliff. One died of the plague in the year of two comets. One's a slave in Chi'ash-lan – if he's still alive at all. One's the king of Chenameg, or used to be. One went trading east of Ashmolea – for all I know, he's in Yestron. There's none to betray us.'

'So we're safe then.'

'For the moment.'

The moment steadily lengthened. They camped on a rock ledge above water level. They drank from a slow-dripping seepage filtering through the rocks, but they had no food. Togura whiled away the darkness by playing his triple-harp, softly, softly.

And waited.

He was constipated. He remembered his father, Baron Chan Poulaan, quoting a common little maxim on the subject:

'If you don't eat you don't shit, and if you don't shit you die!'

However, on the third day, when Draven was sleeping, Togura obtained relief. Prospecting for treasure he found it; he cleaned the ring, then hid it away in the toe of his left boot. By now, having listened to Draven lamenting his loss often enough, Togura knew how to use the ring. He only had to put it on his finger, and turn it, and he would be inside the green bottle which he had stolen from Elkor Alish.

Togura was tempted to experiment, but did not. Though he was very, very hungry by now, and knew there might well be food inside the green bottle, his priorities were simple: Safety first.

CHAPTER 42

They waited in hiding for three days, then slipped back to an unsuspecting harbour and stole food, some barrels of water and a two-masted sealing boat.

As they toiled north in the open sealing-boat, Togura learnt more about sailing then he'd ever wanted to know. He learnt under the worst possible conditions. The boat was too big for two men to handle easily. It leaked. The seas were rough. It rained. An autumn storm beat them about like milk in a butter-churn. They lost their water-barrels overboard. They ran out of food.

And Draven, impatient, bad-tempered, screamed, shouted, cursed and roared abuse. Togura, sleeping between lurches of the sea, sometimes had nightmares in which Draven — swollen to the size of a giant — roared at him:

'Gazzen the hull-skit! Batten the lee! Clabber the gasts, the legs are slipping! Sheet the wind, you spittle-spawned moron! Dirk up the kneecaps!'

And he would wake to find Draven screaming at him in some half-coherent sea-jabber; sometimes, stumbling about the boat with the seas washing around his ankles, he found it hard to say when Draven's talk ended and the dreamtalk of nightmare began.

The sea was endless.

The sea was a windstalking wasteland where waves ate each other and hungered for the bones of men. It was empty,

empty, empty. No place to sleep; no place to lie down. They were always cold, they were always wet, they were always tired, they were always hungry. Heartsick, sea sick, sick of the roiling waves and the slathering spray, Togura longed for land.

'Turn east,' he said, when the weather favoured them with a sunrise.

He knew the coast of Argan lay to the east. They could make land easily, and swiftly. But Draven kept them driving for the north.

'We need to make Sung,' said Draven.

'Why Sung?' said Togura.

It was his homeland, true, but all he wanted now was some land which wouldn't buckle under him from moment to moment.

'Log Jaris is the man to help us now.'

'Log who?'

'You know. You met him. The man at D'Waith with the head and the horns of a bull.'

'Oh, him!' said Togura. 'I thought I'd imagined him.'

'Dream on. And while you're about it − bail.'

He did bail.

He bailed the boat dry.

It rained.

'Good,' he said, drinking.

'Very good,' said Draven, slaking his own thirst. And then, to the sky: 'Okay, that's enough now! You can give it a shake and put it away!'

But if this advice was meant to stop the rain, it failed. The rain grew worse. So did the wind. Soon the boat was thrashing about in a regular storm.

Night, at last, fell, and with the coming of night the storm abated somewhat. Soon it was dying, then dead.

'You steer,' said Draven, yielding the tiller to Togura. 'I'm going to sleep.'

'Which way do I steer?' said Togura.

'I don't know where we are or where the hell we're going,' said Draven, completely disorientated by the shifting stormwinds. 'So just keep the winds behind us.'

'But what if we're going the wrong way?'

Draven, weary, almost too tired to think, scanned the sky for stars, finding none. Sunrise would give them their direction. Till then . . .

'You're right,' said Draven. 'Let's haul down the sail and we'll lie ahull.'

That they did, and were soon sleeping sweetly while the boat drifted through the night. Much later, they woke, almost simultaneously, to the sound of surf breaking on rocks.

'Braunch out!' screamed Draven.

'What?' cried Togura.

'Zelch the pringles!'

Togura, not knowing what a pringle was, or how to zelch it, stood there wringing his hands. The next moment he was flung face-first to the deck as they went surfing into the rocks. Timbers grunched, graunched, despaired and tore open. Smash-batter waves pummelled their way into the boat. Draven, with a cry, was swept overboard. Togura heard his screams jousting with the surf, then − silence.

Silence, at least, from Draven. The wood-wave cacophony continued. With a dreadful sound of rending timbers, the boat broke apart. Togura clung to a piece of wreckage. He was swept away into the sea.

Where was the green bottle?

With Draven.

Wet, cold, shivering, frightened, he clung to his bit of wreckage, swearing and sobbing, cursing sea, waves, wind, water, pirates, quests and adventures in general.

Incautiously, he let his feet drift down.

He touched something underfoot.

He screamed:

'Gaaaa!'

And wrenched his feet up, in case the sea serpent below felt them and bit them off. The waves knocked him around a bit, but he was so terrified that he hardly felt them.

For a while he floated around in a state of helpless funk, then, slowly, logic began to assert itself. They had ripped the

293

boat apart on some rocks. He had now been swept past those rocks, but still . . . rocks usually suggested land. So . . .

Togura put his feet down again, and touched the bottom. He whooped with triumph. A wave smashed him in the face. Blinking away water, he peered through the night, and saw a line of white breaking in the distance. Slowly, he began to wade toward it, and eventually dragged himself up on a sandy beach.

The sky was growing light.

Togura, shivering, shuddering, warmed himself as best he could, dancing round on the beach, singing, slapping his thighs, shouting. He was still at it when Draven, stumbling along the beach, found him.

'Ho, madman!' said Draven.

'You!'

'None other,' said Draven. 'Have you got the green bottle?'

'No, I thought you had it.'

'Pox and piles!' said Draven. 'It's lost!'

They spent half the morning beachcombing, and, at last, found it. But what now? They were, in all probability, on the Lesser Teeth.

'No other coast in these parts has such long, sandy beaches,' said Draven, distinctly gloomy.

Togura did not need to be told that, if the people of the Lesser Teeth got hold of a genuine pirate like Draven, he would probably come to a sticky end.

So there they were, marooned on a hostile foreign shore, with wet clothes, no food, no water, no tinder box, no shelter, and precious little hope of a friendly reception from the natives. It was, without a doubt, time to use the magic ring and get into the green bottle, no matter what the dangers.

Togura took both his boots off, retrieved the ring, massaged his feet, wrung out his socks, put socks and boots back on, and, by the time he had gone through that rigmarole, had nerved himself up to act. Draven would doubtless be furious to find that Togura had kept the capture of the ring secret from him, but the green bottle was alleged to have all kinds of food and other good things inside, and that, with luck, would mollify the angry pirate.

'Draven,' said Togura.

'What?' said the pirate.

'I've got something to show you,' said Togura, taking him by the arm as if to lead him somewhere.

And, his arm linked with Draven's, Togura turned the ring on his hand. A moment later, they were in—

A green chamber, not very well lit.

'Blood's grief!' cried Draven, shocked.

A moment later, something in the shadows by a jumble of empty barrels sat up. It was a man. A warrior!

'Hold fast!' shouted the warrior, drawing his sword.

Draven drew to meet the challenge. And Togura turned the ring again – and was back out on the sands.

He blinked at the light, gasped, shuddered. That was close! It had never occurred to him that there might be someone already in the bottle. And where there was one, there might easily be a dozen.

What now?

If he went back in, he might well be killed by the guard or guards inside. If he stayed outside, he might die of cold and hunger. He looked around. The tide was beginning to go out; the wind was still blowing strong and chill, sending eager little waves scrabbling up the beach.

Togura set off at random, determining to walk until he dropped, hoping that he would find shelter before he dropped. He was rewarded; at mid-morning he came upon a derelict little cottage with a little smoke rising from its ramshackle chimney. There was no door; Togura walked right inside. An old man tending a little fire turned and stared at him with sharp, bright eyes.

Togura cleared his throat.

'Good morning,' said Togura, lamely.

'A rather cold wet miserable morning, if I'm not mistaken,' said the stranger. 'Here's a blanket. Get out of those wet clothes and wrap yourself up in it.'

Togura obeyed.

'Here,' said the stranger, opening a leather bag. 'Here's breakfast. What have we got? Black bread. One boiled egg.

Some dried fish, I wish she wouldn't give me that horrible salty-shrivelled muck, still if you're hungry you'll eat it.'

'Are you sure . . . '

'Am I sure of what? Am I sure I can spare it, you mean? Of course I can. I don't live here, you know! I'm a little richer than this. I'm just here to check on the property, Skyhaven we call it, my uncle's place till he died. My name's Gezeldux. And yours?'

'Togura,' said Togura. 'Togura Poulaan.'

Gezeldux asked no further questions until Togura had eaten. Then, bit by bit, he heard the whole story. By the time Togura had finished telling his tale – Gezeldux was an inquisitive old man, and a diligent interrogator – it was evening.

'You know,' said Gezeldux, when Togura had finished, 'I think you may have done better than you think.'

'How's that?' said Togura.

'Why, if there's any such thing as a Universal Language, it has to be music. Get that triple-harp of yours to Keep, and, three crowns to half a pickle, it'll bring your odex to order.'

'You mean I've found it? I've found the index?'

'Go. Try. See.'

'But how do I get to Sung?' wailed Togura.

'Any boat can stretch across to Sung, no problem. Now rest. Sleep. You're overwrought. Sleep deep, and tomorrow we'll walk back to Brennan.'

So Togura slept, and Gezeldux, an honest and honourable man, made no move against him, that night or after.

CHAPTER 43

Keep!

To Togura it looked small − he no longer thought of it as a city − but marvellous.

'Oh frabjous little town!' cried Togura.

Gaining its narrow little streets with their sloping-slanting rickety-arthritecky buildings, Togura did a dance of triumph.

'Yip yip!' he shouted. 'Hurrah! Callooh! Callay! Skray skray! Oh Halloo-Schlag! Jeronimo!'

These exultations came to an abrupt end when someone at an upper-storey window emptied a bucket of dirty water over him. Muttering dire imprecations, Togura stalked away.

He was still somewhat damp when he stalked into the Wordsmiths' compound.

'Take me to Governor Troop,' said Togura grandly.

'And who might you be?' said the servitor he had confronted, looking him up and down.

'Togura Poulaan,' said Togura, boldly. 'Sword-master, death-dealer, dragon-tamer and questing hero extra-regular, extra-provincial and extraordinary. And, by the by, a Wordmaster in this organisation. So take me to Troop, my good man, or you'll be knucklebone soup in no time.'

'Don't play the red cockerel with me, young strop,' said the servitor, who was bigger and older than Togura. 'We all know about Togura Poulaan. His brother Cromarty paid out good gold for his body's wreckage some six moons back. I saw the muck and mess myself.'

Togura promptly punched the fellow, knocking the wind out of him. It must be noted, with regret, that close acquaintance with the Orfus pirates had caused a certain deterioration in Togura's grasp of the finer points of etiquette.

'It's half-brother, snot-head,' said Togura, as the servitor doubled up, gasping. 'I'm back from the dead, alive and breathing – which is more than you'll be, unless you come to order, pronto.'

Very shortly, Togura was in the presence of Governor Troop.

'Who are you?' said Troop, surveying the stranger in front of him – a hard-faced young man with a scarred nose and a raggedy beard.

'I,' said Togura, 'am Togura Poulaan, also known as Barak the Battleman and as Forester. I am, in case you don't remember—'

'Why, boy, of course, of course!' said Governor Troop, rising, beaming, taking him by the hand. 'How foolish of me! Our questing hero! You've found the index, have you?'

'Not so fast!' said Togura, keeping hold of the Governor's hand, and squeezing it a little, trying to feel the bones through the fat.

'We have a problem?' said Governor Troop, twisting free. 'Why, my boy, I'm sure we can easily sort things out. Sit down and have a drink.'

'We don't have time to drink,' said Togura grimly. 'My men are waiting for me to return with news of satisfaction.'

'Your men?' said Governor Troop.

'My hand-picked killing guard,' said Togura, bluffing without a blush. 'They're waiting out in the wilds. The rest of my legions, of course, are still on the Lesser Teeth.'

'Your legions?'

'Don't look so startled, man!' shouted Togura. 'It's near enough to three years since I left here. Three years of world-wandering, of challenges, courage-tests, heroic deeds. Is it any wonder I've got a following? I've fought dragons. I've killed men in combat, my hands armed or empty. I've commanded troops in the Harvest Plains, I've—'

'Peace!' begged Governor Troop. 'Peace, don't hurt us, don't, please, what do you want?'

The soft fat little butter-plated man disgusted Togura. In a loud, hard voice he made his demands:

'My agent, the wizard of Drum, made an agreement with you and yours. I was to risk all — toes, kneecaps, cock, balls, heart, guts, stomach, neck — to recover the index. Not an easy task, my man! Not with monsters, mad wizards, invading armies, sundry assorted barbarian slaughter-specialists and other hazards to contend with.'

'Yes, yes, I know, I know.'

'In return,' said Togura, 'you and yours were, among other things, to force Cromarty to withdraw the reward offered for my head. I now know — don't try to tell me different! — that that reward was paid out.'

'But you've still got your head.'

'That's not the point! You and yours were supposed to deal with Cromarty. Instead, I've still got to do the job.'

'I'm sure you're more than equal to it,' said Governor Troop, with something like a purr in his voice.

'That's not the point!' said Togura. 'You reneged on our agreement. You broke the contract. That being so, since you're in dereliction of your contractural obligations, I'm in no mind to settle for the paltry eleven per cent my agent settled for.'

'I think—'

'Don't! Listen, now. I'll settle for fifty per cent. Fifty per cent of everything that comes out of the odex. Fifty per cent by value. Take it or leave it.'

Shortly, Togura had extracted a written contract from the Wordsmiths. He departed, saying he was going to confer with his men in the hills. Instead, he went and sought out Raznak the Golsh, one of the most powerful men in the Suet clan. They had a long discussion together.

In return for a small cut of Togura's income from the odex, Raznak the Golsh promised Togura armed protection against

Cromarty, and assured him he would certainly have Day Suet's hand in marriage if he could recover that young adorable from the odex.

The next morning, Togura presented himself again to Governor Troop, then went to try his triple-harp, the putative index, on the odex. Now was the moment of truth. Would it work or wouldn't it?

The odex looked just the same as ever: a thin grey disk, invisible when viewed side-on, a mirror when seen from an angle, a discordant swirl of kaleidoscopic colour when seen from directly in front.

'Ahyak Rovac!' screamed Togura, testing the odex with a fighting-phrase he had picked up on his travels.

Out from the odex came a fang-gaping ilps, a vicious manxome monster which Governor Troop demolished with five well-placed immaculately-timed questions.

'Sholabarakosh,' said Togura, saying the Word needed to open his enchanted casket.

The odex spat liquid jade. Fortunately, it missed both Togura and Governor Troop. The jade hit the ground, hissing, and hardened swiftly. Togura took his triple-harp from the casket.

'That's the index?' said Governor Troop.

'Watch,' said Togura.

And he began to play. He tried high notes and low notes, chords and crescendos. He played something by the way of melody, and something by the way of outrage. He played a caterwauling fugue of his own invention. The music excited the odex. Ilpses came bubbling out, some hard, some lumpy, some focused, some frothy, some with five mandibles and some with seven, some hairy, some glossy. Chased by questions, these fugitive apparitions streamed up into the sky; in the streets beyond, dogs began to bark and howl.

Finally, Governor Troop laughed.

'Well, boy,' said the Governor. 'It seems you haven't done as well as you thought. This is no better than shouting at it.'

'I'm not finished yet,' said Togura.

300

'You are for the moment. Sit over there, boy. We've our daily petitioners to deal with.'

Togura sat to one side, sulking, while various petitioners entered and were permitted – for a small fee – to cast things into the odex. In went a bundle of squalling kittens which someone had been too soft-hearted to drown. In went an unwanted baby of female gender. An old man, wheezing with emphysema, was hauled off his stretcher and flung into the odex. ('Not dead but merely resting,' said the young priest who supervised this operation.)

'Okay then,' said Governor Troop, when this was finished. 'You can try again.'

Togura did try.

Vigorously.

He made music and unmusic pour forth from the triple-harp, but all that came out of the odex was more ilpses – all grinning with high hilarity – a small dead fish, a single false tooth and one thin book. The book proved to be full of entirely incomprehensible squiggles (it was, in fact, an antiquated timetable of tides for the Penvash Channel).

'Well, boy,' said Governor Troop, 'a good try, but you haven't succeeded. Not this time. We know there's other places you might find an index, though. When are you going to set off?'

'Oh, pox and piles!' shouted Togura.

Frustrated beyond endurance, he was about to smash the triple-harp to pieces. Just in time, he restrained himself. It was, after all, valuable in its own right.

'Play some more pretty music,' said Governor Troop. 'The ilpses like it, after all!'

'Oh, shit shit shit!' shouted Togura, losing his temper entirely.

And he hurled the triple-harp into the odex.

'Oh, buggeration!' said Togura, as the odex swallowed the triple-harp. 'Now look what you've made me do!'

'I?' said Governor Troop, with the merest hint of a giggle in his voice. 'Boy, I made you do nothing!'

Togura was tempted to draw steel and kill him.

But before Togura could reach a decision on the matter, the odex spat out the triple-harp.

'There, boy,' said Governor Troop, in a condescending voice. 'Don't fret now. It's given you your music back.'

Togura stooped, and picked up the triple-harp. Of its own accord, it began to play. Not music, exactly, but a weird series of disjointed notes, some high, some low, some flaunting after bat-squeak pitches, some rumbling low to challenge earthquake. And, as it played, the odex began to disgorge things.

Out came the old man wheezing with emphysema.

Out came the unwanted girl baby.

Out came the bundle of squalling kittens.

Out came a bucket-burden of breakfast slops.

'All right,' said Governor Troop, 'you've proved your point. Now stop it.'

'No!' said Togura, who couldn't have if he had wanted to, because he didn't know how.

Out came a heap of slag and ashes.

Out came a blind woman with a battered face.

'You will stop it, you know,' said Governor Troop, advancing on Togura.

Togura drew steel.

'One step further and you're dead!' shouted Togura.

He kept the Wordsmiths at bay for just a little time, then needed to keep them at bay no longer, for things were pouring out in such a flurry that nobody could get near him. He held his station beside the odex as things vomited forth: blood, spittle, urine, dung, ashes, rags, mouldy bread, stones, a mad dog, fish bones, a madman, a cripple, a three-headed calf.

All the filthy, obscene, dirty, unwanted, unloved, despised, hated, feared and abominated objects the world had seen fit to dispose of came surging, screaming, fighting, biting, shouting, reeking, piddling, lurching, slurching and slumping out of the odex. Soon Togura was ankle-deep in filth, then knee-deep. The Wordsmiths fled as things half-dead and half-alive blundered about the courtyard, seeking and finding ways of escape.

Suddenly a familiar voice cried:

'By the hell, you pox-blighted Suets!'

'Paps!' screamed Togura.

His father, the redoubtable Baron Chan Poulaan, turned and saw his son, and waded toward him.

'Pox of a demon!' roared the Baron. 'What is going on here? Where have those dog-buggering Suets run away to? What's all this — blood's corruption! What a stink!'

'Paps!' said Togura, almost weeping with joy and relief.

'Don't call me that!' said his father savagely. 'What's making this mess? What's that music-thing?'

'It's commanding the odex,' said Togura.

'Then stop it.'

'I can't,' said Togura.

'Can't?' said his father. 'I'll show you can't!'

And he snatched the triple-harp from Togura.

'No, paps!' screamed Togura.

But his father put the triple-harp on his knee and smashed it with his mailed fist. The music jangled away into silence. One last thing fell out of the odex: a black-clad Zenjingu fighter and the young and beautiful Day Suet.

'Day!' shouted Togura.

'Help me!' screamed Day.

The Zenjingu fighter looked around, bewildered. As far as he was concerned, he had jumped into the odex — which had been described to him as a Door — just a moment before. That had been at night. Now broad daylight shone down, revealing—

The Zenjingu fighter saw what he was standing in, and swore. He picked up Day Suet and threw her into the odex. Then he jumped in after her, and was gone. An ilps popped out of the odex, giggled, and hauled itself into the sky.

'Well,' said Baron Chan Poulaan, briskly. 'So much for that. Come along home, Togura.'

Togura turned and smashed him. Or tried to. What actually happened was that his father caught his fist in his hand.

'If you want to play fisticuffs,' said the Baron, 'do it with

303

someone else. Coming? No? Well, we'll see you when you get hungry, no doubt.'

And with that, Baron Chan Poulaan strode for the exit.

'Wait about!' said Governor Troop, intercepting him. 'You haven't paid the resurrection tax yet.'

'Resurrection tax?' said the Baron, in tones of outraged incredulity.

'You've been in the odex three years, you know. You owe us three years' rent, as well.'

'It was you who let those pig-licking Suets throw me into it in the first place!' roared the Baron.

'That doesn't alter your obligations,' said the Governor.

And he grabbed hold of the Baron, who smashed him with one mail-clad fist, breaking his collar bone. As Governor Troop slumped down in the muck, the Baron stalked out of the Wordsmiths' compound; Togura thought it safest to follow him.

He found a quiet corner then sat down and wept bitter tears of hate, spite, self-disgust, self-pity, remorse, frustration and despair.

CHAPTER 44

What now?

The only thing Togura could think of was to go to the island of Drum and get help from the wizard of Drum. Somewhere, other indexes were hidden. He would have to go and get one. He had to!

Anyway, first things first.

Furtively, Togura stole water from someone's rainwater barrel, and cleaned himself up. Then he went and sold his sword, to get some working capital. He still had a knife, after all, and lack of food would kill him sooner than would lack of a sword.

With a little of the money, he bought some roasted chestnuts, and wandered about, eating slowly, and brooding. While he was still undecided as to what to do next, he was hailed:

'Hi there!'

Looking around, Togura saw his half-brother Cromarty approaching with half a dozen grinning scungers flanking him.

'Long time no see, little brother,' said Cromarty.

'Pax,' said Togura, offering peace.

'Oh, we could always have pax with your bones, suppose suppose,' said Cromarty.

And advanced on him, with evil his obvious intent. Togura turned and fled. Whooping, Cromarty's mob followed. Then ran him to earth near Dead Man's Drop. Caught in a cul-de-sac, Togura turned at bay, his back to the wall and a knife in his hand.

Cromarty drew to meet his challenge.

'This is the end, methinks methinks,' said Cromarty, closing with him. 'So it's goodbye little Tog-Tog.'

Steel against steel, they clashed, slashed, lunged, parried. Panting, they thrust and counterthrust, dared for a blink, hacked, countered, feinted, tried for a scalp.

'Blood his eyeballs, Crom!' screamed one of the mobsters.

'Bollock him!'

'Rivet him!'

'Into him, Crom!'

'A throat-tattoo! Teach him!'

Then Cromarty slipped. Togura put in the boot. Cromarty went backwards. Togura stamped all the wind out of him, then grabbed him, knife to throat.

'Yield!' hissed Togura, digging his steel in just a little deeper than a tickle. 'Yield!'

Cromarty slowly got his breath back. He croaked:

'I yield.'

'Good,' said Togura.

And stood, and sheathed his knife. Cromarty's sidekicks promptly grabbed him.

'Let go!' shouted Togura, kicking, punching, wriggling, scratching, biting — all to no avail.

'Good,' crooned Cromarty, mustering up a smile. 'Very good. What shall we do with him?'

'Throw him over Dead Man's Drop,' suggested one.

'An excellent idea!' said Cromarty, beaming.

Togura started to scream with hysterical panic as they carted him through the streets to Dead Man's Drop. Nobody took any notice—private quarrels, after all, were private quarrels.

They reached the Drop.

'Take off his boots, boys,' said Cromarty.

They took them off.

'Hold him over the edge,' said Cromarty.

Togura was held.

'Watch,' said Cromarty, sweet satisfaction in his voice.

He lofted first one boot then the other into the air. They went sailing down, falling away to the pinnacles far below. Togura, sick with fear, vomited weakly. His whole body was trembling.

'Please don't,' he begged. 'Please please please don't. I'll do anything!'

Cromarty tore the green bottle loose from Togura's belt, where it had been tied on with twine. He threw that over too.

'We're brothers!' screamed Togura.

'I'm no brother of yours, son of a whore,' said Cromarty pleasantly.

'Don't don't don't do it,' said Togura, almost too frightened to speak. 'I'll do anything.'

'Will you lick my boots?'

'Yes!'

'My arse?'

'Yes!'

'Well,' said Cromarty, sweetly, 'I don't want any boot-licking arse-lickers in my family. Throw him over, boys!'

They began to swing Togura back and forth.

'One!' they chanted.

'Two!'

Togura moaned with terror.

'Three!'

On the word 'three', they tossed Togura into the dizzy gulf. He fell, screaming. His arms flailed. His legs kicked. Down, down, down he went.

And remembered the ring!

The ring on his hand, which, if turned, would get him into the green bottle!

Desperately, he turned it.

It didn't work!

The earth swept up to meet him.

He turned the ring again.

No good!

He went hurtling toward the slaughtering rocks.

And turned the ring. And—

The rocks came slamming toward him—

But—

'Aaaah!' screamed Togura.

And walls of softly glowing green echoed his scream back to him.

He looked around, shivering. He was on his hands and knees in the green bottle. He was alive. Wasn't he? He thumped the floor with his fist. Real solid bottle-rock. He really was alive!

'By my grandfather's sperm,' muttered Togura.

Then fainted.

CHAPTER 45

When Togura woke, he found himself in the green bottle. Bit by bit, he remembered – reluctantly – what had happened to him. Presumably, the green bottle was still lying at the foot of Dead Man's Drop. Presumably, if he used the ring again, he would arrive outside the bottle.

And then what?

Then he would either have to run away or return to Keep and kill Cromarty. At the moment, the latter course seemed infinitely preferable. He wanted Cromarty dead.

'No mercy!' shouted Togura.

Then he wished he hadn't shouted quite so loudly. After all, there were at least two other people in the green bottle – the pirate Bluewater Draven and the unknown warrior he had last seen drawing steel, perhaps with murderous intent.

Those two were dangerous.

Or, on the other hand . . .

They might just possibly prove to be an asset.

If he met them, Togura would have to explain a number of things. First, why he had concealed the ring from Draven. He could say he had swallowed it, and had only recovered it shortly before first using it. Second, why he had left Draven in the bottle. He could say he had been captured (and tortured, and cut to pieces and resurrected afterwards) by people on the Lesser Teeth. Third, why they should help him. He could say he could reward them with his inheritance when he became baron, which was true enough.

As plans went, it was a little shaky.

Still, if Draven turned murderous, Togura could always bring him to heel by mentioning the dralkosh Yen Olass Ampadara. That had brought him to order once, and might well do so again.

And, whatever the dangers of seeking out Draven and his sparring partner, it was certainly much safer than trying to take on Cromarty and all his fellow-murderers single-handed.

'Anyone home?' cried Togura.

Nobody answered.

'It's me!' he shouted. 'Togura Poulaan! Barak the Battleman! Forester! I can explain everything!'

Still no answer.

Togura found a set of stairs, and started downwards. Below, he found the remains of a storeroom. From the empty crocks, barrels and wineskins lying about, it seemed there must once have been a considerable supply of food here. Ferreting about, Togura managed to uncover a bit of smoked pork and some wine. Well – not wine exactly, more like vinegar. But it was still drinkable.

He ate.

He drank.

Then, fortified, descended.

He followed a series of stairways downwards from one level to the next, into increasingly larger chambers. After a while, he quite lost count of the number of levels he had descended.

Then, a while later, the chambers started to get smaller. What did that mean? It meant, perhaps, that he was getting near the bottom. And still no sign of the two men he was looking for, or, for that moment, any others.

Perhaps he had better go up.

The stillness and the silence within the green bottle were uncanny. Unnerving.

On the other hand, it was a long, long way up. There was nowhere the two men could have disappeared to. They had to be down below.

'Courage!' said Togura to Togura.

And, though still apprehensive, continued his descent.

He went down one last set of stairs and found himself in a small chamber which seemed to be the bottom, as there was no way out of it. Trapped in a cage built into the wall of the chamber were two men. They seemed to be dead.

'Gods!' said Togura.

At his voice, the men stirred. Snorted. Woke. One was Draven and the other was a burly stranger of middle years.

'Togura!' roared Draven. 'Get us the hell out of here!'

From the vigour of the pirate's voice, Togura deduced that he had not been trapped in the cage for very long.

'Who put you in there?' said Togura, glancing about nervously.

'Nobody put us in here, boy,' said the second man in the cage. 'We stepped in here, and it closed on us. Say . . . don't I know you from somewhere?'

'I've seen you before, I think,' said Togura, puzzled. 'But I couldn't say when or where. Why did you get in the cage?'

'There was no cage to start with,' said Draven. 'Just a hole in the wall. I went in. Then he joined me. Then the bars caged us.'

'Why did you go in anyway?'

'Oh, pigs buggeration!' said Draven. 'Quit the questions and open the cage!'

'I only asked a civil question,' said Togura mildly.

'Why you—'

'Silence!'

At a word from the stranger, Draven fell silent. The stranger held up a blue bottle.

'Boy,' said the stranger, 'we came down here looking for a way out. We found this blue bottle in this hole. We think perhaps it's a magic bottle. We were on our hands and knees looking for the ring which might command it. The bars trapped us.'

'You didn't find the ring?'

'No, boy,' said the stranger. He held up a small casket, marked with the sign of a heart and a hand. 'Just this.'

'I want that!' said Togura sharply.

311

It was another magic casket. Inside, there should by rights be another index.

'Then you shall have it,' said the stranger. 'Once we have given you our assurances, and you have let us out of here. I will give you my assurances first. My name is Guest Gulkan. I am the rightful heir to the leadership of the Yarglat horsetribes, the rightful heir to the rule of Tameran. I swear, by the secret name of the Horse who was Horse, by the blood of the Rider who was Rider, by the Witness within the Wind and by the Witness beyond the Wind, by the honour of my dynasty and by the honour of my own heartbeat's blood, that I will do you no harm.'

'And,' said Togura, 'that you will yield up that casket.'

'I will,' said Guest Gulkan of Tameran.

'And,' said Togura, 'that you will help me kill my half-brother Cromarty.'

'Sure,' said Guest Gulkan, unable to conceal his contempt for a man who could not do his own killing. 'And rape your half-sister, too, if that's your requirement.'

'I've got a rightful claim to Cromarty's head!' shouted Togura.

'Peace, boy,' said Guest Gulkan, his voice soothing. 'I'm sure you have. Once we're out, you can tell us all about it. Draven, give the boy your assurances. Come on now!'

'I swear to your safety,' muttered Draven. 'By a pirate's honour.'

'Pirate's honour!' said Togura. 'What kind of honour is that? I saved your life once, and you had me thrown overboard to sea serpents. I showed you how to get control of your ship at Androlmarphos, and got precious little thanks afterwards. And what kind of honour did you show—'

'That's enough!' said Guest Gulkan. 'I'll vouch for him. He'll honour his oath or my steel will dishonour his neck.'

Togura bowed.

'You, my lord,' said Togura, 'I trust.'

And Togura began to hunt around for some way to open the cage. He explored the bars of the cage, then the surrounding walls, where he found a little catch hidden in a small

312

indentation. He pulled it. The cage opened. Draven and Guest Gulkan came out, Draven scowling, Guest Gulkan smiling.

'Here,' said Guest Gulkan, handing Togura the magic casket. 'Here's the first part of my oath fulfilled.'

'Thank you,' said Togura.

At that moment, a wall of rock crashed down, blocking the way up the stairs.

'Grief!' said Draven.

The wall growled. And began to grind its way toward them. Its entire surface came alive: became a seething mass of grinding graunching teeth.

"Yaa-hoo!' screamed Guest Gulkan, drawing his sword and attacking the wall.

It munched his steel without faltering, and continued to chomp its way toward them. Togura turned the ring on his finger, once, then again, then again, hoping to get out of the green bottle. But it was useless. He was trapped.

He was going to die.

Raging at his death, Togura, screaming, picked up the blue bottle Guest Gulkan had dropped, and threw it at the wall.

The wall munched into it.

The teeth faltered.

The teeth closed around the blue bottle began to vibrate. The bottle began to crack. So did the teeth. Suddenly the bottle shattered. The teeth, unco-ordinated, began to chatter. The wall tried to continue its advance. But something was wrong. It was vibrating badly. As they watched, it shook itself to bits.

And, suddenly, with a roar, all the walls around split open. Gravity shifted. They were flung head over heels and spilt out through a crack, landing in the mud and muck and detritus in amongst the pinnacles at the foot of Dead Man's Drop.

'By the blood of a weeping virgin!' muttered Draven, looking around. 'Where are we?'

Arching overhead was a huge, curved green wall, with gaping cracks in it, some big enough to permit a mammoth entrance and egress. It rose at least three hundred or so paces high, and seemed to curve away for the better part of a league or so.

'I think,' said Guest Gulkan, quietly, 'we're looking at the wreckage of the green bottle. I think we broke it open by smashing the blue bottle inside it.'

'Well, right or wrong,' said Draven, 'we're out. What now?'

Togura salvaged the magic casket from the mud at his feet. He spoke the Word. The casket opened. Inside was a triple-harp – or, to call it by its other name, an index.

'Now,' said Togura, with determination, 'we've got to set the world to rights. First by taking revenge!'

'First,' said Guest Gulkan, corecting him 'we get our hands on some weapons. And a meal before that, if possible.'

'Come,' said Togura. 'We're going up there. See? It's a long walk, and we've not much daylight left – but I know what to do when we get there.'

He explained all as they went along.

It would probably be night by the time they had traversed the roundabout roads leading back to Keep. Their first move then would be to go to see Raznak the Golsh, of the Suet clan, who would be sure to provide them with weapons, a meal, a bed for the night, and, if necessary, with reinforcements.

CHAPTER 46

The story of how Togura Poulaan encompassed the death of his half-brother Cromarty would not be a pretty tale. It was a singularly sanguinary event. Suffice it to say that the pigs got his kidneys, his thighs went for dogmeat and the rats managed to make off with his eyes.

Shortly afterwards, there was another death when Togura retrieved Day Suet and the Zenjingu fighter from the odex. Guest Gulkan met the Zenjingu fighter, blade against blade, killed him, then hacked off his head.

'All's well that ends well,' said Togura, with some considerable degree of satisfaction. 'Hello, Day, my love.'

'Who are you?' she said, blankly.

'Togura! Your true love, minx! Your questing hero!'

Day Suet, when finally persuaded that the bearded, limping, scar-faced young stranger was Togura Poulaan, fell into his arms, and they made passionate love to each other forthwith. That is, they kissed and they cuddled: copulation would have to be delayed until a more opportune moment.

For the moment, Togura had a practical problem to deal with: how to stop the odex, which was still spitting out junk, rubbish, dead dogs, rats, rotten potatoes and assorted articles of disgrace. He did not want to smash the triple-harp. He was sure there had to be a way of stopping it without destroying it. But how?

He talked to it, shook it, tried to conjure his own

315

independent music from it – all to no avail. Finally, in desperation, he threw it into the odex. His experiment paid immediate dividends. The odex spat out the index: and the index was silent.

Togura had learnt how to start it, and how to stop it. Finer control might come with time: he would see. For the moment, he had other things to attend to.

'Kiss me,' said Day Suet.

And he did.

Three days later, they were married. After riotous festivities which lasted from dawn to sunset, they retired to a house in Keep which had been lent to them by Raznak the Golsh. There Togura and his true love Day stripped each other naked; there they engaged each other in marital combat.

Shortly Togura, outraged, was thinking:

— Is that all?

'You were wonderful,' said Day, nuzzling against him.

She spoke with such ardour and conviction that he almost let himself believe her. As she fondled his body with her hot little hands, soothing his ego with her voice, he heard an ominous sound of rupture and breakage at street level.

Who could it be?

Bluewater Draven? Guest Gulkan? No, surely not – both those worthies had left the day before, determined to head back to the Greater Teeth (Draven, it seemed, was going to try and blame his disappearance on Togura).

'Tog!' said Day. 'Something's happening!'

'A small subsidence, dear,' said Togura, his voice soothing. 'Nothing to worry about.'

At that moment, the door downstairs burst open, and a huge slobbering voice roared out:

'Bring me my man! Slerma has come for her hero!'

Day squealed in alarm.

As Slerma began to bulk up the stairs – forcing the walls apart as she climbed – Togura slammed himself into his clothes, bundled Day into something warm, then led the way out of the window and onto the roof.

'Life,' muttered Togura, 'goes on.'

THE WIZARDS AND THE WARRIORS
By Hugh Cook

CHRONICLES OF AN AGE OF DARKNESS. 1:

'I ask all of you here today to join with me in pledging yourself to a common cause,' said Miphon. Elkor Alish laughed, harshly: 'A common cause? Between wizards and the Rovac? Forget it!'

And yet it had to be. Though Alish never accepted the alliance, his fellow warrior Morgan Hearst joined forces with Miphon and the other wizards. The only alternative was the utter destruction of their world.

The first volume in a spectacular fantasy epic to rival THE BELGARIAD and THE CHRONICLES OF THOMAS COVENANT

0552 125660   £2.95

THE BELGARIAD

DAVID EDDINGS

David Eddings has created a wholly imaginary world whose fate hangs on the outcome of a prophecy made seven thousand years earlier. The fulfilment of this prophecy is entrusted to a young farm boy named Garion, aided by his aunt Pol and the mysterious Mr Wolf. Together they embark on their quest to retrieve the stolen Orb of Aldur and confront the ageless malice of the god Torak.

The story of their quest unfolds with a magical blend of excitement and enchantment. *The Belgariad* is an outstanding piece of imaginative storytelling, destined to achieve the classic status and following of Tolkein's *The Hobbit* or Stephen Donaldson's *Chronicles of Thomas Covenant*.

Pawn of Prophecy	0 552 12284 X	£1.95
Queen of Sorcery	0 552 12348 X	£2.50
Magician's Gambit	0 552 12382 X	£2.50
Castle of Wizardry	0552 124354	£2.50
Enchanter's Endgame	0552 124478	£2.95

CORGI BOOKS